# DELUSION
# ROAD

Also by Don Aker

*Running on Empty*
*The Fifth Rule*
*The Space Between*
*One on One*
*The First Stone*

# DON AKER

# DELUSION
# ROAD

Harper*Trophy*Canada

*Delusion Road*
Copyright © 2015 by Don Aker
All rights reserved.

Published by Harper *Trophy* Canada™, an imprint of HarperCollins Publishers Ltd

First Canadian edition

The author is grateful for financial support from the Province of Nova Scotia through the
Grants to Individuals Program of the Department of Communities, Culture & Heritage.

HarperCollins books may be purchased for educational, business
or sales promotional use through our Special Markets Department.

HarperCollins Publishers Ltd
2 Bloor Street East, 20th Floor
Toronto, Ontario, Canada
M4W 1A8

*www.harpercollins.ca*

Library and Archives Canada Cataloguing in Publication
information is available upon request.

ISBN 978-1-44342-416-5

Printed and bound in the United States

RRD 9 8 7 6 5 4 3 2

*For Siyah,*
*who transformed our lives*

THE TRUTH MAY HURT, BUT DELUSION HARMS.

—JAN MILLER

# CHAPTER 1

He tried to block out the sound of his parents' voices. Not that ignoring their words made a difference—he'd heard variations of the same argument before:

—*I can't believe you're actually considering this.*

—*Haven't I done the safe thing all my life? Look where it got me.*

—*But you know what these people are capable of.*

And so it went until one of them would storm out, doors slamming in the aftermath.

But as much as it remained the same, the argument this morning was different. More intense, as though they'd reached a turning point of some sort. And they hadn't confined it to their bedroom like they usually did, their voices barely muffled by the thin walls of their dilapidated row house on East 52nd Street. They'd continued quarrelling downstairs in the kitchen.

"You should have talked to me first."

"There wasn't time and I might not have gotten another chance."

"But why take the chance at all?"

"After what we've been through? How could I not?"

"Please don't go back there."

"I have to. I think I can get even more."

"If you don't walk away from this now, I will! And I'll take the boys with me."

There was no blocking out that last part.

Sitting on the edge of his bed, his backpack on the floor between his feet, he felt his guts clench. He'd been afraid it would come to this. The last year had been hard on all of them. They'd lost everything, starting with cable, Internet, and cell service, then anything they'd bought on credit, like the home theatre system his dad had spent months researching before finally getting at Best Buy on West Roosevelt. Then the bank had taken both cars and, finally, the house. He heard people were getting great deals on places that banks had foreclosed on, and he thought about the families who'd lost those homes, hoped they'd torn them to shreds before they left. That's what he wished *he'd* done the day they'd walked away from theirs—wished he'd ripped out light fixtures, smashed windows, kicked holes in every wall. But his mother had told him they were better than that.

"You're giving me ultimatums now?"

"If that's what it takes."

"What happened to till death do us part?"

"That's exactly what I'm afraid of."

"Look, no one suspects a thing. I was careful."

His mother laughed at that last comment. That's what it sounded like, anyway. Later, he would wonder if it was something else—a choked sob, maybe—and he would wish that somehow he could be sure. It was the last sound he would ever hear her make.

He listened to the sounds that followed, the closet door in the hall being yanked open, hangers clattering to the floor as his father grabbed his jacket and shouted upstairs for him to get his brother if he still wanted that drive to school. "We haven't eaten yet!" he called down, but his father had already stormed outside.

He hated the old Dodge Stratus his dad had picked up at an auction for three hundred bucks, but he hated riding the bus even more. Hoping he had enough money on him for a breakfast burrito, he grabbed his backpack and crossed the hall, collecting his brother and heading downstairs with the child in tow. He stopped at the kitchen door on his way past, poked his head in to see his mother by the sink. She stood with her back toward him, her head down, her arms making triangles on either side of her slim body as she gripped the worn countertop. As if trying hard to hang on to something neither of them could see.

He took a step toward her, but then the Dodge's horn blared and his brother began to whimper. He turned and tugged him toward the front closet, grabbing coats to put on in the car. Moments later, all three of them were in their seats, his father's mouth a thin, hard line as he eased the battered sedan into traffic.

He stared out his passenger-side window as if actually seeing the buildings slide by instead of his mother's knuckles white against the scarred countertop, so different from the gleaming granite in the house the bank had taken. He tried not to think of that house with its state-of-the-art appliances and ensuites off every bedroom, tried to push aside memories of their backyard with the in-ground pool, the manicured lawn and raised flower-beds, the red maple towering above them all. Despite the cold still clinging to the Midwest, that tree would bud soon, evidence that there really were things that never changed. Unlike every-thing else in his life. He tried to focus on the laboured whine of the car's engine instead of his mother's voice in his head. *And I'll take the boys with me.*

He felt the explosion before he heard it—absurdly gentle, like a house-sized hand nudging the Dodge forward—and then came the sound, a single boom that was its own endless echo, ragged and rolling. "What the h—?" he began, but fingers gripped his arm like talons. He turned to see his father gaping horror-struck in the rear-view mirror, so he swivelled in his seat, saw through the back window the nightmare behind them. "*Jesus!*" he cried.

Nearly bald tires shrieked against the pavement as his father braked and swung the car in a tight U-turn, narrowly missing an oncoming CTA bus. Heartbeats later, the Dodge swerved around flaming debris and slowed in front of what remained of their house, its roof and front gone, fire licking at what hadn't been obliterated by the blast.

He groped for the door handle, but his father jammed the gas pedal to the floor, the smooth tires throwing off ribbons of smoke as the car leaped forward.

"What are you *doing*? *Stop*! We have to go *back*!"

His father's voice was a cracked and ruined version of itself. "It's too late."

"But she's *in* there—"

"It's too late," his father repeated as the houses blurred past them. He was sobbing, too. Only the boy in the back seat was silent.

# CHAPTER 2

Griffin Barnett handed the fare to the cabbie and got out, tugging his collar up against the late March wind that whipped off Lake Michigan and funnelled down the Chicago River. Having grown up in and around Little Rock, Arkansas, Griff hated how a gale could blow nonstop in this city for what seemed like weeks at a time. He'd overheard one guy joke that, on the rare occasions when the wind died down here, the dogs fell over. But Griff saw nothing funny in being sandblasted by grit swirled up from the street. Despite having lived in the Windy City for two years, he hated Chicago every bit as much as on the day he'd arrived.

He had to admit, though, that the bridges were cool. Of all eighteen on the Chicago Loop, Griff liked the one he was looking at now best. Sure, the Franklin Street bridge wasn't the longest or widest or oldest or busiest, but it was special nonetheless. It was where he'd dumped the body of the first person he'd killed in this christly place.

Walking toward the bridge tender house on the northwest corner, Griff saw a passing man glance at him and then scattergun the air with his eyes. There was a time when he'd been bothered by strangers' reactions to his appearance, that moment of unguarded revulsion before looking away. Now he just watched as their eyes took in his six-foot-five, muscled frame before they noticed the thick line of ruined flesh snaking diagonally from his chin to his right ear, barely missing his lips. If he tilted his head to the right, the scar looked a little like a wide second mouth, a crooked pink grin. That's what Morozov's girl had told him last night, anyway, as she lay sprawled on the bed beside him. She was one of those whores who liked to talk afterwards. He'd just wanted her gone. He'd never liked being around women for long, and the talking was only part of it. Mostly it was how they put him on edge, made him feel like they expected something from him that he could never quite figure out. He preferred cash-and-carry hookers who knew when to shut the fuck up and disappeared when the deed was done.

A short but powerfully built man standing by the tender house reached out to pat him down. "Yo, Barnett," he said, his mouthful-of-marbles accent betraying his New Jersey roots. "Colder'n a witch's tit out here."

Griff shrugged. He wasn't good at small talk, could never see the point of it.

A black town car idled by the curb, and New Jersey moved toward it. Griff followed, and the bodyguard opened the rear door for him before getting into the front passenger seat. Griff slid into the back, barely getting the door closed before the car pulled out.

It was a good thing Pavel Morozov's reputation preceded him, because he wasn't much to look at. People expecting a big, brawny man with swarthy features and a penetrating gaze would have been disappointed by the person sitting beside Griff now. In his late forties, Morozov was no more than five foot eight, maybe a hundred thirty pounds soaking wet, and his pasty complexion suggested either an allergy to sunlight or albino DNA. He rarely looked people in the face, a habit that might give the impression of shyness, but Griff had never known a man who unnerved him more.

The lack of eye contact had set off warning bells the day Griff met him. Among the many "uncles" who had rotated in and out of the Barnett household when Griff's mother was alive was a guy named Gil Atkins, who had a similar habit of looking anywhere but at you when he spoke. At first Griff thought the guy had some kind of physical condition, maybe a lazy eye like the kid in his eighth-grade class he'd bullied constantly. But it wasn't that. There were things going on in Gil Atkins's head that you could see in his eyes if he forgot himself and let you look long enough. Things you didn't *want* to see. Things you couldn't even bring yourself to believe until pets started disappearing from the neighbourhood. And then there was the little girl after that. Pavel Morozov had Gil Atkins's eyes.

But it was Morozov's voice that made Griff's skin crawl, an emotionless monotone so soft you had to listen closely when he spoke. You wouldn't want to make Morozov repeat himself.

"Good you could come on such short notice," murmured Morozov. Griff felt gooseflesh pucker the back of his neck.

"No problem, Mr. Morozov." In fact, Griff had welcomed his boss's phone call, which had given him an excuse to send the whore on her way. She'd already served her real purpose, being his alibi if he ended up needing one.

Morozov raised his right hand, studying his paper-white

palm in the grey light that struggled through the tinted window. "I'm sure I don't need to remind you how important this morning's job was."

"No, sir."

Morozov turned his hand over, examining his thin fingers as if checking for hangnails. Or blood. "The prick had it coming to him."

"Yes, sir," said Griff, although that didn't matter to him one way or the other. It was a job. End of story.

"Nobody fucks with Pavel Morozov and gets away with it."

In the last two years, Griff had taken out enough pricks who'd had it coming to know the truth in that. "No, sir," he agreed. Where was this heading?

Morozov let his hand fall to his lap, where it formed a small, white fist. "Then why is he still alive?"

Griff blinked. "He—isn't. He couldn't be. None of them could."

Morozov turned to face him, and Griff felt his guts coil when eyes pallid as death met his own. Something flickered behind those eyes, and once again Griff thought of Gil Atkins. A second little girl had disappeared before the cops finally figured out what Griff had already guessed.

Morozov reached into a leather case on the seat between them and, for a heart-stopping moment, Griff expected him to pull out a gun. Instead, the man handed him a tablet, an Apple product that wasn't even on the market yet. The guy who supplied Griff with his tech had shown him a prototype stolen from an R&D lab.

Morozov reached over and dragged colourless fingertips across the screen, enlarging a black-and-white image. It was grainy, probably taken by a traffic cam, but Griff could still make out the features of the person behind the wheel of the old Dodge. A time stamp at the bottom right showed it had been taken minutes after the bomb should have exploded. "Son of a bitch," Griff muttered. He looked up again, forcing himself to meet those pallid eyes. "I tested the detonator a dozen times. No way could it have failed."

"It didn't," said Morozov, his toneless voice dropping a register. "Apparently, he left the house early."

"But he *never* leaves early. I made sure of it. You could set your watch by the guy."

"And yet there he is," said Morozov, nodding toward the tablet in Griff's hands before returning his gaze to the fist in his lap. Griff watched as the fist opened, the fingers unfolding like thin white worms writhing in the grey morning light.

Not a lot could push Griff's buttons. You didn't grow up with a mother like his, didn't share space with guys like Gil Atkins, didn't make a living the way Griff did now without developing a kind of armour. But the sight of those white fingers unfurling sent a tremor through him that reminded him of something he'd learned five years ago—not all nightmares come to you in your sleep. One was sitting beside him in the back of that town car. "I can take care of this, Mr. Morozov," he said, handing back the tablet.

"My people warned me that a twenty-year-old was too young for this job," murmured Morozov.

Griff opened his mouth to respond, but the small man silenced him with a wave of white fingers. "I didn't listen to them," he continued. "I reminded them how important youth could be, how your facility with technology was superior to most, how eagerness and enthusiasm could trump lack of experience." He sighed wetly. "Was I wrong?"

"No, sir," Griff assured him. "You weren't wrong. I can fix this."

"The clock's ticking," said Morozov as the driver pulled the car over to the curb.

"I'm real sorry—"

"Not nearly as sorry as you'll be if this matter isn't resolved."

"Yes, sir." Griff opened the door and saw they'd come full circle, arriving back at the Franklin Street bridge.

The wind tore at him like claws.

# CHAPTER 3

Pulling into Brookdale High's student parking lot, Willa
Jaffrey rolled her eyes at the words scrolling endlessly
across the school's electronic message board: "Welcome new and
returning students." What was supposed to be *this* returning
student's best year ever certainly wasn't starting out that way.

First, she hated how she looked. After lying in bed until noon
all summer, she'd found it hard getting up early that morning, and
she should have given herself more time to get ready. Especially
since her long blond hair, which had an irritating natural wave,
hadn't cooperated with her flatiron.

Her black mood also had to do with the vehicle she wasn't
driving. She'd spent days that summer poring over brochures
from her dad's dealership, deciding which car she liked most and
choosing the options she wanted. He'd promised that her early
graduation present would be delivered in time for the first day
of school but, instead of sitting behind the wheel of a sexy new
Camaro—Victory Red with graphite racing stripes—she was
driving a black SUV that practically shrieked law enforcement.
"There was a production glitch at the factory," her father had
explained when he'd handed her the keys ten minutes ago, Willa
glaring at the vehicle's dealer plate: *Jaffrey 3.* "Your Camaro won't

be here for a few more weeks." *Weeks?* She'd been tempted to pitch a tantrum in the middle of the dealership's parking lot—one of those nuclear meltdowns she'd thrown when she was little—but she knew it wouldn't do any good. Even her dad couldn't pull a brand-new Camaro out of his ass.

And on top of everything else, she hadn't spoken to Wynn for days.

Like every summer, Willa and her parents had spent the week before Labour Day at their cottage on the Bay of Fundy. Although she'd loved the place when she was younger, that particular stretch of rocky shoreline along Delusion Road was a technological black hole, one of the handful of places in Nova Scotia still without Internet or cell service. And since the cottage didn't have a landline, the past week had been like living underwater, so she'd been relieved to hear her phone chirp repeatedly with messages as bars finally reappeared on the display during their drive home last night. Oddly, none of them were from Wynn. She'd tried calling him but kept getting his voicemail and, by the time they reached Brookdale, she'd begun to worry something terrible had happened. But her fears had vanished when she'd seen what was waiting on their doorstep—a bouquet of yellow roses celebrating their five-month anniversary.

Her mother had been quick to point out to Willa's dad how long it had been since she'd received flowers from *him*, but Willa tried to ignore his "For Christ's sake, not *this* again" and her mother's "Would it kill you to put *me* first for a change?" rant, which she'd heard so often in the last few months. Instead, she'd carried the roses to her room and tried calling Wynn to thank him, but it went to voicemail again. Sometime after she'd gone to bed, he'd sent her a text saying how much he'd missed her and telling her he'd see her at school in the morning.

So, yeah, what with her hair, no Camaro, and missing Wynn, it had been a lousy beginning to her best year ever. And obsessing about it now made her miss the parking spot she'd just driven past. "Damn!" she muttered, braking and shifting the SUV into reverse.

If it hadn't been for the beep of the backup alert, she would have struck the guy who suddenly appeared on the dash's large touch screen. Willa slammed on the brake and the vehicle seesawed momentarily. Her heart in her mouth, she pressed a button on her armrest to lower her window. "I almost hit you!" she shouted to the tall guy with the hoodie who'd crossed behind her.

He didn't even glance back, just kept walking toward the school, his head down.

"Jerk!" she grumbled, then turned completely around to see if there was anyone else behind her before easing into the space.

She was getting her things out of the SUV when she heard a honk from a VW Golf as Britney Lamontagne pulled into a space a few cars over. In a moment, Willa was on the receiving end of hugs from her and Celia Waters.

"We missed you!" her friends trilled.

"You have no idea," said Willa, "how many times I reached for my cell to call you guys."

"How'd you stand being in the dead zone?" asked Celia.

Willa grimaced. "What was worse was listening to my parents bicker for seven days." Hearing them snipe at each other so often, she'd wondered why they'd chosen to spend the week together. She'd even asked her father about it one evening, but he'd just said that all couples squabbled. "I bet you and Wynn get on each other's nerves from time to time, right?" he'd said.

But he was wrong—Willa had lucked out in the boyfriend department. During the five months she and Wynn had been together, they'd never had a single argument. Not one. Wynn d'Entremont had moved from Halifax to Brookdale a little more than a year ago to live with his remarried dad, and it had taken zero time for the muscular, blue-eyed son of the town's mayor to fit right in. There was no question that he was the best-looking guy at Brookdale High, not to mention the top athlete and the sweetest boy she'd ever dated, the roses being a perfect example. Sure, no one was more aggressive than Wynn on a hockey rink or soccer field or rugby pitch, but that was just his competitive nature, which had led all three of his Brookdale teams to district championships and earned them two provincial titles. When he wasn't trying to score a goal, he was a total gentleman. In fact, he could be *too* much of a gentleman sometimes. When it came to the physical side of their relationship, he always stopped at second base despite her growing willingness to run to home plate.

"Don't talk to me about bickering," Celia moaned. "I had to babysit my dweeb brother while Mom went out with her eHarmony hookup."

Willa grinned. Following her divorce from Celia's dad, Rachel Waters had started dating with a vengeance, and Celia was forever entertaining her friends with stories of the losers who'd been seeing her mother. Two weeks ago, when yet another new guy had arrived to take Rachel out for coffee, Celia had snapped a photo of him so the three friends could compare it with his eHarmony profile. Thanks to Celia's mother using the same password for everything she did online, the girls surfed unhindered through her matches until they found Dewayne Eisner. The picture he'd posted wasn't recent and, although his bio said he loved to exercise, that description could only have been accurate if, as Britney suggested, he worked out at Dairy Queen. Willa had snorted over the guy's blatant lies and given silent thanks for Wynn, who never tried to be anything other than what he was.

Reluctantly shelving thoughts of her boyfriend, Willa asked, "How'd you spend *your* Labour Day weekend, Brit?"

"You don't wanna know," warned Celia.

Britney sighed. "I cleansed my colon."

"Ew!"

"Not much else to do with Todd away in New Brunswick," said Britney.

"Now *there's* someone who could use a colon cleanse," offered Celia, nodding at a rusted Hyundai Accent that had been circling the parking lot and was now pulling into one of the few remaining spaces.

Britney snickered, and all three watched as the driver—an overweight senior named Russell Shaw—killed the motor and got out. "Jeez," murmured Britney, "he's even fatter than he was in June."

Celia snorted agreement. "Nice to see you, Russell," she cooed as their chubby classmate approached them. "Lookin' good, man."

His ample cheeks reddened as he passed them. "You, too," he mumbled, turning to give the girls a shy smile. But the toe of his no-name sneaker caught the edge of a drain grate and he nearly went down.

"Walk much, Russell?" Britney called after him, to Willa and Celia's giggled delight.

Russell gave a pained shrug and kept going.

"Loser," muttered Britney, turning again to her friends. "Hey, I heard there's fresh meat in our class."

"More international students?" asked Willa.

"Besides them. A girl and a guy."

As the three made their way toward the east-wing entrance, Celia said, "Man, wouldn't that suck? Starting your senior year in a new place and not knowing anybody?"

Willa couldn't imagine anything worse. Sure, a small-town school like Brookdale High couldn't offer all the programs available in bigger communities, but she liked knowing everybody inside its walls. Well, *almost* everybody. Ahead of her, she could see the tall guy she'd nearly run down earlier, and she was pretty sure he was one of the imports. No one from Brookdale would wear a jacket in early September—already the air felt like a moist second skin, and the heat would only worsen as the sun climbed higher. This guy even wore his hood up. "There's one of them now," she muttered.

"Who?" asked Britney.

Willa nodded toward the figure moving up the steps ahead of them. Even with his shoulders hunched and his head down, he towered over most of the people he passed.

"You mean Son of Lurch?" Britney asked. "What dumbass wears a hoodie this time of year?"

"The kind of dumbass who can't be bothered to watch out for cars," replied Willa, filling them in on what had happened.

Celia scowled. "Hey, you!" she called. "Stretch!"

Everyone on the steps turned, with the exception of the guy

in the hoodie, who'd made it to the top landing and was now reaching for the door.

"Lankenstein!"

He turned, confusion etched on the part of his face Willa could see under the hood. She was right—he was an import. "You talking to me?" he asked.

"Yeah. You."

"What d'you want?"

"A word."

Willa wasn't surprised to see the now-silent crowd on the step part, making room for him to pass. Most nodded and smiled at the three friends below them as they moved aside, but two in the group—Russell Shaw and Greg Phillips, a gangly guy with galloping acne—glanced quickly down as if suddenly mesmerized by their feet.

The guy in the hoodie sauntered down the steps. "What's up?"

Celia tilted her head toward Willa. "My friend here needs something from you."

He looked at Willa. "What d'you need?"

Willa flushed, wishing she'd kept her mouth shut.

"An apology," said Celia.

"What for?"

"Seems you don't know much about parking lot protocol," Celia drawled, stretching out the moment, and Willa could tell she was enjoying herself. Celia had always liked an audience.

"What're you talking about?"

Celia recounted what Willa had told her and Britney, embellishing the incident with details that made Willa's experience sound almost harrowing.

The guy just stared at her. "You're kidding, right?"

Celia lasered him with narrowed eyes, and Willa could feel the crowd on the steps studying them with growing interest. Then, as if coming to the same sudden awareness, the guy looked at Willa again. "Sorry," he muttered, then turned on his heel and strode off before Willa could respond.

Celia turned and raised her hand in the air for Britney and Willa to high-five. "You two bitches ready for the best school year ever?" she asked.

As her palm slapped Celia's, Willa watched the tall guy disappear, his shoulders hunched even more than before. *Man, wouldn't that suck? Starting your senior year in a new place and not knowing anybody?* How about being humiliated in front of strangers before you even stepped inside the building?

She pushed that thought aside. After all, she had better things to think about. Best school year ever? You bet.

# CHAPTER 4

Less than two minutes on the school grounds and he'd already ruffled some bitch's feathers. *Christ.* Waiting in the lineup at the school's main office, Keegan Fraser stared at his feet, trying to ignore what had happened outside. But he couldn't. Molten lead roiled inside him, waves of throttled wrath crashing against the wall of his chest. And behind each wave was a feeling even worse than anger. Regret. Getting noticed like that was the last thing he needed, and he could just imagine his father's reaction to it, not to mention Forbes's. Hadn't Forbes repeated his prime directive again and again?

Keegan forced himself to look up, his eyes drawn to the person in front of him. She was more than a foot shorter than he was, and he found his gaze drifting to the top of her head, where her thick black hair parted in a ruler-straight divide before falling to her waist. Although he couldn't see the girl's face, she reminded him of—

He ground his teeth together, trying to bite back the surge of self-pity that joined the anger and regret seething inside him. It was pointless to let his mind go there. He looked again at the black-haired girl and noticed a bruise on her coppery forearm that the sleeve of her blouse only partially concealed. She looked athletic, so maybe she'd whacked it playing sports. The way she balanced on the balls of her feet made him think basketball or volleyball, but she could be a dancer or—

"No hats."

Keegan turned to see a man in a chipmunk-brown suit glaring at him, pointing toward the wall behind the counter, where a secretary waited on the guy two people ahead. A sign showed the black silhouette of a life-sized baseball cap with a red circle and diagonal line superimposed over it. Keegan shrugged.

The suit approached him and yanked his hood from his head. "You have trouble reading signs?" he asked.

"It's not a hat," Keegan replied, fresh anger churning inside him.

"If it covers your head, it's a hat."

"You find that on Wikipedia?" muttered Keegan. Judging from all the white faces he'd seen so far, he could tell that Brookdale lacked the large Middle Eastern population at his last school, and he would've liked to see the suit apply his definition to a hijab.

The suit bristled. "You're new, aren't you? What's your name?"

Keegan told him.

"I can't say I care for your attitude, Keegan. I'm Mr. Caldwell, the vice-principal, and already you're on my radar. Not a great way to start the school year."

Keegan felt the heat in his belly work its way to his face, and he'd have given anything to tell the guy what he could do with his radar, but he noticed that others had turned to watch their exchange, and Forbes's prime directive echoed in his head. "Sorry," he muttered. His second *sorry* in his first four minutes at Brookdale High.

The vice-principal appeared almost disappointed by the sudden apology, perhaps eager to make an example of someone on this all-important first day. He nodded crisply. "I'll be keeping an eye on you," he warned as he stepped back, his attention moving to the growing crowd in the corridor.

"Someone needs a happy pill."

Keegan turned to see the black-haired girl smiling up at him. "I don't think they come that big," he said, grateful for the swell of sound beyond the office that masked their murmured comments.

"If it's any consolation, it's my first day, too," she said. "I'm Raven."

"Keegan," he replied.

"Yeah, I heard."

"Why Brookdale?" he asked, eager to keep the conversation going so he'd feel less alone.

"You mean what's a nice girl like me doing in a place like this?"

He grinned. "Something like that, only not as cheesy."

"I wanted to see it first-hand."

"See what?"

"Rampant cocklaphobia."

He blinked at her. "Rampant what?"

"Fear of hats. Judging from that sign, it must be epic around here."

Keegan snorted, drawing another glower from Caldwell. "That's really a word? Cocklaphobia?"

"According to answers.com it is," she replied, "although doesn't it sound more like a condition affecting lesbians?"

Keegan's sudden bray of laughter drew looks from even the harried secretary. To hell with the prime directive—it had been a long time since he'd laughed. He wanted to talk longer, but the secretary said "Next?" and it was Raven's turn.

"Nice meeting you, Keegan," she said before pivoting and handing a sheet of paper across the counter.

When it was his turn, the secretary sorted out Keegan's schedule conflict and looked up his locker number and combination, which he'd gladly taken. Finding his locker would help him kill time before the assembly. He'd already gotten dozens of *Uh, new guy* glances from people he'd passed in the corridor, a definite disadvantage of attending a school with only seven hundred students. There were more than four times that in his school back home.

He frowned. *Home.* As if that word had any meaning now. He dug in his pocket for the paper the secretary had given him, pulled it out, then began scanning the numbers on the lockers he passed.

Sudden activity at the end of the corridor caught his attention, a flurry of high-fiving and fist-bumping as some guys greeted each other, followed by a squealed "It's about *time* you got here!" and "Where *were* you last night?"

Keegan arrived at his locker and tried the combination while glancing at the scene unfolding thirty feet away. The bitch he'd had to apologize to had wrapped herself around a big muscular guy who, because his hair was as blond as hers, might have been her brother. That is, if it weren't for the lip-lock that suggested he was trying to remove a kidney with his tongue. Judging from the way everyone else was staring at them, he guessed they were The Couple, the godlike duo in every senior class that everyone else in the building wants to be half of—or, failing that, wants to be around. Keegan tried not to give in to the anger he'd felt earlier, focusing instead on retrying his combination.

"Sorry, Wills," Keegan heard the blond guy say when the two came up for air. "I was helping Dad move stuff up to the community college for Casino Night. Took way longer than I thought."

"You didn't even answer your *phone!*" the bitch named Wills— *Wills?*—pouted.

"Changed my clothes and forgot my cell in my jeans. But I heard your messages when I got home. You liked the flowers, huh?"

"I *loved* my yellow roses!" she gushed, and Keegan got the feeling she was making sure everyone around them could hear her. Yellow roses. Big deal.

A bell rang and Keegan sensed everyone in the corridor give a collective shrug. Spinning the dial on his lock one more time, he watched out of the corner of his eye as The Couple headed in his direction on their way to the assembly, and he saw they had an entourage—the bitch's two girlfriends and two buff guys, clearly athletes. One of them was wearing a Bears cap in clear violation of the no-hats rule, and Keegan watched with interest as a male staff member came out of his classroom and followed the six down the hall.

The teacher made no mention of the offending hat.

# CHAPTER 5

Griff opened his eyes and, like so many other mornings, couldn't believe he'd made it through another night. It had been more than five months since he'd botched that hit, and those months had taken a toll on him. He'd lost weight, his scar now pulling up into the hollow beneath his cheekbone, tugging the ragged line askew and making him look haggard. And more intimidating, too, judging from the reaction of the woman standing in front of him at Starbucks the other day—glancing up into his face, she'd promptly dropped her cup, the liquid splashing all over the floor. She'd apologized again and again, but she'd avoided looking at him each time she'd said "I'm sorry."

Griff had lost track of the times he'd repeated those words to Morozov in the past five months. But apologies meant nothing to the guy. Sooner or later, Griff would be getting a visit from one of his goons, which was why he now slept with his Smith & Wesson in his hand. So far, though, the only thing that disturbed his sleep—besides his usual nightmare—was the memory of Morozov's voice that day in the car: *The clock's ticking*. And Griff was no closer to finding the target than when he'd started.

But as surprised as he was to wake up alive each morning, he could guess why Morozov hadn't iced him yet. Because that's what a sick fuck he was. Years ago, Griff had watched a cat play with a mouse for over an hour before finally killing it, and he figured Morozov took some kind of kinky pleasure in knowing Griff woke up each morning wondering if this was the day he'd slip under the wheels of a CTA train or kiss the grill of a transfer truck. Never a knife in the back or a bullet to the head—Morozov liked his hits to look like accidents, which was why Griff had gone the extra mile to make the job on East 52nd look like a gas leak.

Griff wished now that he'd stayed behind that morning to make sure the target had been offed, but the whole point of using explosives was so he wouldn't be there when the hit went down. With traffic cams everywhere, he didn't like taking a chance on being recorded near the scene if somebody happened to suspect arson. It wasn't likely—Griff had spent hours perfecting the mechanism to ensure the C-4 would wipe out any immediate trace of it—but you never knew.

Morozov had wanted the target's wife and kids killed, too, probably to send a message to anyone else who might be thinking of doing what this guy had done, so Griff had watched the family for days. To maximize his equipment's kill quotient, he needed all four to be in the same room when it detonated, which meant weekends were a wash because the family followed no schedule on those days. During the week, the target often worked late, which meant evenings were a problem, and since nobody in the family came home for lunch, midday wasn't an option, either. Breakfast was the obvious choice. It was the only meal they routinely ate together during the workweek, and always from seven fifteen to seven thirty. Never before and never after.

Except that day.

It was bad enough that Griff had failed to take out the target. Worse, the explosion had tipped the guy off to the fact that Morozov was on to him, which explained why he'd covered his tracks so thoroughly. He was in the wind.

Griff had considered disappearing, too, but he was pretty sure that Morozov's people—who included at least three cops on the Chicago force—would eventually find him. And if that happened, getting run over by a CTA train or pulverized by a transfer truck would seem like a lottery win compared to the end that Morozov would arrange for him. The guy was all about sending messages.

Surprisingly, Morozov's huge network had been no use finding the target, who had somehow managed to vanish along with his digital footprint. He must have gotten help, because Griff had seen no evidence the guy had the know-how to scour his electronic tracks so cleanly, a skill Griff had spent the last five years mastering.

In the beginning, Griff had been confident that the facial recognition algorithm he'd created would do its job—considering the sheer volume of graphic uploads that were posted online daily, it was only a matter of time before he'd get a hit that would pay off. But days became weeks and then weeks turned into months and it still hadn't happened, despite Griff's continual retooling of the FRA to broaden its search parameters.

Although he was certain the FRA would eventually come through, Griff had pursued the target in other ways, too. His first step had been the obvious one—tapping into traffic cam footage and visually tracking the route the guy had taken—but the three-second delay between some surveillance bursts had made the process unreliable, creating too many gaps the target could have driven through unrecorded, and apparently had. Undaunted, Griff had searched state DMV sites looking for updates related to the target's licence and vehicle registration number. He'd hacked bus, railway, and airline manifests along with digital clearinghouses that made hotel and motel bookings, bringing up all three-person occupancies within the relevant timeframe. And finally he'd begun to consider long-term scenarios, infiltrating private and government sites across the country and uploading sifters that combed through records of new employees, rental agreements, even school board funding for specialized support personnel. But so far none of it had panned out.

Griff swung his legs over the side of his bed and reached for the laptop on his nightstand, its screensaver cycling through images of orchids. During the past few months, he'd fallen into the habit of mentally reciting five words before touching the screen, and today was no exception. Please bring me that fucker, he thought as he brushed the display, the orchids vanishing to reveal the FRA that ran continuously in the background. But besides the usual handful of doppelgangers whom Griff quickly checked and ruled out, there was nothing. Not a goddamn thing.

Grimacing, he tapped the Facebook icon. Griff hated Facebook, and not because he didn't have any friends. He just couldn't understand why people posted such detailed information about themselves for complete strangers to see. Because not everyone you friended was who they said they were. For over four months now, Griff had been Kayley Sheridan, a seventeen-year-old girl who attended school on North Ashland Avenue. Using selfies he'd copied from a Bulgarian teenager, his fictional persona had gathered an impressive number of real-life friends. It was amazing how many people not only accepted his requests but actually submitted their own to him. Not that he gave a shit about them. There was only one person he was really interested in.

Time for Kayley to do her stuff.

# CHAPTER 6

Willa thought the assembly would never end. They'd already listened to the usual welcoming remarks from Ms. Stevens, the principal; they'd endured the reading of the school rules by Mr. Caldwell, the vice-principal; and now they were suffering through the We Are a Family of Learners speech from Ms. Flynn, the senior guidance counsellor, who was reciting the same stuff Willa had heard every year on the first day of school.

"Christ!" muttered Celia beside her. "How much longer?"

Willa rolled her eyes. "She hasn't even gotten to her caterpillar metaphor, and then there's the whole 'vision for the future' bit."

"Shoot. Me. Now." This from Britney, who sat on the other side of Jay, the only one in their group who hadn't complained about the length of the assembly. He'd fallen asleep ten seconds in, his head lolling back and his mouth wide open. Only Celia's frequent jabbing kept him from snoring.

More than anything, Willa longed to pull out her phone and respond to some of the many texts she'd received, but one of the school rules that Caldwell most delighted in enforcing was "No cellphones during classes or assemblies." The VP gleefully confiscated offenders' phones and, since Willa had replaced hers with the latest model only a week ago, she wasn't willing to risk losing it now.

Finally, Flynn finished and Caldwell returned to the podium to announce homeroom allocations. Not that it would be a surprise which ones she and her friends were assigned to—seniors were always grouped alphabetically by last name. The real news was which teacher each group would be assigned to. Last year, she'd had to endure Ms. Ericson, a rail-thin woman who never wore antiperspirant and always had half-moon stains under her arms.

Caldwell cleared his throat importantly as if he were about to announce the Rapture. "All those grade twelve students whose surnames begin with the letters A to E will proceed to Ms. MacDonald's classroom, number 108."

Wynn leaned over and kissed Willa before heaving himself to his feet. "Later, babe," he said, shouldering his backpack and ambling toward the exit.

Embracing his inner control freak, Caldwell waited until all of the students in that first group left the auditorium before continuing, "All those grade twelves with surnames beginning with the letters F to J will proceed to Mr. Richardson's classroom, number 117."

"You got the new English teacher," said Celia as Willa stood up. "Text me what you think, okay?"

Willa nodded. Some staff members were less vigilant about enforcing the no-phones rule. Maybe this new guy would be, too. "See you at the break, okay?" she said.

Out in the corridor, Willa followed her fellow homeroomers as they made their way toward the west wing. They were the usual motley crew, six of whom had been in her class the past two years but never in any of her courses because she'd always been in the accelerated group.

Glancing behind her, Willa saw Bailey Holloway bringing up the rear, sporting the result of what was clearly a home
dye-job, the colour close to rust. At least it drew attention away
from her ill-fitting jeans, which Willa suspected had been bought
at Frenchy's, the used clothing warehouse on Highway 1. "Hey,
Bailey," said Willa.

Bailey flushed a deep crimson and a couple of different expressions flickered over her face before she rearranged her features
into a smile, a reaction Willa found odd. She and Bailey didn't
have a lot in common, but they'd known each other for years and
had been in the same homeroom for the last two.

"Hey, Willa," said Bailey. Then, as if to compensate for her
uneasiness, she added, "Guess we got the new guy, huh?"

"Yeah," Willa acknowledged. "Hope he's a decent teacher."

"Not Richardson," said Bailey. "Him."

Willa looked ahead where Bailey was pointing and spied the
tall guy with the hoodie walking alone. Remembering the scene
at the east-wing entrance, she suppressed a groan. Even if they
had none of the same classes, they would be seeing each other
every single day.

In her head, Willa reminded herself that this was going to
be the best school year ever. Despite all evidence to the contrary.

# CHAPTER 7

The extended homeroom period had been a tedious exercise in filling out endless first-day-of-school forms, but even that was preferable to recess, which Keegan spent hanging around his open locker trying to look busy instead of like The Biggest Loser In The Building. He couldn't keep his mind from drifting toward Hamad, Joaquin, and the others, a lump crowding his throat as he thought of what their first day as seniors must be like, so he was actually glad when a bell warned the break would end shortly. He shut the metal door and gave the combination lock a final spin before heading to his first class. He'd never really enjoyed English, which involved way too much reading for Keegan's liking, but Richardson had seemed okay in homeroom. At least he didn't have one foot in the grave like a lot of the teachers on staff.

Keegan had been hoping Raven might end up in his homeroom, but she hadn't. And the one person he'd been hoping *wouldn't* be there *was*—the bitch he'd had to apologize to. Entering Richardson's classroom now, he could see his luck—or lack of it—was holding: not only was she sitting at the back with her boyfriend, their whole entourage was sitting beside them, and the girl who'd waylaid him on the steps now whispered something to her friends. As if choreographed, they all looked in his direction, smirks on their faces. His miserable morning was morphing into a spectacularly shitty day. Keegan slumped into one of the few remaining seats and forced himself to pull his long legs out of the aisle.

Just as a bell signalled the beginning of class, Keegan saw Raven appear in the doorway. Catching her eye, he pointed toward the empty seat across the aisle from his and she smiled, winding her way across the crowded room and sitting down.

"Welcome, everyone," said Richardson, and the post-recess chatter in the room faded away. After introducing himself, he began calling out names from a class list and marking their owners on a seating chart, during which Keegan learned the names of The Couple—Willa Jaffrey and Wynn d'Entremont—along with Understudy Couples One and Two: Todd Thomas, Britney Lamontagne, Jay Underwood, and Celia Waters. He also learned Raven's last name: Powell.

"It's important," continued the teacher, "that I quickly get to know each of you as learners, but it's also important that you get to know one another because you'll be learning as much if not more from your classmates as you will from me. To that end, I'm going to ask you to pair up with someone you don't know and interview one another. Afterwards, I'll ask you to share with the rest of the class what you've learned about your partner."

"Mr. Richardson?" came a voice from the back of the room.

The teacher glanced at his seating chart. "Willa, right?"

"Yes. Most of us know just about everyone here, so is it okay if I interview one of my friends?"

"I would imagine, Willa," said Richardson, "that there are students here whom you aren't as familiar with as others." His eyes roamed the group, settling on Keegan. "You're in my homeroom."

*Uh-oh.*

Richardson smiled. "Willa—"

*Mother of God, don't—*

"—could I ask you to pair up with"—he glanced at his seating chart again—"Keegan?"

Keegan suffered through three heartbeats of pained silence before hearing a muted "Okay."

"Thanks," said Richardson. "Is there anyone else new to the school?"

Raven raised her hand.

"Welcome," said the teacher, once more glancing at his seating chart, "Raven." He looked around the room. "Who'd like the pleasure of interviewing our other new student?"

"I'll do it."

Keegan turned to see Wynn d'Entremont's hand in the air.

"If it's okay with you, Mr. Richardson," said Raven, "I was hoping to work with this person." She pointed behind her to a girl with rust-coloured hair whose name, Keegan thought, was Bailey Something. And by the look on Bailey Something's face, Raven's plan was news to her.

"Certainly," said Richardson. He let his eyes wander the room. "For the next ten minutes, one of you will interview the other. Try to have an actual conversation with your partner and see where his or her responses take you. At the end of that time, you'll reverse roles. Any questions?"

No hands went up. "Okay," said the teacher, "pair up and keep an eye on the time, okay?"

Chairs scraped the floor as students got up and moved around the room, settling themselves beside their partners. Keegan didn't budge.

# CHAPTER 8

As Willa moved across the room, she replayed in her head what had happened by the east entrance. She was pretty sure working with the guy Celia had publicly humiliated wouldn't be one of those best-school-year-ever moments. She felt herself flush as she approached the seat the new girl had just left, thinking about how quickly Wynn had volunteered to work with the new student, how considerate that was. He'd ended up partnering with Greg Phillips, whose acne-pocked face looked even worse than usual beside the best-looking guy in school. Willa's partner had a face like stone.

Sliding into the seat, she hoped her own face didn't betray how awkward she felt. "So," she said.

"So," he repeated.

Seconds crawled by and Willa could tell he had no intention of making this easy. Screw him. "Do you want to go first?" she asked.

He shrugged.

"Okay, then, I'll go first." She pulled a pen and notepad out of her leather bag and opened to the first page, her hand pausing above the paper. She should have paid more attention when Richardson was reading the class list. "So how do you spell your name?"

"The way it sounds."

She could see in his eyes that he knew she didn't have a clue what it was. "You want to sound it out for me?"

He said nothing for a long moment, then exaggerated "Keegan" into five syllables.

She wrote it down. And waited. She looked up. "And your last name is . . . ?" But he just sat there staring at her. "Look, I know it starts with F, G, H, I, or J because we're in the same homeroom."

"Lucky me."

She frowned. "You always such a pain?"

"I rise to the occasion."

"Okay, so no last name."

"Fraser."

Figures it would be an F-word, she thought, writing it down. "Where're you from?"

"Vancouver."

"Really?" She looked up. "I have a cousin who lives there. Near Maple Tree Square in Gastown. Were you anywhere close to that?"

The guy shrugged again. "No."

"So what part of Vancou—"

"Look," he said, clearly agitated, "we're already down two of your ten minutes. You wanna move on?"

Willa bristled. "What I *want* is to just get through this, okay? It doesn't matter to me where you're from. I'm just doing what Richardson said."

"The conversation thing?"

"You've *heard* of it then?" she snapped. "That quaint ritual where two people exchange—"

"Clock's still ticking," he interrupted.

She glared at him for a long moment, forced her teeth to unclench, then summoned the syrupy tone she sometimes used with old people and very young children. "And what brought you to Brookdale, Keegan?" she asked.

"A plane. Perhaps you've heard of them. They're a quaint means of transporta—"

"Hilarious." She'd had all she could take of this jerk and was about to get up and return to her seat when he spoke again.

"My dad."

She didn't get it. "What about him?"

"The reason we're in Brookdale. He got a job here."

"Must be quite the job to move you clear across the country." When he didn't respond, she asked, "What's he do?"

"He's an accountant."

She wrote that down. "Where's he work?"

"At a car dealership."

"Where?"

"Here in town."

"Brookdale has three," she said. The Hyundai and Ford dealerships were her father's only competitors in this part of the province.

"Valley Motors."

Willa couldn't hold back the satisfied smile that lit up her face, and she settled back in her chair, savouring the moment before offering, "Your dad works for mine."

+ + +

"Time's up," Richardson announced at the end of the twenty minutes, and talk trickled away. "Who'd like to go first?"

Willa expected to sit through an awkward pause, but Bailey Holloway put up her hand. "We will," she said, glancing at her partner, who nodded in return.

"Great," said Richardson. "Why don't you both come up here so everyone can see you."

The two girls walked to the front of the classroom. "This is Raven Powell," said Bailey. "Raven's a member of the Haida First Nation, and she's just moved here with her parents from the West Coast. Her mother accepted a professorship at Acadia University, where she now teaches Aboriginal studies, and her father is a researcher for the federal government. Raven's the youngest of four children and the only girl in her family. Her oldest brother is a woodcarver who specializes in totems, and one of his pieces stands on the grounds of the Parliament Buildings in Victoria. But he's not the only artistic member of their family. Raven paints and plays guitar, but her first love is dance, and one day she hopes to perform with the National Ballet of Canada."

Smiling, Richardson clapped his hands, and others in the room joined him. "That was terrific, Bailey. And welcome to Brookdale, Raven."

"Thanks," Raven smiled. Turning to her partner, she continued, "Now I have the pleasure of introducing Bailey Holloway . . ."

Willa allowed her mind to drift. There wasn't much about Bailey that she didn't already know. Celia called her trailer trash, but that was harsh. It wasn't Bailey's fault that she and her younger sister and brother all had different fathers, none of whom had stayed around long. Her mother, Francine, worked in the hospital laundry, and Britney once joked how fitting it was that the woman spent her days cleaning sheets: "She's a total mattress, right?" Willa figured Bailey would spend her whole life in Brookdale like her mother, and Celia had narrowed that forecast further, predicting that, like her mother, Bailey wouldn't graduate before getting knocked up. She and Britney were even taking bets on the month it would happen.

As Raven continued speaking, Willa grinned again at learning the new guy's father worked for her dad. That little revelation had taken the wind out of his sails. He'd been a complete asshole up to that point, but he'd pulled his horns in once he found out who she was.

She looked down at the notes she'd made and wondered what she was going to say about him when it was their turn. He hadn't given her much to go on. One sibling, a younger brother. Both lived with their father. No mention of the mother, although Willa sensed she wasn't in the picture. Divorced, probably. No surprise there if the dad had to come clear across the country to get a job. Probably as big a loser as his son. Celia once claimed that loser DNA ran in families, and she offered Bailey, Greg, and Russell as proof. Willa had laughed like she always did when the girls said stuff like that, but she'd still felt a twinge of guilt. Bailey wasn't what you'd call a friend, but she'd always been nice to Willa—and to Celia and Britney, too, for that matter—and she didn't think Russell and Greg had ever done anything to offend them. But she never reminded them of that, just smiled or chuckled, whatever the moment called for. Her friends had always been quick to pick up on people's flaws, and their comments had entertained Willa for years.

Lately, though, their remarks had seemed darker somehow, more cutting than comical, and a couple of times in the past few months Willa had wondered what they said about *her* when she wasn't around. But both times she'd brushed that thought aside, embarrassed by her disloyalty. Celia and Britney were her best friends.

Willa looked down at the notes she'd written about the new guy and felt a little sheepish about the assumptions she'd made concerning his family. But he'd been so irritating, frustrating her at every turn. Which was why, once she'd finished recording the little information he'd shared, she hadn't waited for him to ask her questions and began telling him things about herself. He'd just sat there, though, writing down almost nothing, so she'd begun talking about the trip she and her family had taken to Italy just to fill up the time. But his bored expression never changed.

Clapping roused her from her reverie, and she watched as Bailey and Raven sat down. "Who'd like to go next?" asked Richardson.

Willa had no desire to prolong the agony. "We will," she offered, getting up and walking to the front of the room. She was conscious that hers were the only footsteps she heard, and she turned to see Keegan still in his seat. Embarrassed, she waited along with everyone else as he slowly swung his long legs into the aisle, got up, and came to the front.

"Which of you is going first?" asked Richardson.

Willa opened her mouth to speak, but before she could say a word, Keegan began.

"This is Willa Jaffrey."

Willa turned, surprised by his sudden eagerness to share. And interested to hear what he had to say.

"I guess most of you here know all about her," Keegan continued. "For those of you who don't, what you see is pretty much what you get."

# CHAPTER 9

*Christ!* If Griff read one more posting about how cool Sonia Martinez's new car was (if you could even *call* a Nissan Micra a car), he didn't think he'd be able to keep from putting his fist through his laptop's display. Why Sonia was Talia's friend in the first place was beyond him. For one thing, Talia was a hell of a lot smarter—Griff had hacked their school records and found Sonia could barely maintain a C average while Talia consistently pulled off As. For another, their attitudes about guys were worlds apart—Sonia was forever riding the Loser Town Express while Talia still hadn't started dating again. There was something about her loyalty to a person she hadn't seen in months that touched a chord in Griff. If only his mother had had some of that loyalty, perhaps things might have turned out differently for her. For both of them.

Griff looked once more at the selfie Sonia had posted that morning of her standing in front of her car, which looked more like a snot-bubble than a vehicle, then closed his laptop in disgust. If he spent another mind-numbing moment on Facebook he might lose the will to live, so he opted to head over to Garfield Park to clear his head. Of course, that meant getting the evil eye from his super on his way out of the building. Griff was pretty sure the pint-sized prick didn't like him, hadn't liked him from the day he'd moved in. At first he thought it was because he towered over the runt, making him physically uncomfortable just by standing next to him. But Griff knew now that it was more than his size putting the guy off. He could tell by the way he studied Griff when he thought Griff's attention was elsewhere, like when he was getting his mail from his box in the lobby and the super was polishing the floor. Or when Griff was waiting on the sidewalk for a cab and the super was Windexing the glass in the entry. He could always feel the guy's eyes on him, like he was trying to peer inside Griff's head, trying to work out his story.

On the lease he'd signed, Griff had put down his employer as Southside Developers, a construction company owned by Morozov. Griff guessed the super was surprised by the hours he appeared to work—or, more to the point, *not* work. For a guy in construction, Griff spent a lot of time in his apartment. More than once during the middle of the day, he'd walked under the lobby's surveillance camera and imagined the super on the other end of that electronic feed recording the date and time in a note-book. Paranoid? Probably, but in Griff's line of work, paranoia wasn't a bad thing.

Stretching, Griff got up and walked to the sliding door lead-ing to his balcony and stepped outside. As usual, that christly wind off Lake Michigan pummelled him, making his shirt flap like a flag. Ads for apartments in his building always played up their water views, but that wasn't what had drawn him to rent there—it was the five-minute walk to the CTA's Green Line, which made it easy getting to Garfield Park, where he often spent his days when he wasn't in the middle of a job for Morozov.

Sometimes he went early in the morning and returned home late in the afternoon to imitate a workday routine, although that obviously hadn't convinced the super. Mostly, though, he went because he loved the place. Located on the West Side, Garfield Park was 184 acres of some of the most beautiful flower gardens in the Midwest.

Griff's fondness for flowers certainly hadn't come from his mother—her interest in plants had been limited to those she could smoke. Nor had it come from the many "uncles" who'd drifted into and out of their lives. Griff had found his way to flowers via Clovis Lafayette, a retired hardware salesman originally from Louisiana who owned an Airstream a few lanes over from the leaky double-wide his mother rented in Camelot Trailer Park out on Sweet Home Cutoff.

When Griff was in ninth grade, he'd been suspended for bullying and fighting so many times that, by spring, the school's administration recommended he stay home for the rest of the year. Griff's mother had been livid, screaming at him that no good-for-nothing asshole son of hers was going to freeload off her all day, and she made him go door-to-door asking neighbours if they had any chores they wanted help with. He and his mom had been living in their trailer on Lancelot Way for only a few weeks, having been evicted from their last place in Little Rock (his mother always seemed genuinely surprised when landlords expected to be paid their rent on time), and during those weeks Griff hadn't done more than nod to their neighbours. Most of them were a lot older than his mother and, judging from the condition of their trailers, no better off than Marsha and Griff Barnett.

Clovis Lafayette, however, seemed the exception. Yeah, he was old, but his lot on Guinevere Lane was way nicer than most of the others in Camelot. Clovis was forever washing the dust off the exterior of his aging Land Yacht, and he'd covered almost every available square inch of his property with flowers. And not just your standard petunias and impatiens; Clovis's flowers looked like the kinds Griff had seen in the pages of the old *National Geographics* he'd flipped through while he sat in his school's detention room.

During his trek through Camelot half-heartedly looking for work, Griff wasn't surprised to come up empty-handed. People who lived hand-to-mouth on disability and welfare cheques didn't have a lot of extra cash for hiring help, but Clovis Lafayette had once again been the exception. He'd just had several bags of fertilizer and potting soil delivered to him from a garden centre in Little Rock, and Clovis said he'd pay Griff ten bucks to lug the bags to where he needed them and then spread the stuff around. That ended up being the first of many such jobs Griff did for Clovis that spring and, in the process, Griff learned a lot about flowers. Later, when he fell in with Morozov, he'd come to realize how much of that learning applied to his current line of work. For one thing, offing targets was a lot like thinning out plants that had outlived their usefulness or posed problems for those that remained. Like the guy he'd been hunting for months now.

A vigorous gust carrying dirt from the street below scoured Griff's face, and he held up a hand to deflect it. He'd always hated getting dirt in his eyes, even more so after his last moments with Clovis Lafayette. For weeks after Griff buried him in the woods behind the dumpster on Roundtable Road, he couldn't shake from his memory the sight of Clovis's open eyes filling up with soil.

# CHAPTER 10

**C**arrying a tray with a carton of milk, two apples, and a serving of something labelled pasta but resembling afterbirth, Keegan scanned the tables looking for the nearest empty seat to park his butt. Before today, he'd never minded his above-average height but, towering over a lot of the people around him now, he felt like there was a neon sign over his head flashing Loser.

"Keegan!"

He turned toward a hand waving at him from the far side of the cafeteria and saw Raven sitting with Bailey Something and two guys, all four looking in his direction. Relief washed over him and he wove his way toward the group. Raven slid sideways to make room for him on the bench attached to a long table that was one of twenty others in the large, noisy space. Setting down his tray, he awkwardly folded his long legs into the narrow opening between the bench and the table.

"You remember Bailey and Greg from English class," said Raven when he was settled.

Keegan nodded. He'd felt sorry for Greg when he got up to introduce Wynn d'Entremont. Standing beside a guy who could model for Abercrombie & Fitch only emphasized Greg's skinny build and acne-riddled face, which probably explained why he'd hurried through a list of d'Entremont's many awards and accomplishments.

"This is Russell," Raven continued, gesturing toward a short, round guy on the opposite side of the table who occupied far more than his share of the bench seat. He wore a sweatshirt with lettering on it that Keegan assumed was a school motto until he read it: *My cereal bowl comes with a lifeguard.* "Russell," said Raven, "meet Keegan."

"Hey, Keegan," said Russell. "I see you got the pasta. Brave guy."

Checking out their trays, Keegan could see that none of them had chosen that dish. "Bad?" he asked.

"It's not so much the taste as the consistency," said Greg. "It's like tapioca with an attitude."

"I don't think it ever digests," added Bailey. "It'll kinda sit at the bottom of your stomach for the next day or so and then reappear in pretty much the same form it is now."

"I have my suspicions," offered Russell, "that the janitors use it as crack fill whenever some Neanderthal decides to put his fist through a wall."

"That happen much?" asked Keegan.

"Depends on how often they serve the pasta," Russell replied.

Keegan laughed and pushed the offending plate away, taking a bite of one of his apples and enjoying the normalcy of the moment before turning to Raven and Bailey. "Hey, great introductions," he said. "Tough first act to follow."

"Thanks," said Raven. "I'm glad Richardson had us do them. It was a great way to get to know people on the first day." She flashed a smile at Bailey, who returned it warmly.

"That's really something about your brother's carving," Keegan said to Raven. "And Bailey, that stuff about the writing contest was impressive."

Bailey's face turned pink. "Raven's the first person I told about it. She asked so many great questions it just slipped out."

"Writing contest?" asked Russell.

"Yeah," said Greg, and there was no mistaking the enthusiasm in his voice, "she placed second in this year's Atlantic Writing Competition."

"Jeez, Bailey, that's great!" exclaimed Russell.

The pink in her face deepening, Bailey waved away the compliment. "It was just the poetry category, and I don't imagine too many people entered."

"*Nuh*-uh," said Greg, shaking his head and tapping his phone in his shirt pocket. "The minute Raven told us, I checked it out online. There were nearly three hundred entries, Bailey. Coming in second is pretty terrific." Keegan could see Greg's face redden in splotches, his acne emphasizing his own embarrassment, and he wondered if Bailey knew the guy was crushing on her.

"When'd you find out about this?" asked Russell.

"A couple weeks ago," she replied.

Russell's eyes widened. "And you didn't *say* anything?"

Bailey looked down. "I didn't want certain people to, you know . . ."

"Give you a hard time," Greg finished for her.

Bailey nodded.

"I don't get it," said Keegan. "Who would give you grief over something like that?"

Russell leaned toward him, no easy task given his considerable belly. "There are a few seniors—" He stopped and seemed to consider his words before continuing, "Let's just say you don't want to get noticed around here. It's usually best to keep your head down, if you know what I mean."

Keegan *did* know what he meant. There were enough yahoos at his old school who took pleasure in singling out people for their own amusement. One group in particular had been a real problem for two of his friends, Curtis and Lamont, who'd made no secret of the fact that they were gay. But as often as he'd seen it happen, Keegan could never understand the mentality behind the need some people had to ridicule others.

"I don't think he does," Greg said to Russell. "Know about keeping his head down, I mean."

Bailey nodded in agreement, releasing a low whistle as if for auditory emphasis.

"What?" asked Russell. He turned again to Keegan. "Okay, what'd you do?"

Keegan shrugged, figuring Raven must have told Greg about the no-hats incident with the VP in the office. But he was wrong.

"He dissed Willa Jaffrey," said Greg, his voice noticeably lower.

Russell gaped at him. "Seriously?"

"In front of our English class," Greg explained. "Including the whole royal party."

"Oh, man," said Russell. He glanced over his shoulder, then back, an expression of relief on his face. "You're lucky they hardly ever eat in the cafeteria." He shot a look at the others. "What happened?"

Bailey explained the task Richardson had given them. "And Keegan got to introduce Willa," she said.

Now Raven spoke up. "I think I'm missing something. Keegan didn't say anything bad about her. In fact, he didn't say much at all."

"That's the point," said Greg.

Russell groaned. "Tell me you at least mentioned her trip to Italy."

"Look," said Keegan, "I had a run-in earlier with her and her friends. I was pissed, so I thought the less I said about her right then, the better."

"He said," Greg offered to Russell, "what you see is pretty much what you get."

Russell echoed Bailey's whistle. "Oh, man," he said, shaking his head. "You are in some serious shit, dude."

"I probably should've said more," conceded Keegan, "but she got under my skin. Especially after the way she looked at me when she found out my dad works for hers."

"Your dad works for Carleton Jaffrey?" asked Russell.

"At his dealership. He's their new accountant."

Russell and Greg exchanged a look that Keegan couldn't read. "I hope your dad doesn't get too comfortable," Greg said. "After this morning, the royal party'll be on your ass for sure."

Keegan heard Forbes's prime directive echo in his head, and he grimaced.

"Maybe you should apologize to her," Raven offered.

Again? thought Keegan. "For what? Not saying enough about her?"

"Something to think about," Bailey agreed.

Another moment passed, and suddenly Russell grinned. "Jeez, I wish I could've seen the look on her face."

Greg pulled out his phone. "Priceless." He touched the screen and then passed it around. "Use the zoom," he said.

A second later, people all over the cafeteria turned toward the group huddled over their table, Russell Shaw's laughter echoing through the large space.

# CHAPTER 11

Willa stared at Britney's phone. "I can't *believe* you took a picture of that," she moaned.

"I'm taking photos of all of us on our first day back," said Britney from across the table at Subway, where the six had gone for lunch. "Since you were standing up there during our first class of our senior year, I figured what could be better, right?" She reached for her phone and, looking at the screen again, she frowned. "Trust me, I won't be posting *that* one."

Wynn put his arm around Willa. "Listen, babe, nobody embarrasses my girl and gets away with it. If he hadn't disappeared so fast, I would've had a chat with that asshole after class." He made a fist with his meaty free hand to clarify the meaning of *chat.*

Willa let her body lean into his. "Thanks, Wynn," she said, "but I don't want you getting into trouble for me. It isn't worth it."

Todd shook his head. "He disrespected you in front of the whole class, Wills."

Willa reddened again, remembering how she'd reacted to the new guy about his dad working for her father. She'd kind of rubbed it in, clearly pissing him off in the process. "Look, it's no big deal, okay? Let's just forget it." She spied a newspaper lying on the table next to them and reached for it. "Here," she said, eager to change the subject, "let's check out the personals."

"Jeez," said Jay, "do people even *read* newspapers anymore?"

"Yeah," said Celia. "Ninety-year-olds who've never heard of the Internet."

Ignoring their comments, Willa pulled out the classifieds and scanned for the personal ads. "Here's one," she said. "'Phyllis Tidwell is no longer responsible for the debts incurred by Andrew Tidwell.'"

Jay cocked an eyebrow. "Sounds like some old lady finally gave the boot to her slacker son."

Willa looked up. "I'm thinking Phyllis and Andrew were married. She caught him cheating."

"With her best friend, right?" said Britney.

Willa shook her head. "With her brother."

"Ew!" said Celia, and all of them laughed.

Willa scanned a few more ads, then read, "'Thank you, St. Jude, for favours granted. Signed L.J.'"

"Favours granted," murmured Celia. "I'm guessing sexual."

"All you ever think about is sex," Britney teased.

Jay put an arm around Celia, grinning as he drew her close. "And that's a problem how?" he asked.

Willa suppressed a sigh—talk like that always reminded her of what she and Wynn didn't share—and she pondered the cryptic message. "Jude's the patron saint of lost causes." She read the ad again silently and then grinned. "L.J. just won the lottery. Not the big one, but enough to pay off some of his gambling debts. But ten-to-one he's back at the casino tonight."

Still grinning at her explanation, Willa looked up, catching what she thought was the tail end of an eye-roll Celia had given Britney. It was no secret those two had never shared Willa's delight at making up backstories for the anonymous people who posted those ads. They preferred their drama real and starring people they knew. Of course, after her embarrassment in class earlier, Willa knew she was just being overly sensitive, had probably imagined the eye-roll.

She noticed the time on the wall clock behind the cash register. "Uh-oh," she said, nodding toward it. They had only minutes to get back for their first afternoon class.

Celia, however, obviously thought Willa was drawing their attention to the person behind the counter, a girl maybe a couple of years older than they were. "I *know!*" she exclaimed breathily. "Somebody needs to give her some tips on plucking. Those eyebrows look like skidmarks!"

Wynn, Britney, Todd, and Jay cracked up, their laughter raucous in the small space. Willa grinned in agreement, until she looked again at the girl, whose face reddened as she took an order from an old woman with a hearing aid. Rising to leave, Willa hoped that the girl was just flushed from the heat of the ovens behind her, but that hope dissolved when Britney muttered in a voice loud enough for even the old woman to hear, "If they're gonna serve the public, people with eyebrows like that need to take a course in personal grooming."

Outside, the six piled into their cars. Wynn had driven Willa to Subway in his new Thunderbird, which his father had bought last week while she was away. Since it was a two-seater, the other four had taken Todd's Mustang. Both cars were convertibles, and Willa revelled in the feel of the wind in her hair as they raced back to the school. It helped get her mind off the expression she'd seen on that girl's face as they'd walked by her.

The Thunderbird's tires complained against the pavement as Wynn took the next turn faster than he should have. He wasn't worried about getting ticketed for speeding, and for good reason—besides being the town's mayor, his dad was tight with Brookdale's chief of police. Sure, Wynn might get stopped from time to time and given warnings, but none of the town's constables would dare to write him up.

*What you see is pretty much what you get.*

Why couldn't she get those words out of her head?

+ + +

"I don't know why Coach Cameron had to start tryouts this afternoon," Celia whined after last period as she shoved her textbooks into her locker. "It's the frigging first day back!"

"I don't know why our guys should have to try out in the *first* place," muttered Britney.

Willa could understand their complaints, since Wynn, Jay, and Todd had led the soccer team in goals last season. "I guess Cameron's just being fair," she offered, clicking her lock on the hasp.

"But the first day of school?" Celia repeated. "Doesn't he realize that some people have actual *lives*?"

"When Todd told me about the email Cameron sent out to all the boys last week," Britney grumbled, "I thought he was joking."

Having been out of the loop, Willa had only heard about the email that morning and she, too, thought that first-day-of-school soccer tryouts were a little much. But she could understand the coach's reasoning—every school in the district would be looking to take down Brookdale after their amazing performance last year, and finalizing this season's roster even a few days early meant more time for practices. Willa idly wondered if the new guy would be trying out today and, as if her thoughts had conjured him, he suddenly appeared around the corner. Willa groaned softly, and both Britney and Celia turned to look at the source of her discomfort. They whipped back immediately, grinning.

"Be gentle," said Britney, although her tone suggested she meant something quite different. Celia was nearly quivering with anticipation.

It turned out that Willa and the new guy had *two* classes in common that semester, the other one being accelerated math immediately after lunch. Having taken math from Mr. Shedrand last year, Willa wasn't surprised when he'd launched immediately into a mind-deadening lecture on the importance of calculus and then shown them a lengthy PowerPoint containing what he called "essential notes" that everybody had to copy. Out of earshot, his students called him Deadhand because of the pages of notes he gave each day, and Willa's hand was numb halfway into that class. If she could've gotten away with it, she'd have taken shots of his remaining slides with her phone, but Shedrand was infamous for confiscating any cell he saw in his classroom.

During an uncharacteristic pause in the flurry of note-copying that period, Willa had glanced across the room and caught the new guy staring into space, and even from two rows away she could see that the open pages of his notebook contained none of Shedrand's material. The only thing he'd done was doodle something that, from where she was sitting, looked a lot like a campfire. Rubbing the stiffness out of her hand, she'd automatically begun inventing a backstory about his family being outdoorsy, how the father took the two brothers camping as often as he c—

But then Shedrand had advanced to the next slide and pencils were racing once more.

Seeing the new guy walk toward her now, his backpack slung over his shoulder, she assessed his looks. He wasn't nearly as hot as Wynn, of course, and his height—he was at least a head taller than her—made his body look slimmer than she liked in a guy, but even his loose clothing didn't hide his athletic build. His hair, so black it was almost blue, was far too long and hung straight in every direction, as if he couldn't be bothered to deal with it. And his jaw, in her opinion, was much too square, like Buzz Lightyear from the *Toy Story* movies she'd watched when she was a kid. But he wasn't ugly. She'd give him that.

She watched as he ran a hand through that black hair now, dragging it from his eyes, then stiffened when he noticed her, too. Coming abreast of her and her friends, he stopped. "Hey," he said.

Willa nodded. Behind her, she could sense movement: Celia and Britney glancing at each other, waiting.

His awkwardness was almost palpable, and she couldn't help remembering Celia's comment that morning: *Man, wouldn't that suck? Starting your senior year in a new place and not knowing anybody?*

"One day behind us," he offered, then grimaced as if realizing how lame his comment sounded.

But it was also true. Hadn't she thought the exact same thing when the final bell rang? The best school year ever had started out pretty much like every year before. Lousy. "Yeah," she agreed, adding an automatic, "only 194 more to go."

He seemed surprised. "Isn't it 179?"

"Maybe in Vancouver, but not here in Nova Scotia."

He reddened, reminding her of the clerk behind the Subway cash register, how embarrassed the girl had been. Which made Willa think of how she and Brit and Celia had embarrassed him over what had happened in the parking lot. And then how she'd treated him in English class, rubbing in his face about his dad working for her fa—

A hand nudged Willa from behind. She glanced back at Britney, whose expression telegraphed an undeniable *WTF!*

"Look, I didn't mean to hold you up," the new guy said, obviously thinking he'd interrupted something. "But about this morning, what I said when I introduced you, I wanted to—"

"About that," said Britney, her voice like a razor. She stepped out from behind Willa. "You think you can get away with saying shit like that about our friend?"

His face coloured. "I just meant—"

"It's pretty clear what you meant, asshole," said Celia, moving forward to stand on Willa's other side.

He looked at Willa, his expression flickering into something she couldn't read. She was embarrassed all over again, but not by what he'd said in English class. By her friends, who'd hijacked the moment and manufactured a whole new drama. She could feel her own face begin to pink. "Let's not—"

"Willa was humiliated," Celia interrupted, her voice rising as if everyone in that corridor couldn't already hear her clearly. The river of seniors leaving the building had slowed to a trickle, but the remaining students were gawking at them, whispering to each other.

"Yeah, humiliated," echoed Britney. She poked Willa with her elbow. "Tell him, Wills."

Willa was humiliated, all right—by the spectacle they were making now.

"Yeah, Willa," urged Celia, "*tell* him."

Willa glanced at Celia, who was looking not at her but at Britney, her expression similar to the one she'd worn at Subway when Willa thought she'd rolled her eyes. More than similar. It was the same.

Willa turned to Keegan. "Yeah, you humiliated me," she said, her words barely audible.

He glanced away, seemed to take a breath, then turned to her again. "Look, I should've—"

"There's *lotsa* things you *should* have done," snapped Britney. "One of them is watching that mouth of yours."

"First, though," added Celia, "you'd better learn how things work around here."

"How things work," he repeated, his voice now toneless. His expression changed again, but this time Willa could read it. He was pissed. He turned to her. "You're unbelievable."

"Me?" she asked. Why?"

"Waiting here with your friends to ambush me. Christ, that's so middle school. You need to grow up, Jaffrey."

Willa felt her embarrassment flare into annoyance. After all, weren't her friends just standing up for her? But before she could say anything, he spoke again. "You're in for quite a shock," he said.

"Am I?" She heard her own voice begin to rise.

"One of these days, you're gonna find out you're not the centre of the universe."

She blinked at him, her annoyance churning into something stormier. She could feel Celia and Britney beside her waiting, watching, willing her to respond. So she did. "*You're* summing *me* up?" she said. "You've been here how long? A whole *day?*" Her words ricocheted off the lockers like bullets.

"I had you pegged from the moment we met," he said. "What you see is what you get, right?"

Willa felt her face work oddly, as if trying to build three expressions at once: anger, indignation, and something more wounded, like the way you'd look after a stinging slap. But before she could reply, he glanced around to see all the eyes in that corridor focused on him.

"Look, let's drop it," he said. He turned to leave, heading for the exit.

She felt her indignation grow exponentially, like the algebraic function Shedrand had shown them in one of his frigging slides. Which made her think of the drawing in the new guy's math notebook. "You need to put out a fire?" she called after him. She hoped he could hear the sarcasm in her voice.

It was like she'd struck him. His stride faltered and, for a second, she thought he would turn. But he didn't. He pushed through the exit and was gone.

# CHAPTER 12

That bitch! Keegan fumed as he burst out the door. The Jaffrey girl had obviously been plotting payback ever since English class, she and her friends waiting for him in the hallway like a firing squad. What had that Celia person said? *You'd better learn how things work around here.* Oh, he'd had that figured out the moment he'd laid eyes on them. And to think he'd been planning to *apologize* to her again!

Reaching the bottom of the steps, Keegan turned and headed for the walkway that would take him around the front of the school. Avoiding the student parking lot meant avoiding another confrontation with Willa Jaffrey, but that wasn't the reason he was opting for the longer route. He was in no hurry to get home.

Correction: no hurry to get to his *house.* He couldn't imagine ever thinking of it as home.

Shoving that thought away, he replayed the events of the past few hours in his head, imagining what Forbes might say about his first day at Brookdale High. It wasn't as if Keegan didn't understand the importance of the prime directive. Hadn't Forbes hammered it into his head repeatedly? And hadn't his father echoed the same thing that very morning as Keegan left for school?

He reached the sidewalk on Gates Avenue and followed the high chain-link fence separating the street from the school's field, where already dozens of guys stood listening to Coach Cameron. Soccer tryouts were being held this week, something he'd learned fourth period during phys ed. Taught by Cameron, the period had been more of an information session than a class—stuff about safety issues and individual performance goals—and most of the people in his class were guys. Last week, Cameron had sent out an email about the tryouts, but Keegan hadn't received it, probably because new students weren't in Cameron's database yet. Even if he *had* gotten it, though, it wouldn't have mattered. He couldn't play.

Three of the guys taking phys ed were Jaffrey's boyfriend and his two buddies, and all three had given Keegan weird looks when he'd walked in, muttering to one another as he'd passed. Keegan hadn't heard what they were saying, but after that scene a few minutes ago in the hallway he figured he'd been a hot topic of conversation at lunchtime.

A whistle shattered the air, followed by Cameron's deep voice shouting commands, and Keegan watched as guys lined up taking turns performing manoeuvres. Balls arced through the air, some of them bouncing across the grass toward the fence.

"Vancouver!"

He turned to see d'Entremont jogging toward him, trapping a ball neatly with his feet and then dribbling it expertly toward the chain-link. "Yeah?"

"You not trying out for the team?"

Keegan shook his head and kept walking.

"Why not?" D'Entremont paced him on his side of the fence,

the ball constantly moving between his feet. "They don't play soccer out west?"

"They play it," Keegan replied. "I don't."

"Figures." This from Todd Thomas, who had also retrieved a ball and, like d'Entremont, hadn't thought it necessary to trot back to Cameron. It was clear to Keegan that neither of them was too worried about not making the team, which didn't surprise him. Just another example of how things worked around here.

As if proving that point, Jay Underwood loped up, ignoring Cameron's shout to bring the balls in. "Vancouver not trying out?" he asked the other two, as if Keegan couldn't answer for himself.

"He doesn't play," said d'Entremont.

"Doesn't or can't?" Underwood asked.

"There's a difference?" d'Entremont snorted.

Underwood guffawed, and Keegan wished he'd cut through the student parking lot after all. He'd swallowed entirely too much shit for one day. He lengthened his stride.

"What you see is pretty much what you get," said d'Entremont, still pacing him.

Keegan forced himself to keep walking. Why hadn't he listened to Forbes?

"The same go for you?" d'Entremont asked him.

Keegan bit back a reply, kept his feet moving.

"Because if that's the case, you're way outta your league here. You know that, right? If I were you, I'd be checking out bus tickets to B.C. One way."

Keegan's stride faltered. "If you were me," he said, turning to face him. He repeated it more slowly—"If *you* were *me*"—and suddenly found himself struggling not to laugh. He failed.

D'Entremont's face darkened. "What's so funny, asshole?"

Keegan ignored him and resumed walking, the laughter bubbling up from nowhere and everywhere. Behind him, he could hear d'Entremont fuming—"You're lucky there's a fence between us, Vancouver!"—but that only made him laugh harder.

*Lucky.*

If luck was something he'd ever had, it had run out a long time ago.

+ + +

By the time Keegan reached his house on Maple Avenue, his laughing jag had ended, replaced now by anger at just about everything—at his father for bringing him to Butt-Suck Brookdale, at Willa Jaffrey and her merry band of dickwads, at his inability to play soccer, at everything. And even greater than all those combined was his anger at himself for doing exactly what Forbes had warned him not to.

Turning into the driveway of the tiny storey-and-a-half that squatted beneath a large maple, he followed the cracked asphalt around to the backyard, along two sides of which the previous tenants had built a high, L-shaped board fence. It connected a corner of the house with the end of what was listed in the rental agreement as a garage but was little more than a shed that leaned to the left, its roofline dipping toward the centre. Tossing his backpack onto the uneven carpet of weeds that had choked out whatever grass once grew there, he opened the door of the shed, went inside, and returned with a soccer ball under one arm, its synthetic leather panels heavily scuffed. Dropping it, he kicked it directly above his head and, as it fell, he bounced it off his right knee, then his left, back and forth, back and forth, before catching it with the top of his right sneaker, then his left, juggling it from one foot to the other as he moved around the yard.

In the middle of one section of the fence, someone had painted an image of a soccer net, and Keegan turned toward it now, the ball in constant motion. In the distance, he could faintly hear the sounds of the tryouts, the coach's whistle and barked instructions punctuated by shouts of encouragement, and Keegan let his mind drift, amplifying those sounds, morphing them into the shouts of fans watching players race down a regulation field. He let the ball fall to the ground and dribbled back and forth across the yard, his feet constantly moving as he lunged and spun, the ball seemingly fastened to them by an invisible elastic cord. In his mind's eye, he pounded toward the net in the game's final moments, his body a needle stitching through a phalanx of opposing players intent on blocking him. Ahead of him, a powerfully built blond-haired player blocked the net, his face a snarling mask as he waited for Keegan to make his move in the remaining seconds. Keegan could hear the roar of the fans swell in his head as they screamed at him to *TAKE THE SHOT!* and he feinted left before veering suddenly right, connecting squarely with the ball and launching it into the air. His opponent leaped a split-second too late, the black and white sphere now hurtling past his fingertips. The scuffed ball hit the exact centre of the painted image hard, shaking the fence and rebounding with equal force into the face of the child who'd appeared, unseen, beside him.

"*Christ*, Keegan!" he heard his father shout. "Look what you did!"

Keegan turned to see his eight-year-old brother sprawled on the weeds, blood already flowing from his mouth and nose. "Jeez, I'm sorry, Isaac," he said, kneeling beside the whimpering boy and cradling him in his arms. "You okay, buddy?" he murmured, rocking his brother gently from side to side. He could feel Isaac's blood leaching into his shirt, but he didn't give a damn.

"What the hell do you think you were doing?" growled his father, standing over them.

Keegan bit back a *Building a cold fusion reactor, what's it* look *like?* and continued to rock Isaac, making soft shushing sounds until the boy's whimpers began to subside.

Evan Fraser knelt on the ground beside his younger son and stroked his hair, but the boy's attention was already lost to the maple tree towering over them, its leaves fluttering in the September air. Keegan pulled his shirttail out of his jeans and used it to dab at the blood seeping from Isaac's upper lip, and he was glad to see that the flow from his nose had slowed. "I think you're gonna live, buddy," he said softly, pulling the boy to his feet. "Let's get you cleaned up, okay?" Isaac's eyes, however, continued to flicker in tandem with the leaves.

Bending down, Keegan put his hand under Isaac's chin and gently guided it so his brother was facing him. "We're gonna go get washed up now, Isaac. I'm gonna clean you up, okay?"

The boy's eyes continued to flicker, but their movement slowed, and he seemed to focus on some point just to the right of Keegan's face, the closest he ever came to seeing eye-to-eye with another person.

"I'll do that," said their father, taking Isaac's hand and leading him toward the back step.

They'd reached the landing when Keegan spoke again. "It was an accident, all right? I didn't mean to hurt him."

His father turned to him. "But you did, Keegan. You have to be more careful."

Keegan abruptly felt spark inside him the anger that had burned so intensely just a few minutes earlier. "Because of you," Keegan snarled, "my whole *life* is about being careful!"

His father's eyes held his for a moment, the look on his face unreadable, then he opened the back door and gently ushered Isaac inside.

Feeling his anger roil uselessly, Keegan retrieved his backpack, then saw the soccer ball a few feet away. More than anything, he wanted to kick that ball as hard as he could, drive it overhead into the maple where, he hoped, the stalk of a branch would pierce it. He liked the thought of hearing the air rush out of it, seeing the synthetic leather collapse around itself, watching it deflate like every dream he'd ever had.

But instead, he picked the ball up and walked toward that piece-of-shit shed, tossed it inside, and closed the door behind him. Turning toward the house, he realized he no longer heard the sounds of the soccer tryouts on the school field.

You could block out anything if you tried hard enough.

# CHAPTER 13

I nteresting, thought Griff as he stared at the Facebook update. The new boyfriend was a surprise, although he probably shouldn't have been, given how much time had passed since the other guy had been out of the picture. Griff had marvelled at how Talia hadn't moved on right away, admired her decision to wait, respected her sense of loyalty. He wondered what had changed. Had she learned something new?

Griff's fingers flew over his keyboard. Months ago, he'd hacked her computer and downloaded software that alerted him whenever someone accessed her Facebook page or messaged her through any of her social networks, but no alert had been triggered beyond the ones he routinely investigated. Nothing was foolproof, though, which is why he was manually accessing her other media, but half an hour later, he slumped back in his chair, frustrated once again. His efforts had turned up nothing he hadn't seen before, no contact from people he hadn't already checked out. The only difference was that Soccerguy89, whom Talia had friended weeks ago, was suddenly more than just a friend.

Seeing how the target had covered his tracks so thoroughly, Griff figured the man knew how to stay under the radar, which was why he'd switched his focus to the older son. He was sure the kid would fuck up, thinking that after all those months had passed it was finally safe to reach out to her. So when Soccerguy89 first popped up on Talia's page, Griff's instincts had jangled like crazy—the target's son had *lived* for soccer.

But Soccerguy89 was just a seventeen-year-old named Nick Longley whose dad, a major at Wright-Patterson Air Force Base in Ohio, had mustered out of the service and taken a civilian job at O'Hare Airport, resulting in the family's move to Chicago. And from what Griff had learned while accessing the boy's Ohio school records, an okay guy. Certainly nothing like those losers Sonia Martinez was forever hooking up with.

And now Talia and Nick Longley were a couple.

Griff felt a twinge of something he couldn't quite put his finger on. Disappointment? That made no sense. The girl was nothing to him. She could date whoever she wanted, right?

But that twinge was there just the same. Gnawing at him.

Griff studied the photo that Talia had posted with her status update. In it, she and this Nick guy were standing in front of the Chicago Culture Center. He had his arm around her waist, and she was gazing up at him instead of at the camera. She looked happy.

There had been a long period when that hadn't been the case. Griff wasn't completely insensitive—he knew it must have been hard on her after her boyfriend disappeared. And before that, there were the two days it took the medical examiner to confirm that what little remained of the body found in the rubble was female. At least then Talia knew he was still alive. But all those unanswered questions must have weighed on her.

Much to Griff's dismay, arson was suspected and later confirmed, but that was only because the husband had disappeared, a fact that raised a huge flag for investigators. They'd initially found no trace of an incendiary device, but when they combed through the debris a second time, one eager forensic specialist discovered minute evidence of the mechanism's signature. And once that detail was released, there was no end of speculation in the media about what had happened. At first, reporters focused on the possibility of insurance fraud, only to discover later that there was no policy on the wife. No policy on any of them, in fact, since their insurance had lapsed a year earlier. Then there was the suspicion the wife had been having an affair and the husband killed her after finding out, but no neighbours or co-workers could corroborate that theory. There were other stories, too, but of all those generated by the explosion and subsequent disappearance of the husband and two boys, Griff had most enjoyed the terrorist angle: the family had lost everything in a foreclosure and the husband had been planning to blow up the bank that had taken his house, but the device he'd built had detonated accidentally. And since there was no evidence to suggest otherwise—the guy's money problems were, after all, well documented—that one had been bandied about by the media for days until another news cycle had kicked in. Things might have gone differently if the target had had relatives around to defend him and demand answers, but there was no one.

What had pleased Griff about all those stories was that nothing tied the explosion to anyone else, which was probably another reason why he was still among the living. The target had, after all, worked for Battaglia, so there was no direct connection between him and that pasty-faced fuck Morozov. But despite the satisfaction Griff took from how things had turned out, he could appreciate how hard all of those stories must have been on the girl. Which only increased the respect he'd felt for her as she'd continued to wait month after month for news of her boyfriend. There was no denying how attractive she was, and there was probably no end of guys waiting to take his place.

Griff studied that photo once more, looked at the expression on Talia's face, looked at the way this Nick person had wrapped his arm around her, and he felt that twinge again.

# CHAPTER 14

Guiding the SUV into the three-car garage attached to her family's Georgian colonial, Willa replayed in her head the conversation with the new guy one more time: *About this morning, what I said when I introduced you, I wanted to—* It sounded like he'd been about to apologize, but then Britney had jumped in and the whole thing had gone to hell. *You need to grow up, Jaffrey,* he'd said. As if he *knew* her! But as much as that had stung, it was his parting remark—*I had you pegged from the moment we met. What you see is what you get, right?*—that had made her lose her temper.

Getting out, she crossed the other two garage bays. Her father's was empty, but a new Cadillac ATS with dealer plates—*Jaffrey 2*—sat in the space nearest the entrance to the house. Willa sighed, hoping her mother's mood had improved since that morning. Despite the size of their house—nearly six thousand square feet spread over two and a half storeys—Willa had easily heard her parents arguing again before she'd gone down to breakfast.

Willa passed through the mudroom into an enormous kitchen containing sleek modern cabinetry designed and installed by Ferrari, the same company that produced precision-built cars. One of the first of its kind in the province, the kitchen had been featured in *Atlantic Home and Garden* the previous spring. Dropping her books on the large quartz-surfaced island, she opened the commercial-size refrigerator beside the equally large upright freezer and reached for a bottle of orange juice. For all the grocery shopping they did—which wasn't much, since the staples in their house seemed to be juice, yogourt, and cottage cheese—a small bar fridge would have met their needs. But really, how would a bar fridge have looked in a Ferrari kitchen featured in *Atlantic Home and Garden*?

"You're home."

Willa turned to see her mother in the doorway, an empty crystal tumbler in her hand. During the past few weeks, Lenore Jaffrey had taken to delivering cryptic second-person proclamations—*You're home, You're early, You're late*—in lieu of actual greetings whenever her daughter appeared, as if Willa needed play-by-play commentary to narrate her own movements.

"Mm," said Willa, twisting the bottle's cap.

"How was your first day?"

"Same as every other," Willa replied, taking a couple of swallows. Her answer, of course, wasn't entirely true, but she knew her mother wasn't entirely interested. The empty glass told her the reason she'd come to the kitchen.

As if to confirm that deduction, Lenore moved to the refrigerator and placed her tumbler in the ice dispenser, which dropped three perfect half-moons into her glass, and then opened a cabinet and pulled out a bottle of Grey Goose. As her mother poured herself a generous amount of the expensive vodka, Willa couldn't help seeing the changes in her looks. A stranger would no doubt see only a striking, slender woman who still looked youthful despite having celebrated her forty-third birthday in January. Her shoulder-length blond hair was thick and shiny, and between the trips she made to a salon in Halifax, only a few roots ever showed traces of grey. And to anyone else, Lenore's oval face probably still looked as fresh as ever, her smooth features seeming to mirror those of her daughter. But it was the way she now achieved this smoothness that Willa had noticed. Her mother had begun to apply more makeup than usual, to conceal the lines around her mouth and her eyes. Not that it was unusual for the face of a woman her age to begin showing the passage of time, but Willa didn't think the lines were entirely due to aging. She'd first noticed them during the summer when tension between her parents had developed. And those lines hadn't been helped by the glass that, lately, never seemed far from her mother's hand.

Lenore raised the crystal tumbler and took a long swallow of the vodka, then turned to her daughter. "Did you have the new teacher today?"

Willa nodded.

"What's he like?" asked her mother, bringing the tumbler to her lips again.

"I like him. Actually seems to enjoy his job." But she didn't want to think about school anymore. "How'd you spend *your* day?" she asked, although she was pretty sure she knew.

"With Rachel on the links." Lenore and Celia's mother had been friends for years, and the two had taken up golf after Rachel's divorce.

"How'd you do?"

"Kyle says my backswing is improving," her mother replied,

the edges of her words softer than usual. She drained the rest of the vodka.

"Who's Kyle?"

Her mother blinked at her, which made Willa wonder if she was having trouble focusing. "I've mentioned him before, haven't I?"

Willa shook her head. "No. You haven't."

"The new instructor. He's been giving me lessons." She looked at the empty glass in her hand, and Willa thought she could see the lines around her mother's mouth deepen. "Giving *Rachel* and me lessons," she added.

"Does this Kyle have a last name?"

"Of course he has, Willa. Don't be silly." Her mother refilled her glass, then turned and crossed the kitchen, opening the garden door and stepping out into the backyard. She would, Willa knew, lie on the lounger beside the pool until the shade from the trees stretched across the patio telling her it was time to prepare dinner, a process that usually involved either warming up something their housekeeper, Evelyn, had cooked earlier or ordering out. They'd had the Brookdale Heritage Inn's dining room on speed dial for years.

Finishing her juice, Willa collected her books and headed upstairs to her room, where she hoped to finish her math homework before Wynn came over that evening. Setting her bag on the bed, she pulled out her math stuff, sprawled across the duvet, and immersed herself in a series of questions that she suspected Shedrand had created to encourage less capable students to drop out of the course. It was a strategy that, along with Deadhand, had earned the teacher the name If-You're-Wrong-You're-Gone Shedrand.

As she'd expected, it wasn't long before her reams of copied notes were useless, and she reached for her laptop to get some online help. When her Facebook page automatically appeared, though, she thought about her mother's odd response to her question about the golf pro, and she did a quick search for him. She was surprised by how young he was. And how good-looking. Although she wasn't able to access much of his personal information, she learned he was single and "looking for someone special." Judging from the photos the guy had posted of himself, two of them showing a bare chest that had been sculpted by something a lot heavier than golf clubs, she was fairly certain he connected with more than his share of special someones. *What you see is pretty much what you get.*

Recalling that comment, she couldn't help wondering what the new guy had to say about himself, and in seconds she was searching for "Keegan Fraser." There were a lot of them—three looked to be senior citizens, several were men around her father's age, but the majority were teenagers. None of them, however, was the Keegan Fraser who'd insulted her in English class and then again in the corridor after school: *One of these days, you're gonna find out you're not the centre of the universe.*

Well, she thought as she directed her browser toward the calculus site she'd used last year, that makes *two* of us. You aren't even on Facebook!

As she clicked through the introductory page of the math site, another thought tugged at her. Who the hell isn't on Facebook?

# CHAPTER 15

G riff toyed with the wording for nearly half an hour. All during that time, he couldn't help thinking that Gil Atkins would get off on the idea of messaging girls on Facebook. Not that convicted killers on death row had the opportunity. And besides, Griff was nothing like Gil Atkins. He was no pervert. Griff—or, more accurately, Kayley Sheridan—was just sharing a concern about a friend, right? And hadn't they all been friends for months now? That was, after all, the beauty of Facebook.

He read his message once more before finally clicking Send.

It took only moments for Sonia Martinez's reply to appear on his screen: *what've u hrd?*

This, Griff knew, was the tough part. Like Talia, Sonia had met Soccerguy89 weeks ago, and Griff couldn't risk saying something that Sonia would know wasn't true. And having hacked into the guy's computer, Griff had found nothing about the boy that was of use to him. He didn't even surf porn, not the kind that would raise eyebrows, anyway. Good-looking, strong student, terrific athlete—your basic prom-king-in-the-making.

But chances were good that whatever Sonia knew about Nick Longley's background were things she'd learned only from him. And people didn't tell others everything. Griff's own mother was a good example of that—the bit about the abortion had been a jaw-dropper when she'd finally shared it.

Griff began to type, his thick, blunt fingers surprisingly nimble as they moved over the keyboard. Finishing, he smiled and clicked Send.

This time, Sonia's reply was almost immediate: *WTF????????*

# CHAPTER 16

"I was thinking about you last night."

Keegan turned and saw Russell Shaw five lockers down from his own, struggling to get a backpack off his shoulders, the words on his XXXL sweatshirt askew but still readable: *Fat people are hard to kidnap.* Keegan grinned. "Need some help there?" he asked.

Flushed, Russell grinned in return. "Nah, I'm good," he said, finally managing to shrug the backpack off one shoulder, gravity taking over and pulling it to the floor. "These books weigh a ton."

Keegan nodded. "I saw on YouTube that South Korea converted all their textbooks to digital. Their students swapped backpacks for tablets."

Russell leaned against his locker and wiped his arm across his glistening forehead. Already the day was too warm. "I'm looking forward to the day somebody figures out how to swap brains."

"Brains?"

"You know, inserting your consciousness into someone else's body."

"And you want this because . . ."

"It'd be the ultimate motivator."

"How's that?"

Russell looked at him for a moment as if trying to decide whether to say more, then seemed satisfied Keegan's interest was genuine. "Look, you've probably always been in shape, right?"

Keegan shrugged. "I guess so."

"So you know how it feels physically." Russell glanced down at his sweatshirt, pulled taut over his abdomen, and shook his head. "Me, not so much." Wiping at his forehead again, he continued, "Sure, I know all the common-sense reasons for getting into shape, but all that medical stuff is easy to ignore if I happen to be passing, say, a Tim Hortons. When those doughnuts start calling my name, they drown out everything else."

Keegan nodded, impressed that a guy he'd just met yesterday could be so open about his struggle with his size. It explained the sweatshirts. "So you want somebody else's body," he said.

Russell shook his head. "Too *Alien Invasion* for me. I'd just like to borrow one."

"Yeah, like *that's* not creepy," kidded Keegan.

Russell grinned again. "The person would have to agree, right? And I'd only need it for a few minutes."

"Then what's the point?"

Russell sighed. "I've always wondered whether the effort it'd take to whip all this"—he looked down at his gut again, and his face took on a wistful expression—"into shape would actually be worth it. If some scientist could insert me into the body of a guy like, say, Wynn d'Entremont, even for only a few minutes, I'd finally know what it *feels* like to be really fit. It'd be a whole lot easier to pass by Tim's the next time." He shrugged. "And then there's the other benefit."

"What's that?"

Russell lowered his voice. "People like Wynn d'Entremont would understand how it feels to be someone like me."

Again, Keegan was impressed by the guy's openness. During their conversation in the cafeteria yesterday, it hadn't taken him long to realize that Russell and his friends had an uneasy history with Wynn and the other members of the League of Extraordinary Assholes. What was it he'd said? *Let's just say you don't want to get noticed around here.* Looking at the overweight senior now, Keegan could only imagine what he'd had to put up with. It made his own altercation with Wynn on the soccer field yesterday seem trivial.

"So like I said," Russell resumed, "I was thinking about you last night."

"Why?" asked Keegan, eager to lighten the mood. "Am I a candidate for the great brain swap?"

Russell grinned. "You'd qualify, but that's not the reason. I was thinking about how you could patch things up with Willa."

Keegan grimaced. "I think Willa Jaffrey and I are beyond the patching-up phase."

"You guys look *far* too serious for the second day of school," a voice said behind them.

They turned to see Bailey and Raven approaching with Greg bringing up the rear, and Keegan figured that the expression on Greg's face as he watched Bailey walk ahead of him probably wasn't much different from Russell's each time he entered a Tim Hortons. "Hey," said Keegan.

"What's up?" asked Raven.

"Let me guess," offered Greg. "Willa Jaffrey."

"You apologized to her like we said, right?" Bailey asked.

"Yeah, about that . . ."

Greg groaned.

"Look," said Keegan, "it's not like I didn't try. It's just . . . things didn't go quite the way I planned."

"What happened?" asked Bailey.

Keegan had never felt comfortable talking about other people, even people he didn't like. "She pissed me off," he said simply.

"No shit," said Russell. "Welcome to *my* world."

"What'd she do?" asked Raven.

Keegan gave them an abbreviated version.

"No offence," said Greg, "but don't be surprised if I ignore you the next time they're around."

Russell nodded. "Yeah, who needs to get caught in *that* cross-fire?"

"*Jeez*, you guys," said Bailey. "That bunch can be a little hard to take sometimes, but you make it sound like Keegan should go into hiding."

Keegan's body reacted involuntarily. Hoping none of them had noticed the brief tremor that had shuddered through him, he forced himself to grin. "Maybe I'll just try the brain swap."

Bailey laughed. "He's been telling you about that, huh?"

Russell's face was suddenly solemn. "Keegan, what I said before about you qualifying? Don't take this the wrong way, but I wouldn't switch places with you now for anything."

Keegan was grateful for the ringing of the bell that drew Raven, Bailey, and Greg toward their own lockers to prepare for first period. Attaching his lock, Keegan heard those words in his head again: *You make it sound like Keegan should go into hiding.* He leaned forward, momentarily pressing his forehead against the cool metal door, trying to swallow the emotion clotting in his throat.

+ + +

"I want to thank you all for your introductions yesterday," said Mr. Richardson. "Now it's rubber-meets-the-road time." He pointed to a stack of books on his desk. "Few people share the same interests, so you'll have lots of choice in your reading materials this semester, but I always like to begin a course with a core text that everyone will read."

"I haven't read a book in years," said a voice at the back, a comment that evoked laughter all around. "Why should I start now?"

Richardson frowned. "It's Todd, right?"

"Yup."

"Todd, Mark Twain once said that the person who *doesn't* read good books has no advantage over the person who *can't* read them."

"Who's this Twain dude?" asked Todd.

The teacher looked astonished. "How many of you here know the writer I'm talking about?"

Keegan put up his hand. Seeing Richardson scowl, he turned and saw only a few other hands in the air, two of which were Raven's and Bailey's. Another belonged to Willa Jaffrey.

"What can you tell us about Twain, Keegan?" asked the teacher.

Keegan flushed, wishing now that he'd sat motionless. "A writer from Missouri," he said. "Best known for his humour."

"Are you familiar with any of his books?"

"*Huckleberry Finn, Tom Sawyer,* and *A Connecticut Yankee in King Arthur's Court.*"

"Those were novels. Do you know any of his non-fiction?"

Keegan shrugged. "*The Innocents Abroad* and *Roughing It.*"

"Anybody know any others?" asked the teacher.

"*Life on the Mississippi* and *Following the Equator,*" offered Raven.

"I'm glad to see some of you are aware of him," said Richardson. His eyes roamed the room. "Twain did the bulk of his writing during the 1800s, but much of it is still in print today."

"What's a guy who's been dead forever have to say to people like us now?" asked Todd.

"Reading any book, Todd, allows us inside the minds of people who've lived other lives, experienced places beyond Brookdale, like Mark Twain's Mississippi. Reading broadens our world view. But since we live in the Annapolis Valley, I thought it appropriate to start with a novel written by someone who grew up in this area." He turned to the books on his desk and began passing them around.

"What?" came another voice from the back, and Keegan didn't need to turn around to know it was Celia's. "Somebody from *here* wrote a book?"

Richardson nodded. "Ernest Buckler." He held up a copy so those who hadn't yet gotten theirs could see the cover. "*The Mountain and the Valley* is considered a Canadian classic."

"He *really* came from here?" asked Celia.

"Buckler grew up about a half-hour's drive from where you're sitting."

"I thought . . ."

"What?" asked the teacher.

"I thought that writers came from far away," she said.

The room cracked up.

A hand went up on the other side of the room. "So what's the book about?"

"*The Mountain and the Valley* deals with a number of themes," said the teacher, "but it's essentially a story about a young man who feels trapped in a place where he doesn't belong."

Keegan looked down at the book Richardson had given him, his knuckles whitening as he gripped it in his hands.

# CHAPTER 17

Willa glanced around the room at her classmates bent over their novels. After some more discussion, Richardson had given them the remainder of the period to read. Her gaze sliding over the bowed heads around her, Willa suddenly found herself focusing on Keegan Fraser, who brushed hair from his eyes as he read. Looking at him now, Willa once again remembered what he'd said to her yesterday after school. His comments still rankled, and she wasn't sure how she'd handle it if she had to work with the guy again. Was it only yesterday she'd thought this was going to be her best school year ever? Christ.

Wynn had heard what had happened before he came over last night, courtesy of Britney and Celia, who'd told Todd and Jay, who'd immediately passed along the details to Wynn. He'd been livid, of course, offering to give Fraser an epic ass-whupping off school grounds, but she'd discouraged him. For one thing, she'd never liked violence, and for another, when Wynn told her about Fraser laughing at him on the soccer field that afternoon, she'd begun to wonder if maybe there was something seriously wrong with the guy. Sure, he'd only been in school for a day, but that was more than enough time for anybody to figure out that Wynn wasn't the sort of person you'd want to piss off. Was the guy an idiot?

Something told her, though, that he wasn't stupid, which he'd confirmed earlier when he'd responded to Richardson's question about Mark Twain. Willa was pretty sure she knew as much as anyone else in her class about the American author, but she'd never heard of half the books Keegan had mentioned.

Willa glanced sideways at Wynn, and she wasn't surprised to see he had his phone in his lap, pretending to read as he tapped in a text, a frown creasing his forehead. She was glad her own phone was on vibrate, something she always made sure of whenever she entered the school, and she slipped it out of her purse now so she'd be ready when the text came in.

A moment passed, and then another. Willa glanced again at Wynn and saw his phone was still on his lap, but his fingers were no longer moving over the screen. He sat looking across the room. As if waiting.

Then, as though sensing her eyes on him, he looked over at Willa, and his frown unfolded into a broad smile.

Hearing the faint hum of a vibrating cell, she smiled warmly back at him and reached for her phone. Its display, however, was blank.

The faint hum abruptly ended and, when she glanced again at Wynn, his eyes were glued to *The Mountain and the Valley*.

# CHAPTER 18

K eegan watched Isaac eat his peas. Or, rather, roll them across his plate. It reminded him of the way his brother used to play with the abacus their mother had bought him years ago. If you could call it "play"—he was always so serious. So purposeful. The bright green balls on his plate were now arranged in rows, each one pea longer than the row above it. Keegan watched as Isaac began eating the groups in reverse order, from most peas to least. Seven, six, five . . . Like a countdown.

Keegan's morning had been something of a countdown. Part of him kept expecting another confrontation with the Jaffrey bitch or her boyfriend, but then he'd been called to the office at the end of English class and given a message to phone his father immediately. His heart hammering in his chest, his mind automatically racing through the contingency plan Forbes had given them, Keegan had imagined a dozen things that had gone wrong as he waited for his father to pick up. He was nearly weak with relief to hear that Isaac had had a meltdown at his school and, because his dad was tied up in a meeting at the dealership, Keegan had to go get him.

Not that Isaac's having a meltdown was a good thing, of

course. But it was a hell of a lot better than the other scenarios that had streaked through Keegan's head.

After signing out, Keegan had run the two blocks to Brookdale Elementary, where Isaac was in third grade. One of the reasons their father had chosen Brookdale as their new home was the support its elementary school provided children with autism spectrum disorder. Forbes, of course, had cautioned against it—"You realize what this could mean, don't you?" he'd asked Keegan's father that last night in the motel as he'd made the final arrangements—but Evan Fraser had ignored the warning, telling Forbes he had to do what was best for his family. Hearing his dad say that, Keegan had nearly yelled the words he'd been biting back for weeks: *If you really wanted what was best for this family, you wouldn't have—*

But he'd stopped himself. Instead, he had left their room and kicked the soccer ball around the field behind the motel until it was too dark to see anymore.

After checking in at the elementary school's main office, Keegan had hurried toward the resource room where he'd found Isaac with Ms. Tomlinson, the educational assistant who'd been assigned to work with him. She was speaking to him in low, soothing tones, but Isaac continued to move in a tight circle in the centre of the room, flapping his hands and making sounds that might have resembled whimpers if they hadn't seemed so urgent.

"Ordinarily," Ms. Tomlinson had explained to Keegan after he'd managed to calm his brother down, "I wouldn't have called home, but Isaac and I are just getting to know each other. I didn't want to do something that might jeopardize my relationship with him. I hope you don't mind."

"No worries," he'd told the EA as he sat beside his brother on the resource room's carpeted floor. "Do you know what set him off?"

The young woman had shaken her head. "Not really. His teacher was introducing a geography unit, and she'd just started showing the class a video about different kinds of landforms."

Keegan tried to keep his voice nonchalant. "Was there a volcano on the video?"

"Yes," Tomlinson had replied. "A clip of one erupting in Iceland. Are volcanoes one of his triggers?"

"Isaac's always had a thing about them," Keegan had told her, glad she didn't know him well enough to recognize he was lying.

Although Isaac seemed better, Keegan had decided to sign him out and take him home anyway so his brother could have time to decompress. And, truth be told, because Keegan was feeling guilty. He knew that Isaac could sense the tension between him and his dad, knew it was stressing him out and setting him up for meltdowns like this one. And the boy didn't need the additional stress of attending the after-school program that was now part of his day until Keegan or their dad collected him.

They'd spent the rest of the morning and most of the afternoon playing the various games Isaac had created over the years, some of which involved Keegan doing little more than sitting in the same room while his brother lined up objects on the floor or a table. But he enjoyed trying to figure out what Isaac was doing, appreciated the window it gave him into his brother's mind. And he loved what happened when he finally saw the pattern that Isaac was creating, loved the look on his brother's face when Keegan, too, was finally able to add a shape or a colour that continued it.

Isaac never smiled, but it was in those moments that the muscles of his face formed something that at least resembled a smile.

Sure, there was a time when he'd resented his brother, begrudged the constant patience that he required, but it was impossible not to love him. Especially now, after everything they'd been through together.

They'd moved into their new house—the one the bank had eventually taken—at the beginning of Keegan's freshman year, which put him in a different school district, so he'd had to make new friends. He was never sure how people would react when they met Isaac for the first time, but they'd all been great with him. Of course, he'd expected that acceptance from Curtis and Lamont, who knew better than anyone what it felt like to be outsiders, but Hamad and Joaquin and Jermaine and the others had been just as accepting, always trying—as much as they could, anyway—to make Isaac feel like part of the gang when they dropped by.

So had Talia.

Watching Isaac eat his peas now, Keegan forced that last memory away, jammed it deep where it wouldn't hurt as much if—when—he stumbled over it again.

Through the open window, he could hear footsteps padding along the driveway toward the back door. It probably seemed weird to others that his dad worked at a car dealership and didn't have a vehicle, but Keegan understood the reason. And not having one wasn't much of a problem anyway. The dealership, both schools, and the grocery store were all within walking distance of their house. Where else did they have to go?

The door opened and Evan entered carrying his suit jacket,

his face glistening from the heat that had hung on into the late afternoon. Nodding to Keegan, he moved to the table and leaned down, pressing his face against his younger son's forehead. At times like this, Keegan almost didn't recognize his dad. They'd been at loggerheads for so long that seeing him display such tenderness always came as something of a surprise.

Isaac, of course, squirmed out from under the contact and ate the last pea on his plate, the single group of one in his numerical arrangement. Then he slipped off his chair and headed toward the living room, where Keegan knew he'd create more patterns with the objects they'd left on the floor.

"Thanks for taking care of him today," Evan said. "My meeting with—"

"No problem," Keegan interrupted. Standing up, he reached for his and Isaac's dishes and carried them to the sink. "Your dinner's in the oven."

"Think I'll change out of these clothes first, maybe grab a shower before I eat."

Keegan nodded and, hearing his father move down the hallway leading to the stairs, he put a plug in the sink and turned on the hot water. Squirting liquid detergent under the faucet, he set the plates and glasses in the rising suds and, like every time he stood at the sink, fought his last memory of his mother, forcing himself to think of something else, anything else. Gazing out the window above the sink, he tried to imagine the house's former tenants and pictured a young couple in their first home. The kitchen lacked a dishwasher, so they probably did the dishes together every evening, one washing and the other drying as they chatted about their day. He could see one of them playfully splash the other as a mock battle erupted, the room suddenly splattered with soap and echoing with startled yelps turning to laughter.

And then, of course, he was thinking of Talia, the part of him where he'd just buried her far shallower than he'd realized. They'd been eating ice cream at Waldowski's Diner and, without knowing it, she'd gotten a dab of strawberry on the end of her nose. Sitting across from him, she'd looked so beautiful that he couldn't bear to tell her, but then a woman at the next table caught her eye and motioned to her face. Glancing at her reflection in her phone, Talia had been mortified, wiping her nose with a napkin as she got up to leave. Once outside, though, she'd retaliated by jabbing at *his* nose with her cone and, within minutes, their faces were covered with his chocolate and her strawberry, the two of them laughing like idiots on the sidewalk. He remembered everything about that moment—Talia's laughter, the feel of her body against his, the way she tasted as they kissed, ice cream sliding down their faces and dripping off their chins.

Lost in that heartache, Keegan felt sudden heat at his groin and looked down to see the first fingers of soapy water reaching over the sink. "Shit!" he muttered, turning off the tap and grabbing a towel to dam the waterfall, all the while remembering the last words Forbes had offered them: *It does you no good to look back.*

His hair still wet, Evan came into the kitchen and reached for a pot holder to take his plate from the oven. "Smells good," he said as he sat down to eat.

Keegan shrugged. It didn't take skill to Shake 'n Bake chicken breasts and boil potatoes and frozen peas, but the way things were between him and his dad, he was grateful for the compliment. For

Isaac's sake, Keegan decided to risk conversation. "How's the job going?"

"Busy," his father replied. "The guy whose position I took left the books in a mess." Cutting up his chicken, he added, "I finally had a face-to-face with the owner. He was on vacation last week."

"What's he like?"

"He's a force to be reckoned with."

"Sounds like you don't care for him."

Evan spoke around a mouthful. "He knows what he wants and isn't two seconds telling you. But I'd rather work for a guy like that than somebody I'm second-guessing all the time. What you see is what you get."

Keegan groaned involuntarily.

"Something wrong?" his father asked.

Keegan pulled up a chair and sat down. "His daughter's in a couple of my classes."

"That's great. Something he and I can talk about besides work."

"Yeah, well, I wouldn't recommend it."

"Why?"

"She hates me."

His father's face darkened. "Cripes, Keegan, you only started school yesterday. What'd you *do?*"

And that was it. Just like with Isaac and the soccer ball: *What the hell do you think you were doing?* As always, *he* was automatically in the wrong. Keegan glanced down the hallway toward the living room, not wanting to get into another shouting match, especially after what Isaac had been through already that day. But that didn't mean he had to take it on the chin every single time. "His daughter's a pain in the ass," he said simply.

Evan put down his fork and knife. "I thought we'd gone over this," he said.

Keegan looked away. Took a breath. Let it out.

"So you just *ignored* Forbes. And me."

"Look," Keegan said, feeling his irritation swell into something more, "I didn't ignore either of you, okay? I just wasn't going to put up with any of their bullshit."

"*Their* bullshit? *Please* tell me you didn't piss off somebody *else.*"

Keegan looked down at the table, a chrome-and-composite thing posing as retro when it wasn't screaming bargain basement.

"So you *did*," said his father.

Keegan looked up. "Her boyfriend's a prick."

"The *d'Entremont* boy?"

"How do *you* know him?"

"Laird d'Entremont was one of the people at the meeting today. When Jaffrey introduced him to me, he said d'Entremont's son was going with Jaffrey's daughter." He ran a hand through his hair. "Jesus," he moaned. "You pissed off both of them. A slam dunk."

"What's the big deal?"

Evan pushed his chair back from the table and stood up. "D'Entremont's the *mayor*." He took two steps toward the sink and stood looking out the window.

"I still don't see what—"

"Of *course* you don't," interrupted Evan, turning to face him. "You *never* do. You're always so busy thinking about *yourself* and how the world doesn't turn to suit *you*." He ran a hand through his hair again. "Forbes and I asked you to do one thing. But *could* you? No!" He paused momentarily as if building momentum. "For once in your life—"

"Spare me that speech," breathed Keegan, struggling to keep his voice down. "I *have* no life, remember? *You* made sure of that."

Ignoring the last comment, Evan pulled his phone from his pocket. "I know you don't care for the life we have here, Keegan, but it's all we've got, remember?"

"What are you doing?"

"Damage control," said Evan, scrolling for a number.

"*What* damage?"

"What do you *think*? Antagonizing my boss's daughter and the mayor's son."

Keegan's desire to keep Isaac from hearing them argue wavered, and he had to swallow hard before speaking. "I didn't antagonize *either* of them. The girl's a grade A bitch!"

Evan stared at him for a long moment before shaking his head. "I used to admire how you always saw the best in people. Like Curtis and Lamont. I'd think about all the crap they took off narrow-minded jerks and I was so proud of how you always stood up for them. And Jermaine, when he got arrested for boosting that car, you swore to me that he hadn't done it, that the police targeted him because he was a black kid in the wrong place at the wrong time. And you were right." He shook his head again. "That person I admired so much, where did he go?"

"He got shipped off to East Cowlick, Canada," snapped Keegan. "Look, you just said I try to see the best in people. Why am I the bad guy here all of a sudden?"

Evan sighed. "Whether you are or not is beside the point. We have to fix this."

"How?"

"The Rotary Club is holding a fundraiser tonight, and Jaffrey and d'Entremont are members. I was supposed to be there and I was counting on you staying with Isaac, but I'll make my excuses to Jaffrey, tell him Isaac isn't feeling well or something."

"Why?"

"Both his daughter and the d'Entremont boy are helping out, and you're going to lend them a hand."

"No," said Keegan.

Evan pulled up the number he was looking for. "I'm calling Jaffrey now," he said. "I'm pretty sure he'll have something for you to do there."

"*No*," repeated Keegan, his voice stronger.

Evan shook his head. "This is *your* doing, Keegan, not mine. I'm just cleaning up your mess."

"Don't you *dare* talk about messes," Keegan seethed.

He could see his comment had hit home, his father's face creasing momentarily. But, recovering, Evan pressed on. "You'll do as I say, and that's all there is to it."

"I'm not a kid that you can just order around! I'm seventeen!"

A deep sadness replaced the guilt in his father's eyes. "And you think that makes a *difference*? That it *protects* you somehow?" He looked down the hallway toward the living room, his voice suddenly flat. "It isn't just yourself you have to think of, you know."

Keegan felt his fingernails dig into his thighs. "I'm not helping out at any goddamn fundraiser!" he shouted, pushing out of his chair and heading toward the back door.

"You don't have a choice," said his father as Keegan burst

through the door and slammed it behind him, the glass rattling in its frame.

His feet pounding down the steps, Keegan was barely conscious of the thick clouds that had gathered overhead. He was aware of only one thing—his father's parting comment echoing in his head.

Evan Fraser had been wrong about of lot of things during the past few months, but he was right about that. Choice was a luxury none of them had. Not anymore.

His hands making useless fists, Keegan stood in the backyard and raised his face to the sky, feeling the first drops of rain. In moments, the wind began to pick up and the rain increased, the drops falling faster, stinging his cheeks, forcing him to shut his eyes. But he welcomed them, longed for them to douse his rage and wash away the grief that lived inside him like an unborn twin.

# CHAPTER 19

Willa couldn't help smirking as she saw him pass through the entrance of the community college her father had booked for the fundraiser. Walking with his head down, he was obviously uncomfortable wearing what was likely his father's suit, the dark blue anchoring him among the brightly dressed early birds waiting inside the door out of the rain. She watched as he spoke to Ed Benjamin, one of the dealership's salespeople her father had put in charge of collecting tickets, then saw Ed nod and wave him through. It was that moment she was enjoying now—the look on the new guy's face as he turned to see her waiting for him, the moment like the final seconds of a MasterCard commercial. Priceless.

She hadn't known whether to laugh or cringe when her dad had told her about the guy's father phoning to say he couldn't make it but his son wanted to help out. "Volunteer" is how he'd put it but, judging from the guy's body language now, she could fill in the blanks—the guy's dad had found out how he'd been treating the boss's daughter and this was his way of making amends.

Reaching her, the new guy offered a mumbled "Hi," like he had to swallow a bottle cap to say it.

"Hi," she returned, still smirking. She had no intention of making any of this easier for him.

His face reddening, he looked around, obviously grasping for something more to say. "You've got quite a lineup already, even with the rain."

"There's always a great turnout for Casino Night," she said. There was an awkward beat of silence. Then another.

He dragged a hand through his hair, which fell immediately into his eyes again. "I, uh . . . I hear all this is your dad's idea."

"Yes, it is." She let the silence continue to unspool around them.

His eyes wandered around the space again and then, after a long moment, returned to her. He cleared his throat. "You look nice."

"Thanks," she said, wondering how much that compliment had cost him. But she appreciated it nonetheless—she'd shopped for days before deciding on the designer dress she wore this evening, a low-cut, off-the-shoulder sheath whose emerald colour contrasted dramatically with her blond hair. "What you see is pretty much what you get, right?"

He grimaced. "Yeah, about that," he said. "I, uh, I'd like to, uh . . ."

"Yes?" she asked.

He glanced away, his body visibly tightening. Then, "I'm sorry for what I said yesterday."

"For saying *what* exactly? That I'm unbelievable or that I'm not the centre of the universe?"

He turned to her again. In place of the grimace was something less wounded. Almost cocky. "Everything's easy for you, isn't it? Even this."

"If it makes you feel any better, I occasionally have a bad hair day."

"So there *is* a God."

She suppressed a laugh. "How does it taste?" she asked.

He blinked. "How's *what* taste?"

"The crow you're eating."

"I've had better," he said.

"Too bad. We Jaffreys usually serve only the best."

Now he was the one laughing, and she liked what it did to his face, smoothing out those stern lines on his forehead and crinkling the skin around his eyes, which she noticed were grey. Like pewter with hints of silver melted into it.

He put both hands up as if in surrender. "You think maybe we could start over?" he asked. "Pretend yesterday didn't happen?"

She studied him for a moment, considering his suggestion. After all, he *had* apologized. Besides, there was something about him that intrigued her, something vaguely mysterious, although she had no idea why she'd think such a thing. She held out her hand. "I'm Willa Jaffrey," she said.

"Nice to meet you, Willa Jaffrey." He took her small hand in his large one and squeezed it gently. "Keegan Fraser."

His handshake surprised her, and it was more than the heat of his skin against hers, more than the obvious strength she sensed in his grip. Something else, like the feel of her fingers sliding into a glove that fit perfectly.

She pulled away. "They'll be opening the doors in a few minutes. We should get inside." She turned and led him across the foyer toward the gymnasium.

The space looked nothing at all like the recreation centre it had been two days before. Bolts of rich fabric covered the concrete walls and formed brilliant backdrops for the various gaming tables scattered throughout the huge space. A temporary bar made of dark walnut lined the far wall, and young men and women dressed in black slacks, white shirts, and red bow ties stood behind it involved in last-minute preparations. Positioned on an equally temporary platform was a tuxedo-wearing quintet tuning their instruments, and in the centre of it all stood a sculpture made of roses arranged in the shape of the Rotarian emblem. The place looked spectacular.

Willa couldn't help but feel proud. It was her father who'd come up with the idea of Casino Night five years ago, ditching all those little flea markets and rubber ducky derbies for something much bigger and far more fun. As a minor, she couldn't gamble or drink alcohol, but she didn't care—she was there to support her dad. Besides, Brookdale's social scene didn't offer many opportunities to show off an Arthur Mendonça original.

She found herself wishing once more that Wynn were there with her, but he'd called an hour ago to say he was running late. So, as weird as it was, it turned out to be a good thing that Keegan had shown up. Not that she couldn't have handled her station alone, but it would be far more enjoyable having someone there to make fun of the over-forties with.

Keegan scanned the room. "Where's your boyfriend? Home reading *The Mountain and the Valley?*"

Picturing Wynn hunkered over a book, Willa almost laughed. "He's coming later," she said, then turned and made her way across the large room, leaving Keegan to trail in her wake.

"So, what's my job?" he asked when he'd caught up to her at a long table.

"Punch patrol." She pointed at an enormous crystal bowl

surrounded by dozens of sparkling glasses. "I pour the stuff and make witty conversation. You keep me supplied with punch and clean glasses from the kitchen."

"And you *volunteered* for this?"

"Didn't *you*?" she asked pointedly. "Look, it could be worse. We could be on cleanup duty. Besides, I don't expect we'll be too busy. There's no alcohol in the free stuff."

"My luck," he muttered.

This time her laughter just slipped out.

+ + +

They were a lot busier than she had expected, and Keegan's decision to "volunteer" turned out to be timely because Wynn had cancelled on her—he called to say he was sitting in Valley Regional Hospital's outpatient department waiting to get a tetanus shot. Since the number on the paper he'd pulled from the Please Take One dispenser was 219 and the one glowing redly below the Doctor Is Now Seeing sign was 174, he would be there most of the evening.

Willa couldn't believe it. "Tetanus shot?" she groaned. "What for?"

He'd stopped to fill up his car at Grant's Gas 'N' Go and had gotten fuel on his hands, so he'd gone inside to wash them off. Grant's was one of the valley's oldest independent gas stations, and its washroom was the size of a coat closet. A nail had been sticking out of the back of the door, and when Wynn had turned in the tight space to get a paper towel to dry his hands, the nail had scratched his cheek. It wasn't bad, he said, but the nail was rusty and he didn't want to take any chances.

"Something wrong?" Keegan asked as she returned her phone to her purse.

Sighing, she explained about Wynn being a no-show, and she was surprised when he offered no reaction. He'd already made at least a dozen trips from the kitchen carrying trays of clean glasses and fresh punch, and she thought he'd have welcomed the help. But he hadn't said much of anything since he'd apologized to her. Not that she hadn't tried to draw him into conversation, but she'd grown tired of making small talk and getting little in return. Earlier, she'd pointed out Wynn's father, Laird d'Entremont, explaining how he'd just agreed to run for a second term as Brookdale's mayor, but Keegan had barely nodded. Not long after that, Ms. Ericson had stopped by their table for punch, the armpits of her dress already darkening, and after the teacher had moved off, Willa had made what she thought was a hilarious comment about problem perspiration. Keegan hadn't even grinned, just looked away as though embarrassed. It was like he had no idea how to behave in a social setting.

"Where's that young man of yours?"

Willa turned to see her father appear beside her, handsome in his tux and sporting a broad working-the-room grin. "Wynn's not coming," Willa pouted, telling him about the call she'd just received.

"That's too bad, sweetheart," said her father. "Good thing you had backup," he added, nodding over her head. "You must be Evan's boy."

Keegan shook the hand offered to him. "Nice to meet you, Mr. Jaffrey."

"I'm glad you could help out, but I'm sorry your father couldn't make it. I'd like to have had the chance to introduce him around, have everyone get to know him."

"My dad," said Keegan, seeming to choose his words carefully, "he's not big on the social thing."

Like that's a surprise, thought Willa. The apple didn't fall far from *that* tree. She turned to her father. "Where's Mom?"

He frowned. "One guess."

"Still at Rachel's?" Celia had texted her earlier with news about Dairy Queen Dewayne breaking up with her mother—by email, no less—just before Brookdale's biggest event of the year, and Lenore had driven over to Rachel's that afternoon to console her. Willa had expected her mother to arrive late, but she'd assumed she'd still make it. It was, after all, her husband's fundraiser.

Her father seemed eager to change the subject. "There's some people over there I need to see. I'll check back with you later, okay?" He kissed his daughter on the forehead, nodded at Keegan again, and then moved off to continue mingling.

Moments later, a woman carrying an impressive camera approached them, her hand extended. "Willa?" she said. "I was speaking with your father earlier. My name is Carolyn Pierce. I'm a reporter for the *Chronicle Herald* covering tonight's event."

"Nice to meet you, Ms. Pierce," said Willa, shaking the woman's hand and introducing Keegan.

"Hello, Keegan," said the woman, but her eyes returned immediately to Willa. "That's a fabulous gown you're wearing. Is it an Arthur Mendonça?"

Willa couldn't help preening. "Yes, it is," she said.

"Absolutely stunning." The reporter held up her camera. "Would you mind if I took a picture of you and your friend?"

"We wouldn't mind at all, would we, Keegan?" Willa said, turning toward him.

His reaction surprised her. His face looked drained of every drop of blood, and he stepped backwards, bumping the refreshment table and making the glasses clink. "S-sorry," he stammered, "I, uh—I have to get more punch."

Watching him hurry off, Willa flushed with embarrassment at his rudeness. "I guess it's just me," she said.

The reporter frowned. "I have to be honest, photos of one person tend to look static. Staged." She raised her camera to eye level. "I'll take a couple, but I doubt the paper will use them."

Willa waited in agonized silence while the reporter took two shots, but she was suddenly grateful neither would appear in the newspaper—try as she might to hide it, she was certain her mortification was written all over her face.

The reporter thanked her and moved off, leaving Willa to scan the crowd for Keegan. He hadn't gone to get punch, she was sure of that. He'd simply vanished.

# CHAPTER 20

Keegan stood in the far stall of the men's washroom, his forehead pressed against the cool surface of the metal door. Listening to the muted sounds of music and activity at the gaming tables floating down the hall from the gymnasium, Keegan silently cursed his father again. It was bad enough having to kiss Willa Jaffrey's ass, not to mention being her lackey while she flaunted that goddamn designer dress. But then being asked to *pose* with her for a newspaper pho—

The washroom door opened and a burst of Casino Night noise flooded the room, then diminished as the door whispered shut on its hydraulic hinge, halting footsteps marking a man's unsteady progress toward the urinals lining the left wall. As the guy pulled down his zipper, fumbled in his pants, and began relieving himself, Keegan stood motionless. No way was he going to be found hiding in a washroom stall.

Keegan listened as the stream hitting the porcelain shrank to a dribble, and a moment later the man zipped up his pants and staggered toward the row of sinks opposite the urinals. Through the narrow opening between the stall's metal partition and door, Keegan saw the guy's reflection in the mirror above the sinks, and he recognized the man whom Willa had pointed out as Wynn's dad. Keegan concentrated on remaining silent as he waited for the guy to wash his hands.

He didn't. Instead, he leaned forward toward the mirror, reaching up to touch the pouchy skin beneath his eyes, gently smoothing out the lines beneath his lower lids. When he released it, the skin drooped to its original appearance. "Christ," he muttered.

The washroom door opened as another man entered. "What are you doing hiding in here?"

Keegan winced, wondering what he'd done to give away his presence before realizing the question hadn't been directed at him.

"Everything okay, Laird?" the second man continued, and Keegan winced again as he recognized the speaker: Willa Jaffrey's dad.

Leaning back against the sink behind him, d'Entremont groaned softly. "Jus' fine," he said.

Jaffrey stepped into Keegan's view, his eyes darting toward the stalls. "Anybody else in here?"

The mayor grunted a negative.

Jaffrey cleared his throat. "Laird, if you don't mind my saying . . ."

D'Entremont's eyes seemed to have trouble focusing. "Wha's on your mind?"

Jaffrey looked in the mirror and adjusted his tie, clearly uncomfortable. "It's just—" He cleared his throat. "You've had quite a bit to drink."

D'Entremont straightened, turned around, and held his hands under the faucet, triggering a stream of water. Bending down, he cupped some in his palms and splashed it on his face.

"Look," Jaffrey began again, "I know it's none of my business, but this really isn't the time or place to . . . overindulge."

The mayor grabbed some paper towel from the dispenser and buried his face in it. When he pulled the soggy mass away, Keegan could see the man's forehead was furrowed with misery. He turned to Jaffrey. "She's gone, Carleton."

"Who?"

"Sharon."

"I know," said Jaffrey. "You told me earlier she was visiting her parents in Toronto."

D'Entremont looked at his feet. "Shlefme."

It took Keegan a moment to translate the single word into three: *She left me.* It seemed to take Jaffrey a beat longer. Then his eyes widened. "I'm so sorry, Laird. I had no idea."

D'Entremont swallowed hard. "She lefanote."

"A note? When?"

"Thish afternoon. S'waiting for me when I got home."

"And you didn't know something was wrong before that?"

The mayor ran a trembling hand over his eyes. "I *knew*, yeah, but wha'd she ex"—another hiccup—"exsphect?"

"I'm not following you."

"You can't—" The man's throat worked like he was swallowing an apple whole. "You can't ashk a man to *choose*—" He swallowed again. "But she did." Then he dissolved into sobs, his shoulders quaking.

Keegan could tell that Jaffrey was embarrassed. "Look, Laird, how about I take you home?"

D'Entremont struggled to get himself under control, reached for more paper towel and mopped at his face. He shook his head, the action making him sway on his feet. "Too much ganhanning to do," he slurred, and Keegan had no idea what he meant.

But Jaffrey did. "I think the glad-handing can wait for when you're—when you've got your head clear."

"Though selections don't win 'mselves," said d'Entremont, and Keegan struggled to interpret the drunkspeak: *Those elections.*

"No argument here," agreed Jaffrey, "but better to put your best foot forward, don't you think? What if I take you out the back way? The only person who might see us leaving is Mort Fetter, and he's the soul of discretion."

Keegan remembered seeing a van parked outside marked Fetter Security, with the ridiculous tagline Sleep Better with Fetter.

"Mebbe you're right," murmured d'Entremont.

"Of course I'm right," said Jaffrey. He put his hand on d'Entremont's shoulder, gently turning him toward the door.

In the mirror, Keegan saw the mayor stumble and Jaffrey put his other hand under the man's elbow, steadying him. "Easy does it," said Jaffrey.

D'Entremont hiccuped again and then burped loudly, the sound like the bark of a seal. This time it was Jaffrey who shook his head. "Do you think you can make it outside on your own, Laird? It wouldn't be good for someone to see me holding you up. There's a reporter here from the *Herald*," he added.

D'Entremont nodded and drew a ragged breath. "I owe you, Carleton," he said as Jaffrey swung the door wide for him.

Keegan watched in the mirror as d'Entremont walked unsteadily through the opening. Jaffrey allowed the door to close momentarily, and the smile that suddenly brightened his face was even wider than his daughter's when that reporter had commented on her dress. "I'm counting on you to remember that," Jaffrey muttered, then opened the door again and went out.

+ + +

"Shh," Keegan heard as he came through the front door. He looked up to see his father tiptoeing down the staircase, one finger raised to his lips.

"What's wrong?" whispered Keegan, his heart already jackhammering. He cocked his head to one side, listening for the things he half-heard during the night when fear jerked him from sleep and made him hold his breath until he could identify the barking dog or backfiring car that had entered whatever dream was already slipping away.

"He's been off all night," his father murmured. "I finally got him settled down a half-hour ago. I was just in his room checking on him."

Keegan felt something in his chest release, the anger he'd nursed during his walk home from the community college evaporating. Anger at his father, at Willa Jaffrey, even at Jaffrey's dad for having that goddamn fundraiser in the first place. Keegan had waited in the washroom a long time until he figured the reporter had had time to take everyone's picture. When he'd finally returned to the refreshment table, Willa had refused to speak to him, which had made the next hour with her even more awkward. He figured they'd both been glad when her father came around again and thanked him for his help and said he could go. When Jaffrey suggested that Willa drive him home, Keegan had quickly said he needed the exercise, and the relief on Willa's face wasn't hard to read. Fortunately, it had stopped raining and the sky had cleared, but the blanket of stars overhead didn't lift his mood any as he walked the six blocks home. In fact, his anger seemed to ramp up a little with each block, and he'd been pretty much at full steam when he finally came in the door.

But none of it mattered, of course, in the face of that other thing, the shadow that hung over them, the shadow and the constant fear.

"Is he asleep?" asked Keegan.

His father nodded. He reached the bottom of the staircase and turned into the living room. Keegan followed.

"He got locked into one of his loops," Evan said as he settled himself onto the sofa. Its burgundy upholstery matched nothing else in the room, which also held a blue armchair, a brown vinyl loveseat, and a black coffee table, its bottom shelf crammed with jigsaw puzzles. The room looked a little like the set of one of those early-morning children's TV shows, but the furniture had come with the house, so what could you do? The important thing was that Isaac felt comfortable there.

"Anything set him off?" Keegan asked as he sat on the other end of the sofa.

His father shrugged. "Might've had something to do with what he saw at school this morning. My guess, though, is that your arguing with me didn't help."

Keegan heard the implication in the "your," like *he* was the one at fault. And what had his father said earlier? *It isn't just yourself you have to think of.* Yeah. As if Keegan would ever have the luxury of thinking only of himself again. He felt the anger he'd nursed earlier return, tried not to give in to it, but it was there just the same. "What's it like?" he asked, his voice low because of Isaac asleep upstairs. But there was no masking its intensity.

"What's *what* like?" his father asked.

"Being right all the time. And when things don't work out, knowing that it's always the rest of the world that screwed up."

His father looked away, didn't speak for several seconds. Finally, "What I did, Keegan," he began, but he seemed unable to complete that thought. "After all we'd lost, I was angry. More than angry. Defeated. The bank took everything we had, and then the government bailed the bank out. They ground us up, spit us out, and then got rewarded for it."

"And that justifies what you did," said Keegan. "Excuses everything that happened to us afterwards."

Evan opened his mouth to reply, but no words came. He dragged a hand across his forehead, then pushed himself to his feet. "I'm tired," he said, and left the room. The creak of worn oak treads followed him up the stairs.

Keegan felt the muscles in his face work hard to keep his mouth shut, to keep him from cursing, from letting everything inside him just pour out.

It was several minutes later before he finally trusted himself to get up from the sofa and climb those stairs himself.

# CHAPTER 21

Griff knew it was his own fault. He'd been stupid to try to play Sonia Martinez without being sure. But the girl drove a *Micra*, for Christ's sake. Nonetheless, he'd always prided himself on being thorough, and this time he hadn't been.

He figured the problem was all the stuff in the media about cyberbullying—people were more aware of the consequences of their online actions. At least, Sonia Martinez was. She might be a slut but she didn't spread rumours, which was what Griff had been counting on. Instead of simply passing along to Talia the information he'd sent her about the guy being investigated for rape, implying that was why the family had left Ohio, Sonia had apparently shown Kayley's message to Soccerguy89.

It hadn't helped that the guy's father was former military brass and still heavily connected. Not only had Kayley's Facebook account been deactivated in short order, Griff could see evidence of someone with high-level cyber-savvy tracking Kayley's digital footprints. By now, someone in authority had learned that Kayley Sheridan was a ghost who spent almost all of her Facebook time viewing Talia Lombardi's page.

Griff was confident there was no way they could trace any of this back to him, but that was the end of Kayley, and he really didn't have the time to invent somebody new. He was going to have to find another way to keep tabs on Talia.

Pondering his options, Griff smiled.

# CHAPTER 22

"Are they shooting a horror flick somewhere around here?"

Keegan blinked, suddenly aware that he'd been standing motionless in front of his open locker like he was trying to close the door with mind control. He glanced over his shoulder to see Raven grinning at him. "Why's that?" he asked.

"You and Bailey have this whole zombie vibe going today."

Keegan looked left, then right. No Bailey.

"Just passed her staring at *her* locker," Raven explained. "She looked even more stunned than you do."

Keegan finished shoving into his locker the books he wouldn't need until that afternoon, and shrugged. "Lost in thought."

"Looks to me like you could use happier thoughts."

He grimaced, thinking again about the tension at the breakfast table that morning. He was sure Isaac had sensed it, too. "Math," he lied, glimpsing his calculus text in his backpack as he zipped it shut. "Shedrand's killing me with all the work he assigns."

"Must be true, then."

"What?" he asked.

"I hear he likes small class sizes, and the workload is his way of getting people to drop back to regular math. Calls it 'weeding the garden.'" She lowered her voice conspiratorially. "I'm not taking accelerated math till next semester, so see what you can do to soften the guy up, okay?"

Keegan grinned. "I'm on it," he said as they turned to make their way toward their homerooms.

Heavy footsteps came up behind them. "Where did *you* disappear to yesterday?" asked Russell, falling into step between the two. The front of his XXXL sweatshirt read *When I haul ass, I make two trips.*

"Medical appointment," Keegan replied, choosing not to say anything about Isaac. It was the second lie he'd told in under a minute. Forbes would be proud.

"I'd sure like to have one of those this afternoon," said Russell, a wistful note in his voice.

"Not feeling well?" asked Raven.

"I won't be by then," he sighed, turning into his homeroom without so much as a *See you later.*

"Jeez," said Raven as she watched him go, "what *is* it with this place? Are they slipping benzos into the drinking water?"

Rounding the corner, they saw Greg approaching, his acne-covered face looking troubled. "Have you guys talked to Bailey today?" he asked when he reached them.

"Tried to," Raven replied. "She seemed a little, I don't know, distracted."

Greg nodded, concern in his eyes. "I just saw her by her locker. She hardly said a word to me. Did I do something wrong?"

Remembering the way Greg had looked at Bailey the other day, Keegan couldn't imagine the guy ever doing anything to offend her. "I wouldn't worry about it," he said.

"I dunno," said Greg. "The look on her face—" He shook his head. "Yeah, you're probably right. Like *I* know anything about girls, huh?"

"Trust me," said Keegan, clapping him on the shoulder, "I don't think guys are supposed to."

Raven put her finger to her ear as if activating a hidden communication device. "Code red, girls!" she hissed. "They're on to us!"

+ + +

Keegan stared at the paper that Shedrand had passed out following another lengthy note-taking session. Ten numerical sequences stretched across the page, and the class was supposed to analyze each one and create equations that described the patterns they followed. Keegan had finished seven, but his mind had begun to wander as he pictured his brother enthralled by those patterns. Of course, Isaac wouldn't be able to create the equations, but Keegan was pretty sure his brother could identify the next numbers in each of the sequences. Although Issac was only eight, his ability to recognize patterns was far more advanced than that of, say, Todd Thomas, who was frowning over the task across the aisle. Looking at Todd's furrowed brow, Keegan was pretty sure the paper in his hands was one of Shedrand's garden-weeding tools.

Keegan's eyes continued to roam the classroom, and he found himself gazing at Willa Jaffrey bent over her desk two rows away, her face rapt in concentration. He was surprised to see she was working on the last sequence—he hadn't pictured her as somebody with a lot going on in the brain department. Yeah, she'd enrolled in the accelerated program, but so had every other student in the room, and Keegan was pretty sure that a few of them—Todd Thomas, for one—wouldn't be there next week.

But it looked as if he might have been wrong about Willa Jaffrey. Intelligence-wise, that is. His first impression of her still applied. The girl was all flash and shine, and unkind, too, judging from the cutting comments she'd made about some of the people she'd pointed out last night. The description he'd given his father yesterday—*a grade A bitch*—was no less accurate today. She was just a grade A bitch with brains.

Keegan watched Willa study her paper, a grimace playing at the corners of her mouth as she worked on that last numerical sequence. She repeatedly tapped the keys of her calculator, pencilled notations on the page, and then slumped back in her seat, her lower lip pooched out. Sighing, she tapped the calculator once more, and then her eyes widened. Leaning forward, she made another notation and punched more keys, nodding to herself as she worked. And then she smiled.

Something about her expression in that moment tugged at him. Her smile was nothing like the shit-eating grin she'd given him in English class their first day when she told him his dad worked for her father. Nor was it like her smirk last night as she enjoyed seeing him eat crow à la Jaffrey. This was different, genuine, something that came entirely from inside. Like someone had turned on a light two rows over.

Keegan glanced down at the numerical puzzles that remained unsolved on his own paper. Easier than the puzzles in his head right now. Like why the hell his pulse had started racing.

# CHAPTER 23

"Thank *God* your mother came over last night!" exclaimed Celia as she and Britney found Willa at recess.

"Your mom was a wreck, huh?" asked Willa, shoving her math book into her locker.

"If I ever get to the point where I'm wailing over getting dumped by a loser like Dewayne Eisner, just shoot me, okay?" Celia held up her hand as if she were swearing an oath. "No, scratch that. If I ever get to the point where I'd even *date* a loser like Dewayne Eisner, shoot me. Point-blank to the head. Multiple rounds."

"How was she this morning?" asked Willa.

"Hungover. The two of them polished off a fifth together." Celia looked at Willa, admiration in her face. "Your mom can really put it away."

She's had enough practice lately, thought Willa.

"Too bad she had to miss Casino Night to hold Mom's hand," Celia added. "Must've been a blast."

"Yeah," echoed Britney. "I didn't even recognize the community college gym in those pictures you sent. Why didn't we see one of you and Wynn?"

Willa sighed. She'd intended to phone them when she got home, but she'd been so annoyed at Keegan Fraser and the way the evening turned out that she hadn't felt like it. She gave them an abbreviated version now, ending with the bit about the new guy running off when the reporter asked to take his picture.

"What the hell's his problem?" asked Britney.

"Who cares?" Celia demanded. "What about Wynn's face? Is there gonna be a scar?"

"I hope not," Willa replied, surprised she hadn't worried about that herself. "I haven't seen him yet."

"Why not?"

"He's at the community college. He's got a spare first period, and his dad asked him to help put the gym back together."

Willa felt Britney nudge her. She turned and saw her friend nodding toward a figure passing them—Keegan Fraser on his way to his own locker. She felt her irritation from the previous night resurface.

She'd ignored him when he finally returned and began restocking the refreshment table again, but it was like he hadn't even noticed her silent treatment. Or cared. He'd seemed lost somewhere inside his own head, the way he looked now, his shoulders hunched, his eyes on the floor.

She suddenly remembered her parents taking her and her brother to see Cirque du Soleil in Las Vegas a couple of years ago. Amid the constant flurry of onstage activity was a guy sealed inside a Plexiglas ball, which he continually rolled around the platform, narrowly avoiding the other performers. Keegan reminded her of that guy now, the way he moved around the groups of students milling in the hallway, like he was inside that bubble, a part of the crowd yet apart *from* it.

Weird.

+ + +

Willa looked at the time on her phone again. She'd texted Wynn earlier that she would wait for him at the east entrance, but she could see Caldwell eyeing her from his post at the top of the stairs. Everyone knew the VP was every bit as anal about students being late for class as he was about in-school cell use, which was why Celia and Britney had left for English without her. She sighed and headed there herself.

She got there just as Mr. Richardson was starting the lesson. "So," he said, "what do you think of the book so far?"

Several of the students, mostly guys, groaned. Todd Thomas spoke up. "*Way* too descriptive."

"What do you mean?" asked the teacher.

"People, places, whatever. That Buckler dude goes on and on about *everything*."

Richardson nodded. "Some readers find that a struggle. Since we're on the topic of Buckler's style, has anyone noticed how certain elements reappear in the story?"

Willa looked around the room, but no one offered a response.

"Seriously, people?" said Richardson. "Nobody's noticed a recurring detail?"

Willa was about to raise her hand when she heard a voice. "Rugs?" It was Keegan who'd spoken.

"Care to elaborate?" the teacher asked him.

"The grandmother, Ellen. She's always making them."

"Good observation," Richardson said. He scanned the classroom. "You'll find that rugs are a motif that Buckler weaves throughout *The Mountain and the Valley*. As you continue your reading, I want you to consider what the rugs are made of and how they serve to dimensionalize the story." He turned to Keegan again and grinned. "I imagine you find the term *mountain* rather ludicrous here in Nova Scotia, right?"

"Um . . ." he began, and Willa could see uncertainty on his face. Apparently, so could the teacher.

"My wife and I skied Grouse Mountain and Cypress, too," said Richardson. "I figure since you lived in view of peaks like those, calling what we have here mountains must seem a little absurd."

"Yeah, a little," Keegan said.

But there was something in the way he responded, the way his face flushed as he said it, that seemed off somehow. To Willa, anyway.

+ + +

"I hear the temperature's supposed to climb even higher in the next few days," said Greg as he pulled up his chair and sat down. His acne seemed even more pronounced as his face gleamed from the heat.

Richardson had asked the class to break up into groups of four to share their responses to Buckler's writing style, and Willa had found herself a fifth wheel to Britney, Celia, Todd, and Jay's quartet. As she'd scanned the room for other partners, Raven had appeared beside her asking if she'd like to work with her and Bailey, and Greg Phillips had just joined the three of them.

Raven nodded. "Humidity's supposed to go up, too," she said. "This place'll be an oven."

Willa looked at Greg's glistening forehead and remembered

Ms. Ericson from last night, her gown dark under her arms. "I can only imagine what Ericson'll look like."

"Must be rough on her," said Greg.

On *her*? thought Willa. What about her students who have to look at those crescent-shaped stains?

"Who's Ericson?" Raven asked.

"Teaches political science," said Willa. "The woman doesn't use antiperspirant. Ever."

"Yeah," said Greg, looking at Raven. "My mom knows her really well. She has some kind of environmental illness, so a ton of products make her really sick." He shook his head. "Can't imagine what it's like not being able to wear antiperspirant in this heat."

Willa thought about Ericson's rail-thinness and deathly pallor and remembered the comment she'd shared with Keegan about her. Now it didn't seem so funny.

"So who wants to go first?" asked Raven, reminding them of the task Richardson had given them.

"Why don't *you* start, Bailey?" said Greg.

Willa looked at Bailey, who appeared to be absorbed in the notes she'd made about the novel, but Willa knew otherwise— Bailey didn't want Willa in their group. Out of the corner of her eye, Willa had seen her make throat-cutting gestures to Raven when she'd asked her to join them. And now she seemed to be trying not to look at Willa. More weirdness. Whatever. Like she cared about Bailey Holloway anyway.

"Maybe someone else could go first," Bailey murmured.

"Okay," said Raven. "What about you, Willa?"

Willa was annoyed at how Raven seemed to have appointed

herself the group's leader, but she was bothered more by the awkwardness that seemed to have settled around them. "Sure," she said. She glanced down at the journal she kept for reading assignments. "I think Todd's right. Buckler really goes overboard with description a lot of the time. But in a way I think it serves a purpose."

"How?" chorused Greg and Raven. Bailey said nothing.

"David, the main character, likes to save moments, right? He likes to draw them out longer so they'll last. Like the day when he goes with his father and brother to climb the mountain." Willa opened the book to a place she'd tabbed. "Although he's excited to do it, David thinks—" She scanned the page and then began to read: "'Let's wait. I can be near the mountain and save it at the same time.'" Willa looked around the group. "When Buckler describes things in so many ways, he's making sure we know exactly what those experiences are like. It's as though he's saving those moments, the way David likes to save them."

"I hadn't thought of it that way," said Greg. "I just kept getting hung up on how the author would compare one experience to tons of things. I was more interested in what the characters were doing, but Buckler kept slowing down the action, giving us one comparison after another."

"I think his metaphors are amazing."

They all turned to Bailey, who seemed to have found her voice. "Like that passage you mentioned, Willa? When Buckler writes about David's excitement climbing the mountain, he describes David making a sun-shiver in his mind. That combination of hot and cold at the same time—isn't it perfect? It's more like poetry than prose. And then when his dad builds the fire to make tea—"

She turned to the page. "'The brook water came to a boil in a sudden volcano.' I'd never pictured a pot boiling that way, but when you think of it, isn't a volcano exactly how that bubbling water would look to a little boy?" Bailey's eyes were shining as though she were making a sun-shiver in her own mind. Then her cheeks began to pink. "Sorry, I get carried away sometimes. Somebody else talk now. Please."

"No," said Greg, "I see what you mean."

"Me, too," said Raven. "It's like what *happens* in the novel isn't as important as how people *perceive* what happens. David experiences everything on such a deep level that it makes sense Buckler would pile on the details to help readers appreciate how David sees and hears and feels things. Everyone else in the story misses the beauty that he notices all around him, which kind of comes back to us reading. When we get bogged down in all that detail, we're just like those characters who don't appreciate David's special way of seeing things."

"I know how he feels," murmured Greg.

"How's that?" asked Raven.

He shook his head. "Sorry, just thinking out loud. It's not important."

"No," said Bailey, "I'd really like to hear this."

He smiled at her, and Willa got the impression that he was willing to share only because it was Bailey who'd asked. "I get how difficult it is for him. Like when he tries so hard to fit in but it never works out for him. He's always on the outside no matter what he does." He glanced away, clearly embarrassed.

"I just caught the end of your discussion," said Mr. Richardson, who'd approached them unnoticed, "but it sounds like you made some interesting connections." The teacher smiled at Bailey. "I especially enjoyed your comment about Buckler's writing seeming more like poetry than prose."

Greg nodded enthusiastically. "No wonder her poem won that writing competition, huh?"

Bailey flushed. "It didn't win—"

"Second place out of three hundred entries is a win in my book," he said as he grinned at her.

Second place in a writing competition? thought Willa. Bailey Holloway?

"I'm asking each group," said Richardson, "to choose someone to summarize what you talked about. I'm anxious to see how the rest of the class reacts to your comments." He moved off to chat with another foursome.

"I think *you* should do it, Bailey," said Raven.

Bailey flushed. "Not me. I wouldn't know what to say."

"Say exactly what you said before," said Willa. "It was great." And she meant it.

A cellphone hummed in one of the backpacks at their feet.

"I think that's yours, Bailey," said Raven.

Bailey's eyes widened. "No, it's not."

"Yeah, it is," said Greg, reaching for her canvas bag and handing it to Bailey. "If you don't want to lose it, you'd better turn it off."

Bailey's face blanched, reminding Willa of how Keegan had looked last night when that reporter offered to take their picture. Bailey thrust her hand into the backpack and fumbled around, clearly trying to power down the phone without taking it out, but it kept vibrating. Frustrated, she yanked out the cell, hit Ignore and then the power button, and shoved it back into the bag, a flurry of movement that took only seconds.

But it was long enough for Willa to notice something about the way Bailey had done it. She'd put her fingers deliberately over the display, as if hiding the caller's number.

From Willa.

+ + +

"About *time* you showed up!" said Willa as Wynn slid into the seat beside her. She and her friends almost never ate in the school's cafeteria, but none of them had the energy to go anywhere today, so she'd texted Wynn to meet them there.

"Ouch," said Jay, pointing at the bandage on Wynn's face. "Any stitches?"

Wynn shook his head. "It's not that bad. I'm just keeping it covered for a while so no dirt gets in it." He leaned over to kiss Willa. "Sorry I'm late, babe. Took the Rotary guys longer than they planned to get all the casino stuff out of the gym. Did I miss anything in English?"

"Only Bailey Holloway pretending she's Mensa material," Britney replied.

"Christ," moaned Celia. "I thought she'd *never* shut up about all that metaphor shit."

Everyone chuckled except Willa. "I kind of liked what Bailey had to say."

"Yeah, right," Celia chuckled.

Willa felt herself grow defensive. After all, she was the one who'd encouraged Bailey to speak for the group. "No, seriously. She was pointing out how Buckler's use of imagery—"

"Hey, guys," interrupted Jay, making a time-out sign with his hands. "Class is over, right? We've got better stuff to talk about."

As if proving that point, Todd nodded toward Russell Shaw in the cafeteria lineup, his tray laden with food. "Is it my imagination," he asked, "or is Russ starting to show some definition?"

"If you're talking about his breasts," Britney crowed. "The guy should seriously think about getting a bra."

"They'd have to supersize *those* cups," Celia drawled, and everybody hooted.

Everybody but Willa. She forced a smile, but she was remembering what Greg had said in their group of four, how he understood the way David in the novel felt. *Like when he tries so hard to fit in but it never works out for him. He's always on the outside no matter what he does.*

She was pretty sure Russell Shaw knew how David felt, too.

# CHAPTER 24

The school had grown uncomfortably warm that afternoon, so being out on the soccer field in shorts and a T-shirt was a welcome relief for Keegan as he stood with his classmates in a circle facing the teacher. Among them were Wynn and his buddies, all three eager for action. Keegan could tell, though, that not everyone was so excited. Standing beside him, Greg Phillips looked like he was aching for invisibility—the sheer whiteness of his scrawny legs suggested that he only wore shorts when he was forced to. And beside Greg, Russell Shaw's substantial belly struggled to get out of the cotton T-shirt it strained against. Keegan now understood why Russell had longed for a medical appointment.

"I'd like to get my hands on the asshole who made PE a required course," Russell murmured to Greg.

"Haven't you heard?" Greg muttered in return, his voice thick with irony. "It builds self-esteem."

In his mid-thirties, Mr. Cameron sported a military haircut and physique that suited his drill-sergeant manner. "I hope our classroom work the past couple days hasn't misled any of you," he said. "If anybody thinks senior phys ed's going to be an easy credit, think again."

Keegan heard a soft groan from Greg.

"Today," continued Cameron, "we're going to do some soccer ball-handling drills, which are great for cardio."

Russell quietly echoed Greg's groan.

Cameron spoke to the class about the mechanics of dribbling, finishing with some pointers. "Keep the ball between your legs so it's harder for your opponent to steal. Know where the ball is at all times, but keep your head up. Most important, focus on your opponent's eyes. The eyes give a guy away every time." He looked at Wynn. "D'Entremont, step up here."

Wynn moved forward, grinning at his buddies.

Keegan wondered about the bandage on his left cheek. On anyone else, it might have looked dorky, but not on Wynn. He wore it like a badge of some sort. A testament to testosterone.

"As most of you know," said Cameron, "d'Entremont here is an outstanding ball-handler. That ability is one of the reasons Brookdale won the provincial soccer title last year."

Todd, Jay, and a few others punched the air with their fists and shouted "*Ooo*-rah!" Like they were frigging marines.

Smiling, Cameron waited for the cheers to end. "I'm going to ask him to demonstrate the moves I just described to you." He nodded toward Jay. "Underwood, how about you come and—"

"Coach," interrupted Wynn, "if it's okay with you, maybe we could give the new guy a chance to show what he can do." He smiled at Keegan, but his eyes telegraphed something completely different. The eyes give a guy away every time, thought Keegan.

Cameron nodded and turned to Keegan. "Fraser, right?"

Keegan nodded.

"You played soccer before?"

"A little."

"Your goal is to try to gain control of the ball. And remember what I said about keeping your head up." Cameron looked at Wynn. "Go easy on him, d'Entremont. No need to run him into the ground in this heat."

He reached into a large netted bag filled with balls and tossed one to Wynn, who jogged with it toward the centre of the field.

As Keegan moved to follow him, he passed Todd, who muttered, "Good luck trying to get your feet on *that* ball, asshole."

"Balls between his legs could be a whole new experience for him," snickered Jay, whose voice could be heard by everyone.

"Underwood!" barked Cameron, the warning evident in his tone, and Jay gave him a palms-up pantomime of innocence.

"You ready for this, Vancouver?" asked Wynn when Keegan reached him.

Keegan nodded.

Wynn dropped the ball and began to dribble, the black and white sphere moving constantly between his feet. Keegan made a half-hearted attempt to hijack it, but Wynn feinted right and then drove left, easily keeping the ball out of Keegan's reach while his buddies cheered. "It's all about control, right?" said Wynn. "And knowing your opponent." He wove deftly around him, keeping his eyes locked on Keegan's the whole time as he expertly manoeuvred the ball over the grass. "You have to know the situation, too. The field you're playing." He got his toe under the ball, flipped it over his head and behind him, then spun around to trap it again as more *ooo*-rahs erupted from the sidelines. "If you don't, you might make a wrong move." He zigzagged back and forth, back and forth. "Know what I mean about wrong moves,

Vancouver? You don't want to upset the balance, right? You've gotta be careful."

*You've gotta be careful.*

As Keegan mirrored Wynn's movements, always a heartbeat too late to connect with the ball, those words echoed in his mind. *You've gotta be careful.*

So much like his father's words that day in their backyard: *You have to be more careful.*

And how had he responded to those words? *Because of you, my whole* life *is about being careful!*

Keegan felt his stomach tighten, felt his jaws clench, felt his hands form steely fists. And then something released inside him.

*Fuck* careful!

He lunged forward and toed the ball, surprising Wynn as it bounced away from him. Before he could react, Keegan leaped, twisting in midair and blocking Wynn as he trapped it, shielded it, controlled it, the ball now a blur between his own feet. He pressed forward, spun back, all the while preventing Wynn from making contact again. He could feel sweat rivering from his scalp down his neck and seeping into his T-shirt, and he revelled in the pleasure of unleashing his body. It felt good to open up, to let everything but the ball and his opponent fall away, his feet instinctively making split-second decisions for him again and again. Some part of his brain, however, registered that the cheers from the sidelines had stopped, a stunned silence filling the open space as he dribbled the ball backwards, forwards, his eyes never leaving Wynn's.

The silence was broken by other cheers, this time from Russell and Greg. Then another voice joined theirs, and then another, shouting his name, urging him on. Despite the heat blanketing the field, he felt like he could run forever.

And then a whistle blew. "Bring it in!"

Keegan stopped on a dime, pivoted, and kicked the ball directly into Cameron's hands. From more than twenty yards.

When he reached the group, Russell and Greg pounded his back while some others whistled. The rest of the students, however, were silent, glancing awkwardly at Wynn bringing up the rear. Standing beside Greg again, Keegan watched Wynn return to his position between Todd and Jay, and the darkness of his expression made the bandage on his face seem even whiter, a kite against a thundercloud. Keegan remembered Forbes's prime directive and winced.

"Fraser!"

Keegan turned to see Cameron striding toward him. The guys around him melted away.

"What do you have to say for yourself?" the teacher barked, his face inches from Keegan's.

Keegan shrugged. "I was just doing what you—"

"Forget that! Why in hell didn't you show up for soccer try-outs?"

+ + +

"How'd he make out today?" asked Keegan, collecting his brother's backpack from the back of the elementary school's gymnasium while Isaac pulled on his outdoor shoes. Keegan was glad that Ms. Tomlinson was involved in the after-school program—continuity made things easier for his brother.

Tomlinson smiled. "Fine. There were some stressful moments this morning, but he seemed to settle much better this time."

"He's getting used to you," said Keegan.

"Maybe, but I think spending yesterday with you was what made the difference. He was more relaxed today. The two of you seem really close. It's unusual to see that in siblings when there's such a difference in—"

Keegan expected her to say "cognitive ability," a mistaken conclusion he'd heard too many people draw in the past. But she didn't.

"—age," she finished. "My sister and I were five years apart, and we could barely stand to be in the same room together when we were younger. Now she's my best friend."

Keegan nodded. In many ways, Isaac was *his* best friend, too. And not just because Jermaine, Lamont, and the rest of his buddies weren't around. No, he couldn't carry on a conversation with Isaac the way other siblings did, but Keegan had always talked to his brother, shared stuff about his day as if Isaac might suddenly surprise him and begin responding like anyone else. Not that Isaac didn't communicate in his own way. His laser focus reminded Keegan how interesting even the simplest things could be, and his silences spoke of how connected everything was if you gave yourself the time to think about it.

And, of course, Isaac also reminded him of—

"Ready to go, Isaac?" asked Tomlinson, bending down so she was looking directly into the boy's face. Isaac's eyes, of course, were focused slightly to the right of hers and he didn't respond, but both his shoes were on, their Velcro straps aligned perfectly.

Keegan slung Isaac's backpack over his shoulder along with

his own, then took his brother's hand in his. "Say goodbye, Isaac."

Isaac made a sound that was more wordless murmur than anything else, but even that response was more than Keegan expected, further proof that Ms. Tomlinson was a good fit for him.

Leading him down the hall toward the exit, Keegan remembered her comment: *There were some stressful moments this morning.* No surprise there. Why *wouldn't* there be? Despite the silence that had hung over the table at breakfast, Isaac would have sensed the friction between Keegan and their father.

And now Keegan had once more done exactly what his father and Forbes had warned him against, and he wished he could erase what had happened on that soccer field. His dad would be pissed if he heard, which would only add to the tension. There was nothing that Keegan could do now about his mistake, but he grudgingly admitted he had to try harder to make things better between him and his dad, to make their life here work regardless of how much Keegan missed what he'd left behind. What he'd lost.

Reaching the exit at the end of the corridor, Keegan nodded at a janitor cutting up a cardboard box for recycling, and he remembered the cereal box he'd emptied into his bowl that morning. He thought again about his resolve to try harder, thought about his father having to shop for groceries after working all day, thought about the debit card in his wallet for the household account his dad had set up. He looked down at his brother. "What do you say we make a stop at the SaveEasy on our way home?"

# CHAPTER 25

Best school year *never*, thought Willa, the steering wheel sliding through her hands as she turned back toward Brookdale. Three days in and nothing was going the way she'd hoped it would.

She'd heard from Britney and Celia—via Jay and Todd—what had happened in phys ed that afternoon, the girls nearly breaking the school's hundred-metre record getting to Willa with the story: Keegan Fraser grandstanding in front of everybody, catching Wynn off-guard, making him look like a fool in front of Coach Cameron and the rest of the class. "He purposely held back," said Britney, "stumbling around on the field before pouring on the juice. It's like he was rubbing Wynn's face in it."

Willa hadn't been planning to see Wynn until after soccer tryouts that day but, having heard the story, she'd gone looking for him and found all three guys on their way to the field. She'd expected Wynn to be annoyed, but she'd never seen him so angry. "I hope the prick shows up this afternoon," he'd seethed. "I'm gonna run his fucking ass into the goddamn ground!" According to Jay, Coach Cameron had made a point of asking Fraser to come to tryouts, which had only increased Wynn's humiliation.

"It's not like you have to worry about making the team," Willa had offered, trying to soothe him.

"That's not the point!" he'd snarled. "Losers like Phillips and Shaw were cheering for him. *Cheering!*" he'd repeated. And then he'd stormed off, Todd and Jay jogging after him. He hadn't even kissed her goodbye.

So instead of heading home after school, she'd gone for a drive, hoping to wrap her head around what had happened. And ended up realizing how inconsiderate she'd been. Hadn't Wynn been nothing but supportive after Keegan embarrassed her in class, even offering to kick the guy's ass? And how had she responded to *his* humiliation? *It's not like you have to worry about making the team.* She must have sounded like she was *defending* Keegan, which was absurd. The guy was a jerk, something he seemed determined to prove every chance he got.

And then, as if her thoughts had summoned him, there he was, big as life, walking into the Brookdale SaveEasy. Stunned by the coincidence, she drove by the store before realizing this was her chance. She'd confront the asshole.

Braking, she whipped into the Home Hardware parking lot, pulled a U-turn, and moments later found herself parked in front of the grocery store, wondering what she was going to say to the guy. *Who do you think you are?* sprang to mind, but that sounded way too much like Vice-Principal Caldwell. She mentally sifted through other options as she got out of the SUV and walked through the SaveEasy's entrance, glancing down each aisle she passed. Spotting the jerk in the condiments section, she made her way toward him, the memory of Wynn storming off still vivid in her mind.

Squatting on his haunches, he had his shoulder to her, his attention directed toward a young boy beside him. In each of Keegan's hands was a bottle of barbecue sauce, and he held both up for the boy to examine. "So, buddy, the way I see it, we've got two options here. There's spicy," he said, waggling the bottle in his left hand, "and then there's extra spicy." He waggled the other bottle. "Whaddya think?"

The boy's eyes seemed to wander the shelves on both sides of him, and he offered no response.

"Yeah, you're right," Keegan continued. "Big decision. We don't want to rush into anything, do we?"

The boy's eyes continued to drift, and Willa recognized the disconnect common to some kids with special needs. The career and life-management course she had taken last year had a volunteer component, and she'd spent her required hours at Brookdale Elementary helping the resource teacher, Ms. Trask. One girl on Trask's caseload was autistic, and the boy she was looking at now shared some of her mannerisms.

Keegan stood up. "How about I put them both in the cart and we'll think on it some more? That okay with you, buddy?" Again, the boy said nothing, but Keegan seemed fine with his silence. He laid both bottles in his grocery cart, then gently ruffled the boy's hair.

It was such a simple act, but the gesture tugged at Willa. They seemed to have a closeness she'd never shared with her own brother. Even before Aiden had gone away to university they'd rarely talked, and when they did it was usually to argue about something. She was still thinking that when Keegan turned and saw her staring.

"Hey," he said.

She had to remind herself why she was there. Summoning that image of Wynn striding away, she opened her mouth to give this guy a piece of her mind, but she couldn't help noticing how he laid his hand on the boy's shoulder and drew him close, as though shielding him. From her? "Hi," she said, finally.

They stared at each other awkwardly. Keegan looked at his feet, then at her again. "I would've thought you had people to do this for you," he said.

She blinked. "Do what?"

"Grocery shopping."

"Uh, we do," she said. "Evelyn, our housekeeper. But her daughter just had a baby so she's off for a while." She stopped, surprised by her rambling. She felt off-balance, unsure of herself.

She felt something else, too. Fingers touching her hand. She looked down and saw the boy now standing beside her. She leaned down so her face was level with his. "Hello," she said, but he didn't respond, just stared at her. "Your brother?" she asked Keegan.

He nodded. "This is Isaac. Isaac, this is Willa."

"Nice to meet you, Isaac," Willa said, and she was surprised when the boy brought his hand up. But not to shake the one she held out to him. Instead, he lifted his higher and touched her hair.

"No, Isaac," said Keegan. "Personal space, remember?"

But the boy didn't pull his hand away. Instead, he threaded his fingers through Willa's locks as though combing them. So softly, though, that she barely felt it.

For a brief second, Keegan's face crumpled. Then, "Sorry," he said, gently taking Isaac's hand in his. "He doesn't usually do this."

Willa stood up. "Likes long hair, huh?"

Keegan shook his head. "It's the colour."

"What about it?"

"Our mother had blond hair."

"Had?"

There was a beat of silence before he responded. "She died."

It was like he'd thrown cold water in her face. "I—" She didn't know what to say. "I'm sorry."

But he'd already turned away, taking Isaac and their cart with him.

# CHAPTER 26

C hrist! thought Griff as the elevator doors opened. The god-damned super practically *lived* in the lobby lately.

The little man glanced up from the rows of brushed steel mailboxes to the left of the entrance, a portable label-maker resting on the floor as he applied a new nametag above one of them. Griff wondered why he bothered. Who actually *got* mail anymore, other than those thumb-thick envelopes from charities begging for money? Griff wouldn't be surprised if the U.S. Postal Service went tits-up any day now.

"Mr. Barnett," said the super, nodding as Griff passed.

Griff grunted in return. Prick, he thought, sensing the super's eyes following him out the door. As always, he half-expected the guy to whip out a notebook and jot down the time, mid-afternoon being way too late for somebody in construction to be heading to work. Griff's growing unease about the little weasel made him wonder if maybe it was time he did some in-house investigating to see if he had reason to be worried.

As he opened the glass door leading to the street, a warm gust caught it and nearly tore it from his hands. Lately, the wind off the lake seemed to have picked up strength, doing its best to pry at exposed surfaces, looking for ways to shred any weakness it found. For an odd moment, Griff felt as if he were the weakness the wind was seeking, bearing relentlessly down on him. But that, he knew, was his fear of Morozov carving away at him, not the wind. Bracing himself, he headed for the sidewalk, the fabric of his shirt rippling on his shoulders like malformed wings.

+ + +

Having hacked Talia's and Sonia's texts, Griff knew they often stopped at Bean There Downed That after school. He couldn't have chosen a better place himself: sitting in the coffee shop with his back to Talia, he was close enough to hear all four speak, while the wall of mirrored tiles across from him provided a clear view of most of the group. Talia was the single exception, but it was more important to hear what she said. Besides, it wasn't as if he'd forget what she looked like. Seeing her enter the coffee shop with Soccerguy89, Sonia, and Sonia's new bad boy, Griff suddenly had another reason to hate Facebook—the photos posted there didn't do this girl justice. Long dark hair swept back into a ponytail, white halter top emphasizing her deep tan, a sheen of perspiration like Arkansas dew on her throat and her cleavage—damn. He'd had to force himself to turn away.

His phone on the table in front of him, he pretended to check his email. Not that he ever got anything except penis enlargement ads and offers of money from that dude in Nigeria.

"—so I told him he could kiss my ass," said Sonia.

"Yeah, right," said Soccerguy89, his tone conveying his disbelief.

"No, she did," offered Talia. "I was there."

The boy whistled. "And he didn't *do* anything?"

Raising his face toward the mirrored tiles, Griff watched Sonia's reflection shake her head. "Those rent-a-cops the school board hires are douchebags. *That* one is, anyway. That's the second time he's tried to pat me down."

"You can't blame him for that." This from the bad boy she'd brought with her.

"Look," said Sonia, "I'm not about to let some overweight guy with dandruff and a unibrow put his hands on me for no reason."

Their chatter drifted to other things as they sipped their drinks. Griff had heard Sonia and her bad boy order the house special, a latte that was more sugar than anything else, and Soccerguy89 had gotten something equally disgusting, but Talia had ordered a simple coffee. It was, in fact, the same dark roast Griff was drinking now, and she took it the same way he did— black, no sugar. As the conversation moved on from an upcoming dance to other topics of zero interest to him, his mind drifted once more to the drink she'd chosen, and then to the memory of the sheen on that golden skin, and from there to the arm's length that separated his body from hers. The sudden movement of a man walking by both tables pulled a swirl of scent into Griff's nostrils, and he realized it was Talia's perfume. She smelled like flowers. Nothing overwhelming like the cloying fragrance of roses that old women were partial to, or the heaviness of lilac and lavender he'd noticed on women trying to hide the smell of their sweat. Or the whore-scent of lily of the valley. Talia smelled faintly of wildflowers after a rain.

Lost in those thoughts, he was caught unaware when Sonia and her bad boy got up to leave. "Call me?" said Sonia.

"Sure," Talia replied.

The bad boy did a complicated hand manoeuvre with Soccerguy89 that ended in a fist-bump, and then he and Sonia were gone.

Griff shifted his chair slightly and watched in the mirrored tiles as the boy behind him reached across the table and took one of Talia's hands in his, squeezing it gently. "Thanks again," he said, his voice so soft Griff barely heard the words.

"For what?"

"You know. For not believing that stuff."

Griff could see Talia nod. "I knew it couldn't be true," she said, and Griff saw in those mirrored tiles that it was *her* hand doing the squeezing now.

"After everything you've been through," the guy continued, "I wouldn't have blamed you if you'd never wanted to talk to me again."

Griff watched Talia look away, her gaze directed out the window at heavy traffic he doubted she was actually seeing. A moment passed before she turned to him again. "I spent the last five months believing a lot of things that probably weren't true," she said softly. "I'm not living my life like that again."

A silence settled around them, but Griff could see a question on Soccerguy89's face. And he was pretty sure it was the same thing he was wondering himself. He was right.

"You really never heard from him again?" the boy asked.

Staring intently at the mirror, Griff watched the back of the girl's head as he waited for her reply, which was swallowed by the sudden blare of a horn outside. Turning toward the window, he saw a cabbie shaking his fist at a driver who, apparently, had just pulled out in front of him.

Frustrated, Griff looked again at the young couple, but they were getting to their feet. *Fuck!*

They moved toward the cash register and, as Soccerguy89 paid their bill, Griff watched Talia looking at him, her expression the same one she'd worn in the photo in front of the Chicago Culture Center.

And he felt something shift inside him, felt a heat rise up from nowhere, felt it smoulder in his chest.

He told himself it was because he'd missed Talia's response to the question that had plagued him for months now, that time was running out and Morozov wasn't going to wait forever, that Griff's own ass was on the line here. All of that was true, of course, but he knew that wasn't the reason he ground his molars together as he watched the pair leave the coffee shop, their arms entwined. Scowling, he grabbed his phone and stood up, looking toward the wall of windows to catch one more glimpse of her. And he froze.

The super from his building stood on the other side of all that glass, his eyes locked on Griff. And then he was gone.

# CHAPTER 27

Keegan's fingers felt like they'd parted from his hands two blocks back. The knifelike handles of the plastic SaveEasy bags seemed to saw through tendon and bone as the bundles swung heavily at his sides. There hadn't looked to be this much stuff in the grocery cart, but there was nothing he could do about it now. At least he'd been able to convince Isaac to carry one of the bags. And Isaac hadn't complained once. Hadn't *whimpered* once, which was his brother's usual response to anything that upset him. Keegan was sure that, one of these days, Isaac was going to let loose a barrage of words to make up for lost time, and the first of these would probably be a curse, like the one that had slipped out of Keegan's mouth a moment ago when he'd nearly dropped the bag with the eggs.

"Almost there, buddy," he said as they turned down their street. Even from four houses away, he could tell their father was already home. All the windows were wide open, Evan obviously doing his best to air out the rooms in the hope of cooling them. Even in late afternoon, the heat hadn't abated. And combined with high humidity, the day felt more like a sauna than September, which had made Keegan appreciate the SaveEasy's air-conditioned interior.

Thinking of that store now, his mind painted a picture of Willa's face when she'd met Isaac. Keegan was surprised at how she'd responded to him, not at all the way he was accustomed to people initially reacting to his brother—first, the surprised expression, and then the barely perceptible drawing back as though whatever Isaac had might be catching. Keegan knew he was far too sensitive about people's reactions to his brother's autism, but he'd seen the same thing too many times not to be. Willa hadn't responded that way, though. She'd caught him off-guard, which was probably why he'd told her the truth about his mother instead of the story Forbes had concocted. As soon as he'd said it, he realized his mistake, but there was nothing he could do about it except get out of there.

There was, of course, another reason he had to get away— the lump that had formed in his throat as he'd watched Isaac stroking that long, blond hair.

Sensing one of the stretched plastic handles was about to let go, he shrugged off the memory and glanced at Isaac. "Better move it, buddy!" he said as he lengthened his stride. Beside him, his brother began to jog, and moments later they were in their driveway. "Could use some help here!" Keegan called. His father appeared at a window, then opened the front door as Keegan took the steps two at a time. He raced inside and down the hall-way, making it to the kitchen just as the handle separated, the SaveEasy bag dropping safely to the counter.

He could feel blood begin to flow into his tortured fingers, and he flexed them, his skin tingling. Hearing his father enter the kitchen, he turned to make a comment about maybe rethinking their need for a car, but the look on his father's face stopped him. "What's wrong?" he asked.

Evan said nothing, merely held up one of the cordless phones that served their landline. He pressed a button, and Keegan heard an automated voice tell the user to press "one" for an archived message. His father did, and then another voice filled the kitchen. "Hello. This message is for Keegan. Coach Cameron here."

*Christ, no.*

"That was an impressive performance on the field today," Cameron said over noises in the background. "I'd hoped to see you after school because this afternoon's tryouts are the last ones." Now Keegan knew what the background noises were— the sounds of a scrimmage, guys shouting as they jostled one another for the ball. "But after watching you in class," Cameron continued, "I don't need to see more. If you'd like to play, there's a spot for you on the team. I'll be at school early tomorrow, so if you want to drop by the gym before classes start, I'd like to talk to you about it. Or, if you'd prefer, you can phone me at home tonight." He gave his number and then the call ended.

Evan clicked off the phone, laid it on the counter.

"Look, I know I shouldn't have—"

"Say it," interrupted his father.

Keegan looked away.

"*Say* it!"

His fingers still tingling, Keegan thought of the groceries he'd bought so his father wouldn't have to. It didn't matter what he did, how hard he tried. It was never enough.

"*SAY IT!*"

Keegan could hear Isaac whimpering in the hallway, and he swallowed the pulse in his throat. "Don't attract attention," he said, the words like shards of glass.

"Simple enough, right?" his father asked. "And how many times did Forbes try to hammer *that* into your head? How many times did I tell you *myself*?" Jabbing a finger toward the phone, he scowled, "Apparently, you just don't *give* a damn, do you? Or maybe you *want* us to get caught. You *want* them to find us."

"Seriously?" snarled Keegan. "You're ready to talk about what *I* want?" He waved a hand around the room. "It sure as hell isn't *this*! But that didn't matter to *you*, did it? *No*! The only thing *you* cared about was—"

"*Enough*!" his father roared, and Keegan could hear the whimpers in the hallway become sobs. "The life we have is the life we have. Period. Neither of us can change that. But we can *lose* it. And in a *heartbeat* if you let yourself forget the prime directive. Don't—attract—attention," he said slowly, each word like the thud of a mallet against bone. "*Christ*, Keegan!"

Keegan glanced again at the bags on the counter. He could feel himself reaching back, could feel the muscles in his arm tense, could feel them winding up for the swing that would send all those bags hurtling to the floor. Eggs and fucking all.

But the sobs came again.

Keegan shoved through the back door and was gone.

# CHAPTER 28

"Mr. Barnett," said the super as he peered around the door he held partially ajar. "What can I do for you?"

His face bore an odd expression that Griff couldn't read. He knew it wasn't fear—he'd seen enough of it on the faces of the people he'd offed to recognize that when he saw it. But, he thought, the fact that the super *wasn't* afraid was a good thing. The prick didn't know who he was dealing with. Yet.

"Mind if I come in for a minute?" asked Griff.

The super's face instantly flushed, and Griff could guess what the guy had been up to. Choking the chicken. Griff expected him to excuse himself for a minute to turn off whatever porn he'd been watching, but he surprised Griff by opening the door all the way. "By all means," he said.

Griff glanced left and right to make sure the hallway was empty. It was late, and the super's apartment was in the basement, sandwiched between the mechanical room and the delivery bay, so he doubted other tenants came down here. There was, of course, the matter of the surveillance cameras in the elevator and at the end of the hallway, but Griff would deal with them later. He stepped inside.

The super's apartment was nothing like Griff had expected. He'd imagined something seedy, and not just because its below-grade location offered slit-like windows near the ceiling. It was the guy's rat-like manner that had made Griff picture him living in something dark and disgusting, but the opposite was true. The living room was bright and cheerful, and instead of tattered furniture found curbside or at a Salvation Army depot, a plush leather sofa and matching loveseat and wingback made a cozy grouping around a gleaming coffee table. Go figure.

"Can I offer you something?" said the super as he followed Griff into the room. "A soda maybe?"

"I'm good," Griff replied, shaking his head. "But would you mind if I used your washroom? I'm not feelin' too well all of a sudden."

The super raised his eyebrows. "Uh, sure. It's this way." He led Griff down a hallway and pointed to a door on the left.

"Thanks," said Griff as he entered a bathroom that, although small and windowless, was brightly lit and had a good-sized tub. Closing the door behind him, he pulled a large plastic bag and a pair of rubber gloves from his pockets. He slipped on the gloves, spread the bag on the floor, took a towel from the vanity, and waited.

After several minutes, he heard the super's footsteps approach the bathroom. "Mr. Barnett? Are you all right in there?"

Griff didn't respond, and a moment later the super tapped on the door. "Is anything wrong?"

Griff made a sound that resembled a moan, faint but loud enough to be heard from the hall.

"Mr. Barnett?"

Griff watched the doorknob begin to turn, and he stepped back. Although there was little space for him to move, the opening door shielded him from view momentarily, and a moment was all he needed. The second the super appeared, Griff reached out and grabbed him by the neck, forcing him diagonally floorward in a single motion and ramming his face against the inside edge of the tub, a broken tooth clattering against the porcelain. Griff wrapped the towel around the now unconscious man's head and lowered him to the tile floor.

He worked methodically, turning on the tap in the tub and plugging the drain before stripping the man of his clothes and dropping them into a hamper beside the vanity. A bar of Irish Spring lay in a soap dish, and he placed it under the tap, the flow of warm water forcing a swath of suds outward across the rising surface. When the tub was more than half filled, Griff turned off the tap, put his arms under the super, and hoisted him up. Trying not to look at his genitals flopping uselessly between his legs, he focused instead on the dark stain seeping across the towel as he lowered the man into the tub. Griff was surprised to hear a muffled groan, and he knew the shock of the water was bringing him around. He would have to move quickly.

The towel had served its purpose, ensuring no blood had dripped onto the floor or Griff's clothes. Cradling the man's upper body in one arm, Griff used his other hand to unwrap the cloth from the super's head and dropped it into the plastic bag at his feet before forcing the guy's head under the water. As his bloodied face submerged, his eyes fluttered open, and in them at last was the fear Griff was used to seeing. Careful not to bruise the super's skin beneath his fingers, he held the man's face and torso under, counting in his head. For a little guy, he was wiry and strong, and he continued to flail until Griff got to nineteen and the weakening body finally went limp. Fortunately, the water had muffled his gargled cries, but Griff was still grateful for the apartment's basement location.

When it was over, Griff rearranged the man's position, turning him this way and that until he was satisfied with what he saw. There being no sign of forced entry into the apartment and no other marks on the super's body, police would assume he'd slipped in the tub and knocked himself unconscious. Hadn't all those studies identified falls as the number one cause of accidental deaths in the home? And most of those happened in the bathroom.

Griff grabbed another towel, using it to mop up the water that had splashed onto the floor, then shoved it into the plastic bag along with the bloodied one before tying the bag to his belt. Pulling a cloth from his pocket, he wiped off the doorknob, the only surface he'd touched without wearing the gloves, then went looking for a bathrobe and a clean pair of pyjamas, both of which he hung from a hook on the back of the bathroom door. Perfect.

Having disposed of the super, Griff was now free to look for whatever the guy had on him, and he found the bedroom that functioned as an office. A leather chair sat in front of a large desk holding a computer and an enormous monitor. Three smaller screens connected to the same computer sat on a separate table to the left.

Easing himself into the chair, Griff began by searching the desk's two drawers, carefully removing everything inside each and then replacing the contents one by one. He found nothing out of the ordinary: one drawer contained maintenance schedules, requisitions for cleaning supplies, shit like that, and the other held only blank notepads and a handful of thank-you cards from grateful tenants. A place for everything and everything in its place, but nothing of any significance, so he turned to the computer and was relieved to see it didn't require a password to bring it out of sleep mode. Not that he couldn't have gotten around that, but it would have taken a while and he didn't want to hang around there any longer than he had to.

Even in death, the super continued to surprise him—as the screens powered up, none of them showed any evidence of porn. The large monitor displayed a desktop photo of Chicago's skyline at sunset, while each of the three smaller screens was subdivided into multiple windows showing feeds from the various surveillance cameras on each floor and elevator. Griff located the cameras for the basement hallway and the elevator that had brought him down and, with a few simple keystrokes, tapped into their feeds and erased those segments. Before leaving the apartment, he would reset the timing sequence and copy and paste video loops of an empty hallway and elevator so he could leave undetected.

Confident he'd eliminated any record of his presence, Griff turned his attention to learning how much the super knew about him. The moment he'd seen the guy had tailed him that afternoon, Griff's imagination had leaped toward a couple of scenarios, one of them involving the police. Nothing about the super had activated Griff's podar but, nonetheless, he set about looking for anything that might suggest a law enforcement connection. Inserting a flash drive, he initialized a sifter that analyzed the hard drive for telltale signs of police activity but, as he'd suspected, the scan revealed nothing.

Griff slumped back in the chair. While he was glad to rule out the police, the alternative was no less disturbing: Pavel Morozov. It would be just like that pale-faced freak to put the super on his payroll to keep tabs on him and make sure he didn't try to run. And Morozov hadn't earned the nickname Architect of Accidents for nothing—he would know that Griff had offed the guy, so who knew what his next move would be? Griff could feel the noose around his neck tightening.

Reaching for the keyboard again, he was about to begin reconfiguring the sifter with a new set of search parameters when his fingers hesitated. He thought about the super lying submerged in the tub down the hall, thought about how tidy the man had been, not just in his apartment but throughout the building. A place for everything and everything in its place. On a hunch, Griff opened up a drive search, typed in seven letters, and hit Enter.

Despite the scenarios he'd anticipated, Griff wasn't prepared for what appeared on the screen.

# CHAPTER 29

Sitting in homeroom, Willa sighed. Monday morning already, and she had nothing to show for the weekend except all the schoolwork she'd finished because Wynn was still in a pissy mood—Keegan Fraser hadn't shown up at the final tryouts on Thursday, and Wynn had missed his chance to run the guy's ass into the ground. She'd wondered if Keegan had heard Wynn was gunning for him, because he hadn't shown up at school on Friday, either.

It wasn't as if she and Wynn had argued, but she'd only seen him Saturday evening because Wynn had gotten Todd and Jay and a few other buddies to scrimmage with him until late on Friday and then most of the next day. And their evening together hadn't exactly been best-school-year-ever memorable. They'd watched a movie at Wynn's place, her body curled against his on his king-sized bed, but she could tell he was distracted, his thoughts clearly on what had happened in phys ed. She'd tried to distract him herself but, as usual, her efforts only got so far. The minute their necking grew intense, he'd pulled away from her and said it was getting late, he'd better take her home.

Like all the times before, she'd struggled to hide how hurt she felt, wondering what was wrong with her. A couple of months after they'd begun going steady, she'd mustered the courage to ask why he was reluctant to take their relationship to the next level, and he'd said he respected her too much to take advantage of her that way. It was an answer that should have pleased her, but for some reason it sounded like he was repeating something he'd heard in a movie or read in a pamphlet. She knew Wynn wasn't gay—hadn't she felt physical evidence of his arousal every time they'd made out?—but each time she believed they might actually take that next step, he seemed to recoil as if something about her flipped a switch, shut him down. She'd wanted to talk to Celia and Britney about it but had never been able to work up the nerve—it would have been humiliating to admit how undesirable she was. So, instead, she continued to look for answers on relationship websites, poring over articles like "Ten Top Tips for Pleasing Your Guy." Invariably, though, they only made her feel worse.

She hadn't seen Wynn on Sunday at all—something he had to do for his father, he had told her. That afternoon, as she'd disposed of the roses he'd given her (she was surprised at how unpleasant week-old roses could begin to smell), she wondered if maybe what he was really doing was kicking that damn soccer ball around some more. Willa understood that Wynn's competitiveness was the very thing that made him so valuable on each of the teams he played for but, for the first time, she'd found herself wishing he would just get over himself.

Off to her right, she heard the hum of a vibrating phone and saw Bailey Holloway pull hers out of her bag, glance at the display, and then stab Ignore. Willa wondered who could be on the other end generating that response. Judging from the way Greg Phillips had hung on Bailey's every word during their group discussion last week, Willa figured it might be him, though the guy didn't seem like the type who'd make a girl punch Ignore. But she really didn't know him, did she?

The door opened and Keegan Fraser walked in, handing Mr. Richardson a slip of paper before moving to his seat and sitting down. Missing school on Friday and now arriving moments before first class made it look more and more like he was keeping out of Wynn's way, which surprised Willa. Despite his obvious talent for jerkness, he really didn't seem like someone who'd slink around avoiding a confrontation. But he'd surprised her before, hadn't he? Like on Thursday at the SaveEasy, the way he was so attentive to his little brother. Wynn had a younger brother, too, but the boy still lived with their mom in Halifax, so Wynn didn't see him much. And he hardly ever talked about him.

She studied Keegan's profile and found herself wondering if he looked like his mother. She had no way of knowing, of course, but the woman had had blond hair, not at all like that so-black-it-was-almost-blue mess on his head, so probably not. And then Willa was thinking of the lie he'd told her in that SaveEasy aisle—*She died.*

She'd felt stupid after he'd dropped that bomb on her. So stupid, in fact, that she'd asked her father about the Frasers at dinner that evening—specifically, what had happened to *Mrs.* Fraser. Willa was surprised when her dad said the marriage hadn't lasted and the wife had left years ago, something Keegan's father had shared with him over coffee at the dealership. Why on earth would Keegan say his mother was dead? To make her feel sorry for him? She guessed it made sense—knowing Wynn was pissed at him, maybe Keegan thought she'd get Wynn to go easy on him. But wouldn't he know she'd eventually discover the truth?

Willa sighed again. She was spending *way* too much time thinking about a guy she couldn't even stand.

She heard the hum of a phone and looked to her right. Bailey's again. This time she pressed the power button and a faint melody signalled the phone shutting down. As she shoved it into her backpack, Bailey saw Willa watching her, and her face suddenly reddened.

Willa was about to ask her if something was wrong when the first-period bell rang. Bailey all but ran from the room.

+ + +

"Is it just me," asked Willa, "or are people acting weird?"

"It's Monday, isn't it?" Celia responded, pushing away the remains of her veggie wrap, one of the Brookdale Deli's low-calorie offerings. Celia had announced that morning she needed to lose two pounds and was apparently serious about it, despite being so slim that a stiff breeze could topple her. But Willa could guess what was behind the weight-loss thing—Celia's mom was still wallowing over her breakup with Dewayne, which meant she was probably hoovering through litres of Chunky Monkey. And whenever her mother went on an eating binge, Celia dieted like a demon. It was like she thought fat was contagious.

"No," said Willa, shaking her head, "it's more than just a Monday thing." She paused, thinking about what had happened in homeroom. "Have you noticed anything about Bailey?"

"You mean *besides* the fact that her jeans make her butt look like a barbecue?" asked Britney.

Todd and Celia chuckled. Jay, on the other hand, said, "I don't think her butt's so bad." Celia elbowed him sharply, and he turned to Wynn for support. "What d'*you* think?" he asked.

Wynn just shrugged.

"I'm not talking about her butt," said Willa. "She seems jumpy all the time."

"Seriously, guys?" said Todd, making no attempt to mask his boredom. "Who gives a shit about Bailey Holloway?"

Willa said nothing. She'd googled "poetry competitions" after English last week when she'd learned about Bailey's prize, and she'd found the contest she'd entered along with close to three hundred others. Those poems had been judged by three Atlantic poets whose names even Willa recognized, so apparently there *were* people who gave a shit about Bailey Holloway.

"I bet *I* can guess what's bothering her," said Britney, grinning. "She's knocked up." She turned to Celia. "And it's not even October. I win!"

Willa shook her head. "I don't think that's it."

"You said she was jumpy, didn't you?" Britney asked. "And that would explain the size of her ass, wouldn't it?"

Jay chimed in. "Maybe those calls are from the hospital setting up the appointment. You know, to get it taken care of. And maybe now she's thinking about keeping it."

"Finally!" said Celia. "Something worth Facebooking about."

Willa was sorry she'd brought it up. "I don't think that's a good idea," she said.

Celia slapped Willa's arm playfully. "I'm not going to mention her *name*," she said. "People can fill in the blanks."

Wynn shoved his chair back and got to his feet. "We should be getting back," he said.

Willa glanced at her phone to check the time. "Crap!" she muttered.

"Problem?" asked Britney.

Willa showed her the device's black screen. "I just got this a couple weeks ago but it won't hold its charge. I'll have to run to the phone store after school." She held out her hand to Wynn. "Can I borrow yours for a minute? I want to check if they have my battery in stock."

Wynn handed her his phone, the same model as hers in black instead of white. As the six left the deli, she scrolled through his contacts to see if the store was among them, but it wasn't. Most of the others listed were the same as her own, but there was one that was new to her. It stood out partly because he hadn't assigned a name to it but also because it was a palindrome, one of those numbers that read the same backwards as forwards. She had a thing about numbers, although she'd never shared that with her friends, knowing it would earn her an eye-roll to beat all eye-rolls. But it probably explained why she was good at math, even liked it, despite Deadhand Shedrand's commitment to wringing the joy out of every moment in his classroom.

Sliding into Wynn's car, she pulled up the store's number on the phone's web browser, made the call, then handed the phone back to Wynn. As he took it, she thought she saw something in his eyes that surprised her. Relief?

Jeez, she was imagining weirdness in everyone around her now, even her boyfriend. Maybe it *was* a Monday thing after all.

# CHAPTER 30

"Vancouver!"

Keegan sighed, turning toward the voice. "Yeah, d'Entremont?" He'd known this moment was coming, and he wished he'd gotten it over with before the weekend. But after witnessing the blow-up between Keegan and their dad on Thursday, Isaac had been so unsettled the following morning that Keegan had stayed home with him.

"You didn't show up at tryouts last week," said Wynn, as he and Willa arrived at Keegan's locker. The bandage he'd worn last week was gone, revealing only a faint red mark on his cheek. "Guess you didn't want anyone to see you're a one-hit wonder, right?"

Keegan knew how he had to play this, but it was still hard saying the words. "You got me."

Wynn grinned. "So," he said, "*that's* the problem? You don't have the stamina for team play? The *guts*?" he added, his voice suddenly booming. Others near them turned to stare.

"Look, Wynn—" he began, but then he heard Forbes in his head: *Don't attract attention.* And there was another voice in there, too, except it wasn't saying words. The sounds it made were sobs, the ones Keegan had heard from Isaac as he and his dad went at it Thursday afternoon.

"Got something to say, Vancouver?"

Avoiding Willa's eyes, Keegan tried his best to look sheepish. "You're right," he said, hating the words he could feel his mouth forming, hating himself even more for saying them. "I'd be lousy on the team. No stamina." There. He hoped his father would be happy. Nothing *else* he did ever pleased him.

Wynn's expression looked like something you'd see on a Powerball winner, all teeth and laugh lines. "Well," he said, his tone suddenly magnanimous, "at least you know your limitations." He reached out and slapped Keegan's shoulder, the way you'd pat a dog that had finally learned not to piss in the house. "Better than wasting the coach's time, right?"

Keegan forced down the bile that rose hot and sour in his throat, made himself look Wynn in the eye and offer a smile of his own, although he was pretty sure it paled in comparison with d'Entremont's million-kilowatter. "Yeah," he said. "I know better than to waste anybody's time."

Wynn looked down at Willa, his grin still blinding. "C'mon, Wills," he said. "Places to go, people to do." And he laughed.

Keegan watched the two walk off, a storm of unvoiced expletives raging through his head.

"How's it taste?"

Willa had asked him that last week when she'd teased him about eating crow, and for a moment Keegan thought what he'd heard was a memory surfacing amid that surge of silent swearing. But then a voice repeated the question, and he turned to see Russell looking at him, his expression unreadable.

"How's *what* taste?" Keegan asked, then realized that was the same response he'd offered Willa.

"The shit you just swallowed."

Keegan reached for his backpack on the floor. "Forget it, okay?"

"Like Wynn'll forget it?" asked Russell. "Like you won't hear him all day telling everybody what just happened?"

"You wouldn't understand," muttered Keegan.

"You're kidding, right?" said Russell, his voice bitter. "I wouldn't *understand*?" He pointed at his oversized sweatshirt, which bore the words *When my pager goes off, people think I'm backing up.* "You figure I *like* wearing stuff like this?"

Keegan didn't know what to say. He shook his head.

Russell looked down at those letters, and Keegan thought he saw his lower lip quiver. When he raised his eyes again, Keegan could see the torment in them. "My mom won't buy these for me. I use my own money, get them custom-printed at that silk-screening place on Church Street."

"Why?" asked Keegan.

"The same reason you just told Wynn you suck ass at soccer. To keep him off your back." He shook his head sadly. "What you did during phys ed last week? The way you put him in his place? I can't tell you how much I—" He shrugged the thought away. "But you're no different than the rest of us losers. Welcome to hell." He turned away and moved down the hall. From behind, his XXXL sweatshirt looked like a large white flag.

Keegan looked down at his feet, clenching his fists as he tried to hold in his mind that image of his brother sobbing. But all he could see was the back of Russell's sweatshirt, like the universal symbol of surrender disappearing into the crowd.

# CHAPTER 31

Walking down Mid-Valley Mall's concourse, Willa glanced at her reflection in a store window and sighed. Despite all the time she'd spent straightening her hair that morning, her natural curl had come back with a vengeance. The haze floating over the valley had intensified the heat, and she could only imagine what it must be like on the soccer field, where Wynn and the other members of the newly rostered team were enduring the first of four after-school practices this week.

That thought, of course, reminded her of the scene Wynn had made at the end of lunchtime. She'd felt bad for Keegan, and she didn't know why. It wasn't so much that he had admitted not having enough stamina to be on the team, although that was embarrassing enough. It was more the way his face had looked as he'd said it. There'd been something in his eyes that hadn't seemed defeated, certainly not the way you'd *expect* a guy to look as he handed over his balls on a platter. It was almost as if he—

Forget it. The important thing was that Wynn was satisfied. Maybe life could finally get back to normal—or whatever passed for it in the Jaffrey household. Her mother had called after last class, saying she was on her way to Halifax for a few days, leaving

Willa and her dad to fend for themselves. Celia's mom refused to stop wallowing in her post-breakup Chunky Monkey binge, so Lenore had arranged some time for them at a spa interspersed with some serious shopping to get her mind off Dairy Queen Dewayne.

It took only a few minutes to get her battery replaced and, as she left the phone store, she spied Bailey Holloway walking in her direction. Willa couldn't help thinking of Bailey's weird reactions to the calls and texts she'd been receiving. And then she thought of that palindrome on Wynn's contact list.

There was, of course, no connection between the two. Wynn hardly knew Bailey, barely even spoke to her at school. And the only time he ever spoke *of* her was to make some remark about her mother and the men she slept with, all of which clearly disgusted him. Still, Willa couldn't stop her fingers from pressing that palindrome's digits on her keypad and, almost immediately, she could hear in her receiver the call going through.

And even from metres away in the mall's echoing concourse, she could hear a phone ring.

# CHAPTER 32

The bus lurched to a stop in front of the mall's main entrance, and Keegan joined the handful of people in the seats around him who got off and entered the large glass doors, grateful for the sudden wash of cool air that enveloped them. That cool air was, in fact, one of the reasons he'd decided to head to the mall after school—their house would be oven-like this afternoon. The other reason had to do with Isaac. Their dad was leaving work early to pick him up from his after-school program, thinking that some one-on-one time with him might help his emotional state, and Keegan had decided it would be easier on everybody if he wasn't home. Neither he nor his father seemed to be able to share space anymore without one of them pissing off the other.

But, hey, at least he'd gotten Wynn off his back. He'd been dreading phys ed that afternoon, and not just because he suspected Wynn would reassert his alpha status on the soccer field—Keegan also wasn't looking forward to Coach Cameron's response to the thanks-but-no-thanks message he'd left on the teacher's voicemail last week. Fortunately, the coach had assigned some general aerobic exercise that didn't involve soccer drills, but as soon as he'd gotten everyone in the class performing a series of cardio routines, Cameron had taken Keegan aside and third-degreed him about not wanting to play. Keegan had felt lousy doing it but he laid the blame on Isaac, telling the coach he was needed at home to look after his younger brother, that he couldn't commit to the time required for practices and games. The coach had seemed to accept this, but that hadn't made Keegan feel any better about the lie.

Making his way down the concourse, he passed a skateboard shop that reminded him of the one he and Joaquin used to hang out at sometimes, and he fought the urge to go in. His first time at Mid-Valley Mall, he was about to do the last thing most people would expect of a guy his age—look for a place to sit and read. He was still only halfway through the novel Richardson had assigned them, and he knew he'd be more likely to get a chunk of it read here than in his ninety-degree bedroom. Or whatever that was in Celsius.

# CHAPTER 33

Willa watched as Bailey pulled her phone from her bag and looked at the screen. Closing the distance between them, she could see her deliberating whether to answer a call from a number she didn't recognize. "You want to tell me what's going on, Bailey?" Willa asked when she reached her.

"Hey, Willa," said Bailey, clearly surprised to see her. She held up her ringing phone. "Sorry, got a call."

"No, you don't." Willa held up her own phone and pressed End, silencing Bailey's.

"That was you?" Bailey slipped the phone back into her bag. "What's up?" The question sounded natural enough, but the hesitation in her voice didn't.

"I want to know what's going on between you and Wynn."

Resignation replaced the surprise in Bailey's face. "What are you talking about?" she asked, but Willa could hear the defeat in her voice. She knew she'd been caught.

But caught at what?

"Why has he been calling and texting you?"

"You know about that?"

"Your number." It seemed easier to focus on those digits, her mind unwilling to consider what they could mean. "It's in his contacts."

Bailey seemed to shrink slightly, like a balloon leaking air. "Willa, I promise you there's nothing between him and me."

"And I'm just supposed to accept that?"

"It's the truth."

"Then what's with all the calls and messages?"

Bailey looked at her feet, her rust-coloured hair falling into her face.

Willa was astonished by her silence. "So you've got nothing to say?"

"Nothing you'd believe."

Willa flushed with anger. "You know, I used to think you were different from your mother. I guess I was wrong."

Bailey lifted her head, her cheeks flushed, too. "My mother has nothing to do with this."

"Really? I heard she broke up two marriages, which makes me think she doesn't have a whole lot of respect for relationships. Seems like you and she have *that* much in common."

Willa expected her comment to hit home, but she wasn't prepared for Bailey's reaction. She burst into tears.

"What the *hell*?"

Willa turned to see Keegan Fraser behind her, his face a hard mask. "It isn't enough giving people a hard time at school?" he demanded. "You have to do it here, too?"

Willa's flush deepened as Keegan stepped toward Bailey, extending a hand to comfort her. Bailey flinched, her whole body recoiling from his reach.

He let his hand drop to his side. "Anything I can do, Bailey?" he asked.

The sobbing girl shook her head, pulling tissues from her

bag and dabbing at her tears. Willa could see nearby shoppers pause to stare at them, and embarrassment took the edge off her anger. But she still deserved an answer.

Apparently, Bailey agreed. Visibly struggling to stop weeping, she turned to Willa with red eyes. "You really want to know what's going on?"

Willa nodded.

Bailey glanced around at the faces pointed in their direction. "Okay, but not here."

Moments later, all three were sitting across from a lottery kiosk on a cheap leather sectional that served as a rest area. Bailey had asked Keegan to come, too, and he sat beside her, giving Willa a stony glare. Which pissed off Willa even more. The guy barely knew Bailey, so who'd he think he was, butting in and making *her* feel like the villain?

Because suddenly she *did* feel like that. A little, anyway. She sighed. "Look, Bailey," she began, "I'm sorry for what I said about your mom. I was just repeating gossip, but I—"

"It isn't true," interrupted Bailey. "My mother never broke up any marriages." She looked down at her hands twisting in her lap. "And I'm not trying to come between you and Wynn. I don't want anything to do with him."

"Then why is he call—"

"It began the week before school started. When you were away with your parents. I was at a party and Wynn showed up alone."

Willa knew about that party. Wynn had told her about it, said it was boring and he hadn't stayed long.

"I didn't stay long," Bailey continued, still looking at her lap. "Somebody gave me something to drink and I started feeling,

I don't know, weird. Not myself. So I left." She took a breath. "The party was only a few blocks from where I live, so I started walking. I didn't get far before Wynn pulled up beside me and asked if I needed a ride." She shrugged, a simple movement, but it seemed to take tremendous effort. "Maybe if I hadn't said yes, none of it would have happened. But he was so friendly, nothing like how he'd acted before. He hadn't said a word to me at the party, and here he was offering me a drive. Besides, the fresh air hadn't made me feel any better, and I really wanted to get home. So I said okay."

She raised her eyes to Willa. "I never led him on. You have to believe me. I asked him where you were and he told me at your parents' cottage. He said that Todd and Jay were away, too. He seemed lonely, and I kind of felt sorry for him."

Willa felt her stomach shift uneasily as she anticipated what Bailey would say next. *I never led him on.* She sat waiting for the rest of it, like the blade of a guillotine.

"He got out and opened my door. Nobody's ever done that before, held a car door open and then shut it for me. Afterwards, he didn't bother opening his own, just swung his legs over and slid behind the wheel. Something you'd see in a movie, you know?"

Willa *did* know. She'd seen him do it lots of times during the past week.

"He talked the whole time he was driving," Bailey continued. "Two minutes in that car and he'd already said more to me than he'd said all last year. I guess that's why I didn't notice."

"Didn't notice what?" said Keegan, his voice tentative as if unsure he should pose the question. It was the very question Willa would have asked if she could have, but she was afraid to speak, afraid she'd start saying the kinds of things again that had brought Bailey to tears.

"We'd passed my street," said Bailey. "I figured maybe he didn't know where I lived."

He knows, Willa thought. How many times had she heard Wynn make fun of that dilapidated apartment building? Or, as he called it, *the dump where Francine Holloway spreads her legs.*

"I told him we'd gone by it," said Bailey, "but by that time we'd made it to Valley View Road, and he said it was such a nice evening, why didn't we drive up to the look-off?" She lowered her eyes again, her fingers lacing and loosening as she struggled to continue. "It was a bad idea. You know what people do up there, right? But I was enjoying myself. Here I was riding in a new T-bird with the top down, talking with Wynn d'Entremont—Wynn frigging *d'Entremont*—and feeling really relaxed, so I said sure. It was still early, just starting to get dark." She turned away, staring silently down the concourse for a long moment, and Willa could see she was fighting tears again. Keegan reached for her hand and this time she didn't draw away.

Staring at Bailey's hand in Keegan's much larger one, Willa felt disconnected somehow from the story she'd been listening to. It was like hearing a conversation over a bad connection, the caller fading in—*It was a bad idea*—and fading out—*You know what people do up there.* What the hell was Bailey trying to say?

Keegan squeezed Bailey's hand. "You don't have to tell us any more," he said softly.

A sudden sob racked the girl, and a moment passed before she could respond. "No, I *need* to. I haven't said anything to anyone before now." She cleared her throat, wiped her nose. "There was nobody else at the look-off. The sun was setting, and the view was amazing. It was like you could see forever. I'd never been up there with a boy before. When I told Wynn that, he laughed. Loud. '*Right*,' he said," Bailey's voice thick with the sarcasm she'd obviously heard in his. "He was sure there were some *other* things I'd done before, too. And he wanted me to do them with *him*."

"Son of a bitch," breathed Keegan.

Bailey swallowed hard. "But I've *never* done those things. Not ever." She paused again as if summoning the strength to go on. "I told him no, told him to stop, but he kept putting his hands . . ." She swallowed again. "I opened the door and he tried to stop me, grabbed at me, but my top ripped and I pulled free. I ended up *falling* out. My legs felt like rubber, but I made myself get up and run. I could hear him cursing, shouting for me to come back, but I hid in the trees. I was terrified he'd find me, but he didn't get out of the car. It was like he was afraid something might happen to it if he did. Or maybe he was afraid of the dark." She made a stran-gled sound like choked laughter. "Finally, he drove off. I thought he might be waiting somewhere for me so I stayed hidden for a long time. By then, my head was clearer, and I headed back to the road and started walking. It took me almost three hours to get home. Whenever I saw car lights coming, I'd hide in the ditch. It was after midnight and everybody was in bed when I finally made it. I had to—" Her face twisted momentarily, but she pressed on. "I felt dirty. All over. I took a shower, stood under the water until it ran cold. Afterwards, I put my clothes in the garbage." She lowered her eyes, and her next words were barely audible. "That's how I felt, too. Like garbage."

It was as though that faulty connection had somehow

corrected itself, the words reaching Willa's brain in a sudden raucous burst of clarity. "I don't believe *any* of this!" she said. "Wynn would *never*—" She couldn't even find the words for it.

Looking up, Bailey nodded. "That's what *he* said the first time he phoned me. He's good-looking, popular, the son of the mayor. He could have anybody he wanted, right? Who would believe me over somebody like him?"

She had only said what Willa herself had thought. He could have anybody he wanted. And then on the heels of that thought came another. Why her and not me? She said nothing for a long moment. Finally, "If what you're saying is true—"

"It *is*," said Bailey. "Remember that bandage he wore for a couple days? What did he say happened to him?"

Please don't let that be a lie. "He cut his cheek on a nail."

"Well, there's *some* truth in that." She drew another deep breath, as though preparing for an incline. "I was picking up a prescription for my mother that night. Just as I left the drug-store, it started to drizzle and a car pulled over. It was Wynn, asking if I wanted a lift. I wouldn't even look at him. I kept walking, but he drove along beside me with the window down telling me he just wanted to apologize, put the whole thing behind us. He even said, 'I'm wearing a *tux*, for Christ's sake. Do you think I'd try anything in a tux?'" She grimaced. "You can't believe how much I wanted it to be true. This is our senior year. The best year ever, right?"

Those five words nearly undid Willa, and she struggled not to give in to tears of her own.

Bailey's eyes seemed to plead for understanding. "I didn't want to spend the whole year worrying every time I saw him."

She rubbed her forehead, as though trying to erase a memory. "You want to know the crazy part? I'd begun to think that maybe it was *my* fault. Maybe I'd given him the wrong idea by going to the look-off in the first place."

Keegan shook his head. "None of this was your fault, Bailey. None of it."

She looked down at her hand still in his, seemed to draw strength from it, then began again. "So there I was on the street with a block still to go and it started to pour. I was getting soaked. And I desperately wanted what he'd said to be true, that he just wanted to make up for what he'd done to me. So I got in." Her voice grew small again. "He didn't take me home."

Willa looked away. She couldn't bear to hear any more, wanted to get up and put as much distance as she could between herself and whatever details Bailey was about to share. And as though she'd read Willa's mind—or perhaps because she'd chosen to put *herself* as far from those details as she could—Bailey was brief. "He used the driver's override control to lock my door this time, but I fought back. He—" She wiped at brimming tears. "He was so much stronger than me. But I kept kicking, slapping him, and I managed to claw his face with my fingernails. When he saw the blood on his tux, he suddenly stopped. Practically pushed me out of the car. Called me a slut and a whore and—" There was no stopping those tears now, her body slumping against Keegan's as she sobbed.

Keegan lowered his head to hers and murmured words that Willa couldn't hear. Or maybe they weren't words, just sounds meant to soothe. And they did. After a few moments, Bailey had herself under control.

Witnessing Bailey's torment, Willa could tell that elements of the story she'd heard were true. But she needed to see Wynn, needed to hear his version of those events. Every story had two sides, didn't it? Surely there was another that made sense of all this. Getting to her feet, she knew she should say something, but all she could think of were questions. One in particular. "Why does he keep calling you?"

But it was Keegan who spoke for Bailey. "I think you know, Willa."

Willa wanted to tell him to go to hell, that he was an outsider who didn't know anything about anything. But she didn't. Because Keegan Fraser was right. She did know. "He doesn't like to lose," she said quietly, then turned and left.

# CHAPTER 34

Getting off the bus, Keegan looked up at Bailey still sitting by the window and mustered a smile for her. In return, she did something with her mouth that might have passed for a smile if not for her eyes. They looked empty. He'd seen eyes like those before—his own, viewed in the mirror those days and weeks after his mother was killed. They were the eyes of a person who no longer believed in happiness, no longer believed that life would ever be anything more than something you coped with. The only thing that a person with eyes like those believed in was fear. Because fear kept you safe.

During the ride back to town, Keegan had urged Bailey to go to the police, but she'd refused. "When Wynn started calling and messaging me," she explained, "I threatened to report him. You know what he did? He laughed. The police chief is good friends with his dad, so they'd never charge him. He told me, 'Who's going to believe that I gave trash like you the time of day?' And he's right. No one will. I'll be a joke. A pathetic liar everybody laughs at behind her back. That's not how I want to spend my senior year."

Keegan had suggested that the phone calls and texts could be used as evidence, but Bailey said she'd deleted every message as soon as it came in for fear someone—Willa especially—might see them. And she was sure Wynn could explain away the phone calls somehow. It was clear to Keegan that she was more than just intimidated, more than just afraid. She'd been demoralized. Broken. Her only hope was that Wynn would soon grow bored with her. If you could call that hope.

"I hate the thought of that asshole getting away with this," he'd told her, "but it's your call. I won't say anything. But if he ever tries to hurt you again, you let me know, okay?"

Watching the bus pull away from the curb now, though, Keegan was pretty sure she'd never mention Wynn again.

Walking from the bus stop, he felt *The Mountain and the Valley* in his back pocket, and he remembered his reason for going to the mall in the first place. He certainly didn't feel like reading the novel now, but he didn't feel like going home either, which was why he'd gotten off the bus on Commercial Street. It was a short walk from there to Brookdale's Memorial Park, where he planned to spend the rest of what remained of the afternoon. He hoped the river flowing along the south side of the park would make it feel cooler there.

Minutes later, his shirt damp with sweat, he walked under a large wrought-iron arch bearing the park's name. A path to his left led toward an oval running track at least a quarter-mile around that, according to a sign, had been built with funds raised by the town's Rotary Club. To his right was an open area that stretched to the river, a grassy expanse dotted with flower beds, park benches, and playground equipment that had also been donated by the Rotary Club. Those Rotarians were a busy group, he thought, his mind drifting to Casino Night. And to Willa.

It had been painful watching her react to the things Bailey told her. Not that he gave a damn about Willa Jaffrey, but it must have been tough learning all that stuff about somebody you cared for. Seeing her take it all in, Keegan had wondered if maybe she'd had some earlier suspicions of her own—she was, after all, going steady with the guy—but all of it was clearly a shock to her. What had Coach Cameron said? *The eyes give a guy away every time.* Watching Willa's eyes, Keegan knew she'd had to force herself to sit there, force herself to listen to all the repulsive things her boyfriend had done. And was still doing.

He even understood her need to deny it. As much as he despised Wynn d'Entremont, the asshole could have his pick of dozens of girls who openly drooled over him each time he walked through the school's corridors. Why attack somebody?

What bothered Keegan the most, though, was how he'd chosen his victim. He'd guessed somehow that Bailey wouldn't go to the police. Had, in fact, counted on her not telling a soul, not even her own mother. The only reason she'd said anything today was because Willa had forced her to. How could Wynn be so confident? It was almost as if—

Keegan felt his stomach drop as his brain finished that thought—*as if he's done it before.*

He shrugged that idea away. He had to. If he continued to think about it, he might break his promise to Bailey about keeping silent.

# CHAPTER 35

Griff had no regrets about killing the super. He liked walking anywhere in the building now without feeling he was being watched, although that was a false sense of security since surveillance cameras were still recording everybody's movements. But at least he no longer had to worry about the person who'd be viewing that footage. Or what that person might be doing with it.

Riding up in the elevator a few moments ago, Griff had eavesdropped on a conversation between two other tenants about the super being found dead in his bathroom. "Kind of ironic, isn't it," one commented, "that he didn't install a grab bar in his own tub. Might've saved his life." Griff had kept his eyes on the changing number above the door, doing all he could not to grin.

But he hadn't been grinning that night in the super's apartment. He'd stared open-mouthed at the results his search of the guy's computer had returned: dozens of photos, Griff in every one.

Many of them were obviously screenshots from the building's surveillance videos, some recent and, judging by the clothes he was wearing, some more than a year old. But others had been taken within a few feet of Griff, likely with a hidden camera. Griff didn't give a shit about the *how*. It was what the guy had *done* with them that made his skin crawl—he'd photoshopped himself into each picture, posed with a hand on Griff's shoulder or an arm wrapped around Griff's waist or, most disturbingly, his lips pressed against Griff's cheek. He must have taken hundreds of shots of himself to get images he could insert into each of those moments and have them look real. Because they did. Very real.

Seeing those pictures, Griff had scrambled to his feet, shoving the chair back so violently that it bounced off the wall behind him. He'd stood there trembling, tasting blood in his mouth from biting the inside of his cheek, hearing all over again the sounds of his mother screaming at him, calling him those names as she came for him.

+ + +

He'd just returned from Clovis's Airstream on Guinevere Lane, where he'd been helping the old guy with his latest gardening project: lady's slippers, orchids that grew wild in the Northeast. Not in Arkansas, though—Clovis said they needed soil with high alkalinity, which was why he'd bought the special containers they'd spent that afternoon preparing for the two plants some flower nut from Maine had FedExed him. Griff figured their efforts were a waste of time—he'd googled lady's slippers and found you couldn't grow them artificially—but he admired Clovis for trying anyway.

Despite the nearly five-decade difference in their ages, Griff liked Clovis a lot, liked his easy, soft-spoken manner and the way he took his time explaining things. More than that, though, Griff liked how he listened as much as he talked, really cared about what Griff had to say, something no one else ever did. The old guy didn't have kids of his own—his first wife hadn't wanted children and his second wife couldn't have them—and it was obvious he enjoyed having Griff around. He insisted on paying Griff for the work he did, although Griff didn't always feel good about taking the cash. Lots of times he'd end up at Clovis's Airstream just because it was better than being home—his newest "uncle," Travis Hubley, was a mean drunk, and Griff was grateful to have someplace else to go when the guy tied one on. Some days it was too hot to work in Clovis's flower beds, so they'd just sit outside under the Airstream's awning, drinking Cokes and talking about everything and nothing. And when Griff got up to leave on those days, Clovis would still pull out his wallet and press money into Griff's palm. Griff figured Clovis knew more about what happened in the Barnetts' double-wide than he let on—Lancelot Way wasn't all that far from Guinevere Lane, and raised voices carried easily on still nights. It was no secret that his mother and Travis were easier to get along with when there was money on hand for crystal and booze.

At Clovis's, Griff discovered the first thing he was really good at: computers. Sure, he'd used them lots at school, but only for dumb things like research and writing assignments. His mother had one but it was years old and, since there was no money for Internet, he'd done little more than play lame games on it. Clovis, on the other hand, had a new PC with fibre-optic high-speed, which was kind of a waste since he mostly used it to take part in online flower forums, pay bills, and play the occasional game of Scrabble. But he encouraged Griff to use it whenever he wanted, and Griff did. At first it was just an excuse to keep from going home, but before long being on Clovis's computer turned into something more.

It started when Clovis asked if he'd show him how to use some of the features of his email program he didn't understand, which got Griff wondering about shortcuts, looking for ways to make the technology easier for his friend. Which led him to programming. He liked the logic of it, how you could always depend on the same outcome as long as the input didn't change, something life with his mother and the uncles had never offered. Seeing him so caught up in it, Clovis began buying him books, starting with simple coding tips and working up to volumes on algorithmic information theory—rough going at first, but Google helped whenever he felt like his head was going to explode. He might have flunked ninth grade but, for the first time, he didn't see himself as the idiot everybody thought he was. Everybody but Clovis.

After they'd prepared the planters for the lady's slippers that afternoon, Clovis said he wasn't feeling well and decided to take a nap. As usual, though, he insisted that Griff stay as long as he liked. Sitting at Clovis's computer, he'd lost all track of time, and it was only when the light had dimmed so much he had trouble seeing the keys that he realized how late it was. He'd flown out the door, shouting goodbye over his shoulder to Clovis, who was probably just waking from his nap in the Airstream's back bedroom.

Even before he reached their trailer on Lancelot Way, Griff could tell something was wrong. There were no lights on, not even the flicker from the flatscreen that Travis had gotten at a huge discount because of the scratch in the bottom left corner (a scratch Griff was sure Travis had put there himself when the salesman wasn't looking). And since his mother was between welfare cheques, he knew she and Travis hadn't gone anywhere. "I'm back," he called as he opened the double-wide's aluminum door. Nothing.

He reached for the light switch and the fluorescent tube above the sink stuttered to life, casting a harsh glare over what served as both kitchen and living room. The place had been ransacked: furniture askew, drawers yanked out of cupboards, boxes upended, stuff thrown everywhere. Dishes lay smashed on the floor, and the curtain rod over the picture window was hanging from one end, the mismatched drapes having slid off and puddled on the cheap linoleum.

His heart pounding, Griff spied his mother's legs protruding from beyond the sofa. "Mama!" he cried, striding through the mess, cheap porcelain crunching beneath his feet as he reached her and dropped to his knees.

Afterwards, he would think he should have called an ambulance or at least run for help. Things might have turned out differently. But all he could think to do at the time was get his mother up off the floor. She was drunk, no question about that, and she'd pissed herself and puked at least once, chunks of it clinging to her bleached blond hair. His arm around her neck, he pulled her to a sitting position and she began to retch again, her eyes open and rolling as strings of slime looped from her mouth. He drew her hair away from her face as the retching eased and she floated toward consciousness, her eyes slowly focusing on him.

And then she exploded. "*You!*" she screamed, cuffing him, clawing him.

He fell backwards on his ass, his arms up trying to ward her off. But she kept coming for him, screaming. And it wasn't just booze that was fuelling her rage. Beneath that godawful lily of the valley perfume Travis had bought her, he could smell the burnt-plastic stink of cheap meth on her hands as she flailed at him. "*You* did this!" she shrieked.

*Did what?* he wanted to ask, but he was too busy trying to keep her ruined yellow fingernails from his face.

"He left 'cause 'a *you!*" Her fetid breath washed over him as he tried unsuccessfully to get to his feet, his worn sneakers slipping on the porcelain-littered linoleum.

*Travis*, he thought as he managed to snare her hands between his. One more "uncle" gone from their lives. He was about to say they were better off, but she fell on him snarling, "You sonuva*bitch!*"

He tried to roll away from her, but she clung to his back, screaming profanities and slapping him, punching him. Despite her smaller size, her strength was astonishing.

"*Stop* it, Mama!" he cried, hoisting himself up on his hands and knees.

But she grabbed his neck from behind, her fingers digging into his throat, squeezing as she howled in his ear, "I *loved* him!"

And there it was. Unspoken but clear as day. *Not you.*

All his life, Griff had blindly clung to the notion that all mothers loved their sons, had convinced himself that one day, when these bad patches were behind them, she would tell him exactly what he meant to her.

She had, in fact, done that now.

He meant nothing.

"You drove him away, you sick bastard!" she shrieked in his ear. "He couldn't stand to *look* at you no more! He knowed what you was!"

Prying her fingers from his neck, Griff fought for air. He had no idea what she was talking about and didn't care. He just needed to get up, to get away until the crystal wore off. He tried to shrug her away but couldn't, tried getting to his feet but slipped again and went down with her on his back, those bony fingers once more closing around his neck.

Her voice became a thin growl, raising the hair on the back of his neck. "Waltzin' in here with cash in your pocket, smilin' like a Cheshire cat. You musta took us for fools, laughin' your head off at us after what you done."

This about money? Griff thought dimly as he struggled for breath. Hadn't he given her all of it? What more could she want from him?

"All that talk about plantin' flowers," she spat, her lily of the valley perfume souring the air as her fingers tightened even more. "Travis knew. He tol' me 'fore he left what was *really* gettin' planted over there, how the thought of it made him wanna puke."

Part of Griff finally understood the poison she was spewing in his ear. His own stomach twisted at the lies Travis had told her, the filth the man had let fly just so he could leave like all the others had. And as black dots began to swim in Griff's vision, another part of him understood something else—she wasn't going to stop. If he didn't get up off that floor in the next few seconds, he'd never get up again.

Placing both hands flat against the linoleum, he suddenly pushed upwards, thrusting her back, and he felt her body flop like a rag doll as her grip broke and she fell to the floor behind him. Scrambling to his feet, he found himself trapped in the L of the kitchen cupboards, and he turned to make a run for the door. But she was already up and coming for him, the neck of a broken bottle now clutched in one fist.

"I shoulda done what my momma *tol'* me to do," she growled. "I shoulda had the doctor suck you outta me when I found out I was knocked up! But I figured you was worth the welfare." She brandished the bottle at him. "And now look what I got to show for it. Good for nothin' faggot scum!"

"Mama!" pleaded Griff, stepping back, feeling the countertop dig into him. "Me 'n' Clovis—"

A shriek drowned out his words. "Don't you *dare* say that pervert's name in my house!" she cried. "I ain't livin' with no fuckin' fudgepacker, you hear me? I brought you into this world and I can goddamn take you out of it." She lunged at him, one edge of the broken bottle raking his face.

Oddly, there was no pain as his skin unzipped from his right ear to his chin. That would come later. What came now was the blood. And the certainty that he was dead at fifteen. It was that certainty that probably saved him, made his body react before his brain did, made him lash out to protect himself, shoving her away with every ounce of strength he could summon.

He'd seen lots of movies where the important action slowed down so the audience could appreciate the horror of it, and in the days and weeks and months that followed, his memory would do the same, replaying his mother's fall in slow motion so he could see every detail clearly: the way she jerked back, the way her heels slid out from under her, the way her head hit an overturned lampstand, the way her neck snapped just before her head bounced off the floor.

What his memory couldn't seem to show him was what happened afterwards. He must have stayed with her for hours because he remembered the sun being up when he finally left, the ripeness of her on his skin and his clothes because of the heat in their double-wide. His mother's bowels had loosened when her neck broke, the smell of her shit mingled with lily of the valley and the coppery tang of his own blood.

Somehow he'd gotten the bleeding to slow, but gravity kept pulling the flap of skin from his face, opening the wound to flies. At least, he vaguely recalled buzzing, lots of buzzing, but that might have been the pain. Agony had a way of involving all the senses, so buzzing might have been what pain sounded like in the aftermath of that night on Lancelot Way.

Eventually, he ended up in the only place he had to go— Clovis's Airstream, where another nightmare was waiting for him: Clovis lying dead in his tiny back bedroom. And this time Griff knew the buzzing was real—flies that had found their way through a hole in a screen now crawled over his open eyes and slack mouth.

Griff figured it was a stroke or heart attack that took him, probably as Griff sat at Clovis's computer, unaware of the final drama playing out in the back of that old Land Yacht. Despite the grief that brought him to his knees, Griff decided Clovis's death was a good thing. That way, he hadn't had to hear the lies Travis Hubley had told about him, the lies that had made Marsha Barnett meth herself into a murderous rage.

Griff sat with him until nightfall, holding Clovis's hand,

oddly cold in that Arkansas heat, and then he left to dig the hole behind the dumpster on Roundtable Road. The people who lived at Camelot Trailer Park rarely went there, preferring to let their garbage pile up outside their trailers, so Griff worked undisturbed for hours that night. There were times when he grew faint from loss of blood, and a driving thirst threatened to overwhelm him, but he forced himself to keep going, to keep digging. It seemed important that he do this. He couldn't bear the idea of Clovis buried someplace he didn't know, someplace far from his flowers.

And after he'd dropped the last shovelful of earth on what had been his only friend, Griff had gone back to the Airstream to get the two lady's slippers from their FedEx container. He was as gentle as he could be planting them in that turned earth, and he took care to soak the soil around their fragile roots, but minutes out of their special packing they'd already wilted. Afterwards, Griff figured there was a good chance the stuff leaking from that dumpster was toxic, and the soil's alkalinity was probably for shit anyway. But if anyone could make a lady's slipper grow, it was Clovis Lafayette.

Griff ended up in an institution, of course. The child-care system could find no foster family willing to take in a hulking teenager who had killed his mom, despite a ruined face that proved self-defence. Down deep, everyone else believed the myth that all mothers loved their sons and, regardless of gruesome evidence to the contrary, no one could quite accept the idea that Marsha Barnett of Camelot Trailer Park on Sweet Home Cutoff had tried to kill hers. So Griff spent the next three years at the Idlewood Home for Boys.

He made no friends there—a school psychiatrist said he suffered from "a dissociative disorder arising from a trauma in his fifteenth year that alienated him from others"—but he proved to be amazing at computers, easily outpacing all his classmates. Even his instructors were awed by his cyber skills, particularly his ability to locate anyone using data collection algorithms he created himself. No one suspected, of course, that Griff's interest in that area was motivated by a very private goal: tracking down Travis Hubley and making him pay for what he'd done.

Planning a murder turned out to be a lot like writing computer code—you had to consider all the options and anticipate where each of them might take you, forever keeping in mind *If this, then what?* He spent three years working it out and was three weeks beyond his eighteenth birthday when he tied Travis to a metal chair in the basement of the house the guy was renting in Joliet, Illinois, with a bleached blond who looked a little like Griff's mother. That wasn't what got her killed, though. Travis must have had a thing for lily of the valley because she was wearing it, too, and the minute Griff smelled it, he knew there was no saving her. He didn't make her suffer, though. He saved that for Travis.

+ + +

As Griff unlocked his apartment door and swung it open, automatically performing a series of checks to determine whether the place had been breached, he recalled another Monday afternoon like this one. He knew it had been a Monday because Pavel Morozov made a practice of only interviewing new talent at the beginning of the workweek.

When Griff had finally taken care of Travis and had a chance to think about his future, he knew there was a market for the particular skill set he'd honed at Idlewood, not to mention his aptitude for cold-blooded murder. Trolling the DarkNet that he'd discovered while planning Travis's execution, Griff had learned of people rumoured to hire guys with his special talents, and because Morozov was the closest to Joliet, Griff had set about arranging a meet. It had been easier than he thought—he'd simply hacked into Morozov's email, which had gotten the man's immediate attention. In fact, the first person Morozov had paid Griff to take out was the guy responsible for his online security.

While he'd been impressed with Griff's technological skills, Morozov had been skeptical that someone so young would have the stomach for the kind of work he'd be required to do, which was why Griff had brought to their meeting pictures he'd taken of Travis before, during, and after their time together. Morozov had been impressed by those, too. "It would appear," the man had murmured while fingering the photos, "that youth has its own special capacity for brutality."

Watching his freaky pale hands fondle those pictures, Griff had wondered if maybe he'd made a mistake choosing this guy to work for. But he'd soon learned that no one chose Morozov. It was always the other way around.

And if Griff didn't find the target soon, Morozov would be making another choice. The last choice Griff would ever have to worry about.

# CHAPTER 36

Willa braked and turned into the d'Entremonts' driveway. She'd forgotten to signal, and the driver behind her blared his horn, but she ignored it. After the bombshell that had just dropped on her, she felt lucky to have made it back to town in one piece.

As convincing as Bailey's story sounded, Willa simply couldn't accept it. There had to be some mistake, a colossal misunderstanding. That's what she'd told herself again and again as she'd driven back to Brookdale at a speed well below the posted limit, earning honks from drivers behind her. But she couldn't have gone any faster. With all those thoughts caroming around inside her head, she was lucky to keep the SUV on the road.

Easing the car to a stop, she shifted into park, shut off the motor, and sat staring at Wynn's house, a large saltbox that his father had bought and renovated when he'd left Halifax ten years earlier, following his divorce from Wynn's mother. Although the T-bird wasn't in the driveway, she was sure soccer practice had to be over. The sooner this mess was cleared up, the better. As much as she needed to hear what Wynn had to say, though, her legs felt like sponges that would surely fold over themselves as soon as her feet touched the ground. But they didn't, carrying her somehow to the d'Entremonts' front door.

Willa felt ridiculous ringing the bell. Any other time she'd have walked in and announced herself, something Wynn's father had insisted she do when she and Wynn began getting serious. But now that didn't seem right. She pressed the button again, and this time she heard movement inside. Seconds later, the door opened and Wynn's dad stood in the foyer with a glass in his hand. Scotch, it looked like. At least two fingers. And judging from the redness of his face, she was pretty sure it wasn't his first of the afternoon.

"Willa!" d'Entremont exclaimed, stepping back and waving her inside. The Scotch sloshed in the glass and some of the amber liquid ended up on the hardwood floor, but he didn't seem to notice. "Come in, come in. You can keep me company until Wynn gets back."

Stepping inside, Willa asked, "Is he still at soccer practice?"

D'Entremont shook his head and closed the door, movement that sent more Scotch floorward. "Got home a few minutes ago. I shent"—he grinned stupidly and tried again—"sent him on an errand."

"When do you expect him?"

"Shouldn't be"—he hiccuped—"more than a few minutes. He's dropping off something for me at the town hall. The agenda for tonight's council meeting. I'm gonna miss this one." He took a swallow of the Scotch, swaying slightly, and Willa figured that his absence from the meeting was probably a good thing for everyone involved.

"Come sit down," he said, leading her into his library, all four of its walls lined with floor-to-ceiling shelves jammed with books. He gestured toward the leather loveseats on either end of an expensive handmade rug. She pushed aside some papers on one and sat down while he moved to its twin, ignoring the papers piled on it. They crinkled under him.

Besides the papers strewn on both the furniture and the floor, a layer of dust lined the shelves, and the rug looked like it hadn't been vacuumed for some time. Wynn had told her that his stepmother had gone to visit her parents in Toronto and, if the mess was any indication, she hadn't returned yet. Of course, the d'Entremonts had a housekeeper, so that really didn't explain the condition of the library. Was the housekeeper away, too?

"So," said d'Entremont after taking another swallow, "how's the school year shaping up?"

"Fine," she said. She knew he expected more from her, a few meaningless details that would go in one ear and out the other, but she was far too preoccupied to make small talk.

D'Entremont used the moment to drain his glass, the papers under him crinkling again. "Wynn never says much about school," he murmured, the edges of his words soft and slurred. "Never says much of anything. You prob'ly know more about what's he doing than I do," he finished.

Willa thought it best not to say anything.

"Can I get you something? There's Coke in the fridge," he said. "And ginger ale, I think."

"Coke would be nice," said Willa, mostly to give him something to do besides trying to entertain her.

She could hear the Thunderbird rumble into the driveway just as Wynn's father returned. Taking the glass from him, she was surprised to see it wasn't entirely clean. A filament of lettuce or celery was stuck to the outside, possibly glued there by the heat of a dishwasher that had failed to rinse properly. Or maybe the glass hadn't been washed in the first place.

She could hear the back door open and footsteps approach along the hall.

"Here he is now," said d'Entremont. He left the room, and Willa could hear father and son pass each other in the hallway, d'Entremont telling Wynn where to find her.

"Hey, Wills," he said as he entered the room. "Thought I was coming over to your place later." He bent to kiss her.

Without thinking, Willa turned her head away and his lips met air.

"Something wrong?" he asked as he straightened.

"We need to talk," she said.

"Okay." He was moving to plant himself beside her on the loveseat when she stood up.

"Not here," she told him. "Let's go outside."

"Sure, but let me grab something to drink first."

She held out her glass. "You can have this," she said, leading him down the hallway through the similarly untidy living room and out the patio door into the d'Entremonts' large backyard, which was surrounded by a two-metre-high privacy fence. She headed toward the small mechanical shed at the far end of the pool, where she hoped the low whir of the pump would mask their voices. She didn't want Wynn's dad hearing what she was going to say. She sat on one of several wicker chairs grouped beneath a tall oak, and Wynn lowered his large frame into an identical one beside her.

"You gonna tell me what all the mystery is?" Wynn asked.

He'd already drained the Coke, and the empty tumbler in his hand reminded Willa oddly of a pin-pulled grenade. "I just got back from the mall."

"Yeah?"

"I ran into someone there. Someone you know."

He scratched at the thread of lettuce or celery with a fingernail. "You gonna make me guess?"

She thought she could hear something creep into his voice. An edge. Impatience? Or was her imagination just working overtime? No way could he have done what Bailey had accused him of. But she'd come this far, hadn't she? He deserved to know what the girl was saying about him. "Bailey Holloway."

He raised an eyebrow. "You hanging out with that one now?"

She shook her head. "We just ran into each other. Spent some time talking."

"Talking, huh?"

She watched as he shifted the tumbler from one hand to the other, the motion slow and deliberate, his knuckles whitening as though he was gripping the glass. Tightly.

He seemed to notice her staring at his hand, and he set the tumbler on the ground, leaned back in his chair. "I wouldn't think you two would have a lot to talk about." There was that edge again.

"Bailey told me about something that happened to her. Something involving you."

He looked at her for a long moment, his gaze steady.

Ordinarily, she would have thought he was waiting for her to continue, but his silence suggested more than that. His eyes were suddenly wary, and his face bore the same expression she'd seen dozens of times in the past year. He always looked that way when he studied players on an opposing team just before a game, sizing them up. He's waiting to find out what I know, Willa thought.

And then she felt sick. "It's true, isn't it," she said as something inside her crumbled and fell away. "What she told me you did to her."

She'd hoped to see confusion on his face, maybe indignation, even anger. At the very least, something that looked like denial. She hadn't expected him to grin. "It doesn't mean anything," he said. "No need for you to be jealous."

The sound of the pool's pump suddenly seemed louder. It had to be, the whir drowning out words, masking meaning. He couldn't have said what she thought she'd heard. "What?" she asked.

"There's nothing for you to be jealous about," he repeated. "Guys have needs. Some girls are willing to do something about them."

Willa's head reeled with the unspoken accusation—*needs that you don't meet.* She thought of all the times she'd sought advice on those women's websites, all the times she'd returned to "Ten Top Tips for Pleasing Your Guy" and wondered where she was going wrong. "You're blaming this on *me?*" she sputtered, her intention to keep anyone from hearing forgotten as her voice climbed a register. "You've never *once*—"

"I respect you, Willa. I'd never treat you that way."

*That way.*

A wave of nausea washed over her. *That* was his need? To physically attack a girl, make her struggle, make her scream as he overpowered her? *That's* what he needed to get off? "You're sick," she breathed.

Something glimmered in his eyes. "Careful, Willa," he said.

"Or what? You'll do to me what you tried to do to Bailey?"

"I didn't do anything she didn't want."

Willa felt her jaw go slack. "You think she actually *wanted* that?"

"Her kind always does."

"Her *kind*?"

"You know what I mean. Look at her mother. The apple didn't fall far from that tree."

Willa recalled thinking the same thing about Keegan the evening they volunteered at Casino Night. Hearing Wynn say those words now, she knew she'd never use that expression again. "You think you can use her *mother* as an excuse?" she asked, her head whirling.

Wynn raised that eyebrow again. "I don't need an excuse. She got in my car. She was totally into it. If she's saying anything different now it's because she figured out it was just physical, that I'd never give you up for her. She just got mad and went running to you."

But Bailey *hadn't* gone running to her. Willa had *made* her tell, and she'd heard the emotion in Bailey's voice as she spoke, had seen it on her face, on her whole body. No way could she have faked that.

Wynn seemed to think he'd made his case. "If I'd really done something wrong, she'd have gone to the police, right? But she didn't." He grinned again. "Girls like her, it's the only thing they're good for."

Something between a gasp and a sob caught in her throat. How could she not have known this about him? How could she have missed seeing it all this time? Sure, he'd called Francine Holloway a mattress, but everybody in their group had, Willa included, something that now shamed her. As bad as that was, though, this was so much worse. She felt her stomach lurch at the sudden knowledge that this part of him had been there all along, but she'd been so caught up with playing her role in The Wynn and Willa Show that she'd never even suspected it. She pulled herself to her feet.

Wynn did the same. "I thought you'd be grateful," he told her. She gaped at him. *Grateful?*

"Men do it all the time," he said. "Why do you think whorehouses have been around forever?" He seemed to be waiting for her to agree, possibly even to thank him for not expecting her to satisfy his needs. "Bailey means nothing to me," he continued, raising his arm as if to put his hand on Willa's shoulder, but she jerked backwards, fighting a shriek that shared space with the bile in her throat.

"Don't touch me!"

"Look, Wil—"

"Don't even *speak* to me!" She turned, heading toward the gate leading to the driveway, but she stopped in mid-stride to look back at him. "Bailey might not have gone to the police, but I could," she said, her voice shaking.

He looked skyward as if she were a child talking nonsense. "You weren't there," he said. "Anything you'd tell them would be hearsay."

She felt her fingers curl into useless fists. He seemed to know a lot about laws involving sexual assault.

And then something clicked inside her head. "You've done

this before, haven't you? That's why you came to live with your dad last year. Did things get out of hand in Halifax? Somebody press charges?"

He scowled. "Nobody takes people like them seriously."

*People like them.* My God, she thought. I've been going with this guy for five months!

And then she remembered the mess in the library—the dirty rug, the scattered papers, the dust on all those shelves—and the d'Entremonts' housekeeper, a young Jamaican woman who'd come to Nova Scotia earlier that year on a work visa.

"Besides," continued Wynn, "think about how it would make *you* look."

"*Me?*"

"People would wonder what was wrong with *you*, wouldn't they? Wonder why I'd have to go to girls like that for what I need?"

Willa had never been so angry in her life. She felt her hands tremble, but she pressed them tight against her legs so he wouldn't see.

"And then there's the other thing," he said.

She forced herself to say the words he was waiting for. "*What* other thing?"

He smiled, clearly enjoying himself. "Ask your father."

"My *father?*" she seethed. "What does *he* have to do with any of this?"

He just shrugged.

"You son of a bitch." She'd barely breathed it, but she could see in his eyes that he'd heard.

"Easy, Willa. No need to make more of this than it really is. We were due for a first fight, anyway."

She felt the shriek threaten again, struggled not to give in to it. "You and I are *done*," she choked.

He glared at her, his eyes flashing. "We'll see," he said. "By the way, I wouldn't go mentioning this to anybody else," and she could hear the threat beneath the words.

"I thought you haven't done anything wrong," she sneered.

But he wouldn't be goaded. "Coach Cameron told me if I play like last year I can expect to be scouted by all the big universities. I don't need the distraction."

*The distraction.* She could no longer stand to look at him. Pivoting, she hurried across the pool deck and had almost reached the gate when his voice stopped her again.

"Remember, I don't expect anybody else to hear about this."

"Really?" she shot back at him. "I bet your *dad* would like to hear about it. He told me he doesn't know much about what you do. Maybe I should have a chat with him right now."

"Be my guest."

Willa turned and saw Wynn's father standing in the patio doorway watching them, an empty glass in his hand, his face flat and grey like the pool deck she was standing on now.

And all at once she understood that her earlier efforts to keep him from overhearing had been unnecessary.

Laird d'Entremont already knew.

+ + +

Willa eased the SUV into the parking space beside the Cadillac Escalade with the licence plate *Jaffrey 1*. She'd been crying when she left Wynn's, but not because she'd felt heartbroken or betrayed. She'd probably have to face those feelings later, but right now all she felt was anger. Wynn's father *knew*! And so did his stepmother. But at least the woman had done something about it. Or tried to. Now it was Willa's turn.

She reached for her bag and pulled out her makeup case, doing a quick repair job—she'd have to walk the gauntlet of dealership employees, most of whom had known her since she was a child. She shut off the engine and got out, surprised again that the heat and humidity hadn't lessened. Walking past the showroom's plate glass windows toward the main entrance, she avoided looking at her reflection for the first time.

"Well, look who's here!"

She manufactured a smile for Bob Hartley and Ed Benjamin, who sat on the leather furniture in the lounge area, obviously between customers. They were quite the contrast—Bob tall, lanky, and nearing retirement, while Ed was built like a barrel and had yet to turn thirty.

"Hi, guys," she said, hoping they wouldn't sense the forced casualness in her voice.

"What? No gown?" Bob teased.

She tried to smile again, but thoughts of her Arthur Mendonça reminded her of how self-involved she'd been that night, focused only on how she looked, while Bailey was struggling to stop her boyfriend from raping her. "My dad around?" she asked.

"In his office."

"Anybody in there with him?"

"Not that I know of. Want me to buzz him for you?"

"Don't bother. I'll just go right through." She crossed the

expansive showroom, passing a gleaming silver Yukon Denali, then turned down a hallway lined with offices. Through their open doorways, she could see people talking on phones or working at computers.

"Willa! What brings you here?" A smiling Shirley Patterson got up from her manager's desk and hurried toward Willa, giving her a hug. Shirley had been working in the parts department when Willa's dad had bought the business from the previous owner, and he'd kept her on, promoting her several times in the years that followed. Carleton Jaffrey had often said no one knew as much about the various departments in the dealership as Shirley did, and he didn't know what he'd do without her. Willa had always thought of her more as family than as her father's employee.

"You're not having a problem with your vehicle, I hope," said Shirley.

"No, it's fine," replied Willa. "Just here to see my dad. Okay if I go in?"

"Sure. But when you get a moment, stop in and visit, okay? We haven't chatted in a long time. You can bring me up to speed on that young man of yours."

Willa forced a smile. "Will do," she said, continuing toward the door at the end of the hall, its brass plaque proclaiming "Carleton Jaffrey, President" in an elegant script.

She knocked, heard her father say "Come in," and opened the door. He looked up from a large spreadsheet splayed across his desk and smiled. "Well, this is a nice surprise."

The moment she saw him, she burst into tears.

Carleton got up and hurried around his desk. "Sweetheart, what's wrong?"

She moved into his open arms, pressed her cheek against his chest, and sobbed.

He reached out and shut the door, then held her for a long moment before leading her to a comfortable chair and easing her into it. He perched on the corner of his desk, one hand still holding hers as he pulled some tissues from a box and passed them to her. "What's wrong, Willa?" he asked, his face etched with worry.

Willa managed to stop sobbing long enough to say "Wynn—" before the tears came again.

"Did you have an argument? Honey, it's not the end of the world. All couples argue. Look at your mother and me—"

"No," said Willa, finally getting herself under control. "We didn't have an argument." She coughed, blew her nose into the tissue, and then started at the beginning. It took her longer than she'd intended because she'd had to reach repeatedly for tissues, but she managed to get through it.

When she finished, her dad's face looked like he'd been gut-punched, which was pretty much how Willa felt. He squeezed her shoulder gently, then moved around behind his desk and sank into his chair. "My God," he breathed. He sat staring at the spreadsheet in front of him for a moment, then looked up at his daughter. "Did he ever hurt you?"

She shook her head.

"And you have no reason to doubt Bailey's story?"

"No."

He leaned across the desk, taking Willa's hand in his again. His fingers gripped hers so tightly she could tell he was struggling with his own emotion. "I can't tell you how sorry I am, sweetheart. It must have been awful hearing those things."

She nodded, but what had happened to her this afternoon didn't begin to compare with what had happened to Bailey. It was a wonder she'd been able to function at all.

"When I think," said her father, his voice thick with loathing, "how I welcomed that animal into my home—" He seemed unable to finish his thought, but he didn't need to. That same thought had ricocheted around inside Willa's own head since she'd left Wynn's place. And to think she'd actually wanted to take their relationship to the next level. She gave an involuntary shudder.

Her father squeezed her hand again. "At least you're shut of him," he said, and she recognized one of her grandfather's sayings.

But she *wasn't* shut of him. Not yet. Releasing her father's hand, she stood up. "I need to get this over with while I still have the nerve."

"Get what over with?"

She took a deep breath. "I'm going to report him."

"You can't do that."

"I know. Wynn made it clear that any statement I make will only be hearsay. But even if I can't press charges, at least the police will know what's he's been doing. If nothing else, they should be able to scare him into leaving Bailey alone."

"It's a small town," said Carleton. "People will find out what you did."

She walked around behind the desk and leaned down to hug her father, grateful for his concern. "I have to do this, Daddy." Straightening, she said, "I haven't been a very nice person."

He started to disagree but she cut him off, pointing to the photo of her father's parents on the wall. "Remember how Grandpa used to say you can dress up bacon all you want but it's still pig?"

He nodded.

"I've nailed the dressing-up part, but I haven't paid much attention to the rest." She thought of how she'd changed during the past year, how she'd allowed herself to get swept up in her friends' ridiculing of anyone who walked into view, how she'd laughed at Russell Shaw the first day of school and all those other times before, how she hadn't stood up for Bailey when Celia and the others had made fun of her. "I haven't been treating people very well," she told her father. "Mostly because I haven't had to. It's about time I did."

Carleton got to his feet. "Please, Willa, don't do this."

She patted him on the shoulder. "I'll be okay—"

"But *I* won't," he interrupted. "Look, Willa, as much as I'd like to see Wynn pay for what he's done, I can't allow you to go to the police."

"What do you mean you can't *allow* me to?"

"Please," he said, pointing to the chair she'd been sitting in, "just hear me out. It's important."

She sat down but her father remained standing, somehow looking far older than his age. He pointed at the spreadsheet lying across his desk. "This economy is ruining me, Willa. See those figures there? I think you know what it means when the numbers are red." He rubbed his forehead. "I lied to you, sweetheart."

"About what?"

"When I said your Camaro was delayed because of a factory glitch. I never placed the order."

"Why not?" The spreadsheet made the answer obvious but, in Willa's confusion about Wynn, that was the question her brain had made her mouth ask.

"The business is hemorrhaging money. Head office keeps putting more emphasis on client satisfaction, which I know is important, but it's costing me a fortune. Protocol personnel, courtesy cars, customer appreciation barbecues, the list goes on and on. And now the building is showing its age." He opened a drawer, pulled out a piece of paper, and handed it to her. "That's the estimate for the new roof, which the contractor now says needs structural refitting."

Willa was astonished by the figure.

"To make matters worse," he continued, "sales are way down, and the extended warranties haven't been moving the way they should. And the service centre is hurting, too. People who used to bring their vehicles here for repairs are taking them to backyard mechanics who fix them for a fraction of what we have to charge. The dealership is going under, Willa."

"That's terrible, Daddy," she said, putting her hand on his arm. "I had no idea." But, of course, the increased hours he'd been spending at work should have been a sign. "Does Mom know?"

He shook his head. "Please don't say anything to her about it, okay? I hadn't intended to tell you, either, but what you're planning to do changed that."

"I don't get it. What's the dealership have to do with Wynn?"

"Everything," he said. "I have a chance to fix things here. With Laird d'Entremont's help."

Willa groaned.

"Sweetheart, most of Brookdale's municipal vehicles are old, and the town's replacing more than half of them this year, all trucks. It's a major contract and, as mayor, Laird has considerable influence in the town council's final decision. He told me he's willing to recommend the town buy all GMCs, along with the five-year extended warranties. A contract like that is just what I need to keep the dealership afloat until I get over this rough patch."

Willa couldn't believe what her father was saying, what he was asking her to do. Or, more specifically, *not* do. What had Wynn said to her? *Ask your father.* And so she had. Only to learn that a few trucks were all it cost for a free pass to do whatever you wanted with a girl you considered trash.

Carleton seemed to read on her face what she was thinking. "Please don't judge me," he said. "I'm not proud of this." He looked down at his desk, avoiding his daughter's wounded expression. "But I've worked very hard to get to this point in my life, Willa. Too hard to lose it all now."

"But think about what Wynn's *doing*, Daddy."

"I know that. But we're not just talking about me here. This dealership has thirty-six employees, and that doesn't count the freelancers we hire for detailing vehicles, delivering custom orders, things like that. Jobs are hard to come by, Willa, especially here in the valley. When you run a business in a small town, the people who work for you are more than employees. They're family. You have an obligation to take care of them."

"I know that," said Willa.

"I don't think you do. Take Shirley out there. She's the best employee I've ever had, but she's pushing fifty. How many job opportunities do you think are out there for her?"

Willa's silence told him what they both knew.

"Someone like Bob Hartley can retire, but Shirley can't. She still has two kids in university, a mortgage, and an ex who hasn't paid her a cent in years. And then there's people like Ed. He and his wife just found out they're expecting their first kid. How do you think he'd cope with a pink slip right now? How would any of them cope?"

Suddenly Willa understood why her father had been working so hard. Yes, he loved the dealership, but he also cared for the people who showed up there every day. People who worked hard for their salaries and needed to keep doing it.

"Any other time, Willa," her father continued, "I'd just submit my tender like the other dealers and hope for the best. But Laird has the power to veto the council's decision, which is why I can't let you go to the police. Chief Jenkins would be on the phone to Laird before you left the building. He and the d'Entremonts have been tight for years. After the contract is awarded, I'll gladly take you there myself." He shook his head. "To be honest, sweetheart, I can't say I ever cared much for Wynn in the first place. That boy was all show. He treated you like arm candy."

"You never said anything."

He patted her hand. "You seemed happy with him." Then he frowned. "You're sure he never hurt you?"

She shook her head. "So you really think his dad would derail the contract?"

Carleton shrugged. "If you'd asked me that a year ago, I might have said no. But I've seen a change in Laird. For one thing, he's drinking too much. I think Sharon was a calming influence on him, but now that she's gone . . ." He didn't bother stating the obvious. "And to tell you the truth, there's a side to Laird that has never sat well with me. As long as I've known him, he's had a chip on his shoulder."

Her father opened a desk drawer, reached inside, and pulled out a small device. "Latest-generation pager," he said. "I give them to staff so they can contact me if there's an emergency. If Wynn tries anything—"

"I don't think he will, Daddy. But if he did, I'd just use my phone—"

"No," said her father. "Things are slow here today, but there are times when my phone doesn't stop ringing. The pager's only for emergencies, so it'll get my attention. As long as you have cell service, you'll be able to alert me and I'll come immediately. Promise me you'll keep it with you, okay?"

"I promise." She took it, slipping it into the pocket of her jeans. "How long will it be before the deal with the town gets finalized?"

"Laird's presenting his recommendation to the town council this evening. If there's no problem with the vote, and with Laird's support there shouldn't be, I could have a contract on my desk before the end of the week. After that, we can—"

"But he isn't."

"Isn't what?"

Willa grimaced. "Presenting his recommendation. He's not going to the meeting."

"Of course he is. He's the mayor."

Willa told him what had happened at Wynn's house, and it was Carleton's turn to grimace. "When's the next council meeting?" she asked.

"Not for two weeks."

Willa thought of Bailey, her mind once more manufacturing those moments when she'd fought Wynn off, running in the rain toward her apartment. *The dump where Francine Holloway spreads her legs.* "We can't wait two weeks," she said. "We just can't."

Carleton nodded. "You're right. But give me a little more time, okay? The end of the week. I'll think of something." He reached out and drew her to him, wrapping his arms around her. "In the meantime, you stay clear of Wynn. And keep your friends away from him, too."

# CHAPTER 37

Keegan opened his eyes and reached for his phone to check the time, surprised to find he'd dozed off. Good thing he was already deeply tanned. Otherwise, he'd be burnt from having lain for thirty minutes in the early September sunshine. He sat up and pulled his shirt on, picked up the novel he'd let fall to the grass, then got to his feet to head home.

When he reached the park entrance, he saw a black SUV idling in the parking lot. Was that Willa Jaffrey's gas guzzler? As he drew nearer, he could see her sitting in the driver's seat, and it looked like she was crying. He couldn't blame her. That was some pretty heavy shit she'd had dropped on her. Should he do something? No. It wasn't like he was her friend, which made him wonder where Tweedledee and Tweedledum were. Any other time, they'd be hovering around like flies on garbage. Not that it mattered—she wasn't his concern. He'd just walk by, pretend he hadn't seen her.

But he *had* seen her. Christ.

He approached the SUV and tapped on the driver's window. Startled, Willa glanced away, wiping her face and pushing back her hair as if she could hide the fact she'd been sobbing.

"Hey," he said when she finally lowered the window. "You okay?" It was a stupid question, but he didn't know what else to say.

She nodded and tried to smile, but it was a wasted effort. She was a wreck.

"Look," he said, "that was a hell of a thing. I can't imagine how you're doing after hearing all that."

She nodded again. It was clear she didn't trust herself to talk.

"Anyway," he continued awkwardly, "I just wanted you to know I was sorry." He turned to leave, and he'd almost reached the street when he heard the SUV pull up beside him.

"You have anywhere you need to be right now?" she asked.

+ + +

"Not exactly what I was expecting," said Keegan as the SUV swung onto the dirt road. Overhanging branches masked some of the lettering on the sign at the entrance, but he could still make out the words: "Valley View Public Look-off," and below that in smaller letters, "$500 Fine for Littering." That threat hadn't seemed to dissuade many visitors, because the side of the tree-lined road leading up to the viewing area was dotted with several Styrofoam cups, the occasional beer bottle, plastic bags, broken glass, and what appeared to be a T-shirt and a sock.

"Yeah," said Willa, "the place can look pretty rough right after a weekend."

"This is all from *one* weekend?"

"Parks Canada staff takes care of the place part-time," she explained. "Couple times a week, I think. Maybe less." She braked and eased the vehicle slowly around a large pothole.

"I'm thinking less," murmured Keegan, marvelling at their sudden conversation. Silence had hung over them since leaving Brookdale, and he'd been unsure how to break it.

He'd been surprised when she'd asked him if he wanted to go for a drive. "I don't feel like being alone right now," she'd told him, which made him wonder again why she wasn't with Celia or Britney, but he didn't say anything, just nodded and climbed in.

He wasn't surprised, though, when she turned onto Valley View Road—he guessed she was trying to cope with the news she'd learned by revisiting where it had happened. He understood that. Many times during the past five months, he'd wished he could have done the same thing.

He watched as another pothole loomed ahead and Willa manoeuvred skilfully around it. "You're a good driver," he said, more to keep the conversation going than anything else, but it was true.

"Thanks," she said. "Do you drive?"

"I used to in—" He caught himself. "—Vancouver. We don't have a car here."

"Seriously?" she said.

"Yeah, my dad says we don't need one."

"He *does* work at Valley Motors, right?"

He grinned, surprised that she was able to crack a joke after what she'd been through. Ahead of them, he could see sunlight reaching through the trees, and in a moment, the SUV rolled beyond the canopy of branches into a clearing bordered on its far side by a rail fence. "Wow," he said.

The valley beyond the town stretched below them in a panorama of colour: the yellows and golds of grain fields; the reds and browns of others that, having already been harvested, now lay tilled and fallow; the bright greens where stands of trees still grew; the brilliant blue of the Annapolis River; and swaths of every other colour in between. Keegan thought of the hooked rugs in *The Mountain and the Valley*, and he felt like he was staring at the largest tapestry he'd ever seen.

Willa eased the vehicle to a stop, lowered all four windows, and shut off the motor. A faint ticking under the hood punctuated the silence for a few seconds, and then everything was quiet. Despite the heat that had lingered into late afternoon, a breeze through the open windows made the air bearable, bringing with it the smells of trees and wildflowers and something thicker, earthier, but still welcome after the staleness of the air conditioning.

And then Keegan was thinking of Bailey running through the trees behind them, fleeing the asshole in the Thunderbird. He wondered if she'd ever be able to trust another guy, to ever be alone with somebody again without reliving that experience, feeling that same panic inflate inside her.

Willa sat without speaking, and Keegan would have been content to let the moment play out. But then she turned to him. "He brought me here on our first date," she said. "We'd gone to see a movie in New Minas, and he drove up here on our way home. The sky was clear and the moon looked like a white fingernail—"

Her voice caught, and Keegan could see on her face what she was thinking. Fingernails. How Bailey had used hers. And *when* she'd used them—while Willa was standing in her gown at the Rotary fundraiser, waiting for Wynn. Keegan wondered if you could get blood out of a tux. Hoped not.

Her eyelids brimming, Willa opened the console between

their seats and pulled out some tissues, wiping her eyes rather than dabbing at them as Bailey had done. She was smearing her mascara, making her eyes look raccoon-like, but she didn't seem to care. "The thing is," she continued, "Wynn was a perfect gentleman that night."

She paused, but he got the impression that she wasn't finished, that there was more she wanted to say about that evening. He was right.

"There were a couple other cars parked here with their windows steamed up, but all he did was put his arm around me. It was early April so the car cooled down fast when he turned it off, and he kept me warm. He didn't try any of the things other guys do even on first dates, and I was really impressed by that. I felt safe with him." She shook her head, probably thinking of how Bailey would respond to that comment. "He was a perfect gentleman," she repeated. "And he's *always* been that way with me. We've never even—" Her voice caught again, and then she was crying.

Keegan had no idea what to do. Her weeping was a tortured sound, and her shoulders shook as though the ground beneath them was shuddering. Without thinking, he leaned toward her over the console separating them and put his arm around her. And then, remembering what she'd said about Wynn, he was sure it was exactly the wrong thing to do.

But it wasn't.

She leaned into him as her body heaved with sobs, her face buried in his neck, her tears seeping into his shirt. Her golden hair smelled like peaches but somehow *not* like them. Richer, fuller. He felt his body responding to her scent, to the velvety feel of her face against his skin, to the heat rising off both of them. What had she said a moment ago? *We've never even*— How could that be true? How could Wynn never have done with Willa what Keegan suddenly felt himself wanting to do now? But then he remembered how Wynn had responded to Bailey here, remembered what the guy had tried to do to her, and he felt ashamed.

Seeming to sense the change in him, Willa pulled away, wiping her eyes with more tissues before blowing her nose. When she looked up, her raccoon appearance was even more startling. But somehow, he thought, she was even prettier.

"I think I ruined your shirt," she said, still sniffling.

He shrugged. "Forget it."

She blew her nose again, her eyes turned toward the windshield and that amazing view. And then, incredibly, she grinned.

"Something funny?" he asked.

"I just remembered the date."

"Today's?"

"No," she said and began to laugh, the sound like bells ringing as tears glistened again in her eyes. But they weren't like her tears before. "The day he brought me here," she said, gulping as she spoke. "It was probably an omen, but I guess I missed it." And she laughed even harder.

"An omen?"

By now she was wheezing, and when she was finally able to force it out, her answer was a breathless gasp. "It was April first!"

April Fool's Day.

And then both of them were laughing.

+ + +

Standing by the fence, Willa was showing him various points of interest in the valley below. They'd left the SUV a few minutes earlier, and he was surprised at the turn their conversation had taken, but he figured she needed to talk about something different from the horror that was Wynn d'Entremont. Something normal.

She told him a little about the area's agricultural background, which was more than evident from their vantage point now. But not speaking about Wynn didn't mean she wasn't thinking about him, and her talk of the area's history morphed slowly into talk of her own.

Keegan was surprised to learn she hadn't dated much before Wynn, but she explained that the pool of guys her age in Brookdale wasn't large, something he'd seen himself. The few she did date, she said, were "nice enough," but not guys she was actually attracted to. One of them, in fact, was Todd Thomas, who'd gone out with her a few times two years ago before moving on to Britney Lamontagne. Willa had actually been relieved when that happened. "Todd isn't what you'd call deep," she said, something Keegan had figured out from the handful of English and math classes they'd shared. "There are only two topics of conversation that ever hold that guy's attention," she added, and Keegan could guess what they were: sports and sex.

So, she told Keegan, when Wynn d'Entremont had transferred from Halifax to Brookdale a year ago, he'd seemed somehow exotic, far different from most of the boys she'd grown up with. For one thing, he oozed confidence, which drew people to him immediately. For another, he wasn't just a jock—his GPA was nearly as high as hers. "He was the whole package," she said softly.

"Were you in love with him?"

She blinked as if abruptly awakened from a sleep that had lasted far too long. "Here's this great-looking guy," she said, "smart, incredible athlete, comes from a good family, his dad's the mayor, what girl *wouldn't* fall in love with him?"

He said nothing, and she seemed to realize she hadn't answered his question. "I think I was in love with the *idea* of being in love with him. And I liked the way people looked at us when we were together. Like we belonged together. Does that make any sense?" Before he could answer, she finished quietly, "And finally I wasn't the fifth wheel any more with Britney and Todd and Celia and Jay."

He heard the loneliness in her voice then, a feeling he knew only too well, and he wanted to wrap her in his arms again—for himself as much as for her. But then she seemed to draw herself up, straightening her body, and he saw the muscles in her jaw tighten. "You know what they say about hindsight?"

He nodded.

"Not that it makes a difference now," she continued, "but I think all along I knew something wasn't right about him. I chalked it up to competitiveness, that need of his to finish first, always come out on top." She paused, looking out over the valley as if seeking the answer to a question she'd never been brave enough to ask before. "I knew he was dangerous."

"Did he—?"

"No," she replied, shaking her head. "Like I said, he was always a gentleman. But there was an edge to him that surprised me sometimes, unsettled me. Like today, when he ragged on you for not being able to play soccer. I hate to admit it, especially now, but I used to find that part of him exciting." She shook her head.

"Pathetic, right? Like I'm twelve again with braces and a bad-boy complex."

The silence that followed her confession hung in the air between them as he wondered how to respond. Fortunately, he didn't have to.

"But he's more dangerous than I thought," she said, looking up again.

"Yeah," said Keegan, "Bailey certainly proved that."

"That's not what I meant." She told him about the absence of the d'Entremonts' housekeeper. "I think he tried something with her, too."

"You said she's from Jamaica?"

"You see the pattern, right?" she said. "He picks girls who'd have a hard time speaking up for themselves. And what's worse is that he doesn't believe what he's doing is wrong. It's like—" She paused, and he could tell she was trying to find the words for what she'd watched unfold in the d'Entremonts' backyard. "It's like he doesn't even see them as people, as human beings. He feels entitled to do whatever he wants with them."

"Jesus," Keegan breathed. "A sociopath."

"And not only that, I think his father—"

"Knows about him," he finished for her.

She looked at him with startled eyes. "How'd you know?"

Keegan told her about the conversation he'd overheard in the washroom during the Rotary fundraiser, a conversation he only now understood. "That must be the reason his wife left him. She must've given him an ultimatum."

"And he chose Wynn over her," said Willa.

Another silence settled around them, and it was then that

Keegan decided what needed to be done. Earlier, he'd told Willa that Bailey refused to press charges and he'd given her his word that he'd tell no one what Wynn had done. So that left only one resort. If he was going to put an end to Bailey's harassment, he'd have to confront Wynn himself.

He knew, of course, all the arguments against it. This wasn't his battle—after all, he'd only met Bailey a week ago. And taking on Wynn d'Entremont would probably mean taking on Todd Thomas and Jay Underwood and all the other goons who'd cheered for Wynn on the soccer field that day in phys ed. Keegan could expect some serious ass-kicking, which was in direct violation of the prime directive. Visibility like that could blow up in all their faces.

But sometimes you didn't have a choice, right? Sometimes the battle came to you.

# CHAPTER 38

"It has to stop," Keegan told Willa. "I'm going to call him on it. Threaten him if I have to."

"No," said Willa. "You can't." She felt awful, especially after everything he'd done for her that afternoon. She had no idea what she would've done if he hadn't suddenly appeared at Memorial Park. She'd longed to share with her mother what had happened but it wasn't something she could do over the phone, and certainly not with Celia's mom within earshot, so being able to talk with Keegan about her relationship with Wynn had been a blessing—she'd somehow purged herself of whatever feelings she'd had for him. And in a way she didn't really understand, it had actually been easier opening up to Keegan than it would have been with Celia and Britney. She still didn't know what she was going to say to her friends about all this, but that could wait. She had to keep Keegan from confronting Wynn.

Keegan scowled. "Tell me you're not *protecting* that son of a bitch. After everything he's done?"

"Of course not. It's just there are others to think about."

"Others?"

Willa recounted the problems facing Valley Motors and the importance of the upcoming contract. "Wynn doesn't know you found out about this when I did. If you threaten him, he'll think I've been talking to people about what he's done and he'll get his dad to screw up the deal." She wasn't surprised to see Keegan's face darken—it was clear he was reacting like she initially had, assuming that money was buying their silence. "Think about all those people who work for my father," she continued. "With the economy the way it is, not many could find work around here. Your dad probably couldn't. Would another move so soon be good for your family? Would it be good for Isaac?"

The sudden resignation in his eyes told her that last question had hit home. But she could see something else in them, too. "All I can say," he murmured, "is that sick son of a bitch had better not try anything else."

# CHAPTER 39

"Thanks for dropping me off," said Keegan as Willa pulled into his driveway.

He saw her eyes drift toward his house. "Can I ask you a question?" she asked.

Uh-oh, he thought. "What?"

"I was just wondering . . ." She paused. "I know it's none of my business, but why'd you say your mother was dead?"

Keegan flushed, turning away so she wouldn't see the truth in his eyes.

When Willa spoke again, her voice was softer. "Your dad told mine how she left years ago. It's nothing to be ashamed of, Keegan. Half the kids in our homeroom have parents who are divorced or separated."

He nodded, struggling not to give in to the emotion that threatened to overwhelm him. He cleared his throat. "It's easier," he began, already regretting the lie he was going to tell.

"What's easier?" she asked.

"To think of her as dead instead of somebody who'd just leave and never come back."

Willa didn't say anything for a moment. Then, "It must've been tough."

"It's been harder on Isaac."

"Do you think he understands what happened?"

Keegan turned to her again. "I'm pretty sure Isaac understands everything. It's just that he doesn't have ways to show us what's going on in his head. Ways that make sense to us, anyway."

She gave him a humourless smile. "After today, I'd say there's a lot that doesn't make sense."

He nodded. "You know, you really surprised me."

"Me? How?"

"The way you've handled all this. What you were willing to do about it. Gutsy."

She smiled again, but this time it was genuine. "I guess maybe I surprised myself." She brushed a lock of hair from her eyes and, even in the diminishing daylight, her blond head seemed luminous. "You surprised me, too," she continued. "You went out of your way for me, big-time. And I don't even know you. Not really." She reached out and squeezed his hand. "Thanks for listening, Keegan, letting me talk it all through. It really helped."

He nodded, getting out and watching as she backed out of the driveway, then drove down Maple Avenue, waiting at the stop sign for traffic to pass before pulling out onto Main Street. The whole time he stood there he could feel the warmth of her hand on his.

When the SUV disappeared from view, Keegan turned and continued down the driveway. It was only when he reached the back step that he realized he was whistling. He grinned, shaking his head as he opened the back door.

Sitting at the kitchen table, his father looked up from his newspaper. "Your dinner's in the oven. I cooked a roast. I figured we'd had enough chicken for a while. I bought a big one so there'll be plenty left over for sandwiches."

Keegan was grateful for his father's Let's-keep-things-light attitude. After all the crap that had come his way that afternoon, he was happy to pretend everything was okay between them. "Thanks," he said. "I'm gonna grab a shower first." He headed down the hallway, peering into the living room to see Isaac bent over a puzzle. "Hey, buddy," he said, then headed upstairs.

A few minutes later, he returned to the kitchen wearing shorts and a T-shirt. That shower was just what he'd needed, although he'd regretted washing the smell of peaches from his skin. But it remained on his shirt, which he'd decided not to toss into the laundry basket with his other clothes. Taking his dinner plate out of the oven, he grinned at himself. Eighth grade all over again.

"Looks like you had a good day," said his father.

After hearing Bailey's story, Keegan knew he had no right to feel so good, but he did. His afternoon with Willa was the first in a long time that he hadn't spent dwelling on what he'd left behind. "Nice enough," he said.

"Anything special happen?"

Sitting at the table, Keegan debated for a moment whether to say anything about Wynn. That business was going to get ugly, and his father had already made it clear he was on Team d'Entremont. No. It would be better if his father found out about that on his own. But there *was* something Keegan could share that was sure to please him. "I spent some time with your boss's daughter today."

"The grade A bitch?"

Keegan grinned again. "Turns out I was wrong about that."

"Glad to hear it," said his father, visibly relieved. "How'd the two of you end up together? Something for school?"

"We took a drive up Valley View Road."

Evan's face darkened. "Please don't tell me you went to that look-off place."

"Why?"

"Bob Hartley, one of the guys at the dealership, was telling me about it. Apparently, people only go up there for one reason."

Keegan could hear the disapproval in his father's voice, and he struggled to keep the defensiveness out of his own. "Well, yeah, we went up there, but—"

"For heaven's *sake*, Keegan! You *know* she's going with the d'Entremont boy."

Keegan shook his head. "Not anymore."

"Jesus!" his father exclaimed. "*Now* you've done it."

"What? I haven't done anything."

Glancing toward the living room, Evan lowered his voice, but the heat in his words was still evident. "Those two were going steady for months! Until you and she spent the afternoon together at that look-off."

"If you'd just listen to me—"

"Like you've listened to *me*?" Evan shoved his chair back and stood up. "You seem determined to screw *everything* up for us. *Everything*!" This time it was Evan who stormed out of the room, his footsteps like exclamation points in the hallway.

+ + +

Wearing only his boxers, Keegan lay face down on his bed under his open window hoping to catch some semblance of a breeze as he stared at his laptop. After everything that had happened that day, it would have been great to be able to message friends like he used to, immersing himself in meaningless conversation just so his thoughts wouldn't keep returning to Bailey. At one point, he'd even thought about giving her a call to see how she was doing, but he really didn't know her well enough to phone her. For that matter, he didn't know anybody well enough to phone about anything.

Or did he? During his time with Willa that afternoon, he was pretty sure he'd seen a side of her that she hadn't shown many others. And despite the circumstances of their conversation, he liked how she'd opened up to him. Liked it a lot.

Not that he could do anything about it, of course. In the past, he'd never really appreciated how easy it had been for him to make friends, but that wasn't part of the plan for living here. How *could* it be when your whole life was controlled by Forbes's prime directive—*Don't attract attention.*

So he'd spent the evening on homework, finishing a math assignment and reading more of his novel.

Despite the descriptive detail that slowed the action, he found himself enjoying the book, probably because of how he identified with the main character. The guy's father didn't seem to understand him any better than Evan understood Keegan. Richardson had said in class that the disconnect between father and son was a theme found in a lot of Buckler's writing. Although the author had been born more than a century ago, Keegan guessed that some things never changed.

He wished he could say the same about his own life. Sure, homework was a necessary evil, but that's all he ever did with his evenings now. How lame was that? Of course, the upside was that it kept him busy, kept him from doing what he'd been wanting to do for the last five minutes. And for the last five months. He stared at the cursor in his browser's navigation bar, counting in his head each time it blinked: 1, 2, 3 . . .

Both his father and brother were asleep in their rooms across the hall.

. . . 4, 5, 6 . . .

Because of the heat that permeated the house, all their doors were open, and Keegan could hear his father's gentle snores, could hear the wordless murmurs that often punctuated Isaac's slumber.

. . . 7, 8, 9 . . .

Screw it! Keegan's fingers slowly typed the URL into the navigation bar, then hovered over the Enter key.

*It does you no good to look back.* Probably not, he thought, but at least it would answer some questions that had been gnawing at him. For months.

His middle finger lowered toward the Enter key, grazed it, ran the length of it without applying pressure.

*It does you no good to look back.* But who really knew that for sure? Hadn't his tenth-grade history teacher been fond of repeating in a solemn voice, "The roots of the present are buried deep in the past"? Not just buried but buried *deep.*

*It isn't just yourself you have to think of, you know.*

Keegan fought the feeling that crowded his chest. Clicking off the browser, he closed the laptop, reached toward the lamp by his bed, and shut it off, too.

But the sudden darkness did nothing to dispel the image in his head, the face that was as vivid to him now as the last time he'd seen it.

# CHAPTER 40

Griff had never owned a car because vehicles were too easily traced, despite whatever precautions a person might take— the licence-plate switching they did in movies wasn't nearly as effective as screenwriters would have people believe. And with continual improvements in forensics, even something as simple as a tire track could spell disaster for somebody in Griff's line of work. But he enjoyed driving, and the Chrysler he'd stolen a couple of hours ago had proven to be a good choice. He had, of course, been momentarily tempted by the Lexus LFA parked in the same lot, but cars like LFAs got reported moments after being stolen, and what cop was going to get all hot and bothered about a missing eight-year-old Chrysler? Judging by its scrapes and dents, Griff figured the owner would probably get more in insurance than the thing was worth.

Parked fifty yards down from the brick two-storey on West Grace, Griff was certain that Talia's bedroom was the one on the left facing the street. Looking through his Fujinon binoculars, he'd caught a glimpse of her in it twice—first when she'd entered and turned on the light and, later, when she'd stood by the window talking on her phone. Probably to that Longley kid. Griff frowned. The two were together most of the day, so he couldn't imagine what they had to talk about at night. He glanced down at the laptop on the seat beside him and was tempted to activate his RAT and hack the webcam on her computer to listen in, but he didn't. Not because it would be an invasion of her privacy—hell, he'd used his remote access tool dozens of times already to do that very thing. He just didn't want to hear what she was saying to Soccerguy89 tonight.

Griff had made up his mind. Sometime within the next few weeks, Nick Longley was going to have an accident. Griff wanted it to happen sooner than later, but killing the kid too soon after trying to discredit him with the rape rumour would raise flags, especially since his dad was so well connected. Besides, Griff had to arrange to meet Talia first so his expressions of sympathy wouldn't come out of left field.

He'd surprised himself when he realized what his subconscious had apparently known for some time—that he and Talia should be together. And not because of her connection to this job he was doing for Morozov. She was much more than just a means to an end. She was the first girl he'd ever *wanted* to be with.

Since that afternoon at the coffee shop, he'd spent a lot of time imagining their initial meeting. At first, he'd been concerned that his scar would frighten her, and he was tempted to find a way to hide it. So tempted, in fact, that he'd almost walked into Neiman Marcus on North Michigan to speak to a makeup person about how to make it less jarring. In the end, though, he'd decided against it. The only men who wore makeup were queers like the ones he saw in East Lakeview, drag queens whose painted faces made him want to puke. No way was he like them. Besides, he was somehow confident that Talia wouldn't be put off by his face. After months of following every keystroke she made on her phone and computer, he knew her better than Soccerguy89 ever could. He'd followed her as she surfed, watched the videos she pulled up, listened to the music she downloaded, read the posts she made on Facebook and Twitter and her other social networks. Of course, there were still nights when, out of the blue, she'd pull up a search engine and enter the same keywords she'd used the first time he'd surveilled her, but that only magnified his feelings for her. She may have moved on with Nick Longley, but her loyalty to the other guy sent a pang through Griff's chest each time her searches turned up nothing.

He knew other things about Talia too, from monitoring her online activity, like how much family meant to her. At least once a week, she sent a long email and photos to her grandmother in a seniors' home in California. Whenever she had a paper due in one of her courses, she actually wrote it, didn't go to sites like Ultius or EssayShark, where she could pay someone to do it for her. Not only was she beautiful and loyal and kind, she had principles— everything a guy could want in a girl. For the very first time in his life, he felt something deep and true for another human being, and he was sure that Talia would feel the same way about him. When she got to know him.

Sure, there were times just before he drifted off to sleep at night when a voice in his head asked if he was any different from Gil Atkins, who'd watched both those little girls for weeks before he took them, but Griff immediately shoved that thought aside. What Gil had felt for the girls he'd chosen was a perversion, nothing like what Griff felt for Talia. Besides, Gil had barely known them, selecting them at random from the neighbourhood, while Griff knew everything there was to know about the girl in the upstairs bedroom fifty yards away.

Sometimes the voice wondered if Griff would have felt so strongly for Talia had he never seen those pictures on the super's computer. *Got something to prove, Griff?* the voice would ask, and memories of those photoshopped images would swim into memory, making his stomach tighten and his skin crawl.

But Griff had gotten good at ignoring the voice. He knew he could make Talia happy, just as he knew she could do the same for him. Once Soccerguy89 was out of the picture.

# CHAPTER 41

"You broke *up* with him?" repeated Britney, her face reflecting the disbelief in her voice. "Why in hell did you do *that*?"

Willa turned toward her locker, pretending to fumble with her combination so her friends wouldn't see her struggling with the truth. "Wynn is—" she began, groping for something other than *a misogynistic prick who preys on defenceless women*, "not the guy I thought he was."

"Are you *crazy*?" asked Celia. "Of *course* he is. You two are *made* for each other. Anybody with half a brain can see that."

People were seeing all right. Celia's and Britney's body language and raised voices had drawn the attention of several students in the corridor, some even coming out of classrooms to see what was going on. "Look, it's just over, okay?" Her response was more abrupt than she had intended, and she regretted the wounded expression that appeared on Celia's face.

"What did he *do*?" Britney asked.

Willa wanted to tell them, wanted more than anything to unload yesterday's discovery on them so they'd understand and, more important, commiserate with her. She knew she could count on them for the support she needed right now, but she also knew that neither of them could keep a secret, and she couldn't risk having Wynn make good on his threat. People's jobs were at stake here, one of them belonging to Keegan's father. After what Keegan had done for her yesterday, she wasn't willing to do anything that might jeopardize it. She let her silence speak for her.

"You're not gonna *tell* us?" asked Britney.

"I will, but not right now."

"Why not?"

"I just can't."

"Look," said Celia, "you and Wynn *have* to be together."

Willa was stunned by the vehemence in Celia's voice. "*Have* to be? What's *that* supposed to mean?"

"Didn't we say this was going to be our best year *ever*?"

"Yes, but—"

"Then why are you *ruining* it?"

Willa blinked at Celia, astonished. "*Me*? How am *I* ruining it?"

"We had all these things planned, remember?"

"Of course I remember."

"Then why are you throwing it all away?"

"I'm not throwing anything away. We can still do everything we talked about."

"The *five* of us," muttered Britney. "You really wanna go back to playing fifth wheel again, Wills?"

That question cut deep. "We did plenty of things together before Wynn came along," said Willa. "Didn't we call ourselves the three musketeers?"

"When we were in grade *five*," Celia replied, "before we grew *up*."

Willa let the lock drop from her fingers, its metal housing

clanging against the steel locker. "Are you saying I need to grow up?"

Now it was Celia who let her silence speak for her.

Willa felt their betrayal like a slap. "I thought you were my friends."

"We *are* your friends," said Britney. "Which is why we want to keep you from doing something you'll regret later."

Willa struggled to keep her voice even. "This isn't something I'll regret."

"Look," said Britney, "it sounds like you and Wynn just had your first fight. It was bound to happen, okay? Everybody has them."

"Exactly," added Celia before Willa could respond. "No big deal. It'll blow over. These things always do."

Willa suddenly wanted to ask Celia if that mindset worked for everyone in her family, if maybe the person who was giving her Platinum MasterCard a post-relationship workout in Halifax was a *different* Rachel Waters. But she didn't. "This isn't going to blow over," she said simply.

"Of course it will," said Britney. "We're talking about Wynn here, remember? The guy's a sweetheart."

And there it was. *The guy's a sweetheart.* Translation: *You're being an unreasonable bitch.* They'd chosen Wynn over her.

How had this happened? She'd have stood by *them* if they'd broken up with *their* boyfriends, wouldn't she? She wouldn't have made them justify their decision, wouldn't have complained about how it was going to change things.

Or would she?

She no longer felt like the person she'd been only a few days ago. Maybe that Willa *would* have reacted the same way. Until recently, the only person she'd been thinking about was herself. Hadn't she nearly thrown a tantrum at the dealership the first day of school when she hadn't gotten her Camaro? And all the while her poor father had been grappling with the prospect of losing everything he'd ever worked for.

As much as it humbled her to admit it, Willa knew she probably *would* have said the kinds of things Celia and Britney were saying to her now. The kinds of things that *real* regret was made of.

"Wynn would do anything for you, Willa," added Britney.

"He's done enough already," Willa muttered.

"Like what?" Celia demanded. "*Christ*, Willa, why do you have to be so frigging mysterious? You could at least give us a *hint*."

How she longed to, but she was afraid to say anything, afraid that, if she did, she wouldn't be able to stop, everything pouring out of her like it had yesterday with Keegan. She thought of him now, remembering how, even after the lousy way she'd treated him, he'd approached her at Memorial Park and offered to help. So different from the two people she'd always thought she could count on. "Wynn and I are done," she said simply.

Britney and Celia looked at each other, and something seemed to pass between them. "You've got such a great thing going with him," said Celia. "I don't know why in hell you'd go and screw it up."

"Why don't you ease up on her?"

All three turned toward the voice. Her face nearly as bright as her hair, Bailey held her books against her chest like a shield.

"Do you *mind*?" asked Britney. "This is a *private* conversation."

"Then you might want to take it down a notch," said Bailey, nodding toward the students staring in their direction.

Celia's eyes flashed fresh anger. "Why? Somebody change your name from Holloway to Hall Monitor?"

Britney hooted.

"Celia—" Willa began, her tone filled with warning.

"Mind your own goddamn business, Bailey."

The red in Bailey's face deepened, but she didn't back down. "Maybe you should take your own advice," she said.

Celia's eyebrows disappeared beneath her bangs. "And maybe *you* should take a flying fu—"

"Everything okay here, girls?" asked Mr. Caldwell, who had appeared, wraithlike, beside the group.

"Everything's fine," offered Willa. "Just getting ready for first period."

The vice-principal looked at all four of them skeptically before moving farther down the corridor.

Celia glared at Bailey. "Why are you still standing here?" she snapped. "Go!"

"Leave her alone," said Willa.

Britney's eyes bulged. "Leave her *alone*? What, are you two BFFs now?"

"C'mon, Brit," said Celia, her voice icy, "let's go. I'm sure these two have *tons* to talk about." She stalked off.

Britney gave them both a hard stare before trailing Celia down the corridor.

"Sorry," said Bailey when they'd left. "I didn't mean to cause trouble."

"You didn't. They were doing a good job of that all on their own." She gave Bailey a weak smile. "Thanks for standing up for me."

"Glad to." Bailey lowered her voice. "I saw Keegan a few minutes ago. He told me a little about what happened yesterday, what you tried to do. I can't tell you how much I—" She looked away, but Willa could see her swallowing hard.

Willa put a hand on her shoulder and squeezed. "Friends stick together, right?"

+ + +

Moments after the bell rang following first period, Willa found herself alone at her locker. Neither Celia nor Britney had come to collect her the way they always did each recess. Willa could have gone looking for them, but she knew the drill. They were cold-shouldering her, like that day in grade ten when she'd refused to skip last class with them so they could bid on tickets to a Toxic Rosebud concert some scalper had put on Kijiji. Willa had had a test scheduled during last period, and she wasn't willing to risk taking a zero for the chance to see a band she really didn't like in the first place. In the end, Celia and Britney had gotten two tickets for a price even Willa thought was outrageous, and they'd refused to speak to her until Willa apologized repeatedly for letting them down.

Well, she had no intention of apologizing to them this time.

She'd just closed her locker when she sensed someone standing behind her. Large hands settled on her shoulders, strong fingers massaging her trapezius muscles in a way that had always made her weak before. Now those hands made her shudder.

"You can't stay mad forever," Wynn breathed in her ear.

"How about disgusted?" she asked coldly, still facing her locker.

Impossibly, she heard him chuckle. "I told you this doesn't have to change anything."

"It changes everything," she said, biting back the barrage of words forming in her throat. If she didn't keep a lid on, she might end up screaming at him, and who knew what he'd do then? Her father had asked her for more time, and she'd promised him that.

She stepped out from under Wynn's hands and turned to face him. "I don't want anything more to do with you, okay? I don't want you talking to me in school, calling me, texting me, nothing."

He raised his eyebrows. "For how long?"

She fought against the rage welling inside her. "You don't *get* it, do you? We're over, Wynn. Done."

He leaned toward her and she unconsciously took a step back, her locker's hasp digging into her. "We're done when I *say* we're done," he hissed. "You got *that?*"

His voice sent a chill through her, and she was relieved when he stormed off. Watching him go, she saw several students in the corridor step quickly aside to let him pass.

Apparently, she wasn't the only one afraid of Wynn d'Entremont.

+ + +

Tray in hand, Willa stopped beside the cafeteria table. "Okay if I join you?" she asked.

Looking up, Russell choked on a mouthful of his pita, and Greg reached over and began pounding him on the back.

"Sure," said Bailey. Raven was already sliding over to make room.

Russell's choking now under control, he stared wide-eyed as Willa slid her legs into the space and sat down across from Keegan. She felt awkward, certain that the arrival of talking plant-life couldn't have generated a more astonished response from Russell, and she was grateful for the welcoming smile on Keegan's face. More than grateful, actually, feeling a pulse of excitement zither through her. She tried to make her voice sound nonchalant. "So how's it going?"

Raven and Bailey offered casual remarks about their first two classes, after which Russell managed a comment about phys ed, saying that he was thinking about recommending Coach Cameron for Brookdale's annual Teacher of the Year Award for choosing walking as their cardio activity that day. "Anything else in this heat and I'd have been tits-up on the training field." He glanced down at his own considerable moobs as if underscoring the certainty of that outcome, sparking laughter all around their table.

"Russell," said Raven, still grinning, "you just need to build up your endurance. A little exercise every day would do wonders for you."

Willa could vouch for that. She usually spent at least thirty minutes each day on the treadmill in her parents' home gym, and she couldn't believe how sluggish she'd felt after that week of non-activity at the cottage. She'd enjoyed getting back into her routine.

"You run every day, don't you, Raven?" asked Bailey. Rather pointedly, Willa thought.

"Not when the heat and humidity get this bad," Raven replied.

"But I walk." She turned to Russell. "If you'd like a walking partner sometime, give me a call, okay?"

Russell's face again conveyed that same talking plant-life surreality Willa had seen only moments ago, and she found herself smiling. Russell and Raven. Who'd have thought? She wondered what Celia and Britney would make of that combination, imagining their caustic commentary. But she had no right to be judgmental—until a few days ago, she'd probably have responded the same way, or at least laughed at their remarks.

"So how was *your* morning?" asked Keegan.

She read in his eyes what he meant, whom he was referring to. "It was interesting," she replied.

He nodded, seeming to grasp her meaning. "You okay?" he asked.

She thought she was, despite having spent second period boiling inside at Wynn's implicit threat. She was glad they hadn't shared the class before lunch so she could get her anger under control. But that was this morning. Now she wasn't so sure. She felt something pull taut inside her, and suddenly she couldn't speak. Couldn't even shake her head.

Keegan reached across the table and took one of her hands, and the gentle strength in his fingers around hers was exactly what she needed in that moment, melting her paralysis. He smiled at her and, as she smiled back, an unfamiliar clarity washed over her. She recalled a passage she'd read in *The Mountain and the Valley* where the main character marvelled about an abrupt change in a relationship, how his life until then seemed like black and white but now everything was in colour. This moment was like that for Willa.

Growing conscious that silence had settled over their table, she turned to see the others staring at them, Raven and Bailey and Greg grinning broadly. Russell, however, was shaking his head. "Cripes," he muttered, "let the games begin."

# CHAPTER 42

Keegan's head was whirling. All through the previous class, he couldn't keep his eyes from wandering toward Willa and, as a result, Shedrand's PowerPoint slides about the quadratic formula might as well have been in Japanese. Math had always come easily to him, but today he felt like Todd Thomas, who'd finally dropped out of the advanced course. Keegan couldn't concentrate, couldn't make meaning of the notes he'd taken, couldn't figure out any of the problems on the sheet the teacher had given them to work on. He was so screwed.

This wasn't supposed to happen. He wasn't supposed to feel this way. Didn't even think he *could* feel this way again, not after—

No. Forget about before. He had to focus on now.

Now he was screwed.

One thing he *didn't* have trouble figuring out was what his father and Forbes would say if they found out. But it wasn't as if he'd *intended* for it to happen. He hadn't even seen it coming. He'd been so torn up by what that asshole had done to Bailey that he'd been blindsided by this thing with Willa. Sure, he'd known he was attracted to her—a guy would have to be gay or comatose not to feel that—but he really thought he was just being supportive. But then he'd held her hand at lunchtime and—

He was so screwed.

He tried to focus. When English class began, Richardson had passed out handouts containing passages from *The Mountain and the Valley* and asked them to discuss in pairs what they revealed about particular characters, and Keegan had ended up partnering with Willa. He hadn't planned it, but Celia and Britney seemed to be shunning her, and Willa had nearly stumbled over a desk moving away from Wynn when he'd approached her. So Keegan had stepped up. Simple as that.

What wasn't so simple was his reaction to the nearness of her, the way her hair glowed in the light streaming through the window, the way her china-blue eyes moved languidly from Richardson's handout to Keegan's face, the way her lips moved as they—

"—out loud?"

He blinked at her. "Hmm?"

She smiled self-consciously and something in his chest expanded fourfold. "I asked if you wanted me to read the passages out loud as we talk about them."

"Yeah, okay," he mumbled.

She turned again to the handout and began to read, but he couldn't hear the words above the rush of blood in his ears.

He was so screwed.

And he didn't give a damn.

+ + +

"Willa, we need to *talk*!"

Heading toward the classroom exit at the end of the period,

Keegan paused beside Willa, both of them turning to see Wynn barrelling past the handful of students still there. He bumped into Greg, knocking his backpack to the floor and spilling books everywhere, but Wynn ignored him and kept coming, a moving wall of muscle.

Keegan felt Willa flinch beside him. "*We* don't need to do anything, Wynn," she said as he reached her. "*You* need to stay away from me."

The few remaining students froze. Even Greg, bent over his backpack, was motionless.

"You don't wanna do this," growled Wynn, anger radiating off him in waves.

"What she *doesn't* want is to talk to you," Keegan said, trying to keep his voice casual. But all he could think about was Bailey running through the woods on Valley View Road and then fighting him off again on Casino Night, and he was glad she'd already left the classroom. He and Willa were still there because he'd asked to borrow her math notes, certain his own would be useless to him. Neither had noticed that Wynn had held back, too.

Wynn's eyes widened, and then he smiled. It was all teeth, though, the expression never reaching his eyes. They held something far different. "You've been a pain in my ass since you got here, Vancouver," he said, his murmured words like smooth knives in the air. "How about you and I go someplace and sort this out once and for all?" His hands at his sides made fists the size of grapefruits.

Willa stepped between them. "The only thing that needs to be sorted out is you, Wynn. We're through."

But Wynn ignored her, glaring over her head at Keegan.

"How about it, Vancouver? Ready to get your ass handed to you?"

"Interesting metaphor, Wynn. Care to elaborate?"

They turned to see Richardson in the doorway. As he did at the end of each class, he'd stood in the corridor chatting briefly with students as they passed, and Keegan could sense Willa's relief at his return. Keegan, however, was disappointed. He'd have liked nothing better than the chance to slam his fist into Wynn d'Entremont's face.

Wynn shrugged. "We were just fooling around."

Richardson addressed the room. "Would the rest of you mind stepping out?"

The spectators were startled into action and the room emptied in moments, Richardson closing the door behind them. "Is there a problem here?"

Keegan glanced at Willa, but she was looking at Wynn, his eyes aglow with brash confidence as if he was taunting her, daring her. Keegan looked at the floor, mentally willing her to say something.

But it was Wynn who spoke first. "Willa and I were just having a conversation."

"It's the conversation you were having with Keegan that I'm interested in," said Richardson.

"We were just—"

"Fooling around," interrupted the teacher. "So you say, but we both know that's not true." Keegan raised his eyes to see Richardson looking at him. "Care to jump in here, Keegan?"

"This is about me," offered Willa. "I broke up with Wynn yesterday and he hasn't accepted that it's over between us."

"And you're saying that it is?"

"Definitely."

The teacher turned to Wynn. "Look, letting go can be hard, but a person can't force someone to be in a relationship."

Keegan almost snorted. Force was Wynn's middle name.

"Nor," continued Richardson, "can we expect to rekindle a relationship by threatening to hand someone else his ass. Understand?"

Wynn gave a grudging nod.

"Good," said Richardson. "What you may *not* understand is how committed this school is to preventing violence of any kind, including intimidation. If I hear you've harassed Willa or Keegan in any way, I'll report you to Mr. Caldwell, who will then bar you from all extracurricular activities for the remainder of the year. Is that clear?"

Keegan watched Wynn's eyes, imagined something in there writhing as he struggled to keep his cool. "As a bell," Wynn said.

"Good," said Richardson. He turned toward his desk and began gathering up the assignments his students had piled there earlier.

Wynn looked at Keegan and smiled again, his expression almost reptilian. "Later," he said, the word suggesting more promise than leave-taking, then reached for the door, yanked it open, and disappeared.

Keegan and Willa collected their books and made their way toward the corridor.

"I meant what I said."

They turned to the teacher, whose face looked uncharacteristically grave. "If he tries anything, anything at all, let me know, okay?"

"He won't," said Willa quickly, and Keegan was surprised by the conviction in her voice. He doubted she believed her own claim, but he could tell she was keeping the heat off Wynn to give her father the time he'd asked for.

"I hope you're right," said Richardson.

+ + +

The teacher in-service scheduled for the following day made the Tuesday afternoon seem like a Friday, so Keegan wasn't surprised to see the student parking lot nearly empty. The few remaining cars probably belonged to the guys at soccer practice. Wynn's Thunderbird was among them.

"Are you sure you're okay?" he asked Willa when they reached her SUV.

She nodded, but the paleness of her usually tan face said otherwise. "Pretty intense, huh?"

"I'm worried he might take all this out on you."

"I think you're more of a target than I am right now," she said. "But Richardson has him worried. He won't do anything that might jeopardize his playing sports."

"Hopefully," said Keegan, "this thing with your dad won't take much longer. Something needs to be done about that guy soon. Did you see his eyes?"

"I *know*," she agreed. "Freaky." Despite the heat, she shivered.

Without thinking, he draped an arm over her shoulder, then realized what he'd done and stepped back. "Sorry," he mumbled, embarrassed.

"Don't be," Willa said, colour returning to her face. She reached out, laid her hand on his forearm. "I'm not."

Keegan felt his face redden, felt his whole body respond to the contact. More than anything, he wanted to kiss her, but he knew how wrong that would be when she'd just broken up with her boyfriend. And then there was Forbes to think about, not to mention his father. Keegan looked away, and he felt the gentle pressure of her hand on his arm disappear.

"So," she said, an awkwardness entering her voice, "I'd better be going. You sure I can't give you a lift home?"

"Thanks, but I can use the exercise." The tension caused by her touch and their encounter with Wynn had made his body wire-taut, and the walk would do him good, help him work some of it out before he got home. What he *really* wanted was to join in the scrimmage he could hear on the soccer field, but a walk was better than nothing.

She nodded, then turned and got into the SUV. Starting the vehicle, she lowered the windows to let out the heat, the air conditioner churning to life. "Later," she said, then backed the vehicle out of its space and headed toward the street.

He watched as she stopped at the exit, waiting for oncoming traffic to pass, her signal light blinking. But when the street was finally clear, she continued to sit there, as if trying to decide where to go. Then the backup lights came on, and the SUV reversed through the parking lot before rolling to a stop beside Keegan. The driver's window lowered again and Willa's face reappeared, a deep flush adding new colour.

"Something wrong?" he asked.

She shook her head. "Look, are you doing anything tomorrow?"

"Not really. No."

"How'd you like to get out of town?"

Despite what his common sense was telling him, there was suddenly nothing he wanted more. "What'd you have in mind?"

"It's supposed to be even hotter tomorrow and I thought I'd spend the day at our cottage. It'll be a lot cooler there," she added, as if he needed to be persuaded.

Forbes and his father clamoured in Keegan's head, reciting a litany of reasons why this was a monumentally bad idea, but he ignored them. "Sounds great," he said.

"How about I pick you up around, say, eight-thirty?"

"I'll be ready. Should I bring anything?"

"Just an appetite. I'll bring lunch." The window closed over her smile as she shifted into drive again, and the SUV once more headed toward the exit. This time, though, it eased into the street and drove off.

Watching it go, Keegan mentally calculated the hours before he'd see her again.

He was so screwed.

# CHAPTER 43

Morozov's New Jersey muscle finished patting Griff down. "Clear," he said, nodding toward a second bodyguard standing outside Morozov's office. Nearly as big as the doorway, the other guy reached for the handle and opened it, waving Griff through.

Griff hated Morozov's office. Anyone who knew the guy might expect something crypt-like, but the place was decorated with large splashes of reds and oranges and littered with moulded plastic furniture like you'd see in old movies from the sixties. Regardless how many times he went there, Griff always felt disoriented when he walked into it—which, he guessed, was exactly why Morozov liked it that way. It put visitors off-balance.

Morozov was his usual sinister self, his pale hands lying limp on his desk. At least, thought Griff as he entered, he didn't bring me here to off me. The freak never had people killed on the premises.

"Hey, Mr. Morozov," said Griff.

One of those disturbingly white hands gestured toward a red chair, and Griff sat down. It was far too small for him—the moulded plastic wedged his ass-cheeks together like a vise—but that, too, was probably intentional. He gave no sign of his discomfort and waited for Morozov to say something. Griff figured he'd been summoned to give an update on his search for the target, but it was always better to let Morozov speak first.

The little fuck kept him waiting, opening one of his desk drawers and taking out a sheet of paper that he laid on his orange blotter. He leaned back in his chair, lacing his fingers together across his nonexistent belly, and Griff was again reminded of white worms. Finally, Morozov spoke. "Do you believe that things happen for a reason, Griff?" His words had their usual soft, wet sound.

Griff wondered if this was a trick question, a land mine that could blow up in his face if he didn't step carefully. "Never really thought about it."

"Think about it now," said Morozov.

Griff took a moment to marshal his thoughts, and his mind returned to that evening in Joliet, Travis Hubley screaming in his basement each time Griff shocked him back to consciousness. What Travis went through that night had definitely happened for a reason, but he doubted that was what Morozov meant. "I guess it depends," said Griff.

"On what?"

"On who stands to gain from it."

Those empty eyes blinked at him, and then the impossible happened: Morozov smiled. "As it turns out, you're the person who's gaining this time," he said.

Griff cocked one eyebrow but didn't comment, knowing it was better to let Morozov offer what he had to say in his own good time.

"It would appear," said Morozov, "that it was fortunate your device failed to kill the target."

Again Griff waited.

Morozov leaned forward. "I've recently acquired a—" He hesitated for the briefest of moments before continuing, "well-placed associate. Someone who is only too willing to make his considerable resources available to me."

Griff nodded, struggling to hide his impatience, wishing the little mutant would just say what needed to be said.

Morozov pushed the sheet of paper across the desk. "Have a look at what our target was up to the last night he worked for Battaglia."

# CHAPTER 44

Pulling into Keegan's driveway, Willa was grateful all over again that her father had agreed to let her take a guy he barely knew to their cottage for the day. But maybe she shouldn't have been surprised—after all, he'd known Wynn and look how that had turned out. Her mother might have been harder to convince, but since she and Rachel had decided to spend the rest of the week in Halifax, Willa hadn't felt obligated to ask her.

Before she had time to shut off the vehicle, she saw Keegan come out his front door and lope toward her. "You didn't need to bring anything, remember?" said Willa, nodding at the bag Keegan tossed onto the back seat as he got in.

"Just trunks and a towel. I figured we'd probably go swimming." He pointed at the exterior temperature displayed on the instrument panel's touch-screen: twenty-seven degrees. And it was only eight thirty.

Willa laughed. "You've never been to the bay before, have you?"

"Why?"

"You'll see," she replied cryptically. She backed out of the driveway, then hit the brakes, the SUV coming to an abrupt halt in the street.

"Something wrong?" asked Keegan.

Out of the corner of her eye, Willa saw him glance left toward Main Street, the traffic check she herself had just done for cars coming down Maple Avenue, but there were none. "Thought I'd forgotten something," she lied as she pulled away.

Because Keegan had been looking out her driver's-side window, he hadn't seen what the dashboard's touch-screen had just shown her: Wynn's Thunderbird parked in the driveway diagonally across the street. Most of his car was hidden by shrubbery, which was why she hadn't noticed it before. It was only the wide-angle view of the backup camera that had caught it.

Willa knew she should've said something, and she'd opened her mouth to do just that, but the screen had shown Wynn pulling out of the driveway and heading in the opposite direction. He may have trailed her to Keegan's house, but he wasn't following them now. Maybe he could see that she'd moved on and realized he needed to do the same. And if that was the case, why mention it to Keegan now and allow a shadow to fall over their day before it had even begun?

"What'd you think you forgot?" asked Keegan.

"Gas," she lied again, "but we're fine." She pointed to the gauge that showed a full tank. "My dad must've filled it up for me." She was amazed at how easily the fabrication fell from her mouth, but she was determined that Wynn d'Entremont wouldn't ruin their day. He'd ruined enough already.

In moments, they passed a sign that read "You're now leaving Brookdale—Please come again," and she felt tension release inside her. Reaching toward the instrument panel, she pressed the auxiliary function to activate her iPod, which she'd paired with the entertainment system. Because the device was always on shuffle, she wasn't sure what would begin playing.

"Billie Holiday, right?" asked Keegan as the first words of "It's a Sin to Tell a Lie" seeped from the speakers.

She glanced at him, astonished he knew the singer. "You listen to jazz?"

"Yeah," he said. "A lot."

"How'd you get into it? Friends?"

"My mom."

She waited for him to say more. When he didn't, Willa asked, "She a musician?"

"No."

Despite the brevity of his answer, Willa heard something in his voice. Anger at a mother who'd left a husband and two sons? Or irritation at Willa for having opened up an old wound? She couldn't tell. "My dad," she said, wanting to get past the moment, "got me hooked on it. He's been collecting jazz recordings forever. There isn't much he doesn't have."

Out of the corner of her eye, Willa saw him nod. "My mom was the same way. Louis Armstrong, Dizzy Gillespie, Count Basie, Artie Shaw, all the greats." His voice sounded more normal now, although she couldn't help wondering if this was something he was working at. "Okay if I turn it up?" he asked.

"Sure."

He reached for the volume control and Lady Day's voice filled the vehicle warning listeners to be sure when they say "I love you," the sax in the background underscoring that message. They listened in a comfortable silence as the road unfurled beneath the SUV's tires, and when the iPod shuffled up the slower tempo of

Charlie Parker's "Summertime," Willa could feel Keegan's eyes on her. "What?" she asked.

"Nothing. I just—" He paused. "I didn't expect to meet someone in Brookdale who likes jazz as much as I do."

"Yeah, all the really cool people live in Vancouver."

He grinned, and she was glad to have the awkwardness behind them.

The music continued as they drove through farmland, most of the fields already harvested, but from time to time they passed a crop being cultivated: a combine eating its way through cow corn; a mechanical harvester pulling potatoes from the rich, dark soil; people standing on ladders under apple trees that marched in long, even rows into the distance. Willa watched as Keegan surveyed it all with interest. "Are they as big here as in the Okanagan?"

Keegan looked at her blankly.

"The orchards," she explained. "In the Okanagan Valley."

"Um, yeah," he said, turning again to his window. "So," he said, as if speaking to the glass, "I've never met a Willa before."

She wondered momentarily at the sudden change in topic. "I was named after my grandmother, Willamena Jaffrey." He turned to her and she could see a grin tugging at the corners of his mouth. "Yeah," she said, "good thing my parents shortened it."

"I like Willa," he said. "I've only heard it once before. There's a writer named—"

"Willa Cather," she finished. "Yeah, I found her when I googled my name. You want to hear something weird?"

"Always."

"She was buried in New Hampshire in a place called Jaffrey. Quite the coincidence, huh?"

He turned to the window again. "My mom used to say there's no such thing, that coincidence is just life happening. She said people like to see connections even when there aren't any."

"Do you believe that?"

"Do you believe in horoscopes?" he asked.

"Why?"

"That'd be the *ultimate* coincidence, wouldn't it? People all having similar personalities and experiences just because they happened to be born around the same time of year? Give me a break."

"I'm guessing that's not the page in the newspaper you turn to first, huh?"

"You read newspapers?" he asked. "The actual paper kind?"

She nodded. "It's something my grandfather got me into. When I was little, I'd sit on his lap and hold the paper and he'd read parts of it to me. The personals section was my favourite. We'd make up stories together about what led people to write their ads. I still do it sometimes." She grinned self-consciously. "Okay, you're looking at the only person under seventy who reads those things every day."

Keegan's face creased in a broad smile. "Salsa lessons with Armand. Reasonable rates."

Willa's jaw dropped. "That was in this morning's paper! *You* read the personals?"

"They told us we sh—" He stopped, the expression on his face suddenly unreadable.

"They?"

Keegan was clearly uneasy, and she had no idea why. "Those ads," he continued after a moment. "They kind of give you a sense of what the people in a particular area are like."

Willa wasn't sure he'd answered her question.

"So what's up with Armand?" he asked abruptly.

"Not his real name, of course," she said. "I figure male prostitute catering to people who like Brazilian boy-toys."

"I guess they're gonna be disappointed when they meet Mike with his tan-from-a-can."

Willa's laughter joined his, drowning out the soulful sounds of Miles Davis's trumpet.

+ + +

"It isn't far now," said Willa, the SUV's transmission downshifting in response to the incline.

"Didn't you say that half an hour ago?"

She glanced at the clock on the instrument panel, surprised to see it was nine thirty already. Their hour together had flown by. "Yeah, but this time I mean it," she said. She reached out and turned off the music so she could concentrate on the road, which hairpinned back and forth toward the North Mountain's summit. There was a moment when Willa heard a sudden intake of breath beside her. "I used to close my eyes when we reached this part," she said, referring to the sheer drop at the edge of the last curve.

"I hope not while you were driving," he murmured, and she liked that he felt comfortable enough to tease her.

In a moment, the vehicle crested the mountain and began

a much more gradual descent toward the bay stretching pan-
oramically before them. In cooler, drier weather, Willa knew they
would've been able to see the dark line of New Brunswick forty
kilometres away, but today that far shore had disappeared into a
blue haze, giving the bay the appearance of an endless sea.

At the foot of the mountain a few minutes later, the pavement curved right to follow the shoreline, and Willa braked to
slow the vehicle.

"Great name," said Keegan, pointing to a highway sign for
Delusion Road, to the left.

Willa grinned. "They built it during World War Two," she
explained. "Somebody discovered a copper deposit here, and an
American company put up the money for the road so they could
get to the ore. Turned out there wasn't much there, though,
and the whole project fizzled." She signalled left and swung the
SUV down the gravel lane, dust billowing behind them as they
bounced through one pothole after another.

"Why do I feel like I'm in a scene from *Deliverance*?" he asked.

She laughed, recognizing the reference to the cult classic
about a group of businessmen on a Georgia canoe trip terror-
ized by inbred hillbillies. Her dad loved weird movies, and they'd
watched it together last year. Disturbing stuff. "Relax," she said,
"nobody's gonna make you squeal like a pig."

"People actually *live* way out here?"

"One or two," she said, nodding at an old farmhouse with a
barn sagging behind it, both in need of paint and visible for only
a moment before trees blocked their view. "But most of the places
on this road are cottages." Another driveway appeared on the

right, curving down toward the water, but thick foliage prevented them from seeing what lay at the end of it. In a moment, the road began to narrow even more, trees crowding closer on both sides.

"How'd your parents even *find* a place out here?"

"They started looking for shorefront property after they were married, and a realtor found it for them. There was nothing on it but woods and they got a huge chunk of land really cheap. They used to come camping here sometimes and, after my brother was born, they hired a contractor to build them a cottage."

"Long way from Brookdale. Do you get out here much?"

"We used to spend most weekends and every summer here when my brother and I were small, but since my dad expanded the dealership a few years ago, he's lucky to grab a week at the end of August. What he likes most about it is that no one bothers him here."

"No shit."

"I don't just mean because of the distance. Look at your phone."

He pulled out his cell and glanced at the display. "No service?"

She nodded. "No Internet, either."

Keegan shook his head. "I thought places without cell service were urban myths."

She grinned again. "Welcome to Delusion Road."

She continued driving and, a couple minutes later, slowed beside a large boulder at the side of the road with "Jaffrey" chiselled into it. Turning right into a narrow opening in the wall of vegetation, Willa braked for the incline, easing the vehicle down a long sloping driveway, branches brushing the doors. In a moment, the trees pulled away and they rolled into a wide clearing.

"I thought you said they built a *cottage*," said Keegan, looking at the large Cape Cod–style structure perched on the edge of a bluff overlooking the bay.

She put the SUV in park and shut off the ignition as Keegan opened his door. "Hey," he said as they got out, "it's a lot cooler here."

Willa had watched the temperature on the instrument panel fall gradually as they got closer to the bay. At six degrees below the valley's reading, the air here was far more comfortable.

Keegan stepped up onto a wide deck that extended out over the bluff on steel beams, giving the impression it floated in midair. Willa followed him. "I thought the water would be closer," he said, nodding toward the bare rocks below them.

"The tide's out. In a few hours, all those rocks will be under water."

He turned toward the distant waves, and his face registered disbelief. "Yeah, right," he said. "Is this where I start squealing like a pig?"

She chuckled, then remembered an analogy she'd learned in a junior high geography class. "Think of a drinking glass and a wide pie plate. If you poured the same amount of water into both, it would rise higher in the glass, right?"

He nodded.

"In most parts of the world, the water level doesn't change as much between high and low tide because it's spread across the whole ocean. It's like pouring water into the pie plate. Now think of the Bay of Fundy being like the glass. A hundred billion tonnes of seawater flow into it, so it piles up higher, rising and falling more than twelve metres. Twice every day." She recalled a fact she'd read somewhere. "More water flows into and out of this bay than the combined water in all the rivers in the whole world."

He whistled, obviously impressed.

Willa was on a roll. "And did you know that the bay was one of only two places in North America shortlisted for the New Seven Wonders?"

"The new what?"

"The new seven natural wonders of the world. An organization in Switzerland came up with the idea, and the Bay of Fundy was one of the finalists."

"What was the other wonder in North America?"

"The Grand Canyon. But it didn't make the cut, either."

"Hard to believe," he said. "How'd the winners get chosen?"

"Global vote. Anybody with an email address could log on to the site and choose their seven. The ones with the most votes won."

Keegan scanned the area around them. "I'm surprised the site didn't crash when everyone from Delusion Road logged on."

"Funny," she said, feigning offence. "Keep dissing Delusion Road and I won't show you the surprise."

"If it's a guy with no teeth and a banjo, I'm outta here."

Willa's burst of laughter caught her unawares. Holding on to the railing as it washed over her, she was suddenly conscious that she'd laughed more that morning than she had in a very long time.

# CHAPTER 45

"What'd you *pack* in this thing?" Keegan asked, the straps of the large insulated knapsack digging into his shoulders as he followed Willa on the path that wound through the trees. "You expecting company? Is that the surprise?"

"I have a brother, okay? I know how much guys eat." She pointed ahead of them. "It gets a little tricky here. Watch yourself."

She was right. The path took a sudden turn, and rainwater or snowmelt had followed its sloping trajectory, washing away much of the soil and exposing rocks perfect for catching a toe or twisting an ankle. He watched as she moved confidently forward, and he found himself planting his feet in the same places she did. In fact, he was so focused on where he was stepping that he didn't realize the trees were thinning until they were gone.

"What d'you think?"

He looked up, astonished by what he saw. A beach, but like no other he'd ever seen. Even in pictures. "Your dad owns all this?"

"Just down to the waterline." She pointed to where the trees and vegetation ended. "He owns the land around it, but there's a right-of-way at the far end that gives access to anybody who wants to use it. Years ago when the fishery was a big deal and more people lived around here, I guess this place used to rock on weekends. People our age would carry blankets and food down here, have bonfires, play music, stuff like that. I don't think too many come here now, though."

Keegan couldn't imagine a place this amazing not getting more use. To their left, nearly vertical cliffs of solid rock roughly paralleled the shoreline and stretched as far as he could see, forming a natural boundary between the trees growing atop them and the water on his right. Between the cliffs and the water lay an unbroken expanse of blue and grey dunes that, instead of sand, were actually great swaths of smooth, round stones, most of them fist-sized or smaller.

"Beautiful, aren't they?" asked Willa.

"Where do they come from?"

"The cliffs are constantly eroding," Willa said, "and the rock shatters when it falls. Over the years, the fragments get rolled around by the waves, especially during winter storms, and that movement wears down the ragged edges until they end up smooth and round."

"You're right," he said. "They're beautiful."

"Hard to walk on, though," she warned, leaving the path and stepping onto the beach.

She was right about that, too—twice he almost ended up on his ass. The stones continually shifted beneath Keegan's feet, and walking even a short distance involved a lot of concentration. The clatter of rocks rolling out from under their feet made it hard to talk, so they moved in relative silence. "How far are we going?" asked Keegan after several minutes of fighting for footing. The whole beach had widened like the letter V as they walked.

"Not far," she said. "Just around that outcrop." She pointed at a cliff that reached farther toward the water than any other.

"What's there?" he asked.

"The last part of the surprise."

A few minutes later, Keegan's legs feeling like they'd run two miles, they reached the outcrop. On the other side was what Willa had brought him here to see: a narrow waterfall that plunged from the top of the cliff to its base, the smash into stone sending up misty rainbows in the bright, clear air, the roar until now blocked by the massive wall of rock. It was, indeed, a surprise.

"Wow," he said.

"Yeah," she agreed. "When my brother and I were kids, my parents used to bring us here for picnics. It's my favourite place in the whole world."

Keegan could see why. If those people who'd voted online had seen this, he thought, the Bay of Fundy would've been a lock-in for one of those natural wonders.

"You can put that here," said Willa, pointing toward a large flat rock out of range of the waterfall's mist, and he slid the knapsack from his shoulders and set it down. "I know it's still early, but I always work up an appetite after that walk." She unzipped the knapsack and began taking out container after container filled with what looked like cheese, cold chicken, sandwiches, and at least three kinds of salad, followed by large bottles of water and juice. No wonder the thing had felt so heavy.

"Is there an army showing up later?" he joked.

"It's that walk. Trust me."

And that was something else she was right about. Keegan inhaled four pieces of chicken along with two handfuls of cheese and an entire salad, and he was finishing off a roast beef sandwich when he saw her grinning at him. "Okay, definitely worth the trouble schlepping all this here," he admitted. He wiped his mouth on a napkin, took a final swallow of water from one of the bottles, and lay back beside her on the blanket that had also been in the knapsack. The smooth round stones beneath it shifted slightly to accommodate the contours of his body, making the whole lying-on-rocks thing far more comfortable than he would've thought.

Gazing up into a cobalt sky dotted here and there with feathery clouds, he sighed. "Life doesn't get any better than this, does it?" He turned and saw her smiling at him. "What?"

"I was just thinking that very thing."

He noticed something he hadn't seen before. "What's that doing there?" he asked, pointing at a rope dangling from a cliff just beyond the waterfall.

"My dad says the locals put it there in case of an emergency." She propped herself up on her elbows, nodding toward the bay. "See where the water is now?"

He propped himself up, too. "Yeah, it's closer than before."

"This beach is flatter than most of the shoreline around here, so it doesn't take long for the tide to cover it. The part we walked on first is a lot narrower, and so is the part where the right-of-way is," she said, pointing farther up the beach. "If they weren't paying attention, people sometimes got caught here at high tide. Somebody tied a rope to a tree at the top of that cliff so you could climb out if that happened."

"Why not just swim over to where the path is?"

"Not a great idea."

"Why not?"

"For one thing, the water is freezing, even in the summer."

"Are all Nova Scotians pussies?" he teased.

She frowned. "Remember what I said about the hundred billion tonnes of water flowing in and out of this bay? It doesn't stay long enough to warm up. Other parts of Nova Scotia have tons of beaches that are great for swimming, but I dare you to stick your feet in here." Which explained why she'd told him to leave his trunks and towel in the car.

"I think," he said, "if I had a choice between getting cold and getting dead, I'd swim for it."

"The cold isn't the only problem. When the bay's rough, even strong swimmers don't last long in it. Besides the undertow, high waves can toss you against the cliffs. Even Olympic athletes can't swim if they're unconscious."

Looking at the glass-like smoothness of the water now, Keegan found it difficult to imagine the scene she was describing. He glanced again at the rope. "How long do you figure that's been there? Rope rots after a while, right? Can't be very safe."

"Doesn't matter," she said. "We won't be staying long."

That, however, turned out to be the one thing she was wrong about.

# CHAPTER 46

Willa held up the dandelion-chain in the bright sunlight, her fingers stained and sticky from the stems. As uncomfortable as the stickiness was, though, she didn't care. Her chain was longer than her brother's. Aiden's older hands were bigger, his fingers thicker and blunter than her tiny ones, and he had trouble making the twists and loops without breaking the fragile stems. Aiden could beat her at everything else, but she was still the champion dandelion-chain maker. Daddy said so, which made Aiden really mad. So mad that he grabbed the hose and turned it on her, the cold water—

—splashing over her feet, like liquid snow icing her bare skin.

Willa's eyes snapped open, her lungs ballooning from the shock. Turning, she saw that Keegan had fallen asleep, too. "Wake up!" she cried, prodding him as she scrambled to her feet. "We have to get out of here!"

"Wha—" he muttered. He'd drawn up his knees in his sleep, so the surge of water that had woken her hadn't reached him. But the next swell did, and suddenly he was gasping from winter in the form of a wave. "*Jesus!*" he cried, bolting upright. He picked up the blanket and turned to the containers on the rock, jamming them into the knapsack.

"Forget them!" Willa insisted. "No time." Looking down the beach in the direction of the path, she could see that water had already covered most of the blue-grey dunes. Only a thin strip at the base of the cliff remained bare.

"Do we climb?" asked Keegan, pointing toward the rope.

She shook her head. "We can make it if we run."

They didn't run as much as clamber and fall and then clamber some more, and they were only halfway to the path when the rest of the stones ahead disappeared beneath a slow wave. "Keep going!" she shouted, looking back, and it was only then that she saw he'd hung on to the knapsack after all, the end of the blanket flopping from its unzipped opening.

The last leg of their clamber and fall was the worst, as icy water clutched at them. They kept going, though, splashing and staggering through it, and the whole time Willa was grateful for the bay's unusual calm.

She was laughing when they reached the path, but she wasn't sure why. Exhaustion? Her jeans were soaked nearly to her thighs, her sneakers felt like lead weights on her freezing feet, and her whole body jangled from the punishment of the shifting stones. She was wheezing and coughing and groaning, but she was laughing, too. She had never felt so exhilarated. She turned to Keegan, who was staring at her with wide eyes.

"Could've been worse," she offered between choking gasps. "We could've been running from a toothless banjo-player."

Then he was laughing, too.

+ + +

"I'd better throw another log on the fire," she said, but she was reluctant to leave the nest they'd created for themselves in the living room, blankets wrapped around them as they huddled together on the loveseat. From the laundry room beyond the kitchen came the thunking sounds of their sneakers tumbling inside the dryer. Because they knew their footwear would dry faster alone, they'd hung their jeans from a makeshift rack beside the fireplace, and the smell of damp denim was heavy in the air.

"I'll do it," said Keegan.

Which was, in fact, exactly what she had been counting on. She liked watching his body move. She liked seeing his boxers slide up his thighs as he stooped for another birch log, liked how the muscles of his long legs bunched as he crouched down, liked the way his shoulders thickened beneath his T-shirt as he prodded the wood with the iron poker. Liked it a lot.

She justified her reluctance to tend the fire with the simple fact that she was wearing only a thong beneath her jeans. This was, however, something she could have easily remedied. She had other stuff in her bedroom upstairs, but those were her Delusion Road clothes, comfort wear. She'd rather have Keegan see her in her laciest thong than in any of the baggy sweats she usually slopped around in while she was here. Besides, pretending to be self-conscious about her underwear gave her the opportunity to check out his ass.

Watching him rebuild the fire, she marvelled at how connected the two of them were, how they liked the same music, found humour in the same things, even read the same personal ads. More important, though, she thought about how easy it felt to be with him, how safe he made her feel. How *good* he made her feel. From the moment she'd left him yesterday in the school parking lot, she hadn't stopped thinking about him. *Couldn't* stop thinking about him. And now she couldn't stop looking at him. There was only one thing that bothered her—

"Anything wrong?" he asked, glancing at her over his shoulder.

"No, why?" she lied, marvelling once more at how closely attuned they seemed to be.

"You're so quiet." He gave the fire a final prod, sparks flaring and cascading into themselves as the birch caught. Then he stood and hung the poker from its hook before returning to their nest, drawing the blanket up around their shoulders again. Despite the warmth of the day outside, the interior of the cottage was cool and those waves had chilled them to the bone.

"I'm savouring the moment," she explained in response to his comment.

"Which moment would that be?" he asked. "The memory of having cheated death?" He leaned toward her, waggling his eyebrows suggestively. "Or were you just checking out my ass?"

She laughed softly, amazed all over again at how well he seemed to know her. "Do I have to choose one?" she asked.

"I'm willing to offer a both-of-the-above option."

"Then that's my answer," she said, and he grinned.

His face centimetres from hers, she saw how incredibly long his eyelashes were, how his cheeks dimpled as he smiled, how the silver flecks in his grey eyes seemed to blaze as they mirrored the firelight. But then the grin vanished, replaced by something altogether different, his expression now brooding, his eyes filled with what seemed like melancholy.

What was wrong with her? Although her mind balked at

the thought of Wynn right now, she couldn't help remembering she'd had the same effect on him. In the middle of every intimate moment, he'd suddenly pulled away, leaving her confused and deflated, questioning what she'd done—or hadn't done—to ruin it again. She knew now, of course, that there was so much more going on with Wynn than she ever could have guessed, most of it having nothing to do with her, but hadn't the same thing just happened with Keegan? What was *wrong* with her?

She turned toward the fire, despair like its own sudden tide washing over her, and the flames began to blur before her eyes. She swallowed hard and got to her feet, tugging the blanket around her. "Guess we'd better head back." To hell with her jeans—she'd throw on her sweats after all. She turned toward the stairs, then felt a hand on her arm.

"Willa."

She knew he'd gotten up, too, but she couldn't look at him. "My dad probably has something around here that you can wear till we get back to Brookdale." She took a step toward the staircase, but he held on to her.

"Willa," he said again.

She turned, and there was more than melancholy in his expression now. Those silver-flecked eyes seemed filled with misery. "What's wrong?" she asked.

"I'm not . . ." He glanced away as if unsure how to finish what he'd begun.

"You're not what?"

For a long moment, the only sound in the room was the crackling of that birch log in the fireplace. Then he turned to her again. "I'm not who you think I am." His fingers on her arm relaxed and they were standing apart once more.

She swallowed hard again and nodded. "Yeah, I get it."

"Get what?"

Was he really going to make her say it? She took a breath, released it. "That you're not into me. Seems no one is."

He reached for her again, this time drawing her body against his, enfolding her in his arms the way he'd done the day before. "I'm not Wynn," he murmured into her hair, his hands warm against her back, gently caressing her, soothing her.

But it wasn't enough. She leaned away, looking up at his face. "Who *are* you then?" And there it was. The thing that had troubled her before. "These past couple days I've told you more than I've ever shared with anybody, and you've been a really good listener. So good that it's taken me until now to realize I know almost nothing about *you*." She shook her head sadly. "You were wrong when you said you're not who I think you are. I don't know *what* to think. And just so you know, I've had my fill of guys pretending to be someone they aren't."

"What if they don't have a choice?" He'd spoken so softly that she'd had to strain to hear the words.

"Too bad," she replied, the sudden strength of her voice surprising her. She could see it surprised him, too. "I've got zero time for that bullshit."

He nodded, and she somehow felt in those seconds as he stood staring into her eyes that he was making a decision, making a choice of some sort. He reached up, placed his hands gently on either side of her face, and pressed his lips to hers.

Their jeans were bone-dry when they finally got around to putting them on.

# CHAPTER 47

"I was getting worried," said Evan, shutting off the TV and getting up from the sofa.

Keegan remained in the doorway, watching Willa reverse out of the driveway. His back to his father, he hoped he could ignore the disagreement they'd had that morning. Evan had disapproved of Keegan's spending the day with Willa, had even begged him to call it off, but Keegan had gone anyway. "I told you I didn't know when we'd be home," he said. He raised his hand and Willa waved back.

"It's just you're a lot later than I expected."

Keegan turned. "I would've called if there'd been a problem." Actually, he couldn't have without cell service, but his father didn't need to know that.

Evan moved toward him. "What if you hadn't been *able* to call?"

"Then I guess you'd just have to trust me. For once."

His father sighed. "It isn't you I don't trust."

"You're talking about Willa? There's nothing to worry about. I trust her."

"You barely know her."

Keegan's mind flashed to their afternoon at the cottage. "I know her better than you think."

Evan scowled. "You can't have a relationship with this girl. You *know* that. It wouldn't be fair to her."

Keegan's fingers whitened around the strap of the bag he hadn't needed that day, and he forced himself to ease his grip, letting the bag slip to the floor. "And *you* know all about fair, right? You're such an expert on making decisions for everybody else."

Evan put his hands up. "Look, I'm not getting into this with you again. *You* have to trust *me*. You don't realize what your actions could cost us."

Keegan flexed his fingers so they wouldn't make fists. "You ever think about what *your* actions cost us?"

Evan looked as though the words had physically struck him. "Every day," he said quietly. "But I did what I thought I had to."

"Really?" said Keegan. "That *justifies* everything, does it?" He turned toward the stairs. "That may get *you* through the night," he said, his footsteps on the treads like the raps of a hammer, "but it's not enough for me. It never was."

"Son, listen to reason—"

"I'm sick and tired of listening," said Keegan as he reached the landing at the top of the staircase and pushed open his bedroom door. "I'm sick and tired of waiting for my life to happen."

"But you don't understand how—"

Keegan slammed the door behind him.

It was only then that he remembered his brother in the next room. He braced himself for the weeping, but he wasn't sorry.

From now on, things were going to be different.

# CHAPTER 48

Now that Griff was on Morozov's good side again—if, indeed, that weird fuck *had* a good side—his appetite had returned. No longer in immediate danger of being eighty-sixed by one of Morozov's goons, he could taste food again, which was why he'd decided this evening to indulge himself at the Cheesecake Factory on North Michigan. Once he finished the Chocolate Tuxedo Cream Delight he was working on, he intended to order the White Chocolate Raspberry Truffle and then maybe the Ultimate Red Velvet Cake. Looking at the menu earlier, he couldn't help wondering which of those desserts Talia would enjoy most, and he'd decided this was the first place he'd take her. Now that he didn't have a bull's eye on his back, he figured maybe he could focus on his own life for a change.

Forking more of the Tuxedo Cream into his mouth, he thought again about the information that "well-placed associate" had passed along to Morozov yesterday. Despite all the time he'd spent surveilling the target, Griff had had no inkling the guy had the know-how to do what he'd accomplished during his last night at Battaglia's, but Griff's failure to kill him had, indeed, turned out to be a fortunate turn of events. How had Morozov put it? *Things happen for a reason.* Maybe. Or maybe people just got lucky. Whatever the reality, at least it gave Griff a bit of a breather. Not that this development lessened the need to find the target—Morozov's revelation about what the sonuvabitch had done made it even more important that Griff find the guy, get the goods, and off him ASAP. No one knew when that shit was gonna rain down, but it couldn't be much longer. If ever Griff needed to finish a job, it was now.

All the same, though, he was taking tomorrow off. When was the last time he hadn't spent at least part of every goddamn day trying to locate the target? Even when he was working on other hits, he'd still tweak his facial recognition algorithm and then comb through the results it pulled up, all before scouring fucking Facebook. The only positive part of *that* soul-sucking chore was spending time with Talia, even if it was only virtual. In fact, she was the reason he was taking tomorrow off. After all these months of keeping tabs on her, poring over every photo upload and text message, observing her through her webcam, even listening to her talk in her sleep, he'd decided he wasn't waiting any longer. Tomorrow they would meet.

Swallowing another forkful of his dessert, Griff thought about how tomorrow was going to play out. He intended to spend most of it at Bean There Downed That so he could go over his strategy as many times as he needed. He liked the thought of doing his planning less than a block away from where she'd be sitting in some classroom, unaware that her life was about to change. *Both* their lives.

He would arrive early in the morning to give himself enough time to consider every *If this, then what?* scenario, anticipating all the things that might unfold when she arrived later that afternoon.

His main objective, of course, was simply to introduce himself to her, but he wanted to be ready to take things further if the opportunity presented itself. Sure, it was likely that Soccerguy89 would figure into each scenario, but he intended to have options for that, too. Nothing was going to keep Griff from her. Nothing.

From time to time, that inner voice whispered Gil Atkins's name, but Griff ignored it. He was nothing at all like that lowlife. Gil had barely known the girls he'd chosen, and his involvement with them was never going to be anything but short-term—they were just temporary solutions for disgusting urges. Griff was making plans for the rest of his life.

Bringing the final bite of the Tuxedo Cream to his mouth, he was just about to wave down his waitress to order the truffle when he felt his phone begin to pulse. Not vibrate. Pulse. He dropped the fork, heedless of the people sitting near him who turned toward the clatter of cutlery, and pulled the device from his pocket. He knew he shouldn't get excited—he'd had lots of hits in the past, none of which had panned out—but it was hard not to hope, especially in light of what would be happening tomorrow. There was no way he could build a life for Talia and himself until he had put this problem to rest. *Please bring me that fucker.*

He pressed Cancel on the screen and returned the phone to his pocket, then reached for the case under the table and pulled out his laptop. He'd programmed his phone to alert him to any hits, but he preferred to use the computer to check them out, not only because of its faster processing power, but because its larger screen and greater resolution allowed him to verify more easily whatever the FRA had found.

Raising the display, he watched as the laptop woke up, a sense of anticipation building inside him as the retinal scan gave him access and the FRA came online. Please bring me that fucker, he thought again.

# CHAPTER 49

"Looks like somebody enjoyed her day off."

Willa turned from her locker to see Raven grinning at her. "What makes you say that?"

"If your face was a light bulb, I'd have to wear sunglasses."

Willa's smile grew even wider. She'd felt it the moment she'd woken up that morning, and it had returned again and again as she'd showered, dressed, done her makeup, eaten breakfast, brushed her teeth, driven to school. She'd kept waiting for her cheek muscles to start aching, but she guessed that only happened when you forced a smile. This one kept surfacing all on its own.

"Anything to do with a tall, dark-haired someone we know?" asked Raven.

Willa nodded, beaming.

"He's a good guy."

"Yeah," said Willa, "he is." She thought of everything he'd shared with her at the cottage, telling her about Curtis and Lamont, how pissed he'd been at the way others had treated his friends when they came out. And about someone named Jermaine, who'd been arrested for something he hadn't done. Keegan had been talking about his past, telling her about the guys he'd hung out with. Without his realizing it, though, the stories he'd shared had told her far more about Keegan Fraser, about his willingness to defend the people he cared for, his refusal to look the other way if he saw someone being mistreated. Which explained his reaction to Wynn's assaulting Bailey. "He is," Willa repeated, her smile even broader. "A really good guy."

A shadow fell across Raven's face. "Gotta go," she said, turning and moving quickly down the corridor toward her homeroom.

"You don't call, you don't write," came a voice over her shoulder, its humorous tone belying the speaker's true meaning.

Willa turned to face Wynn and the rest of them. She wasn't surprised by the looks Celia and Britney were giving her, but that didn't make it hurt any less as they glared at her. What *did* surprise her were the expressions on Todd's and Jay's faces. They looked embarrassed standing there in the corridor, almost as if they'd been caught doing something they shouldn't. Wynn, of course, looked like he owned the place.

"Hi," said Willa, ignoring his comment and addressing the others.

"Hi," said Jay, but his greeting seemed to fizzle. Other students in the corridor threw the group furtive glances as they passed.

Another beat of silence. Then, "You still doing social work?" asked Celia.

The comment made Willa fume inside. "Bailey's really nice. You'd like her if you got to know her."

Wynn snorted, and Willa felt her face burn. *You asshole!* She seethed silently as his smirk telegraphed his thoughts. He was rubbing her face in what he'd done, confident there was nothing she could do about it. The smile Willa had worn all morning had vanished, but she struggled to resurrect it. "What'd you guys do with your day off?" she asked brightly, ignoring Wynn's sneer.

"Hung out in Wynn's pool all day," replied Todd. "Too hot to do anything else."

"It would've been a lot nicer on the bay," Jay said, then reddened. "That is, you know, if—"

Celia silenced him with a withering look, but Willa had no trouble finishing the thought: *if you'd invited us to your cottage.* "It *was* nice," she said. "We spent the whole day there."

"You and your new girlfriends?" said Britney, the brittleness of her voice making the last word sound like an expletive.

"No," came a voice behind them.

They all turned to see Keegan brush past them to stand by Willa, his face a dark scowl. He took her hand in his. "She spent it with me."

Willa watched Wynn's face change, his smirk mutating into a jagged line like a scar on his perfect tanned face. She looked up at Keegan and suddenly her true smile was back.

Later, she would realize it was her smile that had set him off. Wynn took two sudden steps forward, putting him toe-to-toe with Keegan, his face a misshapen mask. "You son of a bitch," he snarled, his words seeming to carve the air, shape it, give it a pulse, drawing the attention of everyone in that corridor. "I'm so gonna *end* you, asshole."

Keegan smiled at him. "Go for it," he said, and Willa could see in his eyes how much he wanted Wynn to try.

Willa saw Wynn's hands form fists, saw him draw back his right arm, and she opened her mouth to shout at him, but it was someone else who called his name. She turned to see Mr. Richardson hurrying toward them.

Wynn froze, his face working oddly as he glared at Keegan, his body a wellspring of rage. Keegan continued to smile at him.

"C'mon, man," said Jay, tugging at Wynn's arm, "you don't wanna do this."

But it was clear that he *did* want to. Very much.

"Come with me, Wynn," ordered Richardson as he reached them. "Now!"

# CHAPTER 50

"You wanted to see me?" asked Keegan, standing in Richardson's doorway. A secretary had buzzed into Keegan's fourth-period class requesting that he see the English teacher before he left at the end of the day. He'd half-expected Wynn to be there, too, thinking Richardson might try to mediate the situation between them, and he was relieved to see that wasn't the case. Mediation wasn't in Wynn d'Entremont's vocabulary—jerks like him negotiated with their knuckles. Keegan wished he could share with the teacher what he knew about Wynn so someone else would understand what the guy was capable of and, more importantly, could keep an eye out for Bailey. And Willa.

Looking up from the papers on his desk, the teacher asked, "Would you mind closing the door?" Seeing the concern on Keegan's face, he said, "This won't take long. I imagine you probably have someone waiting for you, right?"

Keegan grinned as he shut the door behind him. He was still grinning as he crossed the room to the teacher's desk.

"I wanted to talk to you about this after class today," said Richardson, "but I knew we'd have more privacy after school. I gave Wynn his final warning this morning."

Keegan's grin faltered.

"If it had been anyone else," the teacher continued, "it wouldn't have been a warning. I'd have done what I told him I'd do and started the process of pulling him out of extracurriculars."

Surprised by this admission of preferential treatment, Keegan wasn't sure how to respond. "Yeah, well, thanks for telling me."

"I know what you're thinking," said Richardson, "but it has nothing to do with Wynn being the mayor's son." He picked up a pen from his desk and rolled it between his fingers before he continued. "Remember last week when you introduced Willa? You said what you see is what you get, right?"

Keegan flushed, embarrassed. "Yeah, well, I was wrong. She's a lot more than that."

The teacher gave him a wan smile. "Most people are. It's in our nature to project the persona we most want others to see. We play our cards close to our chest, keep the innermost parts of ourselves hidden. We all have secrets. I'm sure you do, too."

Keegan flushed again, but not from embarrassment this time. He said nothing, letting the teacher's observation hang in the air.

Richardson didn't seem to notice, his eyes returning to the pen in his hand. "It's unprofessional of me to be talking with you about another student, but I think it's warranted in this case. That scene in the hallway this morning raised a red flag for me. I think Wynn's dangerous."

Keegan cleared his throat. "Look, I understand your not wanting to get on his bad side—"

It's not me I'm concerned about, Keegan. I wouldn't be much

of a teacher if I let a student's intimidation keep me from doing the right thing."

Afraid he'd offended the man, Keegan was about to apologize when Richardson continued, "I'm way out of line telling you this, Keegan, but there's something I believe you need to know."

# CHAPTER 51

G riff hated the car he was driving, its cherry-red exterior almost as loud as its sound-enhancing muffler. He'd have preferred stealing something far less flashy, but there were too many people coming and going in that airport parking garage for him to be choosy. He'd checked out three different levels but grew worried that his continued circling of vehicles would draw the attention of whoever was monitoring the surveillance cameras, so he'd settled on the car parked farthest from the elevator on the third level, a Dodge Charger that looked—and sounded— like something out of the *Fast and Furious* film franchise. It had power to spare but it rode like a bitch, thunking along as though suspension had been an afterthought. Of course, the condition of the highway didn't help, one section of it so rough Griff felt like he was navigating an obstacle course as he swerved to avoid potholes. Apparently, whatever passed for public works in Nova Scotia didn't earmark much cash for road repair.

Listening to the throaty rumble of the muffler above the whine of pavement beneath the tires, Griff let his mind roam back over the events that had brought him to this point. Last night when he'd confirmed his facial recognition algorithm had gotten its first solid hit, he'd read and reread the Facebook page the software had pulled up and wondered what the fuck any of it meant. At the same time, he'd cursed himself for not considering the possibility that the target and his sons had left the country. After they'd vanished, Griff had scoured only American employment and education databases; if he'd widened his search to include similar databases in Canada, he might have located them long before this. He blamed this oversight on his FRA's failure to ping their passport photos when they crossed the border, but he could guess now why that had happened: high-level intervention. He wouldn't make that mistake again.

He'd been pissed at having to postpone meeting Talia, but finishing this job was a priority so, sitting there in the Cheesecake Factory, he'd pulled up on his laptop all the airlines with flights departing to Halifax from O'Hare. There were no seats available on any of the direct routes, but an Air Canada flight to Toronto was leaving in just over an hour, and he could continue on to Halifax in the morning. He hated the delay, but he'd booked the flight anyway, paid for his dessert, and then called a cab to take him to the airport.

He hadn't had time to return to his apartment to pack anything, but he'd learned early in his work for Morozov the importance of keeping a set of fake IDs on him, complete with passport and cloned credit card, so he'd had no problem boarding the flight as Leo Forrester from Dixon, Illinois. He'd gotten some strange looks from O'Hare Security when his only luggage was his laptop case, which contained an interesting item in addition to his computer, but no one commented on it, and he had Morozov to thank for that, too.

While waiting for his taxi outside the Cheesecake Factory,

Griff had called Morozov to update him and, at the same time, raise the issue of his firearm. In the past, he'd never had to travel more than a couple of hours to perform a hit, which meant he'd been able to take his Smith & Wesson with him in whatever car he'd stolen. Griff thought of that gun as a natural extension of his body, and he didn't like the idea of going after the target without it. He could, he'd told Morozov, leave it in a locker at O'Hare and steal a gun in Nova Scotia, but that would almost certainly increase his kill time, especially since he'd heard that firearms were harder to come by in Canada. There were, of course, other options, but there was no longer any point in trying to make the hits look like accidents—the distance between Illinois and Nova Scotia meant that local authorities wouldn't immediately connect the killings to Morozov, and Griff planned to make the bodies unidentifiable once he was finished with them anyway. After all, the target's prolonged vanishing act had caused Griff considerable misery, so payback was going to be a bitch.

As Griff had expected, Morozov was thrilled to learn the target had been located—so much so, in fact, that his voice had briefly taken on an almost human quality. Even more surprising was his offer to handle the problem of the firearm, which he did by making a phone call. It turned out that his "well-placed associate" had the means of adding an interesting credential to Leo Forrester's profile: air marshal, one of those in-flight security officers whose position entitled him to carry a gun on a plane. Grateful that he looked old enough to hold a position like that, Griff couldn't help but wonder who the hell this associate might be and what hold Morozov had over him. It had to be more than money that got co-operation like that. Blackmail? Probably.

After purchasing onboard Internet service with his cloned credit card, Griff had spent the first leg of his journey checking out his destination. He was pleased to learn that Brookdale, located in western Nova Scotia, was a small town—good news because Griff had no specific address for the target. But since everybody would know everybody else in a community that size, finding him there wouldn't be too big an obstacle.

Griff had worried he might have a problem with his Smith & Wesson at Toronto's Pearson Airport—security at international arrivals was understandably tight—but Morozov's associate had come through again. A customs official checked the digital document on Griff's phone and compared it with what appeared on her computer, then waved him through, even thanking him for the important work he was doing keeping people safe. It was all Griff could do to keep from busting a gut.

He could have checked into a hotel but chose, instead, to spend the night in the airport. He figured he wouldn't get much sleep anyway—he was pumped about finally getting to off the guy he'd been tracking for months—so he'd stretched out across five seats in the departure lounge, the gun hidden beneath his left arm. Surprisingly, he dozed fairly well until his usual nightmare yanked him trembling from sleep. But he would've had that regardless of where he was.

He'd been relieved when his flight out of Toronto left on time and, shortly after takeoff, he'd again purchased Internet service, this time to check out upcoming events at the Garfield Park Conservatory. He was hoping to find something he could take Talia to see there. Then, his mind already on flowers, he'd googled plants native to eastern Canada and was surprised to learn that lady's slippers were found in undeveloped areas across the region. In fact, Prince Edward Island, a tiny province in the Gulf of St. Lawrence, had chosen the lady's slipper as its official flower.

Reading that, Griff had sat back in his window seat staring out at the clouds and thinking of Clovis Lafayette. Apparently, he'd up and vanished from Camelot Trailer Park and was never seen again. The police had come to the Idlewood Home for Boys a couple of times shortly after Clovis's disappearance and asked Griff about him, having learned they were friends, but Griff had just shrugged, said he hadn't seen the old guy for a while. Which was, in fact, the truth.

Griff's plane had arrived in Halifax a few minutes early, one o'clock Chicago time but three o'clock local time, and fifteen minutes later he was on the road. Driving west along Nova Scotia's Highway 101 now, he allowed his thoughts to return to Clovis, the only friend he'd ever had. Surely the presence of lady's slippers in Nova Scotia was a sign, a good omen of sorts. His mind leapfrogged from there to the lady's slippers he'd planted behind the dumpster on Roundtable Road, and he wondered if at least one of them had survived somehow, defying the odds of alkalinity. And then he thought about the grave he had painstakingly dug that night in the soft earth.

Hopefully, by this time tomorrow he'd be digging three more. But not before he'd had his fun.

# CHAPTER 52

"You sure your parents won't mind me being here like this?" asked Keegan as the garage door closed behind the SUV.

"This from a guy who was ready to go World War Three at school this morning?" she teased.

"Wynn was asking for it," he said. "Parents I don't like to piss off. I want to be invited back."

"Don't worry," she grinned. "While I was waiting for you to come out of the school, I texted my dad that we'd be here, and he messaged back it was okay."

"Your mother still in Halifax?"

"Still," she said, the word sounding more injured than she'd intended.

Keegan reached across and took her hand. "None of this means they're breaking up."

"Maybe not, but you haven't seen them together. Lately, they—" But she didn't want to finish that thought. "Did your mom and dad argue much before she left?"

He looked down at her hand in his, the expression on his face suddenly sombre, and she regretted asking. Of *course* his parents had argued. They'd divorced, hadn't they? "Never mind," she said. "Besides, I didn't bring you here to sit in the garage." She opened her door and slid out, and Keegan did the same.

"Wow!" exclaimed Keegan when he saw the gleaming kitchen cabinetry and the polished quartz countertops that bounced sunlight from the large windows onto the stainless steel appliances.

In the past when a visitor saw the kitchen for the first time, Willa always took pride in the Ferrari workmanship and unique design. Now, though, she just saw how over-the-top it all was. "Want something to drink?" she asked quickly. "There's soft drinks, juices, stuff like that."

"Water's fine," he said.

She got glasses from a cupboard and placed them in the refrigerator's automated dispenser, a sensor adding crushed ice and filtered water, then carried them both to the enormous island, where she sat on one of the sleek air-lift counter stools that were as much modern art as furniture. Keegan sat on the one next to hers, and in that moment she noticed something. "Keegan, do you dye your hair?"

Keegan flushed, and he dragged a hand through the long black strands that hung to his eyes.

"Your hair's brown, isn't it?" she asked, looking at the roots now visible in the bright light pooling around both of them.

"Yeah," he replied. "I thought new school, why not a new look?" He picked up one of the glasses and took long swallows, seemingly intent on draining it.

Willa could tell he was embarrassed, although he had no reason to be—lots of guys coloured their hair. She was just surprised she hadn't noticed it before.

She hated the awkwardness that seemed to have settled around them, and she groped for something to say. "You think Wynn will be back in school tomorrow?"

Keegan nodded. "I meant to tell you. Richardson asked to meet me after last class. That's why I was late getting to you."

It was Willa's turn to flush as she remembered their first few minutes in the SUV after school. They hadn't spent them talking. "What'd he want?"

"To tell me what was happening with Wynn."

Willa nodded. When they'd gone to homeroom that morning following the altercation in the hallway, Wynn was still in there with the teacher. She couldn't hear what was being said, but it was the first time she'd seen anything that looked like worry on Wynn's face, and she guessed it had to do with his getting pulled from the sports program. "What'd he say?" she asked.

"That he'd given Wynn his final warning."

She frowned. "I'm surprised he gave him a second one."

"I was, too. At first." Keegan looked at the now-empty glass in his hand, set it down on the countertop, then turned to her again. "He said that Wynn worried him."

"Richardson's afraid of him?"

"Not in the way you think."

"What other way is there?"

"He thinks Wynn's dangerous."

Willa's eyes widened. "You didn't tell him about—"

"No. I *wanted* to, but I didn't."

"So he's basing this on the fight he broke up this morning? Teachers break up fights all the time."

"It's not just that. He told me about a student he taught a couple years ago in Ontario."

"What about him?"

"Really popular guy. Not athletic like Wynn, but active in student government, drama, debate club, stuff like that. Richardson called him charming."

"What's this have to do with Wynn?"

"Richardson said he had a bad feeling about the guy from the beginning, that there was something off about him somehow. None of the other teachers seemed to see it, but he looked into his background anyway, even spoke to the school's guidance department about him. All their files showed he was the real deal, the kind of guy parents would love to have their daughters bring home."

"I still don't see what—"

"Two weeks later, he took a baseball bat to his mother."

"*What*? Why?"

"Richardson didn't go into all the details, but it boiled down to her not giving him permission to do something he wanted. The thing is," Keegan continued, "he has the same feeling about Wynn, that something's off somehow. And not just because he wants to beat the crap out of me. Richardson's worried there's something darker there."

"So he was warning us."

Keegan nodded. "And explaining why he gave Wynn another chance. He's worried what the guy might do if he has nothing to lose. At least the threat of getting kicked off his teams gives him something to think about."

"Why hasn't Richardson just gone to the VP about this?"

"About a feeling?"

"Yeah," she acknowledged. "It sounds crazy when you say it like that."

"Richardson felt bad talking about another student, but he couldn't take the chance of saying nothing in case his hunch turned out to be right."

Willa sighed. "I just wish we could get Bailey to go to the police. Everybody needs to know what that guy's capable of."

Keegan drew her close. "Right now," he said, his tone lighter, and she could tell he was trying to cheer her up, "what's important is what *I'm* capable of."

She smiled up at him. "You sure you're up for this?"

He raised his eyebrows in mock offense. "Willa Jaffrey, are you questioning my considerable prowess?"

"Considerable?" she echoed. "That remains to be seen, doesn't it?"

He leaned toward her, his forehead touching hers. "Prepare to be overwhelmed."

+ + +

She was. The assignment Shedrand had given them that morning would have taken Willa a lot longer to do by herself. She was confident in her own math ability, but Keegan had a way of thinking outside the box that opened up some of the problems a lot faster than if she'd been working on them alone. They finished in under an hour, a record for the homework Shedrand had been giving them lately.

"You want to stay for dinner?" she asked as they packed up

their books. They'd worked in her room, using her laptop to access some of the math help sites she'd bookmarked.

"Thanks," he said, "but I missed having dinner with Isaac last night. I think I should spend some time with him this afternoon."

Willa was moved once more by the bond Keegan shared with his younger brother. "No worries," she said. "Another day. Then you can meet my mom."

"I'd like that," he said.

Willa pushed away from her desk and stood. "I'll drive you home. I'll just be a minute, okay?"

She was, of course, longer than a minute. Several, in fact, after seeing in her ensuite mirror the wreck her makeup had become following their moments in the SUV after school. When she finally emerged from her bathroom, she found Keegan sitting at her desk, closing her laptop. "Anything interesting?" she asked.

He reached for his backpack on the floor. "Just checking to see if the weather's going to break."

Something about the moment didn't feel right to her, although she couldn't have explained why. She pushed the thought aside, chiding herself for her overactive imagination. After all she'd been through with Wynn, she was gun-shy, expecting trouble where there was none.

Later, though, after she'd gotten back to the house, taken a swim, and called her mother, who was in the middle of a spa treatment with Rachel that involved seaweed, she returned to her bedroom to finish her other homework. As she stood in the doorway, the memory of that moment came back to her, and she suddenly knew what had bothered her about it. He hadn't looked at her when he said he'd checked the weather.

She tried to shrug off her suspicion, but it nagged at her the whole time she was reading the last two chapters of *The Mountain and the Valley*. When she finally put the book down, she glanced over at her laptop and scowled. Moving to her desk, she lifted the screen and the processor woke up. She stared at the desktop image, a photo of the bay she'd taken in August from the deck of their cottage, and she remembered Keegan standing there yesterday. And then later inside the cottage, the silver flecks in his eyes blazing with firelight. She closed the laptop and reached for her history homework.

But he hadn't told her if the weather was going to break, had he?

*I'm not—*

She turned back to the laptop.

*—who you—*

Her fingers traced the computer's logo as she cursed her suspicion.

*—think I am.*

She raised the screen again and touched her browser icon. Opening the Internet Options tab, she scrolled down to History. There was none.

It had been deleted.

# CHAPTER 53

Griff unlocked the door of the motel room, finding it nicer than he'd expected. An hour ago, he'd pulled off the highway and driven through a community called New Minas looking to buy some equipment he'd need and then decided to spend the night there. Brookdale was only a short drive from New Minas, and he thought it safer not to stay in the town where he would carry out the hit. People had a tendency to remember you more clearly if you overnighted in a place.

Besides the bag of items in his left hand—most of them were electronic, but there were some old-school tools in there, too— he carried in his right a bag containing two Big Mac combos. Rather than eating at a restaurant, where someone might recall seeing him, he'd decided on takeout, and McDonald's was the first drive-thru he'd seen. Besides, he was interested to see if takeout from the Golden Arches in New Minas tasted anything like McDonald's in Chicago.

After he'd eaten—and damn if the stuff hadn't tasted exactly the same—he took a long shower. Towelling himself off afterwards, he could hear his phone pinging—the signal that someone had accessed Talia's Facebook page, someone who had never viewed her profile before. Not that this meant anything. Complete strangers checked out other complete strangers all the time. But Griff had long since learned to trust electronics more than people, and he pulled his laptop out of its case, powered it up, activated the retinal scan, then logged on to the motel's free Wi-Fi.

A few minutes later, having tracked the IP of the computer that had triggered the pinging, he could barely contain his excitement. Reaching for his phone, he entered the street address into his GPS, then lay back on the bed. He'd heard somewhere that bedspreads in hotel rooms contained more germs than toilet seats, and here he was lying naked on one of those cloth cesspools. But Griff wasn't the one living dangerously tonight. That person was viewing Talia Lombardi's Facebook page on a computer in Brookdale.

Hadn't he said it over and over again? Sooner or later, everybody fucked up.

# CHAPTER 54

Keegan saw the number on his cell's display beside the low-battery icon but ignored it. He would call Willa back later. Right now, he was reeling from the news his father had just delivered. "I'm not moving," he said. "Not again."

Evan's mouth was a thin line. "I'm their accountant, remember? I've just gone over the last of the books. It's only a matter of time before the dealership goes under."

"Willa's dad is working on that. He—"

"Would need a miracle," finished Evan. "And in case you haven't noticed, times are nearly as tough here as they were back home. I have to think about *us*, which is why I'm calling Forbes to arrange something. It'll look less suspicious if I tell everyone I got offered another job. Judging from those books, the rest of the staff will be looking for work soon, too."

Keegan glanced toward the living room, where he and Isaac had been working on a puzzle together. He didn't want to lose his temper like last night. Isaac had stimmed for over an hour after that. "I'm not moving," Keegan repeated, his voice as even as he could make it.

"That's not your decision."

"Right. You're the only one in this family who gets to make those. And we all know how great that's been working for us."

"Son, if I had it to do all over again—"

"Don't you goddamn *dare*!" Keegan fumed, trying to keep his voice down. "You don't get to talk to me about do-overs. *Ever!*"

His father looked away, and Keegan could see his words had hit home. A moment passed before he turned back. "I accept that you don't care what happens to me. I even understand it. But are you willing to risk Isaac's life, too?"

"I'm not risking anyone's life. I'm trying to *have* one. Is that so wrong?"

"Of course it's not wrong. But it's not possible here."

And that was it. To hell with what anybody else wanted. Or needed.

Keegan felt his fingernails dig into the flesh of his palms, felt his pulse throb in his ears, felt curses pile up in his chest like cars bottlenecking a lane. And then he thought of Isaac.

He turned and pushed out through the kitchen door and down the step. He was running before he reached the street.

# CHAPTER 55

What were the chances? thought Griff, watching the girl pull out of the driveway and accelerate past him. A fucking blond. Sitting in the Charger, parked down the street from the address he'd traced the night before, he felt his skin crawl and tried not to think of it as another omen. A bad one this time.

Judging from the house she'd just left, Griff was pretty sure the target didn't live there. He'd have been crazy to put himself up in something so flashy. Then again, Griff was sitting in a cherry-red Charger with sound-enhancing muffler, wasn't he?

A man in a suit had driven off a few minutes earlier, and Griff had identified him from online photos as Carleton Jaffrey, the girl's father, who owned a GM dealership on Commercial Street. Which explained the SUV the girl was driving now. A bitch like that you'd expect to see in something like a Camaro.

Seeing her drive off, he resisted the temptation to follow her, deciding to watch the house a little longer just in case the target surprised him and appeared after all. Several minutes later, Griff had detected no one else, neither outside nor within—the windows in the place were so large that, had anyone been inside, he was certain he'd have seen them moving around.

Only the two of them living in that huge house? he thought. He momentarily wondered where Jaffrey's wife was but, having seen photos of her online, too, he could guess. Another blond. The bitch had probably divorced him and was making some-body else's life miserable now.

Despite his near-certainty that the target wasn't inside, Griff knew he couldn't leave without being absolutely sure. Turning off the ignition, he reached for the bag on the seat beside him and got out. From the look of the place, Jaffrey was probably paying an arm and a leg for his security and monitoring systems. Too bad none of them were worth shit.

+ + +

Thirty minutes later, having been over every inch of the place, Griff was confident that, not only was the target not in the house, he didn't live there. Which meant only one thing: his older son had used the blond's computer to access Talia's profile. So he and the girl must be friends. Mind you, that relationship might not be present-tense, given the stuff his FRA had found on Facebook, but Griff was confident his theory was solid. The girl was the key to finding the whole family.

Standing at the rear entry and grateful for the high fence around the pool that blocked the neighbours' views of the back-yard, Griff reset the alarm and closed the door behind him. Coming around the side of the garage, he peered over the gate to see if anyone was on the street, but he saw no one. People who lived in neighbourhoods like this were either already at work or still in bed.

His hands moist inside his plastic gloves, he walked nonchalantly toward the Charger and got in, turning on the engine and air conditioning once more. Gripping the wheel, Griff thought again about the Jaffrey girl, wondering how he could get the target's address from her. He had no time to do his usual planning, work out all the angles, anticipate every scenario. Not if he wanted to see Talia soon. There was only one way.

He slid the gearshift into drive.

# CHAPTER 56

Keegan looked like crap, and the question Willa wanted to ask him—*Where were you last night?*—suddenly didn't seem as important as the state he was in right now. She'd thought about driving to his house that morning to pick him up but, since she hadn't heard from him, she'd waited for him in the student parking lot. Sitting in the SUV beside her now, he looked very different from the confident guy who'd stared down Wynn d'Entremont the day before. He looked worried. Agitated, in fact. And were those the same clothes he'd been wearing yesterday? "What's wrong?" she asked.

He shook his head. "My dad and me. Difference of opinion." He reached across the console to take her hand. "Sorry I didn't call you last night. My battery died."

Not exactly the excuse she'd been hoping for. Weren't there other phones in his house?

As if reading her mind, he added, "I wasn't home last night. I was afraid I'd blow up and send Isaac over the deep end."

"Where'd you go?"

"Memorial Park. Slept on a bench."

She reached up and stroked his cheek, the stubble on his face rasping her fingers. "You could have come to my place," she said.

"Trust me, I wouldn't have been good company."

*Trust me.* She wanted to, but there was still that thing with her laptop. She'd checked her Internet Options again to see if maybe she'd inadvertently changed a setting, possibly checking the "Delete browsing history on exit" box. But she hadn't. There was no question: Keegan had used her computer to access the Internet and then erased his tracks afterwards. But why? There could be any number of reasons, the most obvious being porn, but he really didn't seem the type. Of course, Wynn d'Entremont didn't seem like the type who'd get off on assaulting girls, either. But something—she wasn't sure what—told her that Keegan hadn't been surfing X-rated sites. He'd been looking at something else. Something he didn't want Willa to see.

She'd planned to confront him about it as soon as she saw him, but she knew now wasn't the time. And, deep down, she was hoping he'd tell her without her having to ask.

*Trust me.*

Okay, she'd give him some time.

But she wasn't going to wait long. Wynn had made a fool of her for months. She wasn't about to let that happen again.

+ + +

"Okay," said Mr. Richardson, "now that you've all finished reading the novel—" He stopped, pointing to the calendar on the wall. "This being the deadline I gave you for finishing it, I'm working on the assumption that everyone has."

There was a sudden chorus of emphatic "Sure"s and "You bet"s, and the teacher grinned before continuing. "As I said at the beginning of this novel study, I asked you to pay attention to the rug motif that Buckler threaded throughout his narrative."

"About that, Mr. R.," Todd interjected. "I had a real problem with that Ellen character."

"Problem? Why?"

"She was a grandmother, right? *Way* too old to be hooking."

Willa noticed less of a response in the room than she'd have expected after a comment like that. The little laughter she heard seemed strained, almost obligatory. Perhaps everyone was sapped from the continued heat.

Or maybe people just didn't think the Wynn Crowd was all that funny anymore.

Richardson ignored the comment. "Any other thoughts?"

Bailey put her hand up.

"Yes, Bailey?"

"Ellen uses bits of the characters' worn-out clothes to make her rugs."

"And what does that suggest?"

"That they're kind of a physical representation of the way Buckler tells his story. The pieces of clothing are all woven together, and Buckler does the same thing with the lives of his characters. They're all interconnected, like the pieces of clothing in Ellen's rugs. Each piece reminds her of a particular moment in time, which got me thinking that, in a way, the novel is like one big rug, a patchwork of the experiences that made Buckler's characters who they are."

"Excellent point," said the teacher, and Willa saw Celia roll her eyes at Britney.

"Does anyone have anything to add to that?" asked Richardson. Glaring at Celia, Willa raised her hand.

"Willa?"

"Ellen always made her rugs out of scraps of things. She never used anything new, or anything whole."

"Did that have any significance for you?"

Willa tried to ignore Britney murmuring to Celia behind her hand. "Nothing is ever completely gone. It might be worn or tattered, but a part of it always remains, like in Ellen's rugs. Isn't that the same with the characters in the story? So many of them are influenced by events in their past. It's like they can't shrug them off and move on. They're continually shaped by them."

"Another excellent observation." The teacher looked toward the back of the room. "Yes, Wynn?"

"What Willa said. It made me think that maybe the rugs are bigger than just how they work in this story. They kind of represent the way our world is now."

"How so?"

"The rugs show how all the characters are connected to each other, right? Doesn't the Internet do the same thing?"

"Definitely, from a communication standpoint," agreed the teacher. "Can you bring that analogy back to the novel?"

"I was thinking about the sites that people post stuff on. The things they write about themselves. And the things they write about others. They're like the scraps that Ellen uses in her rugs."

"In what way?"

"The rugs last, right? Even when the actual clothes are gone, the rugs are still there, so the pieces of those clothes are still there. It's the same way with web pages. Anything that somebody puts online is there forever. Even if they delete it, it's still out there on a server somewhere, waiting for somebody else to uncover it, to find out stuff about them. Maybe even stuff they don't want other people to know."

There was something in his voice, something like the edge Willa had heard that day by his pool, and she turned to look at him, half-expecting to see him staring at her. But he wasn't. He was looking at Keegan, his eyes burning a hole in the back of Keegan's head.

And he was grinning.

+ + +

"Do you want me to come with you?" asked Keegan amid the recess chatter in the corridor.

Willa shook her head, thinking about Mr. Caldwell. The vice-principal's epic obsession with attendance and tardiness had grown even more pronounced during the past week. Because of the hot weather, a lot of students had been skipping classes, and Caldwell was even more vigilant about ferreting out offenders and assigning detentions. "I don't know how long this'll take," she said. "My dad'll write me a note if I'm going to be late getting back, but you could get into trouble."

He nodded. "Any idea what he wants?"

She shook her head, glancing again at the text she'd just received: *can u come to dealrshp now?* She was hoping it had something to do with Wynn, that maybe they'd be able to go to the police now, and she could see in Keegan's eyes that he was thinking the same thing.

She reached into her bag and pulled out her math assignment. "Would you give this to Shedrand if I don't make it back before the break ends?"

"Sure," he said. Taking it from her, he leaned down and kissed her.

"Cripes, you two. Get a room."

Willa turned and grinned at Russell's mock grimace. The guy never failed to make her smile. Although they didn't share any classes this semester, he usually managed to connect with them during their breaks, and she'd liked getting to know him, enjoyed his sense of humour. She wished she knew him better, though, because she'd been wanting to talk to him about his shirts. Like the one he wore today, which announced *When I go to the zoo, the elephants throw* me *peanuts*. She'd come to recognize them as his way of highlighting his size before anyone else could. She wanted to tell him that his size didn't define him, that he had so much more going for him. Besides that great sense of humour, he had a natural empathy, always seeming to know how others were feeling. And it was easy to see how much he liked Raven. Unfortunately, for all his empathy, Russell seemed completely clueless that the feeling appeared mutual, and Willa had been waiting for an opportunity to tell him. And to let him know that those shirts weren't necessary. He was so much more than any of those put-downs, something she wished she'd realized herself a long time ago.

Despite Russell's protestation, Willa gave Keegan another

kiss, then hurried toward the exit. Four minutes later, she was pulling the SUV into the Valley Motors parking lot. "My dad around?" she asked Bob Hartley when she entered the showroom.

"In his office with a client."

"I don't want to interrupt, but he asked to see me."

"I'll let him know you're here." He stepped into his office and Willa watched through the glass as he picked up his phone and spoke into it.

In a moment, her father appeared in the showroom. "Thanks for coming, sweetheart," he said, kissing her forehead. He took her hand and led her outside, the sun even more intense as it reflected off the rows of shiny new vehicles.

Her heart lifted at her father's obvious need for privacy, and he seemed to read on her face the conclusion she had drawn. "Sorry, Willa, this isn't about Wynn. I need your vehicle."

"What for?"

"I have a client in my office who's thinking of buying it. He wants to test-drive it today."

She glanced at the seven brand-new, same-model SUVs lined up at the far end of the parking lot, two of them black like hers. "Why doesn't he—"

"He's specifically interested in yours."

"How does he even know I have one?"

"Bob was talking to him initially. He may have said something about it. It's fully loaded, so that's probably what he's looking for. If he likes it, he's willing to pay the sticker price plus buy the extended warranty."

That was a surprise. Because she'd been driving it, the guy

was entitled to the dealer discount. Wouldn't he know that?

"Business being what it is," said her father, "I can't pass up the sale."

"It's okay," she said, handing him the key. She was surprised by the way she felt as he took it from her. As much as she'd hated the SUV the day her father had given it to her, she'd come to enjoy driving it. A lot. She thought again about Russell and how easily perceptions of people and things could change when you gave them a chance.

He reached into his pocket and pulled out another key, a fob dangling from it bearing the words "Valley Motors Courtesy Car." "Sorry, sweetheart. It's the best I can do. None of the vehicles on the lot are ready for long-term right now. If you can wait around, though, I can get one of the guys to—"

"No problem," she said. And it wasn't. The Sonic that the dealership loaned to clients whose vehicles were in for repairs was perfectly adequate. Tiny, but adequate. "What?" she said as he stared at her.

"Just wondering who stole my daughter and replaced her with you," he teased gently, obviously referring to her near-meltdown the first day of school.

She grinned and took the key from him. "Where's it parked?"

"Around back by the service entrance."

She stood on tiptoe to kiss his cheek, then turned to cut through the showroom—if she hurried, she could just make it back before the bell. Heading down the hallway, she saw a large man in the doorway of her father's office.

"Willa," said her father behind her, "this is Mr. Forrester. He's the person who's interested in your vehicle. Mr. Forrester, this is my daughter, Willa."

She looked up. Way up. Built like a linebacker, the man towered above her, seeming to fill the space. At first glance, he looked to be in his late twenties, but there was something about him—the way his eyes flickered over her, maybe—that made her question that estimate. "Nice to meet you," she said, holding out her hand, trying not to stare at the vivid scar that twisted diagonally from his chin to his right ear.

He took her hand but released it almost immediately, an odd expression on his face that Willa couldn't interpret. "Same here," he replied. "Sorry for any trouble I might be causin' you."

Willa thought she heard in his voice the trace of an accent. And he sounded younger than he looked. "No trouble at all," she said.

"Much appreciated," said the man, smiling. "I've been lookin' for a long time, and you've got just what I'm after."

As she turned to go, she had an odd feeling—there was something about his smile that seemed familiar, but she couldn't remember what. It wasn't until she was pulling into the schoolyard that it came to her. His smile looked like the one Wynn had worn in English class, as his eyes lasered the back of Keegan's head.

+ + +

They appeared to be waiting for her as she approached her locker. Willa hoped so. She was tired of the looks and the comments and the wedge that was Wynn solidly between them. Although the end-of-recess bell had just gone, she was willing to risk being late for Shedrand's class if it meant having the chance to put an end to all this. "Hi," she said.

But the looks she saw on both their faces told her nothing had changed.

"Still slumming?" asked Britney. There was something in her voice besides animosity, besides ridicule. Willa could hear beneath it a trace of the poutiness Britney always used when she was hurt. The implication? That Willa had intentionally set out to wound her, which she'd accomplished by turning her back on her real friends.

Celia, however, showed no similar softness. "You're going to regret this," she said.

"There's a lot that I regret," Willa sighed. "Look, you don't know the whole story."

"And you think *you* do?" Celia laughed, the sound almost shrill in the growing silence of the emptying corridor. "I always thought you were one of the smartest people I know, Willa."

"What's that supposed to mean?"

"You're making a mistake. A big one."

"It's the mistake I made five months ago that bothers me now."

Britney spoke up. "Wynn's the best thing that ever happened to you. I don't know why you can't see that."

"You don't know Wynn as well as you think you do." It was pointless trying to make them understand. She turned to her locker.

"Yeah, like you know Keegan Fraser," scoffed Celia. "No secrets there, right?"

Willa looked at her. "What are you trying to say?"

"It's better if we show you," said Britney.

+ + +

"Took you a lot longer than you thought, huh?" asked Keegan when he found Willa at her locker after school, students hurrying past them toward buses and cars. Then he seemed to notice the look on her face. "What's wrong?"

She'd intended to stay home, which was where she'd gone after Celia and Britney had shown her what they'd found. She was glad her mother hadn't returned from Halifax because she'd needed the privacy, crying for an hour. She'd managed to hold most of it in until she reached the Sonic, wiping the tears away as she drove, but she hadn't given in to it fully until she made it to her room. It was there that she wailed at the enormity of Keegan's deception. Eventually, she'd fallen asleep on her bed, then woken up an hour later and cried some more.

She'd intended to stay right where she was on that bed, too overwhelmed to even think of confronting him. But then she'd gotten into the shower, letting the hot water pulsate against her body for twenty minutes, easing her muscles, and when she'd finally shut it off, she was pissed.

*Trust me.*

She had. Just like she'd trusted Wynn. And look where that had gotten her. Again.

*I'm not who you think I am.*

No shit.

She'd arrived back at school in time to catch her last class, but she might as well have skipped it—she'd spent the whole period imagining this moment. And now it was here. "I know, Keegan," she said, struggling to control her anger. She had a lot to unleash, and she didn't want to dissolve in tears before she'd said all she had to say. *Needed* to say.

"Know what?"

"Everything. I know who you are."

His eyes widened.

"And don't pretend you have no idea what I'm talking about," she said. "The thefts, the violence, I know all of it."

"How?" His voice was a hoarse whisper.

"How do you *think*? Facebook."

His face blanched, and she took a grim pleasure in the effect her words were having on him. "Show me," he said.

It was the last thing she'd expected him to say. The *nerve* of him. She turned to walk away, afraid she'd do something she'd regret if she didn't.

She felt a tug on her arm, and she spun to face him. "Get your hands off me!" His eyes were wild now, and suddenly she felt fear of her own. She reached into her pocket for the pager her father had given her, only to remember it was in her other jeans, the ones she'd taken off when she'd showered. She glanced up and down the corridor, but it was deserted. And why *wouldn't* it be on a Friday afternoon?

"Please," he said, "show me what you found."

"Are you crazy?" After what she'd learned about him, there was a good chance he was. After all, she'd only known him a couple of weeks. Maybe he was even crazy enough to try something here. No, *she* was the crazy one for confronting him by herself. Maybe if she took out her phone to show him what he wanted to see, she could dial 911. But responders would take at least a few minutes to get there, and a lot could happen in those minutes. She needed to get to an adult. Fast. "I'll show you in the library."

Her heart sank when they arrived, but she shouldn't have been surprised to find it, too, deserted on a Friday afternoon. A note on the door from Ms. Ruggles said she'd return in a few minutes—librarian-speak for *I'm in the bathroom*—but Keegan didn't wait, pushing through the entrance.

She realized she'd have to humour him until Ruggles returned, so she headed toward the bank of computers, pointing to a chair.

"No," he said, dragging a hand through his hair, "you do it."

Willa glanced toward the door. Still no librarian. She forced herself to sit down, touching the monitor in front of her, which lit up with a login screen. She typed in her student number and password, then brought up the browser, opened Facebook, and located the page that Celia and Britney had shown her. She could hear Keegan's rapid breathing above her as he began to read.

"What—?" He reached over her and touched the screen, scrolling through the text.

As much as it hurt her, sickened her to read it again, she once more scanned the information that had been posted by a retired Vancouver nurse whose home had been robbed months earlier. A widow, she'd arrived home earlier than expected, interrupting the break-in. The burglar had beaten her badly, smashing out two of her teeth and leaving her with a concussion, a dislocated shoulder, several cracked ribs, and bruises over most of her body. The seventeen-year-old multiple offender had been apprehended quickly, yet, when the case went to court, he'd received a year's probation—"a slap on the wrist," wrote the former nurse, who still suffered from post-traumatic stress disorder and had lived in fear ever since, certain her attacker would return for his revenge.

In defiance of the Youth Criminal Justice Act, she had posted the teenager's name—Kevin Fredericks—and photo so others would be on the alert if they saw him. Willa had recognized the guy immediately. It was Keegan.

# CHAPTER 57

"This is what you were looking at on my laptop last night, isn't it?" demanded Willa.

Reading the information on the screen, Keegan wasn't surprised by the venom in her voice.

"Gloating over what you'd gotten away with?" Before he could answer, she continued, "You and Wynn must've been separated at birth."

"Willa, none of this is true. You have to believe me."

She glowered at him. "Yeah, because believing in liars has been working so well for me."

"I'm not lying. Somebody made all this up."

"Is your name Keegan Fraser?"

Anger and disbelief blazed like twin bonfires in her eyes, and he knew he had only one chance. She would know if he tried to lie. "No," he said softly.

"And yet none of this stuff here is true," she said, her words seared with scorn. She turned away, and he could tell she didn't want him to see the tears that threatened. "You disgust me."

"Willa, please," he said, "I know how it looks, but—"

"I don't give a damn how it *looks*. I only care how it *is*," she said, and he could see she was about to get up.

He moved closer, towering over her so she couldn't stand, and he saw her flinch, saw something else join the anger and disbelief. She'd turned to the doorway, and he knew she was looking for the librarian.

"Please, Willa," he begged, dismayed by the realization that she could fear him, *did* fear him. "I'm not that guy! I'm *not* Kevin Fredericks!"

Turning back to the computer, she jabbed her finger at the screen. "Isn't that *you?*" She pointed to the photo of him standing outdoors, the easy grin on his face suggesting what he already knew—he was unaware of being photographed. "See the caption?" she asked. "'Taken outside the courthouse.' No wonder you were smiling. A slap on the wrist must've felt pretty good compared to what they could have given you. *Should* have given you."

Seeing her look toward the doorway again, he could tell she was no longer willing the librarian to return. She was looking for a chance to bolt. Keegan fought the urge to put his hands on her shoulders to keep her in that chair. Instead, he leaned over her again, peering more closely at the screen. And then he saw it. "Look," he said, pointing at the bottom left corner of the photo.

Willa continued to face the door.

"*Please*, Willa. *Look!*"

Cringing from the intensity of his voice, Willa turned toward the monitor. "What do you want me to—"

He dragged his fingers across the screen, doubling the size of the image he was pointing at. In the photo, he was standing beside a black vehicle, only a small portion of which could be seen.

She leaned closer to the monitor. "Is that—" She enlarged the photo even more. On the back of the vehicle was a sticker bearing a stylized V and M. The logo of Valley Motors. "It's the SUV from my dad's dealership. How——?"

"That photo was taken here in Brookdale." He zoomed out again, pointing to the corner of a building in the background. "And look. That's my house. I'm standing in my driveway."

Willa turned to him, her face furrowed with confusion.

"I've never been to Vancouver, Willa."

She looked at the image again, clearly trying to reconcile what she'd seen with what she thought she knew. "But you *came* here from Vancouver."

"That was our cover, a story they created for us."

"Who?"

He shook his head. "It's better if you don't know."

"Look, a few minutes ago I told you I'd found out about the thefts and the violence, and you asked me how I knew. You're caught up in something, aren't you? Something bad. What is it, Keegan?" She frowned, tears springing again to her eyes. "Or *whatever* your name is."

He could hear his father in his head warning him once more against doing the very thing he'd longed to since their afternoon together at the look-off. "It doesn't matter what my name is. You just have to know that I would never do anything like this." He pointed at the monitor. "Trust me."

She wiped savagely at fresh tears on her face. "Like I trusted Wynn?"

He winced.

"Tell me this, then," she said. "What were you looking at last night in my bedroom?"

"What do you mean?"

"You were on my laptop and then deleted the browser history. What were you looking at?"

"It's not important."

"It's important to me. If you want me to start believing you, tell me. If you don't, I'm out of here."

A part of Keegan knew now that his father was right, the part that had lived in fear for months, terrified by what had happened and what still lay out there waiting for them. But there was another part, the part he'd thought was gone but had come roaring back to him in that cottage on Delusion Road. That was the part he listened to now. "I was on Facebook. I wanted to check on somebody."

"Who?"

"Someone I knew from before I came here."

"*Who?*"

He sat down in the chair beside her, taking her hands in his. She flinched, pulling away. "A girl," he said. "Her name's Talia."

She said nothing, her silence its own condemnation.

"She was—" He paused, unsure now what to say. So much could happen that changed what you thought you knew, what you thought you felt. "She was someone I cared for."

Willa looked down, but not before he saw fresh pain in her eyes. "Do you still care for her?"

Keegan didn't want to make her flinch again, but he reached out anyway and gently raised her face toward his the way he often did with Isaac. "Not like I used to," he said softly. "Not like I thought I did."

The lines on her face changed direction. "Then why were you—"

"On her Facebook page? I wanted to make sure she'd moved on. This thing between you and me, I couldn't feel good about it if I wasn't sure she was okay, too."

This seemed to satisfy her for a moment. But then, "Why not just call or message her? Why use my laptop to creep on her?"

"I can't have contact with her."

He felt her draw back again. "What did you *do* to her?"

"I didn't do anything, Willa. None of what happened had anything to do with me."

"*What* happened?"

"I can't tell you. It's not safe for you to know."

"You're scaring me," she said, her voice suddenly small.

"I'm glad." Seeing her grow more alarmed, he knew he had to tell her some of it, the part that would make her understand. "There are people after my family, Willa."

"The police?"

"*No*," he insisted, his voice more forceful than he'd intended. "Bad people. *Very* bad."

"Why?"

"It doesn't matter. What's important is that no one can know we're in Brookdale."

Willa's eyes widened and she pointed at the monitor. "What about that?"

"It's okay. It says I'm in Vancouver."

She scrolled to the bottom, and the place where people could post comments came into view. There was only one, probably written by whoever had shown the page to Willa: *This asshole now calls himself Keegan Fraser and he's living in Brookdale, Nova Scotia.*

"Christ!" Keegan groaned. He jumped up, felt tears of his own threaten. His father had been right all along. "We have to leave."

"Why?" asked Willa, standing with him.

"They'll find us."

"How?" she asked. "If you're not Kevin Fredericks or Keegan Fraser, anybody looking for you would never find this page."

He pointed at the photo. "They would with facial recognition software. That's why my dad doesn't have a car. He couldn't chance getting a driver's licence because they would've found his picture in the DMV database. And it's only a matter of time before they see this—" He froze. "Oh, no," he moaned.

"What?"

"I used your laptop to check out Talia's Facebook page. They'll have your IP address."

"But tons of people probably click on her page." Then realization shuddered through her. "If they know you're in Brookdale—" She didn't finish. Didn't need to.

"May I help you two?" They turned to see Ms. Ruggles in the doorway.

"We're just leaving," said Keegan, reaching for Willa's hand and tugging her behind him. They brushed past the librarian and started down the corridor, but Keegan stopped. "Wait!" he said, and darted back into the library. He could feel Ms. Ruggles's eyes on him as he clicked off that Facebook page, then deleted the browser's history. Deep down, though, he knew it was a wasted effort—people all over town were probably posting links to that page now, increasing the likelihood that *they* would find it.

Back in the corridor, he said, "I have to warn my dad. What's the dealership's number? I should know it, but—"

She told him and he punched it in, listening to the automated voice list the directory of employees. When he reached his father's office, the phone rang several times before going to voicemail. He clicked it off. "He's not there. Is there someone else who—"

She took the phone from him, calling the dealership again. "Hi, Shirley. I'm looking for Dad's accountant, Mr. Fraser. Can you—" She listened for a moment, then thanked her and hung up. "He went home at noon."

Keegan nodded. "He walks home to eat lunch. For the exercise."

"But he didn't come back, Keegan. No one's seen him since. And he didn't call in."

An ice pick lodged itself in Keegan's chest. "I have to go," he rasped, turning and running for the exit.

He heard her running behind him. "It'll be faster if we take my car," she called.

Bursting through the exit door into the sunshine, they veered toward the parking lot. When they reached it, there were only two vehicles left, and he saw that neither of them was—

"This one," she told him, running toward a small blue car. She hit the remote entry button on her key and they piled in.

Willa started the vehicle and shifted into drive, both their heads snapping back as she floored the gas. Whipping the car into the street, she asked, "You know who posted that page, right?"

Keegan hadn't had time to think of it, but now he nodded. "Wynn," he said.

"Wynn," she echoed, her voice a jagged knife. "That miserable son of a bitch."

In less than a minute, she tore into Keegan's driveway, and he was out of the car before it even stopped moving, bounding up the front steps. Finding the door unlocked, he pushed inside, his senses assaulted by the damage he found. The living room was a shambles: furniture overturned, the coffee table broken, pieces of a puzzle scattered everywhere. A lamp lay on its side on the hardwood floor, and for a moment Keegan's brain couldn't make sense of its colour. It was supposed to be brown, but from this angle it looked red. And then he saw it was lying in a pool of something. That pool was red, too.

"My God." He felt Willa beside him, a hand on his arm. "My God," she repeated, the soles of her shoes making soft squeaking sounds.

He stared uncomprehendingly at her feet, her sneakers pressing scattered puzzle pieces against the hardwood. Puzzle pieces. Puzzle— "I have to get Isaac!" Turning his back on the ravaged room, he headed for the door, Willa on his heels.

Back in the car, he fought the sobs that threatened to undo him and managed to tell her about the after-school program at Brookdale Elementary, and he slumped back in the seat as Willa gunned the car in that direction. As she drove, he was grateful for her stunned silence, which he used to try to get himself under control. He couldn't go into the school looking like this. His appearance would alarm the adults and, worse, upset Isaac.

When they arrived moments later, Keegan thought he could do this. Taking deep breaths and dragging a sleeve across his face, he got out and forced himself not to run through the school's entrance. Arriving at the gymnasium, he found Ms. Tomlinson among the adults supervising the students, most of them playing a game his shock-numbed brain couldn't identify. Isaac, of course, wasn't part of that activity. He sat in the far corner amid several brightly coloured plastic disks, Ms. Tomlinson kneeling beside him chatting. Looking up, she gave Keegan her usual broad smile and got to her feet.

As he approached, though, her smile faltered. "Is everything all right, Keegan?" she asked.

He nodded, afraid to acknowledge whatever it was about him that she'd seemed to notice. "Hey, buddy," he said softly as he squatted beside his brother. "Time to go."

Isaac, of course, gave no indication he'd heard him, merely reached for another disk and added it to one of three rows he'd made.

Keegan tried again. "Isaac, we have to leave." He expected to have to repeat himself, to take Isaac's chin in his hand and establish eye contact to draw him back from wherever he was in his head, but his brother surprised him. He looked up.

Keegan passed him his outdoor shoes and was relieved to see him begin putting them on. He turned to Ms. Tomlinson. "I'd help you clean this up, but—"

"No need," said the EA. She held out Isaac's knapsack.

"Thanks," he said, taking it. He knew he'd never see her again and he wanted to say more, wanted to tell her how much he appreciated the way she'd cared for his brother, but there wasn't time. He took Isaac's hand and led him out.

Keegan expected to have to do some major convincing to get his brother into the unfamiliar car, but Isaac surprised him again. Once he saw Willa behind the wheel, he opened the back door and climbed in. As Keegan reached across him for the seatbelt, Isaac's eyes never left her, ignoring Keegan as he drew the belt down and fastened it.

"What now?" asked Willa as he got into the front seat. "Call 911?"

Keegan shook his head. "They might be monitoring emergency calls in this area."

"Then what do we do?"

Keegan had no idea. He couldn't keep his mind from returning to their living room, to that overturned lamp that used to be brown. "Just drive, okay?"

He'd been such a fool to think they could ever be safe, to think he could have a life here or anywhere else. The night before last as he'd lain on his bed doing homework, he'd even let himself make plans, his thoughts wandering again and again to Willa and the part she would play in them. He'd had to force himself to concentrate on those last few chapters of *The Mountain and the Valley*. Watching the streets slide by now, choking back the fear that threatened to engulf him, Keegan realized that book had been a warning of sorts. He just hadn't recognized it at the time.

It was the first novel he'd ever read where the main character died at the end.

# CHAPTER 58

Willa forced him to tell her everything. And if she hadn't seen the condition of his living room, she might have thought Keegan was summarizing a movie, one of those crime dramas that included a parental advisory about violent content. But even if she *hadn't* seen that living room, the call Keegan placed to a guy named Forbes made the whole thing blood-chillingly real.

The moment they'd left the elementary school, Keegan had pulled out his phone, but his hands were trembling so badly he'd messed up the number three times before banging the cell against the armrest again and again, cursing.

"I have hands-free," she'd told him, grateful she'd paired her phone with the car's Bluetooth that morning. She pressed a button on the steering wheel, and an automated voice said, "Number, please."

Keegan had spoken the number slowly, and after the voice asked for confirmation, the connection was made. A man had answered almost immediately. "Special Agent Forbes."

Keegan had opened his mouth to speak, but suddenly he was sobbing and Willa had had to leap in, telling what little she knew. The FBI agent had immediately given her the third degree, but eventually he'd seemed satisfied she was no threat. He'd asked her if there was someplace safe she could take Keegan and his brother and she told him yes. She'd been about to give him the location, but he'd cut her off. "Can you tell me without telling me?" he'd asked, and she realized what he was saying, the warning he was giving her. She'd thought for a moment. "Fundy," she'd said finally, hoping the agent had access to her parents' information. He did. A few seconds later, he'd said, "Got it. I'll coordinate with local law enforcement and send support there as soon as I get Canadian clearance. You're sure it's safe?"

"I'm sure. Is it okay if I phone my dad and tell—"

"Too dangerous. You can call him after the team arrives." His next words hadn't been for her. "Keegan," he'd said, his voice strong, confident, "we'll find your dad. I promise." And then the connection was broken.

Willa had continued to drive, unsure what to say. Keegan was no longer sobbing, but he'd given no indication he'd heard Forbes's comment. "That was reassuring," she offered, trying to sound as positive as she could.

But Keegan had turned to the window. "He just said they'd find him. He didn't promise they'd find him alive."

She'd had nothing to say to that, and she'd driven in silence for a few minutes before once more trying to get him talking, to keep him talking. She was hoping that the energy involved in explaining would keep his mind from that scene back at his house, the blood on the floor, but she was unprepared for the story he shared with her, for the loss that had followed his family and then all but destroyed it.

They had been living in a well-to-do area of Chicago until his father had lost his job as a result of corporate downsizing when the markets tanked—"increasing shareholders' profits at the expense of employees," Keegan told her, his voice a muted monotone. And because of the lousy economy, no one was hiring and his father had gone without work for months, depleting their savings before forfeiting on car payments, mortgage, everything. They'd lost it all.

And then a ray of hope—his father had gotten a job with a trucking outfit on the West Side owned by a guy named Battaglia. Less than a month later, the feds contacted him.

"The feds?" Willa asked Keegan.

"A special task force. They'd had Battaglia on their radar for a long time."

"What'd they want your dad to do?"

"To keep an eye out for anything that didn't seem right. To call them if he found something."

"And he did?"

"He was getting ready for an audit, and he discovered problems with some of the accounts, money that didn't seem to jibe. My mom—" He turned toward the window again.

"Were she and your dad still together then?"

He nodded.

"How'd she feel about him reporting to the feds?"

He didn't answer right away, the silence spooling out as the Sonic ate up the road, and Willa began to wonder if Keegan had heard the question. Then he spoke. "She said he shouldn't get involved, that he was lucky to have a job. They—" He stopped, and seconds passed before he continued. "They argued about it. A lot. But he called the FBI anyway."

Willa understood now. "So that's why she left him." When he offered no comment, she struggled to keep the conversation going. "What happened then?"

She watched as he raised a hand to the window, his index finger moving against the glass as if following a pattern visible only to him. "My dad traced the money to a guy named Pavel Morozov."

"Morozov," she repeated. Why did that name sound familiar?

"Calls himself a businessman, but he's into everything. Drugs, racketeering, prostitution, weapons smuggling, the whole nine yards."

Now it came to her—she'd seen something about him in the newspaper. "Wasn't he indicted for something?"

Keegan shook his head. "He was arrested, but the case they had against him fell apart. Their witness—" It was like he couldn't say the words. But he didn't have to.

"What did your dad have to do with Morozov?"

"He figured out how Morozov used Battaglia's company to launder his drug money. He collected evidence that proved it."

"Wasn't he worried they'd find out?"

"The feds said they'd protect us."

Willa needed a moment to let everything she'd heard sink in, but she was reluctant to let silence fill the car again. "When did all this happen?" she asked.

"The end of March."

"So your father's already testified against Morozov."

"No."

"Why not?"

There was a long pause before Keegan replied. "Dad refused to until the feds got us set up with new identities, and it took time working with Canadian authorities to place us here."

"But why Canada? Why not just stay in the States?"

"After what happened, they figured we'd be safer out of the country."

Willa waited for him to say more, but he didn't. "After *what* happened?"

He turned to the window again, his finger moving slowly against the glass once more. "Battaglia suspected something." He paused again, as if getting everything straight in his head. "Forbes figures that Morozov had cops on his payroll, but the FBI didn't know it then. They made that connection after."

"After what?"

His index finger curled into his palm with the others, his hand now a fist pressed hard against the glass. "After they killed my mother."

The car's right tires dropped onto the shoulder, gravel and dust billowing behind them as Willa fought to get them back on the pavement, and her hands were trembling when she finally got the vehicle evened out. But not from their near accident. She wanted to respond, wanted to say she was sorry, but it didn't seem enough. "Keegan—" she began, but she had no more words.

"Morozov's men blew up the house we were renting. Made it look like a gas leak. She was the only one inside."

Willa didn't have to look at him to know he was struggling with the memory.

"All four of us would've been killed if my dad hadn't left

earlier than usual that day. They'd been arguing again, and my dad got fed up, stormed out. He usually gave Isaac and me a drive to school—" He made a sound like his throat was closing over, and she knew he was sobbing again, silently this time.

Willa's hands gripped the steering wheel as she remembered their first day in Shedrand's class, how instead of copying notes Keegan had been drawing a campfire. But it wasn't. She'd just seen him draw and redraw the same thing on the window, and she now knew it for what it was. She thought of those flames, his mother trapped inside them, and she struggled against a sob that crowded her own throat.

"You know what the worst part is?" said Keegan after a long moment, his voice thick.

Can there *be* a worst part? thought Willa. "What?" she asked, dreading his answer.

"One of the last things my dad said to me was that he knew I didn't care what happened to him."

Yes, she decided, there *is* a worst part.

"But he was wrong," said Keegan. And then he was sobbing again, his hands over his face, his shoulders quaking.

Something flapped in the back seat. Her vision blurred by tears of her own, Willa looked in the rear-view mirror, shocked to find that she'd forgotten all about Isaac. He'd been completely silent the whole time, motionless behind her, but no longer. His arms bent toward his chest, he flapped his hands repeatedly, whimpering.

"Keegan?" she said. "What's happening?"

The sobs beside her diminished, and Keegan pulled up the bottom of his shirt, wiping his face with it. When he spoke, his voice was like gravel. "He's stimming," he explained. "He does it when he gets overwhelmed. It's my fault." He turned toward the back, rearranging his features into an expression that was supposed to be reassuring but, to Willa's mind, looked grim. "Hey, buddy," he said softly, "it's okay. Everything's gonna be okay."

But Willa could see in the mirror that Isaac wasn't convinced, his hands flapping faster and faster. The sounds he was making seemed less like whimpers now, their rise and fall becoming more distinct, almost repetitive. And then she recognized they *were* repetitive, the same series of sounds coming again and again. But they were more than just sounds. They were words. Numbers.

". . . two eight dot one nine four dot two five three dot one one seven dot one two eight dot one nine four dot two five three dot one one seven dot one two eight dot one nine . . ."

"What's he saying?"

Keegan didn't reply, and when she pulled her eyes momentarily from the road to glance at him, she saw astonishment ripple across his face. "I don't know," he said finally, his words hushed, almost reverent. "I've never seen him do this. He doesn't speak."

"Never?"

"A little when he was younger, but not for a long time."

". . . one two eight dot one nine four dot two five three dot one one . . ."

"What do you think it means? It's the same sequence over and over, right? Is it some kind of phone number?"

"Two many digits. Unless it's an international number, but then there's those dots." He shook his head. "I have no idea."

Willa remembered what Keegan had said about his brother the afternoon she had driven him back from the look-off, a moment that seemed a million years ago now. "You told me you think he understands everything. He just doesn't have ways to show people what's in his head, right?" Looking at Isaac in the mirror again, she asked, "Do you think this has something to do with your father?"

"Maybe," said Keegan. "I don't know how, but maybe."

As Willa turned the car north and the Sonic began climbing the mountain, the boy continued to recite the pattern only he could understand.

# CHAPTER 59

As the car bounced along the gravelled surface of Delusion Road, Keegan was both relieved and troubled that his brother had suddenly stopped talking. Relieved for obvious reasons—hearing that sequence repeated over and over had frayed his nerves, made him want to press his hands to his ears, turn on loud music, shout, anything to drown out those numbers that cycled through the vehicle again and again. But troubled, too, because he couldn't help wondering if his brother would ever speak again. As Keegan watched the trees crowd in upon the vehicle, he knew he had far more pressing things to worry about right now, but still there was that echoing sense of loss.

"We're here, Isaac," said Willa, turning the car into the driveway. "I was hoping to bring you sometime anyway, so maybe we can have some fun while we wait, okay?"

The car rolled to a stop in front of the cottage, and even before Willa had shut off the motor, Keegan was out and leaning in the rear door to unfasten Isaac's seat belt. "C'mon, buddy," he said. "You'll like this place." He turned and looked toward the bay, large whitecaps rolling across its choppy surface.

As Isaac got out, Willa came to stand beside them, her hair

whipping out behind her in the brisk wind. "Do you think he'd like something to drink? I'm parched."

"Yeah, I think he would." He took Isaac's hand and led his brother up onto the deck.

"That's weird," said Willa when they reached the entrance.

"What?"

Her hand turned the doorknob. "I thought I locked this before we left."

He was about to assure her she had when the door abruptly swung inward. "Took you long enough," said a hulking figure towering in the foyer.

By itself, the scar on the large man's face would have made him seem menacing enough, but it was the gun in his hand that turned Keegan's legs to liquid. Instinctively, he stepped in front of Isaac to shield him while, beside him, Willa stood stunned and motionless, gaping at the guy with what looked like recognition on her face.

"I ain't got all day," the figure growled, waving them inside with the gun. "Get the fuck in here."

There was nothing else they could do. Keegan led the way, Isaac sandwiched between him and Willa.

As he entered the living room, Keegan's heart leaped. "Dad!" he cried, seeing his father sitting in one of the wooden dining chairs. His arms were pulled behind him, clearly bound, and his dress shirt was covered in blood from the beating he'd endured— his face was a pulpy mass of abrasions, one eye swollen shut and his right ear mangled. Keegan saw a bloodied pair of pliers on the table beside him, and his stomach dropped.

"Keegan," moaned Evan, blood seeping from his mouth. "I'm—I'm so sorry."

"So *now* you're sorry," muttered the guy with the scar. "Asshole, you don't know the *meanin'* of sorry. But you will."

Something in the way he spoke, the way the heat in his words made his threat sound somehow personal, made Keegan realize the guy was younger than he'd first thought, no more than three or four years older than himself. *This* was the killer Morozov had sent for them? Maybe they had a chance after all.

"Please," Evan slurred through the blood, "don't hurt them."

"I won't have to if they give me what I want."

"They don't know anything."

"Then I guess we'll have to go with Plan B, won't we?"

Evan struggled against his bonds and the scarred guy brandished the gun meaningfully. "Sit still and shut the fuck up."

"How'd you know we'd come here?" asked Willa.

Keegan turned to her, surprised by her question and even more surprised by the calm in her voice. But he could guess what was going through her mind—like him, she was thinking of the support that Forbes was sending, hoping to keep the guy talking as long as she could.

The guy grinned, making the scar on his face contort repulsively. "I test drove your car this mornin', remember? Downloaded your GPS data and found out where you'd been the last few days. This place is so far off the beaten path it was a given you'd run here. But even if you hadn't shown up, it's still a great place to have a conversation." He gave Evan an exaggerated wink. "No one around for miles to hear the screams."

"Why'd you go after *her*?" asked Keegan. He already knew

the answer, but he was taking Willa's cue, trying to keep the guy yakking. He also needed to derail that talk of screams, struggled to keep his eyes from drifting to the pliers.

The scarred guy sighed. "I knew it was only a matter 'a time before you checked out your girlfriend back in Chicago, even if you used somebody else's computer to do it." There was a slight softening in his voice as he continued, "I can see why, though. Talia's quite the girl."

"You stay the hell away from her!"

The guy's ruined face registered amusement. "Look around, asswipe. You ain't exactly in a position to tell me what to do, are you? Besides, don't you worry about Talia. I'm gonna take real good care of her for you."

The thought of that monster anywhere near Talia made Keegan's heart lurch. But before he could respond, a sudden pounding on the door shattered the moment. Forbes's men already? Hope rose like wings in Keegan's chest—

"Open this fucking door! I know you're in there!"

—only to vanish when he recognized the voice.

The scarred guy was faster than his size suggested, and he was at the door before Keegan was even aware he'd moved, the gun in his hand still pointed at all of them. As the pounding resumed, he yanked open the door and the new arrival stumbled inside.

Wynn d'Entremont blinked at the scene before him, trying to make sense of what he was seeing, but the scarred guy grabbed him by the shoulder and shoved him forward into the room. "Join the party, asshole!"

Wynn moved as if wading in deep water, unsure of his footing, and whatever emotion had drawn him to follow Willa's car to Delusion Road was gone, replaced by fear. Keegan could see it on his face, the same fear that was on all their faces. Except that of the scarred guy. He just looked pissed.

"Uh," Wynn began, "whatever's going on here, I don't have anything to do with—"

"Shut up," growled the guy with the scar. "Gimme your car keys."

"My what?"

"You heard me."

Wynn fumbled in his pocket, finally producing his keys and handing them over, his trembling fingers making them jangle on the ring. "Look," he continued, "I don't know what the deal is here and I don't *wanna* know. I'm just an innocent bystand—"

"I said shut the fuck up!" The gun still covering all of them, the scarred guy stepped to a window and opened it, wind off the bay making the curtains billow crazily. Punching his fist through the screen, he tossed the keys out, and Keegan thought he could hear a splash before the sash slid back down.

"Please!" Wynn's voice took on a pleading tone, and a part of Keegan—perhaps the only part not paralyzed by the horror of their situation—wished Russell and Greg could hear him now. "Let me go. My dad's an important—"

The butt of the gun struck Wynn squarely on the side of the head, and Brookdale's star athlete went down like a bag of rocks, blood already seeping from his temple as he lay in a heap on the floor. Only the shallow rise and fall of his chest showed he was still breathing.

"As much fun as all this is," said the scarred guy, "I figure it won't be long before we have some other visitors, so let's get down to business, okay?"

"Business?" asked Keegan, surprised he still had a voice. He'd put his hands on Isaac's shoulders and was gently turning his brother's body into his own, keeping him from looking at the unconscious figure on the floor and muffling the boy's rising moans against his shirt.

The scarred guy sighed heavily, clearly bored. "Your old man has somethin' I need, but he's havin' trouble rememberin' where it is. To tell you the truth, he's held out a lot longer than I thought he would."

Keegan tried not to think of the pain his father had already suffered. "That's because he doesn't know anything," he said.

"Really? You're goin' with that?" The man turned his scarred face toward Evan again and shrugged. "Guess it's time for Plan B."

"Plan B?" asked Willa. Once again, Keegan was astonished by her composure. She had seemed so fragile in the library, and he could only imagine the effort it was taking for her to maintain the calm she projected now.

Without warning, the scarred guy pivoted and grabbed her, one massive arm around her throat as he held the gun to her head, and whatever composure she'd displayed was gone as she gasped and struggled to break free.

And whatever slim chance Keegan thought they might've had now vanished. But he had to try something. Gently moving Isaac aside, he took a step forward. The gun, now pointed at his face, stopped him.

"Sorry, sweetheart," the scarred guy hissed in Willa's ear, "but

I'm workin' my way up the food chain. You and that asshole on the floor there are what's called least leverage. Since he's outta commission, you're on tap." He looked at Evan again. "I got zero problem puttin' a bullet in this one. Now, are you gonna tell me what I wanna know or not?"

"Tell him!" Keegan pleaded.

Evan's good eye blinked sadly. "He's not letting any of us go, son. You have to know that."

"Dad, please!"

"Looks like somebody needs some convincin'," the scarred guy muttered. He tightened his arm, making the cords in Willa's neck bulge as he pressed the muzzle of the gun against her temple. Her face began to redden and she flailed at his arm, but her efforts had no effect. She was choking.

"Please—" Keegan begged again, then sensed sudden movement behind him.

"What's he doing?" snarled the scarred guy.

Looking around, Keegan saw that Isaac had begun to stim again, his hands flapping wildly. "He's autistic. He can't help it."

"I don't give a shit. Make him stop."

"Listen, buddy," said Keegan, his heart hammering as he knelt before his brother, "you need to settle down, okay? Everything's gonna be all right."

Isaac clearly knew otherwise. His hands flapped harder.

"I said make him *stop!*"

Keegan looked up. "He's upset. He does this when he's stressed."

"Then it's a good thing I got a surefire stress suppressor here."

The gun was aimed at Isaac now.

"Please!" Keegan pleaded, standing and stepping in front of his brother. "Don't!"

"One two eight dot one nine four dot two five three dot one one seven dot one two eight dot one nine four dot two five . . ."

Keegan saw his father's good eye widen, and then he heard him groan.

The scarred guy grinned. Turning to Evan, he said, "Looks like your bad memory ain't gonna be a problem after all."

Keegan could see he had eased his grip on Willa, who was eyeing a pair of heavy brass candlesticks on either end of the mantel, one of them almost within her reach. If only he could distract the guy. "Those numbers mean something?" he asked.

The guy grinned even more broadly, the scar on his cheek writhing. "Seems your old man here scanned some documents and uploaded them as insurance to a secure server somewhere. I know my way around a computer, and my boss has a lotta other talented guys on his payroll, but no one's been able to track 'em. I figure he used a combination of onion routing and mirror sites to do it." He glanced at Evan. "The feds show you how to do that?" When Evan didn't reply, he continued, "Don't matter. We know you ain't handed the stuff over to them yet or Morozov would have been arrested by now. He figures you were makin' sure the feds got the three of you set up safe first. Was he right?" Evan nodded and the scarred guy turned to Keegan again, clearly pleased with himself. "We needed that IP address, and it looks like we just got it." He spun Willa around to face him. "My laptop's in my car. Show me a computer."

"There isn't one here," she said, rubbing her throat and

coughing, and Keegan saw her use the movement to disguise the small step she took toward the mantel.

"Liar," the scarred guy snorted. "Like you could last ten minutes without one."

"There's no Internet."

"Bullshit. Everybody's got Internet."

"Not on Delusion Road," she said.

He scowled, reaching into his pocket and pulling out a phone.

"No cell service, either," said Willa.

He held it up. "Christ!"

His eyes on the phone's display, he didn't see Willa move closer to the mantel. Keegan held his breath as her hand inched toward the candlestick, then grabbed it. She swung as hard as she could.

Because of the guy's much greater height, the heavy brass object glanced off his jaw rather than the side of his head, but it was enough to throw him off balance. *"Fuck!"* he bellowed, swaying to his left and nearly dropping to one knee. Enraged, he brought the gun back up to point at Willa but, in that brief moment when all his attention was directed toward her, he didn't see Keegan leap.

Tackling him, Keegan propelled him backward against the mantel and they went down in a mass of thrashing arms and legs, the gun knocked to the floor. The scarred guy grabbed for it but Keegan kicked it away, the weapon sliding easily across the polished hardwood as he scrambled to his feet. But the scarred guy was faster, and he landed a haymaker to Keegan's midsection that doubled him over. Gasping for breath, he looked up to see the guy lift the poker from its hook, raising it high overhead. Keegan closed his eyes and prayed it would be quick for all of them.

"Drop it!"

Keegan opened his eyes again and saw Willa pointing the gun at the guy. She gripped it with two hands, both of them shaking.

"I said *drop* it! Or I'll blow your goddamn head off!"

The guy glared at her, then lowered the poker to the floor. As Keegan got to his feet, he could see the guy's expression had changed. He was smiling. "From the way you're holdin' that thing, sweetheart," he said, "I'm guessin' you don't know much about guns."

"I know which end the bullets come out of, asshole."

He smiled again. "There's a whole lot more you need to know than just pointin'. Like recoil, for instance. How it can affect your aim."

Keegan watched the guy's body shift incrementally toward her. "Willa," he warned as the scarred guy continued, his voice smooth, almost hypnotic.

"And then there's the matter 'a mechanism. Most guys in my line 'a work prefer semis, but I've always liked a forty-five, like that double-action you're holdin' there. It's got great balance, but you gotta be careful how—"

Willa pulled the trigger, the explosion deafening as a bullet winged into the wall to the guy's left, the acrid smell of gunpowder now filling the room. Keegan could see her hands were shaking now almost as fast as Isaac's were flapping. "Stay back!" she shouted. "I know what you're doing. Don't move a muscle."

The scarred guy froze, the smile on his face a sudden slash.

"Sweetheart, this'll end a whole lot easier for you if you don't make me mad. I gotta thing about blonds."

A second bullet whizzed past him within an arm's length. "Shut up and sit your ass down or the next one will be in your crotch!" Willa gestured with the gun at a chair behind him.

The guy with the scar stared at her for a long moment, then sat.

Isaac's hands were a blur as he recited the IP address at warp speed. Clutching his stomach, Keegan moved toward his brother, doing his best to murmur soothing words. Uncharacteristically, Isaac leaned into him, his face pressed to Keegan's shirt, and Keegan resisted the urge to hold him. "Dad needs us," he said softly. He led Isaac to Evan, weaving around Wynn's still unconscious form, and then knelt by their father, untying the rope around his wrists.

Both Evan's eyes leaked tears. "I'm so sorry, son. I never meant—"

"I know," said Keegan. "We need to get you to a doctor."

Evan shook his head. "We need to call Forbes."

"Done," said Keegan. "He's sending help."

Wincing, Evan gingerly pulled himself to his feet. "This guy's car is parked down the road where you wouldn't see it." He limped toward the seated figure. Although Willa still had the gun pointed at the guy, Evan kept his distance. "I want your keys. Now."

The scarred guy ignored him.

Willa waved the gun. "Give him your keys! I wasn't kidding about your crotch."

Despite the gravity of the moment, Keegan grinned at Willa's fierceness. After today, he thought, Wynn d'Entremont had better watch his sorry ass.

Scowling, the scarred guy reached slowly into his pocket, fumbling for a long moment before finally pulling out a key ring, tossing it to Keegan's dad. His reflexes impaired, Evan missed, and he gasped as he stooped to pick it up.

"I got it, Dad," said Keegan, reaching for it and handing it to his father, never taking his eyes off the scarred guy, who seemed to be studying their every move.

Wavering on his feet, Evan said, "It isn't safe here. There could be more coming." He looked at Wynn on the floor. "I'm not sure what to do about him."

Remembering how Wynn had begged to be let go, to hell with the rest of them, Keegan kicked the guy in the ass. Wynn groaned. Keegan kicked him a second time, and Wynn's eyes fluttered open.

"Get up," ordered Keegan.

Wynn turned to see the scarred guy sitting in the chair, Willa covering him with the gun. He pulled himself slowly to his feet, clutching the side of his head and groaning again. "What the hell—"

"Just so you know," Keegan snarled, "this is your fault. You nearly got us all killed!"

Evan put a hand on Keegan's arm. "There'll be time for that later. Right now, I want you to take him, your brother, and Willa and drive until you get a signal, then call Forbes again. He'll tell you what to do. I'll wait here for the people he's sending."

Keegan shook his head. "You're hurt. I'm not leaving you."

Evan sighed. "The only other choice is for all of us to drive out of here together."

"*Nuh*-uh," said Willa. "No *way* am I getting into a car with that freak." Although her hands were steadier than before, Keegan could still see them tremble. The weight of the gun wasn't helping. He considered offering to take it from her, but he was pretty sure what her response would be.

"Maybe we could just tie him up and leave him here," suggested Willa.

"He's a professional," said Evan. "He'd be out of here in minutes."

Keegan had another option. "Dad, you need a doctor, and Isaac is traumatized." He nodded toward his brother, who remained by the chair where their father had been tied, his open eyes unseeing. "Forbes's support shouldn't be much longer now. You take Isaac, Willa, and Wynn and go make that phone call. I'll wait here with him."

"*No!*" said Evan. "I'm not leaving you alone with that—that monster."

"I'll stay," said Willa. Wynn, however, said nothing. He moved toward the door and stepped outside without looking back.

Keegan turned to her. "No. This isn't your fight."

"Seriously?" she asked. "He was going to kill me here in my own place. Look, Mr. Fraser," she said, her eyes still on the guy in the chair, "Keegan is right. You need medical attention and Isaac needs to be away from here. The key to my car is in the ignition. We'll be okay. This jerk is going to sit right where he is with both of us watching him every second."

"I can't let you—"

"Do I need to remind you who's holding the gun?" she asked, and Keegan was surprised to hear her crack a joke after what she'd just gone through, what all of them had just gone through. She was frigging amazing.

"Dad," he said, "we'll be careful. Go call Forbes."

Evan looked at them both, clearly unwilling to move, and then turned to Isaac and his unseeing eyes. "Your father is going to kill me, Willa," he said.

"Now *there's* an expression I can do without hearing again," she murmured, and Keegan grinned.

Evan moved toward Isaac, tenderly taking his hand in his. "Time to go," he said, and Keegan recognized the same gentle manner he'd always used with his younger son—he could just as easily have been getting the boy ready for school. Leading him toward the door, he paused and turned to Keegan. "Promise me—"

"We'll be careful," Keegan finished for him.

Wincing, Evan raised his arms and pulled Keegan to him. "I love you. You know that, don't you?"

Mindful of his father's injuries, Keegan resisted the urge to hug him back as hard as he wanted to. "I love you, too, Dad. Now go."

As the door closed behind them, the scarred guy spoke. "Christ, I'm in a rerun of *Dr. Phil*."

"Fuck off," said Keegan.

"You eat with that mouth?" The guy smirked.

The sounds of Willa's car starting and pulling away from the house gave Keegan strength. "Go to hell."

"Ignore him," said Willa. "You know what he's trying to do, right? He wants to rattle you. Rattle both of us."

"Don't try to get inside my head, sweetheart," the scarred guy said. "You don't know me. But I know *you*," he said to Keegan.

"Bullshit," Keegan said.

The guy's eyes gleamed. "So you weren't the ones livin' in that dump on East 52nd?"

Keegan's blood ran cold.

"Too bad about your mother. Pretty thing, except for the hair."

Keegan tried to hold on to Willa's warning—*He wants to rattle you*—but he felt like he'd been haymakered again. "You shut your mouth."

"I set the device under the kitchen counter. Thought I'd get all of you at breakfast." He shrugged. "My bad."

"Keegan," said Willa, her voice clear, urgent, "Forbes's people will be here soon. Don't let him get to you, okay?"

The guy's grotesque face creased in a parody of a smile, as if he'd just remembered something. Something important. "She used to stand at the sink a lot, didn't she, looking out at the street. You suppose that's where she was when it went off?" He laughed then, the sound like rocks colliding in his chest. "I wonder if she felt anything when it blew her to pieces."

Keegan knew he was being goaded, provoked into doing something stupid, something he'd regret. But knowing that and caring about it were two different things. This was the guy who'd killed his mother. Had blasted her into oblivion so there was barely enough left for the authorities to cremate. And now here he sat gloating, laughing, rubbing it in Keegan's face, daring him to do something about it.

Keegan remembered Wynn doing the same thing in the school corridor after Keegan had embarrassed him in phys ed. Remembered Wynn taunting him, ridiculing him, showing everyone how pathetic he was. And Keegan had been forced to take it, had swallowed his anger and even smiled before turning and walking away, listening to the laughter echo behind him.

Not this time.

He strode across the space between them, Willa's cry— "Keegan, don't!"—drowned out by the blood pounding in his ears. Reaching for the scarred guy, his only thought was to wrap his fingers around his windpipe, to choke off the words spewing from his mouth, to finally give himself the peace that eluded him whenever he recalled the last time he saw his mother, the way she'd stood at the sink with her head down, her hands gripping the countertop. Inches from the device that would obliterate her. "I'm gonna shut you up for good!" he roared.

And in the split second when his hands reached for the guy's throat, the split second that separated misery from peace, he saw the knife.

# CHAPTER 60

Willa screamed as the scarred guy thrust the blade into Keegan's chest, the gun discharging into the ceiling. Then he was on his feet, tossing Keegan's bleeding body aside and coming for her. In her panic, she shot wildly, pulling the trigger again and again, gunfire reverberating around the room and in her head until all she could hear was clicks.

"*Fuck!*" cried the scarred guy, looking down at his left leg, where blood streamed from a hole in his jeans just above his knee. "You *bitch!*" He grabbed her arms and knocked the empty revolver to the floor, shaking her hard, then backhanded her before throwing her onto the sofa.

Willa's face was broken—it had to be. She had never known such blinding pain, and her ears, already ringing from gunfire, now jangled from the blow. But all of this was secondary to the terror that clutched at her now, rending her, ripping at her core as the scarred guy raged above her. Some part of her subconscious now understood deer frozen in the sweep of headlights. She was paralyzed by the fear coursing through her, unable even to cry out.

"Don't say I didn't warn you, bitch," he snarled, his words shredding the air. "That thing I have about blonds? It ain't a good thing."

It wasn't his words that shattered her paralysis. It was the look in his eyes. Yes, he was going to kill her. But afterwards. And it was her sudden knowledge of the part before that, the horror between what was now and what would follow, that galvanized her, made her think of Bailey at the look-off and again on Casino Night. Beneath her surging terror was an anger she'd never known she was capable of feeling, and it clawed at her throat. "You talk and *talk!*" she shrieked, unsure where the words were coming from, just letting them flood out of her. "You compensating for a tiny *dick*, asshole? Or maybe you don't even *like* girls and all this is just for *show!*"

Roaring, he lunged at her, and that single moment of unguarded fury gave her the chance she was hoping for. Drawing back her foot, she drove her heel into the wound on his leg.

He didn't go down—that's how powerful he was—but he staggered back a step, bellowing in agony, and she rolled from the sofa and ran. She kept her eyes up, not just to avoid running into furniture but to keep from looking at the body on the floor, the pool of red expanding around it. She was sobbing when she reached the door, tearing it open and launching herself into sunlight.

# CHAPTER 61

That fucking, fucking *bitch*! She'd *shot* him!

The pain in his leg razored through him, making each step a singular agonizing nightmare. But despite the overwhelming, all-consuming power of it, there was a part of him that was numb, that didn't feel it, that was somehow removed from the excruciating confluence of bullet and flesh and bone. It was the same part of him that had stood in a double-wide trailer on Lancelot Way watching his mother come for him, brandishing the broken bottle, screaming, *I brought you into this world and I can goddamn take you out of it!* The part of him now keeping the pain at bay was the same part that had kept him from shattering when he'd heard *I shoulda had the doctor suck you outta me when I found out I was knocked up!*

But the thing was, she'd been coming for him nearly every night for the past five years, screaming names like "fudgepacker" and "faggot scum" in dreams that, even after all this time, still left him sweat-drenched and shaking. And now she had come for him here. *Maybe you don't even* like *girls and all this is just for* show*!* Out of nowhere, Gil Atkins's voice had suddenly echoed his mother's, reminding him of those photoshopped images he'd deleted from the super's computer. But he hadn't deleted them from his head, no matter how hard he'd tried, and they only fuelled his rage, his whole body quaking from the sheer effort not to fracture at its centre.

A more rational part of him realized that it wouldn't be long before the cops arrived, that he still had time to get away if he left now, even with a bullet in his leg slowing him down. But that rational part hadn't watched his mother's neck snap, hadn't buried his only friend behind a dumpster in the dark, hadn't spent three years in the Idlewood Home for Boys planning how to torture Travis Hubley before putting a bullet through his forehead. Because no rational human being could have done any of those things and survived.

But survival was the last thing on Griffin Barnett's mind right now. He would make that blond bitch pay for all of them if it was the last thing he ever did.

# CHAPTER 62

Unbelievably, he was right behind her, his feet pounding across the wooden deck and along the gravel driveway, his hands reaching for her, grabbing at her blouse. Willa shrieked and dove forward just beyond his grasp, some part of her brain—the part that solved whatever math problems Shedrand threw at her—screaming, *How can he run with a bullet in his leg?*

"When I get my hands on you, bitch," he howled, "you'll wish you'd never drawn a breath." And there was her answer. Fuelled by adrenalin and rage, he was beyond pain, and he was going to catch her if she didn't get somewhere he couldn't fol—

Willa abruptly veered right, plunging down the path she and Keegan had taken what seemed a lifetime ago. Branches tore at her arms and face and her lungs screamed for air, but she kept going, a river of roared epithets in her wake. Reaching the part of the trail where soil had washed from the path, she tripped on a rock and almost went down, but the harsh laughter behind her kept her on her feet and running.

Bursting through the trees onto the beach, she anticipated the give and slide of the polished stones, keeping her balance despite their constant shifting beneath her feet. Behind her, she could hear the scarred guy stumble, loose stones rolling, clattering toward the water, and she knew she now had the advantage she needed. She allowed herself to look back, saw pain engraving his face, slowing him down, and it gave her strength. He yelled something at her but his words were garbled, the sound more animal than human, lost in the wind off the bay as the distance between them increased. Twice she almost went down herself, her ankle rolling on the smooth round stones, but she knew she could do this, could outrun him, could live.

The waterfall was approaching, and she picked up speed, knowing safety lay beyond the outcrop that blocked it from view: the right-of-way at the far end of the beach. He couldn't possibly catch up to her before then, and the lead she was acquiring would allow her to lose him in the thick forest that lined the shore.

It wasn't the spray from the waterfall as she passed it that made her suddenly shiver. It was icy realization. Rounding the outcrop, she could see the tide had already reached the cliffs between her and the right-of-way, waves crashing against them, sending up spumes of seawater and foam. She was trapped.

She heard maniacal laughter behind her, and she turned to see the scarred guy fifty metres back, bent over, his hands on his knees. He'd obviously seen what she had. "Looks like you got a little problem, bitch!" he hooted, the sound more cackle than laughter. He lowered his large body onto those smooth fist-sized stones. "Don't worry," he called. "Take your time, sweetheart. I'll wait right here for you."

Willa didn't fight the sob that tore at her. She gave in to it, allowed it to rise up, to surge through her, to sound her defeat like the exasperated wail it was.

And then she saw the rope.

Sucking back her despair, she ran toward it, grabbing the end of the woven line. *Rope rots after a while, right?* she heard Keegan say in her head. *Can't be very safe.* As if she had an alternative. She gave it a strong yank and, mercifully, felt nothing give, then turned back. Knowing her voice probably wouldn't carry to him above the wind and pounding waves, she thrust her fist into the air, flipping him the finger.

She was glad for all the running she'd done on the treadmill, glad she'd been increasing the incline and speed rather than relying on the same settings. She liked pushing her body to the limit, seeing what she was really capable of. What she'd never liked, however, was climbing. Ladders, trees, you name it—she preferred her feet on the ground. Britney and Celia had often coaxed her to go with them to Cliffhanger, the rock-climbing facility in New Minas, but each time she'd sat and watched from the juice bar as her friends scaled that four-storey edifice, encouraging them from the sidelines as she sipped her Apple Mango Supreme.

Now she wished she'd tried it at least once.

Looking at the sheer stone wall looming above her now, Willa took a deep breath, then gripped the weathered cord and pulled, bracing her toes against the rock.

Six metres up, her arms and shoulders were killing her, her hands were numb from clutching the rope, and she was nearly sobbing from the effort, but she was doing this. *Fuck* Cliffhanger.

Then she suddenly swung out and back, banging into the rock, the impact jarring the breath from her.

Glancing down, she saw the scarred guy gripping the end of the line, yanking it from side to side. "Careful when you fall, bitch!" he called. "I wanna be the one to break your fuckin' neck."

# CHAPTER 63

I t was all falling apart. The life he'd built for himself since
Idlewood, the life with Talia he'd dared to let himself imagine. All of it, slipping through his fingers. He knew he should
run, should get someplace where he could deal with the bullet
and the blood, call Morozov and give him the location of those
documents and let that sick little fuck deal with the target himself. Once and for all.

But he couldn't.

All that mattered to Griff now was the bitch dangling above
him, clinging to the rope that he swung left then right, left then
right. She couldn't hold on forever. When she fell, he was going
to twist his fingers into her blond hair and lift her body clear of
the ground, spitting in her face and wrenching her so hard her
neck would snap.

With any luck, he'd rip her goddamn head clean off.

# CHAPTER 64

The rope swung out and back, describing ever greater arcs before banging Willa against the cliff again and again. Her right shoulder shrieking in pain, her grip loosened and she began to slip, the rope burning her fingers and palms as she struggled to halt her descent. Then something bounced off the rock wall near her head. A stone. He was throwing stones at her. The next one caught her in the small of the back and she cried out.

She fought sobs. She'd come so far. After everything else, it couldn't end like this. She looked frantically around her, searching for a loose rock, anything she could kick loose to fall on him.

And then hope bloomed in her.

"Know anything about the tides around here?" she called to him as her body collided with the cliff once more. Pain scissored through her as she nodded in the direction they'd come from. Waves crashed over the beach they'd run on only minutes before. "I hope you can swim, asshole!"

"You fucking—"

"Bitch?" she finished for him. Her whole body was in agony and trembling from exertion, her hands and fingers raw from the burn. But she revelled in the barrage of profanities he hurled at her now. It meant he wasn't yanking on the rope. She inched upward.

There was another tug from below but, looking down, she saw he wasn't trying to shake her off anymore. He was attempting to climb. *Rope rots after a while, right?* She shuddered, sure it couldn't support them both. She tried climbing faster, the rope jerking dramatically in her hands, and she imagined him below heaving his own bulk upward.

Then, "*FUCK!*"

When she looked down this time, relief swept over her. He lay sprawled on the stones. Even somebody as strong as he was couldn't climb with so much blood draining from him. He cursed again, but the wind tore away his words. Pulling himself to his feet, he gave a final vicious yank on the rope before turning away, limping back along the beach.

Willa focused again on the task at hand, trying not to think of the distance yawning beneath her, nor the distance that still stretched above. Her eyes on the rope, she sucked down a deep breath and strained, lifting herself higher.

Before long, she heard a strangled cry carried on the wind, and she turned to see the breakers pummel him, tossing his flailing body like a rag doll against the cliff. Oddly, she felt no satisfaction at the sight, instead forcing herself upward, gritting her teeth with each pull. When she finally reached the top, clambering, gasping over the lip before collapsing on the ground, she allowed herself to look down once more.

He was gone.

# CHAPTER 65

. . . face against hard floor, strange warmth pooling beneath him, spreading like a scarlet tide . . .

. . . wet, ragged wheezing he didn't recognize as his own . . .

. . . clamouring sounds, strident, intensifying, ratcheting the air and his brain . . .

. . . a crescendo of voices, indistinguishable in their shared urgency . . .

. . . a sense of suspension, of being cradled and carried, lifted and lowered . . .

"Can you hear me, son?"

Keegan understood the words but not their meaning, felt them drift over him as he himself was drifting, sliding from the now into the after—

"Can you hear me?" A hand gripped his own, drawing him back into the moment.

Keegan tried turning toward the voice, but something ripped him in half. Gasping, he clutched the hand holding his, tried to telegraph his awareness. But surely there was more to awareness than the pain slicing him now, more to consciousness than the piano on his chest making every breath a struggle, as if air were iron that he sucked through a straw.

"Easy, son. This'll help."

Keegan felt a jab in his arm and, heartbeats later, the pain lost its clean, vivid edge. He could breathe again.

And remember.

His heart stuttered in his chest. "Where is she? Where's—"

+ + +

"—Willa?" he murmured.

But time must have passed between the beginning and end of his question. The noises and voices were gone. So was he— from where he had been, anyway. He lay now in a room filled with machines, tubes entering his left arm, a monitor by his bed displaying numbers that changed before his still-focusing eyes.

"Keegan?"

Keegan shifted slightly, not wanting to bring that piano crashing down again. His father sat on the other side of the bed, holding Keegan's right hand in his, relief written across the few parts of his face not covered by bandages. His ear was swathed entirely in a white dressing and much of his exposed skin was purple and swollen, but he could see out of both eyes now. And the bloody shirt was gone, replaced by a clean one. "Thank God you're back," he breathed.

"Willa?" he croaked.

"Safe," said his father.

And then he was drifting again.

+ + +

"We've been calling you Rip Van Winkle," said the nurse when he opened his eyes. She was hanging a fresh IV bag on the pole by his bed.

"Mm?" His head felt filled with sand.

"Don't worry," she said, moving to the monitors. "Completely normal after a trauma like yours."

He watched as she tapped buttons, then allowed his eyes to slide to the window behind her. Through it he could see tall steel-and-glass buildings, visual confirmation of what he already knew—he wasn't in Brookdale. Not that it mattered, of course. Not after what had happened, what he'd brought roaring down on Willa. He released a hitched sigh that made his chest flare with pain, and he moaned softly.

"Anything I can get you?" asked the nurse.

Keegan reached deep inside, grappling for the word he wanted. "Thirsty."

She pulled a straw from a paper sleeve, placed it in a Styrofoam cup sitting on a table by the bed, then brought it to his lips. He sipped greedily, the cool water luxuriant on his tortured throat. As he drank, she said, "I finally got your father to step out for a bit. He went to get some—"

As if completing that thought, the door swung open revealing Evan, a coffee in one hand as he guided Isaac inside. "How long's he been conscious?" he asked, concern clouding his face.

"He just woke up."

Evan directed Isaac toward one of the two chairs beside the bed, then sat in the other, setting his coffee aside.

Having finished her tasks, the nurse turned to him. "My

break's coming up," she said. "I could take Isaac if you'd like some time alone with Keegan."

Evan offered her a polite smile. "That's very kind of you to offer, Patti, but I couldn't impose."

Keegan saw that her tag said "P. Nelson," and he wondered how long he'd been lying in that hospital room for his father to be on a first-name basis with the staff.

"It's no trouble," she said, smiling. "I have three teenaged daughters. It'd be nice to spend some time with a young person who isn't accusing me of ruining their life."

He seemed to consider it. "It would probably do Isaac good to have a little distance. He hasn't been out of my sight since—" He shook his head as if casting that thought away. "Yes, if you're sure it's no trouble, I'd really appreciate it." He turned to his younger son. "Isaac, Ms. Nelson here—"

"Please," she said, "Ms. Nelson is my mother-in-law. Does he like ice cream?"

Evan nodded. "Patti is taking you to get ice cream, Isaac. I'll be right here the whole time, and she's going to bring you straight back to me afterwards, okay?"

Keegan watched his brother's eyes do their usual circle of the room, and then the boy said, "Chocolate." The nurse extended her hand and Isaac took it, allowing her to lead him out.

Keegan's astonishment must have been evident on his face.

Evan nodded. "Yeah, I know. Pretty amazing. Only a word now and then, and most of the time it makes no sense, but I'll take what I can get." He shrugged. "It's like he finally decided he had things to say." He paused for a moment, reaching across the bed to take Keegan's hand in his. "I have some things to say, too." But he didn't speak right away, swallowing thickly before continuing, his voice becoming husky. "I'm not sure what you remember, but thank God Forbes sent that helicopter. The doctors—" He stopped, swallowed again. "They worked on you a long time. Hours. You'd lost so much blood. You nearly—" He made a sound that was somehow both sigh and sob. "I can't tell you how sorry I am," he finally whispered, leaning forward and pressing his lips to Keegan's hand. Then his shoulders were shaking.

Mindful of the tubes, Keegan cautiously raised his other hand and placed it on his father's head, stroking his hair. The effort pulled at something in his chest, and he clenched his teeth to keep from groaning. "S'okay," he whispered.

Evan sat up, wiping away tears with his sleeve, and shook his head. "It's not okay. You were right all along. I should never have—"

"No," said Keegan, the scarred guy's gloating voice swimming suddenly into memory: *She used to stand at the sink a lot, didn't she. You suppose that's where she was when it went off?* "I was wrong," he continued, summoning what little strength he had left to force out his next words. "People like that . . . need to be stopped." What had run through his mind that afternoon he spent with Willa at the look-off talking about Wynn? Sometimes you didn't have a choice, right? Sometimes the battle came to you. He took a deep, painful breath. "Nail those bastards."

Evan's eyes filled again, and he leaned forward to kiss his son's forehead. "I love you," he whispered. "Now you rest. I'm just going to sit here, okay? You try to sleep."

Keegan humoured him by closing his eyes, although he knew it was pointless. After all the sleeping he'd done, there was no way he could possibly—

+ + +

The scarred guy's arm circled her neck as he brought the gun to her temple. "Sorry, sweetheart," the man hissed, his mouth against her ear, "but I'm workin' my way up the food chain. You and that asshole on the floor there are what's called least leverage." Her face reddened as his arm tightened against her throat. If the bullet didn't kill her, the lack of oxygen surely would.

"Willa!" called Keegan, his heart pounding.

A hand gently prodded his shoulder. "It's okay, son. You were dreaming."

Keegan opened his eyes. "Dad?"

"Yes?"

His father had told him that Willa was safe, but he hadn't said whether—

Keegan took a breath. "Was she hurt?"

"Bruises, and she was shaken up pretty bad, but she's okay. She's a remarkable young woman." He seemed to consider whether he should say more. Then, "None of us would be alive if it weren't for her. She saved us all."

Keegan felt the hammering in his chest begin to ease—

*She saved us all.*

—as sleep's dark arms wrapped round him again.

+ + +

"Keegan?"

He heard the voice, but it was too far away. Or perhaps it wasn't a voice at all, merely the tendril of another dream disguised as consciousness, memory masquerading as waking thought.

"Keegan?" the voice came again.

Keegan's eyes fluttered open. Beside him, the chair was empty. Though he knew his dad and Isaac must be nearby, neither was in the room with him now.

"Over here."

Keegan turned slightly to see the man standing at the foot of the bed. More mountain than man, his imposing frame somehow contained in a navy blue suit. Special Agent Forbes.

"Mm," Keegan replied.

"I hear you're doing better. I'm glad."

*I'm glad.* It was the first time Keegan had ever heard the man mention feelings, his own or anyone else's. Since the day the FBI agent had appeared in their lives, Keegan had only ever heard him talk about protocol and procedure, restrictions and rules. He was good at his job, never allowing emotion to cloud his view of a situation. *I'm glad.* Keegan wondered if the sky was falling.

"I have something for you," said Forbes. "And you should know that I'm giving it to you against my better judgment." He placed a thick manila envelope on the foot of the bed. "I'm sure I don't have to remind you that nothing has changed." He moved toward the door, hesitating for a moment before pulling it open. He turned back, and Keegan thought he could see the trace of a smile on that stone face. "She's persistent, I'll give her that." And then he was gone.

Keegan wondered who he was talking about, wondered even more what might be in the envelope, but there was no way he could possibly reach it. He couldn't bend his body that far. Leaving it beyond his grasp was so like Forbes, the King of Can't.

Keegan considered pressing the call button to ask a nurse to get it for him, but before he could put that thought into action, he was drifting again.

+ + +

Keegan opened his eyes to find his father in the chair by his bed again, Isaac in the other one with a large tray on his lap covered in puzzle pieces. Both were dressed in different clothes, and Keegan wondered how long it had been since he'd last seen them. But the passage of time had done him good. He felt a little stronger.

"Hey, buddy," said Keegan. "Where'd you get the puzzle?"

His brother gave no indication he'd heard the question, merely continued to mesh pieces with other pieces.

"Patti brought it in," explained his father. "It's been a god-send." He pointed toward the table by the bed. "I see somebody brought you something, too."

Keegan turned to see the manila envelope on the nightstand and idly wondered who had moved it. "Forbes," he said.

His father nodded. "I saw him in the hall yesterday. Here." He reached for the envelope and handed it to Keegan.

It bore the official insignia of the Federal Bureau of Investigation and was heavier than he expected. He remembered getting one like it before they moved to Brookdale. He let it drop from his fingers to the bed.

"You're not opening it?"

Keegan shook his head. He wasn't interested in the new identity Forbes had created for him. There'd be plenty of time later to learn about the person he would become. To start from scratch all over again.

"It's not what you think," said his father.

"He told you?"

His father nodded. "I think Special Agent Forbes might be mellowing with age."

His interest piqued, Keegan pushed the envelope toward his father. "Open it for me?" he asked. He wasn't sure he had the strength to hold it for long.

His father nodded. Tearing off the end, he slid the contents onto the bed beside Keegan, smaller envelopes of various sizes containing what looked like cards. Lots of them. Keegan reached for one and opened it, and he had to look at the signature twice to trust his eyes: *Jay Underwood*. Between the name and the canned Hallmark greeting was a brief, handwritten note: *I'm really sorry for everything that went down. I know it doesn't seem like much of an excuse now, especially after what happened to you, but I didn't know what he was really like. None of us did. Get better, okay?*

There were lots of other cards, some from people he barely knew who were in the same classes he was taking. Classes he *used* to take, he reminded himself. Many bore only signatures, but a few cards contained long personal messages that he'd have to read later. Already he could feel weariness seeping into him, and he pushed the rest aside. As he did so, though, his hand brushed something heavy at the bottom of the pile—a thick packet of envelopes bound by a rubber band. Keegan reached for it, curious why they'd been separated from the others. And then he knew. These cards were from Russell, Greg, Raven, Bailey, and Willa, their bulkiness suggesting letters inside each. Willa's envelope was far heavier than the other four, and for a long moment he simply stared at it. He didn't realize his hands were trembling until his father steadied them with his own. "I can't—" Keegan began, but his throat locked and he could only shake his head.

"You didn't do anything wrong, son," Evan said gently.

Yeah, Keegan thought, if you don't count nearly getting her killed.

"Go on," said his father. "Open it."

Keegan continued to stare at it, uncertain if he could bear to read what she'd written. Jay Underwood had every right to feel guilty, which explained the positive message, but Willa had done nothing wrong except trust him. He could only imagine her letter's contents: the utter betrayal she must have felt at discovering the lies Keegan had repeatedly told her, the absolute terror she'd experienced in the grip of the scarred guy who must surely have haunted her dreams since that day because he continually roamed his own. But what had Forbes said? *She's persistent, I'll give her that.* Of course she was. After what Keegan had put her through, she had every right to unload her shit on him. But still he lay there, unmoving.

Finally, his father took the envelope from him, opening one end and pulling out a folded sheet of paper that he passed to his son. Drawing a breath, Keegan unfolded the paper to find only a few words on it: *I'm glad you called Forbes from my car. I never would have reached him if my phone hadn't stored his contact number. He wasn't thrilled to hear from me—*

Despite his apprehension, Keegan smiled at this understatement.

*—but I kept blowing up his voicemail and I finally wore him down.*

Keegan turned the paper over, but there was nothing more written on it, and he looked questioningly at his father.

Evan smiled, reaching once more into the envelope and pulling out a phone. "It's a burner. Untraceable. Forbes said you'll only be able to use it once." He smiled again. "He even programmed in her number."

Eyes wide, Keegan now understood his father's earlier comment about the mellowing of Special Agent Forbes. He took the phone, opened up the contacts page, and saw the sole name revealed on the screen. He held his finger above the Call key.

"Take all the time you need," said his father. "Your brother and I'll be down the hall. Come, Isaac," he said, getting up and lifting the tray from his younger son's lap. "We can work on this together in the waiting room."

Isaac stood and followed his father toward the door, then abruptly stopped. "Willa," he said softly, and Keegan's own surprise was reflected in their father's face. Then they were gone.

Exhausted, he let his head sink into the pillow. His eyes fixed on the ceiling, he drew another deep breath, bracing himself. Finally, he pressed Call and brought the phone to his ear.

She answered on the first ring. "Hello?"

His heart stumbled in his chest. "Willa—" he began.

"Keegan? Is that you?"

Yeah," he said. "It's me."

"Hang on a second."

Keegan could hear muffled exchanges and then Willa's voice,

bell-like in its clarity: "You do whatever you have to, okay? I'm taking this call." A few more moments passed before he heard her say, "You still there, Keegan?"

"Still here. Was that—"

"Yeah, Shedrand."

"You're in math class?"

"Not anymore. I walked out."

Keegan attempted to whistle his surprise, but the sound came out a breathy moan. "But Caldwell—"

"Screw Caldwell." He heard a sudden creak of metal and knew she was pushing out the exit door at the end of the school corridor. "How're you feeling, Keegan?" she asked.

"Good," he said.

"Liar. I saw you just before they airlifted you. I thought—" There was a sound on the line he couldn't identify. "I thought you were dead," she whispered, and then he knew what that sound had been.

He felt his apprehension evaporate. "I'm okay."

There was a pause before she asked, "Does it hurt much?"

"Only when I laugh," he said.

She didn't miss a beat. "So not at all then."

"Mm," he said. He doubted he'd have anything to laugh about for a long time. Maybe never. Right now, though, there were things he wanted to say, questions he wanted to ask her. "Nobody here has told me what happened, just that you saved us. How did you—"

"I can't—" she began, then paused, and for a few seconds only silence connected them. Finally, "I'd rather not talk about it," she said. Her words were straightforward enough, yet Keegan could hear the anguish beneath each one.

"You're okay, though, right?"

There were more seconds of silence, and he regretted his question. Like anyone *could* be okay after what she'd been through. "I'm so sorry, Willa," he said. "I shouldn't have let the guy get to me like th—"

"Stop it, Keegan," she interrupted, her voice firmer. "He would've used that knife no matter what you had done, probably on me first because I had the gun." He could sense her shudder. "Those awful things he said about your mother. That's what evil sounds like, isn't it? What it looks like." Before he could reply, she added, "At least he can never hurt Talia or anyone else again."

So the guy was dead. Good. Keegan wanted to ask how it had happened, wanted her to tell him it took a while, that the guy had suffered right up to the end, but he let the question go unspoken. Her earlier refusal to talk about it was only part of the reason. He needed to let it go. All of it. His mother would have wanted him to. He knew that now.

"Hey, speaking of mothers," she said, obviously wanting to change the subject, "mine's back. And, *man*, was she pissed when she got here."

"No shit," he said. He could only imagine how the woman had felt coming home to find her daughter nearly murdered by a hired killer. Not exactly an episode of *The Real Housewives of Brookdale.*

"Yeah, major panic attack over what happened at the cottage. She refilled her Xanax prescription. But once she got the worst of it behind her, she was super pissed at my dad."

"Why? None of what happened was his fault."

"Not about that. She thought he was having an affair."

"Was he?"

"No, of course not."

"I don't get it."

"All that time he was spending at work, she thought he was seeing another woman. When she got back from Halifax, she confronted him about it, and he finally told her about the trouble the business is in."

Keegan had never met Willa's mother but, judging from the luxuries she enjoyed from the dealership's profits, he could well understand how she'd feel about its closure. Willa seemed to sense his thinking. "It wasn't the money," she explained. "They used to work side by side when they were first married. They bought the business together, developed it together, but when Aiden and I came along, Dad encouraged her to stay home. With Aiden gone now and me graduating next spring, she's been wallowing in almost-empty-nest syndrome, spending a lot of time obsessing over things that aren't true."

"She must've been glad he wasn't cheating on her."

"Yeah, but she was furious he hadn't shared how bad things had gotten. She accused him of not caring about her enough to tell her the truth."

Keegan looked at the ceiling, hearing those last words echo in his mind, wondering if they were in some way directed toward him. But he needn't have worried.

"So she's working now," continued Willa. "She took over your dad's job. She used to do the accounting there years ago."

Listening to her speak about the dealership, Keegan suddenly remembered what had been foremost in his mind before everything had fallen apart. "Did your dad get the contract for those vehicles?"

"No. After what happened at the cottage, Dad said to hell with it. Getting Wynn out of circulation was more important."

He felt relief sweep through him. "So you went to the police?"

"Someone beat me to it."

"Who?"

"Raven and Bailey."

"Raven? I don't underst—"

"Wynn had assaulted her, too."

Keegan was dumbfounded. "When?"

"A few days before school started. She likes to run really early in the morning to beat the heat, and she'd gone to the track at Memorial Park. Wynn was jogging there."

"Did he—? Was she—?" He didn't know how to ask the question, didn't know if he should.

"She was bruised pretty badly—"

Keegan remembered the discoloration he'd seen on her arm the first day of school. That bastard.

"—but it's a good thing she's a runner."

Keegan pictured that tiny figure outdistancing the hulk that was Wynn d'Entremont, and he imagined Wynn's frustration in that moment. For a star athlete, he'd certainly underestimated both girls. "Why didn't Raven report it before?"

"Yeah, we talked about that. She'd just moved into the area and didn't know anybody. It's hard enough being the new student—*you* know that, right?—but then she learned she was the only Aboriginal person in the whole school. She didn't want to make her final year even harder by wearing a Victim sign on her back, too."

"Doesn't Canadian law protect the identities of people who've been assaulted?"

"Yes, but Wynn called her names that—" She paused. "Let's just say he doesn't have a very high opinion of First Nations people, so the attack would have been treated as a hate crime. That kind of thing gets lots of press, and in a place as white as Brookdale, Raven wouldn't have to actually be named for people to know who she was."

What had Bailey said that afternoon on the bus? *That's not how I want to spend my senior year.* Keegan could understand that. And, apparently, so had Wynn. He'd known exactly which people he could prey on.

Yet they had gone ahead and reported Wynn after all. "So what made her and Bailey go to the police?"

"When Raven heard about Wynn's imposter page nearly getting us killed, she confided in Bailey what he'd done to her. And then Bailey shared her story with Raven. They both decided they couldn't stay silent any longer."

Looking at the ceiling, Keegan found himself thinking the impossible. As horrible as that day on Delusion Road had been, some good had come of it after all. But his pleasure at this news was only momentary. "Is Wynn giving them a hard time?"

"No one's seen him since the first morning back at school after—" He heard her voice catch, and he waited for her to continue. When she did, he could hear disgust in each word. "Get this. That douche came in wearing a big bandage on his head and telling everybody how he'd saved us all."

"Where's he been since then?"

"The school board's anti-bullying policy meant his web page got him a two-week suspension. And now with these assault charges, there's talk that he's out for good."

"His dad must've hired a hell of a defence team."

"Probably," said Willa. "He'll need it. We're hearing rumours there may be more charges involving girls in Halifax."

"So you were right about there being others," he murmured.

They were both silent for a moment, and when she spoke again, her voice was lighter. "You haven't heard the best part."

"What's that?"

"Russell and Greg beat the crap out of him."

"*What?*"

"Before Raven and Bailey went to the police, they told the guys what Wynn had done to them. They were waiting for him at school that morning, and they went apeshit on his ass."

"Russell and Greg?" Keegan was astonished.

"Yeah, I know. Hard to believe, right? Mind you, it took both of them to do it, but they're still pretty pleased with themselves."

"Our Russell and Greg?" Whatever weariness Keegan had felt earlier vanished as he tried to comprehend what he was hearing.

"Yeah. According to Greg, Russell's SDR is a thing of beauty."

"SDR?"

"Stop, drop, and roll. He bowled Wynn over like a tenpin in the school corridor, and then both of them went postal on him. Caldwell stopped it before any bones got broken, but not before most of the senior class saw Wynn get shellacked."

"Anything happen to Russell and Greg?"

"Two-week suspensions, but they're treating it like a vacation from phys ed."

Keegan grinned. Remembering the note on Jay's card, he asked, "I'm guessing Todd and Jay didn't jump in to help?"

"You guessed right."

He thought about the rest of the League of Extraordinary Assholes. "Have you seen Britney and Celia?"

"They came by as soon as they heard what had happened."

"And?"

"They apologized for everything. Hoped we could put it behind us."

"You've been friends for a long time."

"We were *together* for a long time, but I'm not sure that's the same thing. I don't think real friends would have turned their backs so fast." Then, as if to change the subject again, she said, "Speaking of friends, did you get the cards? I sent a package that Forbes promised to deliver, but I'm thinking get well greetings probably aren't an FBI priority."

"He brought them with the phone I'm using," replied Keegan. "I haven't had a chance to look at all of them yet. There's a ton."

"That's Mr. Richardson's doing," she said. "He's the one who suggested it to the other seniors. He said it didn't seem right for you to leave Brookdale without knowing you'll be missed."

And there it was. The opening he'd been looking for, hoping for during this whole conversation. "Do *you*?"

"What? Miss you?"

He let his silence answer for him.

"Keegan, how could you ask me that?"

He was suddenly embarrassed. "You didn't say in your note." In fact, she hadn't said much of anything.

"I wanted you to *hear* me say it. That's why I made Forbes get you the phone."

Keegan grinned, imagining Forbes being *made* to do anything. *She's persistent, I'll give her that.*

He heard her take a breath. "Keegan Fraser, or whatever the hell your real name is, I miss you. A lot."

The sudden tightness in his chest had nothing to do with the surgery that had repaired his wound. "I miss you, too," he said, imagining her with her phone to her ear, her blond hair framing her face, lifting slightly in an afternoon breeze. Was it afternoon where she was? He hoped so, hoped it was the end of the school day so they could talk as long as they wanted. "I was afraid that—" He began, then stopped, too embarrassed to finish that thought.

"Afraid that what?" she asked.

"Nothing."

"Seriously? Forbes comes through with a phantom phone that you get to use only once and you're clamming up on me?"

He groped for words. "It's just," he began, thinking of his initial response to the package she'd sent him, "after everything that happened, I was afraid you'd never want to speak to me again." He lowered his voice. "You almost died because of me."

"*Both* of us almost died, but not because of you. None of this was your fault."

"But if I'd never shown up, you wouldn't have been in danger in the first place."

Silence once again filled his receiver. Then, "If you'd never shown up, Keegan, I wouldn't have met this incredible guy who likes the same music as me, who gets a charge out of the same crazy personal ads, who—"

"You're forgetting what a prick I was when we met. I totally misjudged you."

"No, you didn't," she said. "I was a bitch."

"Willa—"

"No, let me finish. I've had a lot of time to think about this. Before you showed up, I'd gotten into the habit of taking things for granted. Taking *people* for granted. And there was so much that I believed was true but wasn't. Like how I felt about Wynn. I imagined it was so much more than it was, *wanted* it to be simply because it made *sense* to be. I thought I had friends I could count on, no matter what happened. I thought my dad was this amazing guy who could magically make everything perfect, but all this time he was fighting to keep the dealership afloat while his marriage was crumbling. Nothing was what I thought it was, and you were there to help me pick up the pieces when everything began to fall apart. Do I wish things hadn't turned into a shitstorm the way they did? Of course I do, but I don't regret a second of the time we had together. Not one second. My only regret—" She stopped, and he thought he could hear a quaver in her voice, a struggle between her words and the emotion that fuelled them.

"What do you regret, Willa?" he prodded gently.

"That this is all we get," she said, her voice catching, but she cleared her throat and tried again. "I was just getting to know you. Just getting to—"

This time Keegan didn't prod her. It wasn't necessary. He felt exactly the same.

"It isn't fair," she continued finally. "If I could find some way to convince Forbes to—"

"Willa Jaffrey!" a voice boomed. "Come with me at once!" Even over the phone, Keegan recognized the speaker: Mr. Caldwell.

"Yes, sir," said Willa, "as soon as I—"

"I want your phone, young lady."

"But I haven't finished talk—"

"That's not my concern. Mr. Shedrand tells me you took a call during his class and then walked out without his permission."

"Yeah, I did, but he didn't understand who—"

"What *I* understand, Ms. Jaffrey, is your complete disregard for the rules. Your phone, please."

"But—"

"Your *phone!*"

Keegan listened to a brief muffled exchange, followed by a dial tone.

Christ! He brought Willa's number up on the screen again and pressed Call, but nothing happened. The words now scrolling across the display read *No Service*.

# EPILOGUE

"We should start a club," said Russell. He leaned back against the bench, his outstretched arms covering part of the words "Property of Brookdale Memorial Park." Although it was the last week of September, temperature and humidex records were still being broken, so instead of a sweatshirt, Russell was wearing a T-shirt today, orange lettering across the front claiming *Poets have been mysteriously silent on the subject of cheese.*

Willa sat to his right, the humidity having played havoc with her hair, resurrecting its natural wave, but she hadn't bothered straightening it. She kind of liked it the way it was. "Club?" she asked.

"For badasses," he said. "Of course, you're kind of in a class of your own, aren't you? There can't be too many people around who've beaten up a vice-principal."

"I did *not* beat him up," she insisted.

"Right," grinned Greg, sitting on the other end of the bench. "He got that black eye and broken nose from walking into a door."

Willa rolled her eyes. The truth about what had happened—Caldwell trying to grab her phone, the phone falling to the ground, both of them reaching for it, and the back of Willa's head striking Caldwell in the face when she stood up—hadn't played nearly as well as the rumours that had circulated in the days since Willa had been suspended. She sighed, resigned to her notoriety.

Thankfully, her parents weren't as upset as they might have been, considering the gravity of the charge she'd been suspended for, and there were a couple of reasons for that. First, of course, was the circumstance under which Willa had walked out of Shedrand's class. She'd told her parents in advance about Forbes's deal with the phone he'd supplied Keegan—it could make only one call before being rendered useless—so they understood that she'd have to answer her own phone whenever and wherever it rang. Mind you, they felt Willa could have been more forthcoming—not to mention polite—in explaining to Shedrand her need to take the call, but the circumstance was what it was.

The second reason her parents hadn't gone ballistic had little to do with Willa. Since her mother's return to work at the dealership, her parents had spent more time together in the past few days than they had in months, and they were—in Willa's mind, anyway—uncomfortably enthralled with each other. It was embarrassing, really, the way they'd gaze into each other's eyes when they were supposed to be poring over accounts or revised business plans, but Willa hadn't heard them argue once, so it was all good. That is, if you could ignore the claims of being tired that took them to bed earlier than usual. Gross. But the upside was that happy parents made for more agreeable ones, and instead of her suspension getting her grounded at home, she was free to come and go during her days out of school. Which explained her sitting in Memorial Park now with two other fledgling badasses.

"So," said Greg, "is this club gonna cost me anything? Are there, like, dues or something? Because I gotta tell you guys, I'm broke."

Both Russell and Willa nodded sympathetically. Greg's hours stocking shelves after school at the Bulk Barn had been drastically reduced, something that couldn't have come at a worse time, since he'd just made what his parents called a "staggeringly expensive purchase" without their knowledge. With some clandestine help from Raven, he'd managed to get copies of most of Bailey's poems and had taken them to a printer in New Minas, where he'd paid to have them published in a print run of twenty hardcover books complete with illustrations that he'd created himself. One of Willa's all-time favourite photos was the picture she'd taken of Bailey on her birthday last week when she'd opened the heavy box Greg had given her at Subway, where they'd all met for lunch since three of them were barred from school. Absolutely stunned, Bailey had begun to laugh and cry at the same time, and before long all five of them were doing the same, a shared emotional release triggered by everything that had happened to them. They'd drawn a lot of weird looks, but Willa couldn't have cared less—she'd never before felt so connected to a group of people, and as she'd watched Bailey plant a kiss on a wide-eyed, red-faced Greg afterwards, she'd realized only one thing was keeping that moment from being perfect—Keegan wasn't there to share it with them.

"Nah," said Russell now, "badasses don't pay dues. They might, however, want to bring snacks to the meetings—"

He made an *oof* sound as Willa jabbed him in the ribs. Russell was into his second week of doughnut withdrawal and claimed to be getting calls from Brookdale's Tim Hortons complaining about a drastic drop in their revenue, but he was determined that this diet was going to last. He and Raven were dating now, and he'd confessed privately to Willa last week that he was already thinking ahead to prom and wanted her help in getting into a size 42 tux by then. Willa had happily agreed and, besides being his conscience when it came to calories, she'd started him on a daily exercise program that included him walking around the Memorial Park track while she ran the oval. He complained constantly, but she knew he was grateful for her support, and she'd gotten Greg to join them when he was available, which was quite often, given his suspension and the reduction of his part-time hours.

The cutback in shifts at the Bulk Barn was just another indicator of how tough times were in the valley. The town had decided not to go ahead with plans to replace its aging vehicles, choosing to keep the ones they had for at least another year, so it turned out that none of the dealerships had gotten the contract. But rather than lay off staff at Valley Motors, Willa's parents had chosen to inject some personal capital into the business to keep it viable until they got over this hard patch, capital that was coming from the sale of their place on Delusion Road. After what had happened, none of them could see themselves ever spending time there again, so they'd put the house in the hands of a broker who had close ties to the European real estate market. Surprisingly, within twenty-four hours the broker received a solid offer from a wealthy German buyer who'd learned about the Bay of Fundy during the New Seven Wonders competition and was eager to own such a large property on its tidal shoreline. The details were still being ironed out, but the broker was confident the sale would go through, and her parents planned to put the money into a contingency fund that would prop up the dealership for a few more months while offering them tax breaks on their personal incomes. They were confident that GM's upcoming introduction of two affordable electric vehicles would turn things around for them, and Willa hoped they were right. For now, though, she was just glad to see them getting along again.

A young mother pushing a stroller smiled at the friends and said "Good morning" as she passed their bench, her response to the presence of three teenagers in the park on a school day definitely atypical—most people gave them wary glances, as if fearing a sudden swarming. All three offered a simultaneous "'Morning" in return, watching in comfortable silence as the woman followed the path down to the water's edge. The lengthy stretch of hot weather had lowered the level of the Annapolis River markedly, but it was still one of the nicest places to be in Brookdale. Seeing the water slide slowly by, a person could let her imagination go wherever it wanted, and today Willa's was working overtime.

"What are you grinning about?" asked Russell.

"I'm not grinning," said Willa, but her beaming expression said otherwise.

Greg turned to face her. "Okay, what's up?" he asked.

She feigned innocence. "I don't have the slightest idea what—"

"I've seen that look before," said Greg.

"So have I," offered Russell. "The day you told us you could get somebody to give our letters to Keegan."

As always, Willa was surprised by their perceptiveness. In the few weeks they'd spent together, they'd come to know her better than Britney or Celia ever had.

"You've heard from him, haven't you?" said Greg.

"He's not allowed to contact me," she said. "You know that." Her repeated googling of Chicago businessman Pavel Morozov had brought news that he'd finally been arraigned on numerous charges, news that Willa had shared with the others.

"You didn't answer my question," said Greg. "You've heard from him, right?"

She tried to keep from smiling again. She really did. But she couldn't stop thinking about the personal ad she'd read and reread during breakfast that morning: *WHERE THERE'S A WILLA, THERE'S A WAY.*

She got to her feet. "C'mon, badasses," she said. "We have work to do."

# AUTHOR'S NOTE

'm often asked how long it takes to write a novel, and my answer to that question is always "It depends"—usually on how much research is required and what other projects I happen to be working on at the time. *Delusion Road* took more than four years to write, but it's been percolating in the back of my mind for more than four decades.

When I was growing up, my parents never moved from the community where we lived, so I was fortunate to graduate with friends I'd known for many years. In fact, I attended a rural high school where everyone knew everyone else, so strangers in our midst were readily apparent. I recall sitting in an assembly during the first day of my senior year and seeing someone I didn't recognize sitting alone a couple of rows ahead of me. Even all these years later, I vividly remember thinking how horrible it must have felt for that person to be "the new kid," having had to leave all of his friends behind and start from scratch in what was supposed to be his best school year ever. That memory is one of the seeds that grew into *Delusion Road*.

Often, of course, there is more than a single seed that results in a novel, and another that influenced and informed the writing of this one is my environment. I live on Nova Scotia's Bay of

Fundy shoreline, and the study where I write is only a few metres from the water, which is an ever-changing landscape of incredible beauty. Twice each day, I watch the ocean rise and fall a vertical height of more than ten metres, a spectacle I never tire of. Not only is it an astonishing sight, but the force of those tides is nearly incomprehensible, possessing the kinetic potential to generate electricity for 100,000 homes once it is harnessed. No small feat, though—a few years ago, a test turbine costing ten million dollars was destroyed in a matter of weeks by the sheer force of the bay's powerful currents. Having heard many accounts of people—usually tourists—trapped along this rocky shoreline by a rapidly incoming tide, I knew I would one day write about that experience. And so I have.

The third seed that gave rise to *Delusion Road* was, for me, the most compelling—the prevalence of violence against females, especially those of Aboriginal heritage. Statistics Canada tells us that half of all women in our country have reported at least one incident of physical or sexual violence since the age of sixteen. Just as staggering is the statistic that less than ten percent of all sexual assaults are reported to police. This societal problem simply cannot be ignored, and the more I encountered stories about it in the news, the more I realized I needed to address it in a story of my own imagining. If *Delusion Road* does nothing else, I hope it gets people talking about the victimization of women and what each of us can do to ensure a better world for our daughters, our partners, our mothers, and our friends.

As important as seeds are to a story, however, nothing beats the support an author receives during the actual writing of it, and I would never have completed this one without the encouragement of my wife and my daughters. In addition, every writer should have the very good fortune to work with an editor as talented as mine, and I owe an enormous debt of gratitude to Hadley Dyer, who gently but unerringly guided me through this novel. As always, I am as grateful for her endless patience and her wonderful sense of humour as I am for her extraordinary understanding of story.

Finally, I offer my sincere thanks to the person reading this now for choosing *Delusion Road* from among the countless other novels beckoning from shelves and websites. You are, quite simply, the reason why I get to do the thing I love most—create characters and follow them wherever they choose to lead.